Albemarle

Photo # NH 57270 CSS Albemarle

Albemarle

An Epic Novel Depicting One of the Greatest Missions in American Naval History

by Jim Stempel

www. Fireshippress.com

Albemarle by Jim Stempel

ISBN-13: 978-1-61179-333-8(Paperback)
ISBN -978-1-61179-334-5(e-book)

BISAC Subject Headings:
FIC0012000FICTION / Action
FIC014000FICTION / Historical
FIC032000FICTION / War & Military

Cover work by Christine Horner

Address all correspondence to:
Fireship Press, LLC
P.O. Box 68412
Tucson, AZ 85737
Or visit our website at:
www.fireshippress.com

Table of Contents

1864

Preface

It is winter, 1864. The American Civil War has raged for three bloody summers, yet no end appears in sight. The preceding summer, the Federal Army had won what appeared to be a decisive victory over Robert E. Lee's Army of Northern Virginia at Gettysburg, but that victory was not aggressively followed up, and Lee's army slipped back to safety in Virginia. For the intervening seven months, George Meade's Army of the Potomac has dogged Lee at a distance, but has not struck a decisive blow. Thus, the war in the Eastern Theatre has devolved into what might be considered an uneasy stalemate, and now the weather has forced both armies into winter quarters.

The campaigns in the Western Theatre have shown some promise for the Northern cause, but, as in the East, the war seems nowhere near a successful completion. The successful Federal siege of Vicksburg, Mississippi, followed by victories at Chattanooga, Knoxville, Lockout Mountain, and finally Missionary Ridge, have opened a pathway into the deep South; but in Washington City, Abraham Lincoln knows that a pathway south and ultimate victory are two very different things. One clear result of these victories, however, is to solidify the reputation of Ulysses S. Grant as the most energetic and successful of Union generals. That fact has not been lost on Abraham Lincoln, for Lincoln is much in need of successful generals.

On the high seas, the war effort has fared far better for the Federal cause. During the first three years of conflict, the Federal Navy radically increased in size, and its blockade of Southern ports has proved a critical success. By 1864, the only three Southern ports open for blockade running are Savannah, Charleston, and Wilmington, North Carolina, yet even at these locations the blockade has greatly reduced seaborne commerce.

For the Federal Navy, Wilmington has proved the toughest nut to crack; this because the city itself lies well inland on the Cape Fear River, with two channels that lead from the river out into the open seas, giving blockade runners a distinct advantage. Thus, it is toward Wilmington and the Eastern counties of North Carolina that the Federal Navy will turn increased attention in the coming year. And, conversely, it is this same territory that Southern war planners know must be held if the Confederate cause is to survive.

In roughly the next twelve months, the fate of the Confederacy will be decided. Great, bloody, and desperate battles will be fought on land, while some of the most daring and remarkable missions in the history of the war will be launched on the rivers of North Carolina. These clashes, large and small, will soon spell the fate of the Confederacy. In far larger terms they will also begin to shape the nature of the nation that will ultimately emerge from the carnage of the American Civil War.

"The destruction of the rebel ram Albemarle by Lieut. Cushing proves to be one of the most daring and romantic naval feats of history"

New York *Times,* November 3, 1864

Chapter One

February 29th – Morning

Cooke stood back and watched for a moment as workmen scurried over the ship's emerging structure – bolts being carried aloft, hammers ringing, iron plates being fixed firmly into place – and felt a sudden surge of pride in what he had finally been able to accomplish. It had not been easy. The morning sun was rising now, casting a fine, red glow over the misty Roanoke River, and as he watched the plates of iron being hammered into place, James Cooke knew for the first time that the ironclad would be ready on time.

General Robert E. Lee had developed a plan for regaining many of the eastern counties of North Carolina from the Federals, but everything depended on this ship being finished on schedule. For almost two years he had struggled to overcome every difficulty, but now, at long last, he could see that it was all falling into place. Indeed, within only weeks they might be headed downriver. For months, Richmond had been on his back to push the the ram to completion, but demands were not iron plates, and ships, he knew, could not be hammered together simply by means of fortitude alone. It had been tools, equipment, and iron they had always lacked, but those hardships had been overcome and now the ironclad sat before him, a dream at long last realized.

James Wallace Cooke had been born in Beaufort, North Carolina in August 1812, and had lost both his mother and father at a very young age. Raised by his uncle, Cooke received an appointment to the old Federal Navy when only a boy of fifteen, and had spent most of his life at sea. That navy had been a stagnant, moribund affair, dedicated to the rulebook, offering little if any chance of advancement. It had been a navy bereft of pluck and imagination, vision or fortitude. In over twenty-seven years of service, despite all his time and effort, he had not risen beyond the rank of lieutenant. It had been a life of aimless missions in nameless ports. As one officer had succinctly put it, "the navy list was encumbered with ... worn-out men without brains."

So, when war came, in 1861, Cooke joined with some 375 other Southern officers and resigned his commission, promptly offering his services to the Confederacy and his native North Carolina. But Cooke soon found that the Confederate Navy existed in name only. When Stephen Mallory, the Confederacy's Secretary of the Navy, took the oath of office in 1861, he took over a service that listed not a single ship. Facing virtually insurmountable manufacturing and transportation obstacles, the Rebel navy chose to not even attempt to match the Federal build-up of warships. Rather, they concentrated on a few fast cruisers that could wreak havoc on the Union merchant marine, while hoping to construct a limited number of imposing ironclads that might instantly render both the wooden Federal fleet and the blockade that it enforced obsolete.

James Cooke's first action had come with the "Mosquito Fleet," a small group of reconfigured tugs and paddle steamers that fought the Federal navy in and around the North Carolina sounds during the winter of 1862. It had been a hopeless affair from the start. Entirely overmatched in their makeshift craft, Cooke was in command of the small tug, *Ellis,* when the Mosquito Fleet made its final stand not far from Elizabeth City. When the *Ellis* became disabled due to heavy fire, he rigged explosives to take the tug down, but his plan went awry, and the charges never blew. So when the Yanks came storming aboard, he yanked out his cutlass and fought until the Yankees overwhelmed him. Wounded badly, he was taken captive, but luckily paroled only five days later. Cooke then returned to his home in Portsmouth, Va., where, with the loving care of his wife, Mary, he slowly regained his health. But he never really got over the loss, and while his body eventually recovered from the wounds, his heart did not. Defeat, Cooke realized, had a bitter taste.

The *Ellis*, he learned later, had been quickly refitted by the Federals and given to a young lieutenant by the name of William Cushing. Cushing had developed quite a reputation for himself as an aggressive fighter on the inland rivers, but soon he too had run into trouble on the New River in North Carolina and had to finally scuttle the boat. So the *Ellis* was no more, but the memory of her loss still haunted him. Since Cooke's return to active duty he'd been assigned to the completion of the formidable new ironclad the Confederacy had under construction on the Roanoke River, and good work it was.

For James Cooke, the ironclad had become a holy mission of sorts. Conceived by the young shipbuilder, Gilbert Elliott, the ship represented something entirely new for the Confederacy, and for Cooke, a chance to redeem his career. She was far more than just another boat to captain, representing a substantial innovation in design.

The ironclad was 158 feet long, and 35 feet in width, but drew just 8 feet of water. She was constructed of 10-inch-thick stout pine timbers, overlaid with solid pine sheathing, which in turn was covered with two layers of iron plating. The sides had been sharply angled to repel even point blank shots, and on the bow she featured a sturdy ram, covered in iron, and tapered to a knife-like point. The ironclad was powered by two 200 horsepower engines, and once completed would boast a pair of Brooke rifles – one fore, one aft – that could swing in a 180° arc from side to side. The ship was of the standard *Virginia* class design, and a formidable design it was.

Yet its draft, not its firepower, was the ironclad's most remarkable feature. Drawing only 8 feet of water, she would be able to maneuver in the shallow rivers and sounds where no Federal ironclads could manage. Like a giant wolf with no natural predators, the new Rebel ironclad would enjoy an open season against the outdated wooden Federal warships, and her appearance, Cooke thought, would mark a significant change in the trajectory of the war.

The plan was a simple one. The ironclad, along with her sister ship, the *Neuse*, would cruise south – one on the Neuse River, the other on the Roanoke – to New Bern and Plymouth respectively, where, in conjunction with infantry from Robert E. Lee's Army of Northern Virginia, they would defeat the Federal garrisons and reclaim the towns for the South.. The ironclads would be virtually invulnerable to anything the Union forces could throw at them. Thus, the defeat of the Federal garrisons seemed only a question of time.

That accomplished, the sounds would soon be reopened, for with the christening of the Confederate ironclads the local Federal inland water fleet would at once become obsolete. Some of the most fertile counties in the Carolinas would be recovered. Supply routes north to Richmond would reopen and soon be teeming again with much-needed food and supplies for the Confederate cause. While the port of Charleston, South Carolina had not yet fallen, the

Federal Navy had so effectively sealed it off that blockade running in that area had been limited to but a trickle. Thus, the South had only Wilmington, North Carolina left as a point of entry along the east coast for its blockade-runners. The supply of food, supplies and munitions had naturally trailed off as a consequence, but the ironclads' completion and deployment would soon rectify much of that. Lee would need his troops back for the coming spring campaign, so if the trap was to be sprung, Cooke knew, it would have to be sprung soon.

Cooke decided to rest his legs. He sat back carefully on a crate, sipped his coffee, and watched the work as it progressed, enjoying the simple buzz of activity, the almost joyous ring of hammers in the early morning air. The rudder was now fitted out, and the shell room, magazine, officers' quarters, and berth deck completed. The iron was in place, the ship already afloat, and the engines would be ready for their initial firing in perhaps no more than a week. The Brooke rifles, cast at the Tredegar Iron Works in Richmond, were expected to arrive any day now. Like a wondrous dream, the ship was finally taking shape, coming to life before his eyes.

It had not been easy. While the original contract for the ironclad's construction had been signed in January 1862, construction had not begun for over a year. Bereft of almost all necessary shipbuilding facilities, the construction had inched forward gradually in a cornfield at Edward's Ferry on the Roanoke for month upon month. Iron, of course, had been the principal problem, for the Confederacy lacked the North's manufacturing capacity, and those few ironworks that remained open were overwhelmed with orders from the land armies. Cannons, rifles, and the ammunition to feed them were in constant demand, and in light of the dire circumstances that faced the Rebellion daily on land, the needs of the infant navy had little resonance in Richmond.

Cooke had solved the problem himself, sending out parties far and wide to scour the countryside for every scrap of iron they could put their hands on. Bolts, rakes, picture frames, wagon wheels, nails – whatever amount and in whatever form they could uncover he confiscated from the good people of North Carolina. All that iron was promptly melted down and turned into metal sheathing for the ironclad, but it had taken months of hard, often hostile, work. Soon he was known far and wide as the "Ironmonger Captain." Well, he'd been called worse.

More than once the stress and strain had gotten to him. Cooke, now in his fifty-first year, had long ago contracted a debilitating illness on one of his many voyages into the Caribbean, and often, like the ocean he loved, the sickness rose up in waves to overcome him. For long periods of time he would feel well enough to hope of recovery, only to succumb suddenly to another wave of illness. Then he had fever, chills, and often pain in his joints and legs. But Cooke – a short, slim, intense man – overcame the illness with the same determination he had brought to the completion of the ironclad. He mentioned the sickness to no one, kept the problem to himself, and focused instead on the job at hand. For him, it was a matter of mind over matter. If his body continued to cooperate and if God remained willing, he would see the thing through to completion. Much, he knew, depended on it.

One of the workers turned and spit out a plug of tobacco. "What's the next spike, Commander?" he yelled, cupping his hand around his ear.

Cooke stood up straight, thought for a moment, and recalled the plans. "Drive number six!" he yelled back.

The man waved, and the work went on again.

In a navy short of boats, James Cooke was building what might soon be regarded as one of the most fearsome vessels ever launched, and he knew its impact on the war for Southern independence might well be incalculable. His heart throbbed with the notion of returning to the scene of his previous defeat, capture, and humiliation; of storming through the Federal fleet like a hot knife through warm butter; of seeing his name written high in the papers; of beating the Yankees once and for all at their own game. In just a few weeks he planned on delivering to the Yankee fleet, to Mr. Lincoln in Washington City, and to all of the North a message they would not soon forget.

James Wallace Cooke had every intention of making history, so he had named the vessel after the North Carolina sound where he had met his initial defeat on board the *Ellis*. Soon that body of water would reverberate with his thunderous return. Of this he was sure. The boat was being built for the Confederacy, but in his heart it seemed crafted for his own personal redemption. The name had come to him like a vision in a dream, and the next day he limped painfully down to the dock in the still of the evening and privately, silently, christened the ship. The name seemed perfect; simple, yet rife with meaning for the fifty-one year old commander. He named it the *Albemarle*.

Chapter Two

February 29th– Afternoon

Lincoln watched curiously as bursts of sunlight danced and then disappeared on the hills just across the Potomac River. Great white clouds came tumbling swiftly overhead, casting sudden shafts of dazzling light that were followed quickly in turn by somber, whirling curtains of darkness that dappled the snowy ground as they made their chaotic journey east. The scene he thought fascinating, and he put down his pen and watched for a moment. Here were earth and sky, locked once again in the eternal struggle of light and darkness, day and night ... life and death. He concentrated, laboring to discern a pattern in it all, some inkling of meaning or intent, but soon the clouds blew away and he was left with only the bright snowy landscape, and just the faintest recollection of motion. He sighed, felt a surge of emptiness sweep over him, brooding and bitter, but he managed to fight it off. Abraham Lincoln looked up into the afternoon sky and wondered ... Why? Why war, why so much ... death? But there would be no answer on this late February afternoon. Abraham Lincoln knew that, for the time being at least, he would have to forge the answers himself.

This marked his third winter of war, and far off in the distance he knew the competing armies were hibernating through the cold and darkness in their winter quarters. Like great, slumbering beasts, they were marshaling their strength through the short, dreary months in order to be ready once the sun and warmth of spring returned. Winter, spring, summer, fall .... Was there any meaning to the endless rhythm, or was it, as Mr. Charles Darwin had concluded, merely the mindless interplay of dirt, wind, and water? He wondered, brooded, felt forever uncomfortable with the question.

He closed his eyes, felt the terrible pain of grief rise in his chest, almost overwhelming. Not many months before he had buried the second of his own sons – little Willie – and the pain of that was never far away. His wife Mary had been driven nearly crazy, locking herself away in her room for months in mourning, and the suffering of it seemed to fall steadily now like a dark rain in the halls and rooms of the White House. It seemed so heavy that there were times when he actually felt he could reach out and touch the misery in the air around him. Now Mary confided that she often spoke with Willie, actually carried on normal conversations with him in her room, and he feared for her sanity. The dark rain seemed to fall thicker and heavier by the hour, day after day.

While his own grief remained almost unbearable, he knew he had no particular right or privilege in that regard. He was, after all, the one man above all who had leaped headfirst into the vortex of dynamic, ungovernable forces that had led directly to civil war. Now that war raged from Texas to Pennsylvania, and in three years more men had been consumed in the conflagration than could ever be counted. So what special right did he have to mourn, when almost every home and cottage across the country had been touched by the hand of death? None. Indeed, there were times when he thought Willie's death nothing more than a grim form of justice enforced by an all-knowing Providence. If he was going to insist on the consummation of this bloodbath, then he could not hope to remain immune to death and suffering himself.

Yet pain, suffering and death were hardly new to Abraham Lincoln. Born to Thomas and Nancy Lincoln on Nolin Creek, Kentucky in February 1809, in his early years Lincoln had lived the "hardscrabble" life of the American frontier. There he briefly studied his ABC's before being uprooted and moved to Indiana, where his family passed the winter in an open lean-to, scarcely better off than the wolves that howled at night. It was not until Abraham was eight years old that the family finally moved into a small log cabin with a fireplace. Soon he learned to handle an axe, worked long hours on the farm, and slept soundly in the loft at night above the fire. In 1817, an epidemic swept many of the settlers away, including his mother. He but vaguely remembered her funeral. A year later his father left for Kentucky and returned months later with a new wife – Sarah Bush Johnston, and her three children. Sally proved to be a fair, straight, energetic woman, and years later Lincoln recalled her as a "good and kindly mother." But life remained hard, and the reality of the graveyard was never far away.

His family moved again, to Illinois, and over the years Abraham grew into a tall, angular, athletic youth, who was fast and powerful in body, yet awkward and homely in appearance. He often despaired of his looks, but cherished, above all else, his insightful, curious mind, and felt a burning desire to understand everything around him. He attended school irregularly, but whenever he did he was an excellent student. Lincoln learned to read and to write poetry, and generally lost himself in any book he could get his hands on. He ran loads down the Mississippi on a flatboat, had his share of fights with river toughs, and over time developed an ambition for a life beyond the frontier.

Abraham Lincoln hungered for knowledge, understanding, respect. He took up the law, later politics, and discovered he had a natural talent for them both. Through all his early years he had learned to live with poverty, disease, madness, and, above all, the constant, unfathomable, specter of the grave. So while Lincoln had certainly followed one of the most unusual roads to the White House, he was no stranger to want, hardship, and the angel of death.

That dark angel was now surely feasting upon the American landscape, yet in a real sense the seeds of the bloody nightmare known as the Civil War had been sown long before. The founders of the nation had by and large ignored the underlying problem, presuming that over time the "peculiar institution" of slavery would die a natural death. But rather than fading away, it had persisted, and the minds and hearts of those who supported slavery had only been hardened, somehow twisting the wicked institution into a joyous boon, a consecrated way of life, almost a blessing of sorts. Indeed, so infatuated had some in the South become with slavery that they were calling for an end to free labor even in the North, and the institution of white slavery upon the working class. Lincoln thought the notion beyond imagination. How long, he had asked repeatedly, could a nation founded upon the principle that "all men were created equal," blithely ignore the men, women, and children among them in bondage? But these were words that hardened minds refused to hear.

"If slavery is not wrong, nothing is wrong," he had declared. Slavery was, to his mind at least, a grotesque injustice, a festering wound that like a malignant cancer would have to be expunged from the national soul. It could be done reasonably, legally, sensibly – as the Southerner, Henry Clay, had proposed – or else it would explode into violence, just as it had done in Missouri and Kansas. But among the hardened hearts and heads on both sides of the Mason Dixon Line, by 1861 reasonableness had become a commodity hard to come by, and in the end it was the hot heads and hard minds that had carried the day.

War had come, and when it did, it came with an intensity and savagery that few had prefigured. For the causes of union and abolition, that war so far had not gone well, and Lincoln's worst fear was that the bloody nightmare might continue unchecked until freedom and republican government itself might perish in the flames. What civilization had struggled thousands of years to accomplish might well implode in a heartbeat on the North American Continent, never to be heard from again. Surely, Democracy was on trial in this most bitter of wars.

So now he found himself sadly contemplating the dancing forms of shadow and light just across the Potomac, the conundrum of life and death, in this, his third winter of war. In order to save the Union and expunge slavery, it had become evident to him that the war would have to be pressed to a victorious conclusion, but to do that would require a second term on his part; the one would not come without the other. He had not yet openly declared himself a candidate, but already the endless political maneuvering had begun. Sadly, the meanest intrigue against him had come, not only from within his own party, but from within his own cabinet.

Salmon Chase, the Secretary of the Treasury, had been for some time now privately stoking the subterranean fires of his own presidential ambitions. In January, Chase had declared himself available should the nomination come his way, and since then Lincoln had been receiving a steady stream of disquieting reports that Chase was using his position at the treasury to grease his way into the White House. The issue had come to a head just the week before when an anti-Lincoln circular authored by Senator Samuel Pomeroy of Kansas had hit the papers. The letter argued that Lincoln was unelectable; a deterrent to the cause of liberty, and that Chase was obviously the best man for the office. Since everyone knew Pomeroy was no more than Chase's front man, most savvy speculation soon centered on Chase as the true instigator.

Lincoln had accepted Chase's apology over the circular, but refused to accept his resignation. Long ago he had learned that most men involved in politics had strong personal ambitions, and that those ambitions usually could not be thwarted, but at best only channeled. Lincoln himself had been "bitten by the presidential bug," of course, but his agenda was far more than personal. He strove to restore the Union and emancipate the slaves – for a better republic true to its original ideals – but knew that many did not think as he did. So if Chase could be used, then use him he would, and dismiss the rest as inconsequential. What else could he do? In a world overflowing with ambitious scoundrels, he simply tried to harness the ambition and ignore the endless intriguing.

Thankfully, not all men were schemers and scoundrels. Many had already given their lives for union and abolition, and many more were prepared to do so. These came to his office from time to time, but always had a different feel and flavor than Chase, and most definitely a different agenda. It was not that these men did not have ambitions – all men had ambitions – so much as that their ambitions seemed of a higher order. Lincoln could recognize them almost at once and felt quickly at ease in their presence. These were the men who believed in what they were fighting for, and he fancied them a rare and precious commodity.

They came in all shapes and sizes, these men. Indeed, there was no one characteristic they all seemed to share except, possibly, sincerity. He sensed more than figured these men, could feel them across the length of a room just as one could sense true warmth in a smile. Often these days they were military men, generally lesser in rank, mindful only of the task at hand, rarely if ever of their own needs or aspirations. He thought of his friend, the journalist Noah Brooks, of Charles Dana, and of Lincoln's own secretary, John Hay. Usually they were older men, but not always. Indeed, he remembered one – a young naval lieutenant, if he recalled him correctly now – brought over one day by the Secretary of the Navy.

Lincoln leaned back, closed his eyes, thought for a moment. What was that boy's name? He could see him clearly in his mind's eye; tall and handsome, with a lean, intelligent face and bright blue eyes; he had hardly looked to be out of his teens. The Secretary had been particularly impressed with the boy, wanted the president to know there were good, daring fighters in the service. ... Cushing! Yes, that was it. Lt. William Cushing. It had been back in the spring of '63, and the Secretary had brought the boy up to his office, then regaled him with stories of the lieutenant's escapades on the North Carolina sounds and rivers – seems the lieutenant was the youngest in the country's history to command his own ship – while the boy sat quiet as a church mouse across from Lincoln.

Then the Secretary left, and Lincoln chatted with the lad for a good hour or so, recalling his own times on the Mississippi River hauling furs down to New Orleans. He didn't talk of war, didn't think it necessary, still feeling benumbed, in truth, by the most recent Federal disaster at Chancellorsville. He spoke rather as he might to a younger brother or son, to someone very special. And the boy listened quietly, bright eyes clear and focused, taking in the afternoon. Lincoln remembered that the boy never spoke of himself, never boasted, never even tried to make an impression, and Lincoln spoke to him, not as Commander-in-Chief, but as a compatriot. Then the lieutenant thanked him and left. He had not heard from him since.

Lincoln would need many such men if the war were ever going to be won. On his desk now, for instance, was a bill just sent over from Congress for his signature, a measure restoring the old rank of lieutenant general. Lincoln had asked that it be introduced with the intention of bestowing the rank on Ulysses S. Grant. His plan was to have a single, overall commander: one good officer who would coordinate the entire war strategy for the North, not five different generals often working at cross-purposes.

He'd never met Grant, knew him only through official reports, idle chatter, and newspaper accounts. But it was clear that he could fight, and that his fighting produced victories. And since war was about winning, he seemed not only the best, but in the end the only, choice for the job. Lincoln had heard the rumors, of course, that Grant was coarse and rough – an alcoholic. So he'd sent Charles Dana out to tag along with Grant's headquarters, and all the reports had come back solid. Now Grant was headed east to be promoted to lieutenant general, and once the snow melted and the roads dried, Grant would be out after Lee.

Lincoln could only hope and pray that Grant would fare better than the handful of Union generals who had preceded him – McDowell, McClellan, Pope, McClellan again, Burnside, Hooker and finally Meade. The war was costing the nation almost $2,000,000 a day, yet often his generals seemed to do nothing but sit. The previous summer Meade had soundly defeated Lee at Gettysburg, but had failed to follow up on that victory, and Lincoln had become at first furious, then despondent. Lee's shattered army had been allowed to slip across the Potomac River unmolested, and now it appeared the war would drag on for at least another year. If Lincoln were going to be reelected, the war effort would have to improve considerably. If the Union was ever going to be restored and the slaves freed, the war would have to be fought to a conclusion, yet Lincoln was the only candidate willing to press the bloody thing to that difficult end. So, in that sense, all his hopes were now riding on Grant.

Lincoln signed the bill, set it aside, then stood and went to the window. Across the river, they would soon be burying Union boys in long rows on the rolling landscape of Arlington, Robert E. Lee's sprawling Virginia estate. How many more rows and acres would it take, he wondered, before the thing would finally be over, the tents struck, and the armies at long last mustered out? He had become so mortified by the death rolls and long casualty lists, that now he searched for a reason to grant clemency for almost every offense that came across his desk. The army officers howled, of course, but he didn't care. Enough death. Lincoln preferred mercy to harsh justice, had never felt comfortable with bloodshed. Yet here he was prosecuting the bloodiest war in the nation's history. Lincoln winced at the irony.

He could still recall that day in Indiana when as a boy he'd run off for the gun when a wild turkey had approached the cabin. He yanked it down, took proper aim, cocked the hammer, then pulled the trigger. The turkey was almost shredded in a torrent of buckshot, and his young soul was simply horrified by the sight. He dropped the gun and backed away, staggered by what he had done, appalled by the sheer senselessness of his own act. After that, he had always kept his distance from guns and bloodshed, and the irony of this bloody civil war was not lost upon him – a man of essentially peaceful, nonviolent sensibilities presiding over the most sanguinary episode in the nation's short history. And it gnawed at him. In response to a letter from a group of Quakers, for instance, he'd written that, "Engaged, as I am, in a great war, I fear it will be difficult for the world to understand how fully I appreciate the principles of peace inculcated in this letter and everywhere by the Society of Friends."

And while he had good reason to feel a measure of optimism over Grant's imminent arrival, Lincoln knew the general's promotion guaranteed nothing at all. For three long years Robert E. Lee had outfought and outmaneuvered every general officer Lincoln had sent against him, and Lincoln seriously doubted that Lee was in any way awed by Grant's reputation. The Rebels had fought well, and Lincoln knew they would continue to fight well. Lee was building his strength over the winter, and Lincoln had heard reports that the Rebels were constructing two ironclads on the rivers in North Carolina while contemplating a spring offensive in that area as well. If true, a Confederate success in eastern North Carolina might reopen the supply lines to Lee's army, and prolong the war almost indefinitely – in short, it would be a disaster.

Lincoln closed his eyes, rubbed his face, then slowly opened his eyes again. In the window glass he spotted his own reflection, and the sight gave him a momentary start. Thin, worn, and entirely bedraggled, he could hardly recognize his own image anymore. At times he felt as if the weight of the world was sitting on his shoulders, and that the burden was far more than one man could bear. "This war is eating out my life," he had told Owen Lovejoy, perhaps his best friend in Congress. Despite that, he would not put the burden down and walk away with the job only half finished. No, he intended to see it through to the end. That meant a second term, but a second term would only come his way with success on the battlefield. Peace could only be gained through war, justice through blood – darkness spinning into light, death into life, ... on and on. He frowned.

In the end, he knew, there was really no making sense of it, no use wondering why. What would be would be. God's intentions, it seemed, were beyond his reckoning. For some odd, imperceptible reason Providence seemed to have selected him of all people to lead the nation through this disaster of civil war. Why him? Why now? Who could say? But this much was clear to him: the terrible toll of hate, anger, and death seemed to be slowly but steadily killing him too. Not a grave was dug on American soil these days – North or South – that he did not feel the earth shift under his own feet, and his heart break once again.

He recalled his last day in Springfield then, the day he'd packed and took the train out to Washington to take the oath of office. Before boarding the train with his family, he had wandered back down to his law office for a short chat with his partner, Billy Herndon. Lincoln loved the place, his desk and unorthodox pile of law cases on the floor, and he told Billy not to take the sign down – that just because he was off to be president for a while, didn't mean that their partnership necessarily had to end. When it was over he hoped to come back and pick up right where he'd left off. But as he lay on the sofa studying the ceiling overhead that afternoon in Springfield, a darkness came over him. More than mere thought or shudder, it was a premonition of sorts, a dire understanding of what was and was not to be, and that premonition told him clearly that he would not be coming back to Springfield – alive.

Since arriving in Washington, he had not forgotten that premonition. It had, in fact, been reinforced, supplemented by a host of odd dreams, feelings, and events. So be it. In the end what could he do but soldier on? He had come to understand that the business for which he had been summoned was far larger than any one man, political party, or region. While he labored over emancipation, eventual reconstruction, the course of the war and so forth, those things were in the end only singular threads in a much larger fabric. It was that fabric that most men did not see, ensnared in their own private squabbles and prejudices, the larger picture always seeming to escape their provincial gaze. Adrift in a world of political ideologues, his every move seemed to draw fire – he was moving too fast or much too slow, steering the nation toward the reefs of disaster, or totally ignoring the moral imperatives of the day. Practical objectives seemed to interest no one.

So slowly he wove this fabric alone, depleted now through exhaustion and worry, struggling as best he could to place each stitch with painstaking precision. It would have to last, this tapestry of his, to cradle and hold generations yet unborn. It was, to his mind at least, a holy endeavor crafted in blood, heart, mind, and soul, and ripe with wondrous potential yet beautiful to imagine. Indeed its completion gave hope to his nights and inspiration to his days, for its name was the future, and for Abraham Lincoln that future radiated promise no less than the brightest point in God's starry heaven.

Chapter Three

February 29th– Night

Cushing motioned quickly, and all the oars stopped simultaneously, hanging just slightly above the dark river, dripping. He took a single deep breath; he could hear his heart softly beating in his chest like a small drum in the profound, sudden silence. Cushing sat calmly as the boats drifted a few yards through the black night, listening for what he thought had been the snap of a branch along the shore. But in time he realized that there was nothing out there in the darkness, and he slowly lowered his hand. The men were watching him intently, waiting. Then, he raised his hand again, made a circling motion, and the two boats began to come about. It was time to move in.

The gig and the small cutter loaded with Yankee sailors turned around in unison, then started back down the Cape Fear River toward the small town of Smithville, North Carolina, slicing across the water almost silently on the current with muffled oars. So far all had gone smoothly, precisely as planned. They had rowed in from the ocean, slipped upriver past the town, then turned around and started back down so they would appear to anyone who happened to spot them from shore to be Confederates on their way downriver from Wilmington. So far it appeared that no one had. Or so they hoped.

In the distance now, he could just make out the lights of Smithville. There was a hotel sitting not far from the water and a few houses scattered about. He motioned for the men to guide in toward the lights, which were shimmering out toward them over the black river like radiating pools of whiteness, eerie and beautiful, seemingly beckoning to them through the cold morning air. For a fraction of a second he thought the scene captivating, but there was no time for that now, and he put the thought aside.

Then, Cushing spotted a lone sentry on the wharf, sitting motionless on a chair, and he put his hand up again. The boats stopped along the edge of the rippling whiteness, muffled oars once again pulled from the water, and they all drifted in a tense silence as William Barker Cushing studied the sentry from a distance. Small puffs rose from the men's lips, rising into the cold night as they waited, hunched over their oars, silent as statues.

The two boats bobbed on a light chop. Cushing took his time, needing to be sure, watching the sentry until he was certain the man was asleep. Then he motioned them forward again, and the boats slipped in toward the wharf as silently as ghosts, only the gentle slap of water against wood pilings breaking the silence of the night. Far off in the distance a dog barked twice, then fell silent again. The small town seemed motionless, silent, frozen in time. Good. It appeared that no one was expecting trouble.

His twenty men had been handpicked, the very best he had, and they beached the boats quietly, moving like shadows through the night. He left twelve behind to guard the boats, then started up a small rise with the remainder. Just ahead he came to a short bluff; beyond that lay the town. He motioned them down as he kneeled in the sand and studied the scene – the hotel, what appeared to be a fort, the main street winding uphill, here and there a few lights flickering in the darkness. But no one was moving. Everything was still.

Cushing had conceived the mission days before, when Captain Sands had refused permission for him to take two hundred men ashore late at night and seize all of Smith's Island. His original plan had been to hold the entire island until the army arrived, and, while it was a risky venture, success would have sealed off one of the two channels leading into Wilmington that the Rebel blockade-runners regularly used. But Sands – far more concerned with the potential fallout of failure than the benefits of success – proved too cautious, and Cushing's request had been denied. Sands' refusal infuriated Cushing, and he vowed to snatch the Confederate general in charge of the entire area – he was known to reside in Smithville – and bring him back for breakfast with Sands to prove the feasibility of his plan. And, of course, Cushing also intended to show up his commanding officer. So, that night, they had all shoved off around 8:40, without permission; details like orders and permissions were for lesser souls than William Cushing.

William Barker Cushing had been born in the wilds of Wisconsin in November 1842, the last in a line of five sons, to Dr. Milton and Mary Cushing. His father died when Will was only four years old, and the family moved on to Fredonia, N. Y. Educated by his mother – who ran a small private school – at the age of only fourteen Will received an appointment to the U. S. Naval Academy in Annapolis, Maryland.

There, Cushing proved to be an above average student, but a behavioral nightmare, racking up demerits at an almost unprecedented clip. Good fun and hijinks captivated Cushing until a run-in with the Superintendent, combined with a bucket of water dumped from a door jamb onto his Spanish professor's head, eventually got him dismissed from the Academy – all this only months before graduation. A crestfallen Cushing hung around Washington until he was finally able to get his case reviewed by Gideon Welles, then Secretary of the Navy. Welles heard the young man out and was apparently impressed. While he did not send Cushing back to the Academy, he did allow his reentry into the navy with the rank of master's mate. It was a favor Cushing would never forget, and since then his rise through naval ranks had been nothing short of meteoric.

Accounts of his daring and bravery soon reached the highest levels of the Navy Command, and in July of 1862 Will Cushing was jumped two full grades to the rank of lieutenant. Later that year he was given command of the gunboat *Ellis,* and with that he became the youngest officer to command a ship in American naval history. While he had to scuttle the *Ellis,* his performance on the rivers of Virginia and North Carolina was deemed so meritorious that he was eventually given command of the *Monticello,* a sleek, black, ocean going vessel of the highest quality, capable of running down almost any Rebel blockade-runner at sea. And it was from the deck of the *Monticello* that Cushing had set forth on his audacious raid into Smithville that evening.

He studied the town for a few minutes from behind a tree, eyes narrowed, drinking in every detail. From his position below the town he could not determine which house above might belong to the general in charge, and he had to know that before moving on. So he hatched a plan. Slowly, silently he edged his way along the cover of the bluff, eight men stretched out behind him, moving as he moved, at short intervals. Cushing made his way down toward a salt works known to be at the end of the point, and from the top of a small rise spotted a fire burning directly ahead, with two black men seated nearby – just what he had been looking for. Cushing held up his arm, motioned for the column to stop. Ever so quietly he un-holstered his pistol and crawled toward the fire through the shadows until he was only a few feet from the two. They were chatting, laughing, had no idea he was nearby until he stood up suddenly and pointed the gun. He took dead aim.

"Say nothing and do not move," Cushing ordered in a whisper, "and you will both live to enjoy your grandchildren."

Both men drew back, stunned by his sudden appearance. But once they grasped the color of his uniform, they seemed to relax. One nodded that he understood.

"Okay," Cushing whispered. "Can either of you gentlemen direct me to the residence of General Hébert?"

The same man who had nodded leaned forward just slightly, smiled thinly, nodded again.

Cushing smiled back. "Fine, then," he whispered. "And a steamer? Is there a good steamer that we might appropriate from the harbor tonight?"

The men glanced at one another. "No, sir," came the answer. "Least not tonight. Last night maybe, but not tonight. Ain't seen no steamer."

Cushing frowned; he had hoped to grab the general and then spirit him off on a swift steamer out to the *Monticello.* But steamer or no, he was not about to abandon on his plan.

"Well, all right then," he said to the man who had spoken. "Tell me, would you gentlemen like to accompany us later this evening when we leave? If you come along and show me the way to the general's residence, I'll take you both back to freedom with me." He looked again toward the man who had spoken up. "You come with me now. Your friend can stay here for the time being."

Both men nodded vigorously.

"Fine then," Cushing said, nodding to one of the sailors to guard the second black man until the mission was complete.

They slipped gingerly back along the cover of the bluff toward the town, and there Cushing called the rest of his men together. He sent several back to guard the route to the boats, then headed off with the last three. Will put his hand gently on the black man's back as they walked up the street. "What's your name?" he asked.

"William, sir," the man replied, calmly enough.

"Okay, William," Cushing continued, "we'll all follow you. Just lead us up to the general's house. Then you can go back with your friend, and no one will be the wiser."

William smiled. "Okay, Captain. You take us to the North? To Freedom?"

Cushing winked. "You bet."

They made their way quickly up the central street, turned once, being careful to stick to the shadows. They were soon confronted by an enormous white home with a large porch that wrapped around the entire front. It was a dazzling sight in the moonlight, looming above the town.

William nodded toward the house. "Dat be de general's house," he said.

"Yes, good," Cushing answered, looking the place over quickly. Everything seemed quiet, still. He looked closely – there were no lights on inside.

William pointed across the street. "And over there be the fort," he whispered. "Whole bunch o' Rebel soldiers asleep over there. You got's to be careful now, Captain."

Cushing smiled. "So," he whispered, "we'll just have to be extra quiet this evening. Very good, William, my friend. Go back down to the fire with your friend and wait for us. You have done us an invaluable service this evening. I will not forget you."

"Yes, Captain. You bet we wait."

As the slave turned and made his way back down the street, Cushing gathered his men around. He pointed out the house and fort, then assigned one man to guard each exit of the residence. After that he crossed the street and stepped lightly onto the porch. Will halted by the front door for a moment, listening patiently for any sound from inside, but he heard nothing but the steady, rhythmic beat of his own heart. He felt a steely sense of excitement rise in his chest, then noticed that several of the windows all along the porch were open. A breeze was wafting the curtains gently in and out of their frames. Cushing leaned forward, grabbed the door latch, gave a delicate tug, and the front door swung open freely. His heart began to beat harder. He stepped inside, stopped and listened again, hearing no sound but the ticking of a clock off in the corner. It was very dark. He blinked, blinked again, trying to acclimate his eyes to the blackness.

In time, the room began to materialize out of the darkness. Straight ahead he could just make out the shape of a long hallway, above that a very high ceiling, implying, perhaps, a second or even third floor. Just off to his right there was a large room with a table and numerous chairs – probably the dining room – while on his left, above the clock, loomed a set of stairs leading up to the second floor. Cushing moved toward them slowly, smoothly, soundlessly. He found the base of the steps with his foot, took one, stood firmly for a moment, glad that it did not creak. The excitement in his chest was gone now, replaced by an intense sense of concentration, of awareness. There was no fear, no apprehension. He floated nimbly up the remainder of the steps until he reached the second floor.

Here on the landing it was too dark to see, so he pulled a match from his pants pocket and struck it between his fingers. The light flared like a beacon all around him, momentarily flooding the landing with a radiant, orange flash. He looked quickly, spotted several doors, decided to try the first. Just as Cushing pushed the door open he heard a sudden commotion from below. The match burned out. He held his breath. What was going on?

"Captain! *Captain!*" It sounded like one of his men calling urgently. Yes – he suddenly recognized the voice – it was Howorth!

He pulled out his pistol, bounded back down the stairs, turning at the bottom toward the sound of Howorth's voice. Cushing's heart was pounding now, his senses on fire. He raced down another hall, pushed through a door, fumbled through his pockets, struck another match in the darkness. The match exploded like a flare, briefly illuminating the room. There, directly in front of him, not five feet away, was a tall man in a nightshirt holding a chair directly over his head like a truncheon.

Cushing reacted without thinking. He rushed the man, tackling him at the knees, driving him backward to the floor. The force of the collision sent the chair crashing against the wall. Will struggled for control, then forced his pistol up against the side of the man's head with one hand while grabbing his throat with his other.

"Are you Hébert?" Cushing hissed into the man's ear, breathing hard, holding the pistol firmly against his captive's temple.

The man's eyes bulged. He shook his head no.

"Where's Hébert?" Cushing hissed.

"G-Gone."

Cushing tightened his grip on the man's throat. He had no time for games. "Gone where?"

"Off ... to Wilmington for the night," the man replied, blinking. "He's gone, I swear," he went on, breathing hard now, sweat dripping down his face.

Cushing sensed the man was telling the truth. He relaxed his grip slightly. "Who the hell are you?"

"Ke-Kelly," the man stuttered. "Captain Kelly, Chief Engineer."

Cushing struck another match, took a close look at the fellow, felt satisfied the man was not lying. "Well, Captain Kelly," he said with a wry smile, "it's a pleasure meeting you. My introductions aren't usually quite so violent, but I'm afraid it's the nature of our times. No offense intended."

Kelly swallowed hard. "No offense taken… sir."

Suddenly, a door flew open and Ensign Howorth dashed into the room. "Captain!" he cried, "I saw someone running away from the house up toward the Rebel barracks. He must have gotten out a window or something! They know something's up! They *must* know we're here!"

Cushing leaped to his feet. "Damn!" Will took a deep breath, letting his mind settle. "Well, all right," he said, thinking it through. "We have to get out of here. Fast! Grab all the papers you can find – anything that looks official." Then he turned back to his captive. "Put your pants on, Captain," he said. "You'll be coming along with us. And not a word out of you if you ever hope to see Dixie again. Do you understand me, sir?"

"Yes, yes, of course," Kelly answered, climbing awkwardly into his trousers.

The alarm had already been sounded, and outside Confederate search parties were racing every which way, down darkened alleys, checking in the nearby trees, scouring the creeks and farm fields. Cushing watched them for a second or two, mind awhirl. The Rebels seemed to be everywhere. This was not going to be easy. Then it came to him: the Johnnies were looking everywhere but in the most obvious place – so that was the one way out! He grabbed

Kelly by the arm, placed his pistol in the small of his back, and ordered his men to walk slowly, calmly, straight down the main street of town.

They all stared at him as if he'd gone crazy.

"What, Captain?" Howorth asked, rubbing his ears as if he had not heard correctly. "Right down the street there?"

"Trust me. It will work," Cushing replied. "I can't tell blue from grey in the dark. Neither can the Rebs. We'll avoid the light, walk like we belong here. It's the only place they're not looking."

"You sure, Captain?" Ensign Jones asked nervously. "I mean, right down Main Street?"

"Positive," he answered. "But we have to act like we belong here. Just like we have an appointment with General Robert E. Lee himself," Cushing told them. "And we have to go quick. Now!"

They all looked at one another nervously, then started off slowly, walking behind Cushing with a calm, measured gait.

Twice they were almost run over by Rebel patrols racing off on some wild goose chase, but nothing came of it. No one recognized them. Slowly they strolled down to where the two slaves had been moved. Cushing nodded to them both, motioned for them to fall in line, and the small group continued its cavalier walk back to the boats completely unmolested. Not once were they challenged, although frantic Rebels were everywhere.

"What's up, Captain?" one of the sentries whispered nervously, lowering his carbine as the party approached. "Heard a whole bunch of commotion up in the town. Thought you were in big trouble for sure. Rebs running everywhere now."

Cushing smiled. "Nothing much, really," he answered. "Just a little fun." He let the breath out of his lungs slowly. "Now, let's get in the boats and get the *hell* out of here."

They all tumbled into the boats and then quickly shoved off.

"Row like hell!" Cushing hissed, looking back over his shoulder as the cutter slipped away from the shore. The oars struck the water with great power, and they made their way rapidly back out into the channel, out of the faint glow of the town, away from Rebel vision.

Behind them, the Confederate soldiers could still be heard running, shouting, searching for blue ghosts in the night. Shouted orders filled the air above Smithville, but whatever it was they were looking for seemed to have vanished. Cushing smiled, felt the muscles in his neck relax, a sense of pleasure rise up through his chest. Intoxicating.

They rowed quickly, calmly into the darkness and escaped without a shot being fired. At 3:30 that morning they hailed the *Monticello.* Twenty minutes later they were all back on board.

Early in the morning Cushing had Captain Kelly, the Rebel engineer, rowed over to the commanding officer's ship to be presented at the morning meal. An astonished Captain Sands almost swallowed his tongue when the captured chief engineer responsible for all the Confederate fortifications in the area was brought in and seated at his table.

Later that afternoon Cushing sent Ensign Jones back to Smithville under a flag of truce to pick up Captain Kelly's personal effects, and to deliver a note to the Confederate commander. It read:

> My Dearest General:
> I deeply regret that you were not at home when I called.
> Very Respectfully,
> W. B. Cushing

Jones returned later that evening with a copy of the Wilmington newspaper. It had a story on the front page describing Cushing's raid in glowing terms, and in remarkable detail.

"By the way, Captain," Jones said, grinning, barely able to contain his excitement, "General Hébert was not there, but I met with their Colonel Jones. He seemed quite impressed with our little mission."

Cushing smiled. "He was now, was he?"

"Yes, Captain. Did you read the Rebel papers? They're quite complimentary actually."

"No, but I will."

The ensign smiled. "Seems the good colonel would like to meet you someday. He told me so."

"Is that right?"

"I don't think they get much company over there in Smithville," Jones nodded. "Especially late at night."

Cushing laughed.

"But I must tell you, Captain, he also said that you should never try and stage such a stunt as that again. Because the next time, he said, he promises you will not get off the river."

Cushing cocked his head back, hesitated for just a moment. "Oh, really?"

"Well, that's what he said."

The following morning the story of Cushing's Smithville raid made headlines all across the North, and in a single day William Cushing – all of twenty-one years old – became a national hero. But he took no great glory in it. Glory was not, after all, what interested him. Besides, he'd already hatched an even better plan.

Chapter Four

March 8th – Evening

Lincoln folded the newspaper away carefully, pushed it to the side of his desk, and laughed out loud one last time. It seemed like the first he'd really laughed in months, and like a rock sent bounding down a narrow crevice, the pure joy of it rattled his being rib-to-rib and seemed to bring him back to life. Abraham Lincoln had a natural fondness for good humor, relished it just as a hound relishes the shade on a hot summer day. God knows he needed it.

He'd been brooding again, swept away once more on a current of despair, suddenly mindful of a million mushrooming grave markers all given life by this river of blood called Civil War. The image of a nation in flames, of death running rampant across the American landscape, haunted his days and nights. The night before he'd dreamt once again of a crewless ship floating aimlessly through the fog, lost ... adrift … distant voices that he could not quite make out whispering in the background. The dream, as always, had unnerved him.

Many, Lincoln understood, conceived the war as a clash over slavery, union, or even states' rights, and nothing more. While those views were fundamentally correct, in the end, Lincoln knew they were all only half-truths, partial glimpses of a much larger picture. He wished he could make them understand.

Boiled down to its most basic elements, the war was, in fact, a heated confrontation between two antagonists; one an emerging future, the other an inflexible past. That's the way he saw it. In that sense, it was a head on collision between the budding forces of law and reason, and the heavy hand of power that had ruled over civilization since there had been such a thing. The Declaration of Independence, the Bill of Rights, and the Constitution were all creations of the Age of Reason, a blossoming moment in the growth of humankind when suddenly certain truths had become – as Jefferson had so aptly phrased it – "self-evident." And if all creation was, as Lincoln conceived it, the work of God, then reason could only be sensibly interpreted as God's latest manifestation, democratic government not simply another bureaucratic subset, but the latest, and most extraordinary gift of a benevolent Providence.

The simple notion that "all men are created equal" led logically, inexorably to Democratic government, but democratic government that only favored a precious few would never do; was in fact, nothing more than a sad, hypocritical mockery of itself. 'All men' meant just that – *all.* This did not mean, of course, that all people were, in fact, the *same*, only that they were all conceived with the same opportunity to freely pursue life, liberty, and the pursuit of happiness to the natural extent of their own individual talents. No two men, women, or children were born exactly alike in terms of their capacities, but that had never been the point. Freedom had to do, therefore, with the right to certain opportunities, not the results those opportunities might ultimately produce. What's more, it required no elaborate analysis to conclude that reason had not been specially granted to any one nation, culture, or race. The ability to think deeply, to penetrate nature's mysteries as had the minds of thinkers such as Galileo, Kepler, and Newton, was surely a common attribute of humankind in general, and not the province of any one particularly fortunate group. But wasn't nature ultimately just another aspect of all creation, of God, The Divine, or the Common Father – as Lincoln often spoke of the ineffable? And thus wasn't it simply logical that reason had been created by God and bestowed upon man to in some way help him to unravel the mystery of the Divine? And if reason had sprung from God, how could its valid conclusions possibly be evil? It was self-evident that only an abundance of mind separated man from God's lesser creatures, yet it was precisely the abundant use of that instrument that seemed to enrage so many.

Across the globe the discordant voices of a thousand different religions, sects and philosophies often decried and condemned the simple conclusions that naturally flowed from this new Age of Enlightenment. Where logic saw unscientific, unsupportable dogmas, religion proclaimed infallible truth through faith alone. One such odd truth was that insisted upon by many Southern thinkers and politicians; that the right to own other people was, in fact, God given.

Where logic reached out and discovered common spiritual ties that bound all peoples in mutual respect, these thinkers screamed 'heresy'. Those heretical assertions were at times so loud and flagrant, it seemed to Lincoln, that to actually *use* one's God given faculties was considered by some to be tantamount to sin. Instead of embracing a worldwide community of man as being conceived and sustained by a single Divine Spirit, individual religions continued to squabble amongst themselves while tirelessly proclaiming their own superiority. These squabbles often led to self-contradictory declarations, many of which Lincoln found quite amusing.

He had a favorite story, one he loved to recount about a Sunday morning during his Springfield days. Seems a young Universalist preacher had come to town and his teachings concerning the long reach of God's benevolence had infuriated some local men of the cloth. Three orthodox ministers had gotten together and agreed that come Sunday morning they would all "take turns and preach the young fellow down." The first to mount the pulpit in this holy crusade was the Methodist preacher. As Lincoln loved to tell it, "He commenced by telling his large congregation how happily they were all situated in Springfield. Launching into his sermon, the Methodist shouted 'and now comes a preacher preaching a doctrine that all men shall be saved. But, my brethren, let us hope for better things.'"

That story and a hundred more like it were the reasons Lincoln had never seen fit to attend church or join any particular religious group – not because he took religion *lightly*, but because he took it far more *seriously* than most. And he was unwilling to abandon his mind, that one unique piece of human equipment that he prized above all else. He would think freely, exercise his mind as he pleased, and where creed and logic disagreed, he would favor his own good judgment.

Over time it had become his firm conviction that freedom and democratic government represented something far more than just another formula to rule by, but were indeed an expression of the Divine Will. And that was what made this Civil War so terribly important and the burden that he carried so difficult to bear. Very few seemed to understand just what was at stake, but it was not for his lack of trying. On more than one occasion he had tried to convey his heartfelt convictions to various groups. Once he'd told a visiting group of Methodists ministers that the war was "an important crisis which involves, in my judgment, not only the civil and religious liberties of our own dear land, but in large degree the civil and religious liberties of mankind in many countries and through many ages." Some fought for their own state, region, or personal animosities. Abraham Lincoln fought, on the other hand, for posterity, and today, he suddenly remembered, that effort was hopefully to take a great leap forward.

He checked his watch quickly, then stuffed it back into his vest pocket. Tonight there was to be a reception for General Grant in the Blue Room, and for that he dared not be late. The general had come to Washington to receive his new commission, and Lincoln was anxious to meet his new lieutenant general. But there was still time enough – he had not drifted off in thought for too long this time. So he took up the newspaper once more, glanced at the story he'd been reading, and laughed out loud again. And the laughter felt good.

It was a brief, supplemental article on Cushing's Smithville raid of the previous week. Lincoln could not help but enjoy the image of an entire Confederate garrison running around in circles as Cushing marched his captive, along with his own small command, to safety right down the main street of town. That sort of comic calamity had been visited upon his own officer corps on more occasions than he cared to recall by the likes of J. E. B. Stuart or John Mosby, and it was a joy to finally be on the other side of the picture. While Cushing's raid was hardly a major military affair, it certainly played well in all the papers, and it was nice to see that the North had officers capable of making the Johnnies look like buffoons as well.

The door cracked open just slightly, and his secretary, John Hay, stepped into the office. He hesitated until Lincoln looked up. "The reception, sir."

Lincoln smiled; he was feeling better now. "Yes, of course." He folded the paper again, tucked it away in his desk. "I'm looking forward to meeting General Grant," he said.

"Yes, sir. The guests are arriving."

Lincoln thumped the desktop, stood. "Very well, then."

He walked down the long hall to the Blue Room, quickly warmed his hands over the fire, then took his place in the reception line. Most of his cabinet members were already on hand, he noticed, and Mary was there too, smiling pleasantly and looking well. His heart soared to see her so cheerful, and for a moment the sadness that seemed to constantly envelope him melted away like morning mist and he felt a small blossom of joy rise in his chest.

She came and stood by his side, smiling warmly.

"You appear very lovely this evening," Lincoln observed.

She bowed ever so slightly. "Why, thank you, Mr. President."

He could not recall her appearing so radiant since the death of little Willie. "It is a joy to have you here this evening. I am very pleased."

"Washington is buzzing with the news of General Grant's arrival," she said. "Everyone is talking."

"That so?" he replied. "Good. Yes, I suppose that's good."

He'd met her at a cotillion in Springfield, Illinois in December 1839. By then Lincoln had already established himself as an excellent attorney and an up-and-coming politician. But success with men in men's activities and success with women on the other side of the hall were two very different things. Put simply, women confused and bewildered Abraham Lincoln. Coarse, as he fancied himself, ungainly, homely, and shy, he yearned for the company of a woman, but the young debutantes of Springfield might well have come from another world, so foreign and exotic did they appear. Indeed, often he despaired he would never enjoy even a romantic relationship, much less a wife who would love and care for him, and that anxiety only served to increase his fits of despair and diminish his confidence. The more he fretted, the more awkward he acted, until the whole thing just seemed to spiral out of control.

Then suddenly one night she was there: pretty, charming, and witty. If he closed his eyes he could still feel the excitement of that moment, the soft music, perfume, gentle smiles and wood smoke all twisted together to form an intoxicating recollection. She was there on his arm, interested in *him*, and they danced and talked and laughed the night away. Somehow, in some odd way, he discovered he could dance, joke, even flirt with her without the sense of looming disaster he generally felt – like the sword of Damocles – to be hanging just above his head. In that one extraordinary evening he had accomplished the impossible, bridged a gap so wide that previously he'd had no idea even where to attempt a crossing.

Prior to that night he usually just sat on a chair along the edge of the dance floor, hands tucked neatly away under his legs so he would appear less bumbling, and fretted the time away. Sometimes he acted the clown, sometimes the fool, most often he said nothing at all.

Then suddenly he was out dancing, spinning and spiraling with a lovely young lady, as captivated as he could ever imagine. *She* had approached *him*. And it wasn't a prank or clever joke conceived by some vengeful adversary at the bar. With all the other handsome, polished, eligible bachelors around, she seemed only interested in *him*. Miracles, he discovered that night, do happen.

In time, they married. It was not easily accomplished, of course; she a Todd of high social standing, Lincoln of no standing at all. Once, fearing failure and wracked by confusion, he had walked away, retreated to his law practice with a mind to never see her again, but that only sent him spiraling into a bout of depression so deep that many of his friends thought he might never return to himself again. But in time he did. Love guides, it seems, even the most bewildered spirits.

They had experienced good times and hard times, he and Mary Todd. Now the miles, years, and numerous deaths had all taken their toll on her, and in the chatty corridors and back rooms of Washington society the ugly rumors of her flighty ways and tottering sanity were never far away. He paid them no mind. She was the one who had reached out to him when no one else would. In the papers they still called him 'monkey', 'baboon,' or 'gorilla', and while he tried to laugh the derision away, those smears always hurt. But she had seen through all of that, clear into his heart and mind, and he loved her for it, and his love was eternal. That was their special bond, and if some people could not grasp the beauty of such a thing, well then, there was nothing he could do but feel sorry for some people.

Lincoln stood erect, continued shaking hands. The room was filling now. He hovered in the reception line, aloof and distant, his usual mechanical self until around 9:30 when a noticeable stir rippled through the crowd. Almost immediately he spotted Grant emerging through a small group of admirers and walking directly toward him. Lincoln recognized the small general at once from photographs he'd seen in the papers.

Grant was a short, intense looking man, slim of waist, with piercing grey eyes, and an expressionless face. He did not so much walk as hurl himself forward step by step as if life was the enemy and his body the chosen weapon of assault. Lincoln had heard as well that Grant was not much for pomp, but dressed modestly and preferred no fancy airs. If true, he would be a welcome change from the often imperious gentlemen who inhabited the upper echelons of the Army of the Potomac, and who from time to time drove Lincoln to distraction. Lincoln was already in a reasonably good mood, and Grant's entrance only served to amplify it. He smiled warmly.

"Why, here is General Grant!" Lincoln cried, taking the general by the hand and shaking it vigorously. "Well, this is a great pleasure."

Grant bowed. "Mr. President, the pleasure is all mine, I assure you."

They chatted amiably for a while, and then Lincoln introduced Grant to the Secretary of State, William Seward, and then to several other members of the cabinet who were close at hand. In time, Seward took the general over to meet Mrs. Lincoln, and the crowd grew more animated with every passing minute. The excitement continued to grow, people pressing closer and closer to get a good look at the famous officer, until Seward saw fit to grab Grant by the arm and drag him over to the East Room where there would be far more space to move.

"Grant! Grant! Grant!" came the cheers, and Lincoln smiled to think his selection had generated such excitement. He watched from a distance as visitors crowded around the general, calling his name, eager for just a glimpse. Finally, Seward convinced Grant to step up onto a sofa so that he could be seen by everyone, but that only caused the crowd to cheer that much more. It was wild and jubilant, and Lincoln was inspired by it all.

He would speak with Grant later of war and strategy. For the time being Lincoln simply stood back and enjoyed the scene, and hoped with all his heart that it was a sign of better things to come.

The day had ended well, and for the first time in weeks he actually felt optimistic. Deep waters seemed to be moving, shifting, shaping the world to come, using him and others as instruments of change. Who could say where it might all lead? His wife seemed almost herself again, young Cushing was creating havoc on the rivers of North Carolina, and now Grant was here to guide the war to a final, victorious conclusion. He felt the odd, tingling sensation of joy continue to rise in his chest, and for a moment at least his despair lifted. By golly, if there had been music he would have danced. Earlier that day he had noticed that the air had warmed and the snow had begun to melt. Could spring be far away?

Chapter Five

March 11th – Late Evening

Cushing sat on the edge of his berth, fumbled for a match, then relit the lantern overhead. Memories had overwhelmed him, and sleep had once again become impossible. It was almost midnight. Cushing slipped from under the covers, listened to the water slap gently along the flank of the *Monticello* and watched the lights flickering in nearby Norfolk. He loved the sound and feel of the sea, even the slow roll of the ship at anchor in port, but for some reason they were doing little to soothe him tonight.

He touched the portal glass – cold, icy – and drew back. Once again, as with the three nights prior, he could not keep his mind from drifting off to thoughts of his brother, Allie, and with that, misery washed over him like a wave and consumed him completely. He needed to move, he knew, to get back to sea, to tangle with the Rebels again, but for the time being at least, all that had become an impossibility.

Cushing had hatched several good plans for interfering with the Confederate blockade-runners, but now they all had to be put on hold. On March 6, the *Monticello* had been making good time for Beaufort in order to replenish its coal supply, when the acting deck officer thought he'd spotted a runner and changed course to intercept. That officer had taken the Federal ship, *Peterhoff*, for a blockade-runner. With the *Monticello* giving chase, the two had accidentally collided. Thank God, no one had been killed, and all hands were rescued, but the *Peterhoff* took a hard blow at midships and went to the bottom in only minutes. While damage to the *Monticello* was slight, Cushing still had to return to Norfolk for repairs, and it would be weeks before his ship would be capable of venturing out again.

So with nothing much to do or to occupy his thoughts, his mind naturally drifted back and became fixated on that one awful day – the day the bottom had fallen out of his world, the day Allie had been killed. Almost a year had passed now since he had heard the news, but in many ways it seemed like only minutes. He recalled it again with a shudder.

It had been in early July, 1863. Will Cushing was in Washington in command of the *Commodore Barney* at the time, and all the telegraph wires in the capital that day were hot with news from Pennsylvania. Lee's Army of Northern Virginia had moved north across the Pennsylvania line, the Federal army trailing up the dusty roads through Maryland until the two finally collided at a small town named Gettysburg. For two days the contest had been furious, and on the third the issue was still very much in doubt. While messages of the fighting were sketchy, the casualty reports were staggering. The fate of the nation seemed to hang in the balance, and no one was sure which side would prevail.

Alonzo, his older brother, his best friend, and the one person in the world he could not live without, had command of an artillery battery in the Union army. Alonzo – or Allie as Will had always called him – had always taken care of Will, and while they were two years apart in age, they had been the best of friends.

He could recall vividly the day that their father had died. Will was only four at the time, and Allie had taken him under his arm and told him everything would be all right. Allie promised, and Will believed. That's how it had always been.

Allie and Will grew up as close as brothers could be, playing on the streets and wood lots of Fredonia. Allie was the sensible, personable one, Will the daredevil who would fight any kid at the drop of a hat. But they loved and respected one another, worked hard to earn extra money to help the family along, and helped their mother run her small private school. Although Allie was older than Will, they nonetheless had both received their appointments in the same year, Allie to West Point, Will to the Naval Academy. Since graduation, Allie's rise through the ranks had been spectacular. Now he was in charge of a full battery of guns, he'd been commended for bravery many times, and far bigger things were expected soon.

Will was at the War Department when word from the front finally arrived – Allie was dead. He'd been killed at the very height of the last Confederate assault, an attack that would forevermore be known as Pickett's Charge. Will had been staggered by the news, and his initial response was to go to Gettysburg in order to recover his brother's body and assume command of his battery of guns. He simply assumed that his naval rank and reputation would convert into a land commission, so he boarded the train late that day and headed north. It was an honorable, if somewhat foolish reaction.

The ride was grueling, but nothing like what he discovered once he got near Gettysburg. Will Cushing had seen death, battle, and destruction in the navy, but had never even imagined anything on the scale of what he encountered at Gettysburg. Here were literally whole square miles of wasted woods and farmland, dead and dismembered men flung every which way across fields and fences, dead horses, wrecked limbers, the lost and discarded implements of war littering the ground for as far as the eye could see. The hospitals were overflowing, the stench unbearable. It was a maddening, sickening experience.

Cushing was soon directed to Captain John Hazard, commander of the II Corps artillery brigade, and Allie's immediate superior, but Will had already discerned from the scope of the carnage that his hopes were in all probability doomed. As Hazard explained it, his brother had died a hero's death, but Allie's battery had been reduced to splinters during the course of the battle. There was nothing left to command, even if they would allow him to command it. Alonzo's body had already been shipped off under guard to West Point for burial.

So Will could only take the long train ride back to Washington and somehow try and come to grips with a gaping hole in his heart, and a world without Alonzo. It had not been easy. In fact, he remained in a horrible depression for months, and only time and action had seemed to allay his sense of loss. Action worked the best, seemed to focus his mind to a fine point that excluded all extraneous thoughts, but action was not a constant; thus the painful memories of Allie were never far away.

In a way, Allie's death seemed to concentrate his hatred of the Rebels that much more. They were, after all, the ones responsible for his brother's death. Even though he had been able to right himself emotionally to a certain extent, for Will Cushing the conflict soon devolved from being a war with a sensible cause into a hateful crusade. Allie's death had become his reason for fighting, for breathing, for living. But now the *Monticello* was tied up in Norfolk, weeks away from being seaworthy, and he could not keep his mind from drifting again and again to thoughts of Allie.

With Alonzo gone the small circle of people Will both cared for and trusted had shrunk to but a precious few: his mother, who had given everything to keep their family together since the death of his father; Commander Charles Flusser, his mentor at the Naval Academy, and whose glowing reports had secured Will his first command at sea; and Abraham Lincoln, who had treated him like a son when they'd chatted together in the spring of '63. For those three he would do anything. They were the few who now formed the inner constellation of Will's world, but his mother remained in Fredonia, Flusser was in charge of a small Federal squadron on the Roanoke River in North Carolina, and Lincoln sat at the head of the government in Washington.

Like Allie, Will had always been amiable and free with people – even charming at times – but unlike Allie he had rarely made friends. People seemed distant and confusing to Will Cushing. While he cared for his men, there was not one among them he considered a friend. His one true friend was gone, lost forever at Gettysburg.

So now he focused his pain and anger on the Confederate enemy, but with the *Monticello* laid-up for weeks, they were nowhere near. Absent an adversary, he was left with only his misery and bitter sense of loss. There would be no more warm reunions in Fredonia. Allie would not be coming home. Ever.

Will Cushing closed his eyes, listened to the gentle slap of bay water against the ship's hull, and wished with all his might that the weeks of inactivity would hurry by and that spring would come soon. Late at night he felt only the pang of loss, the clanking, hollowness of his loneliness, and at times a wild, unfocused anger. He desperately wanted to be on the water, face-to-face with the enemy, to feel the wonderful intensity of action again. Truth be told, battle was the only place on earth where he felt alive anymore.

Chapter Six

April 17th – Late Afternoon

Cooke waited impatiently for the mechanic to come on deck and give him the latest raft of bad news. He took a puff of cigar smoke, blew it away, then stared off angrily into the black night. His right leg was starting to ache again, but he had no time for it, so James Cooke tried to think the pain away. Then he checked his watch by the light of a burning forge and spit angrily into the water below. It was dark already, good hours were being wasted, and he was falling further behind schedule by the minute. And now the ironclad was foundering, helpless, again. What else, he wondered, was going to go wrong this night?

The CSS *Albemarle* had shoved off late in the afternoon, bound for a confrontation down river with the Federal squadron at Plymouth, still miles south of his current position. General Hoke – one of General Lee's lieutenants – had made an appearance the day before imploring Cooke to take the ironclad downriver as soon as possible. Hoke's land force was arrayed to attack the city come first light the following day, but if the Federal boats were allowed to blast away with impunity from the safety of the water, Hoke's attack would never succeed. The *Albemarle* was needed to clear away the Yankee gunboats and then attack the town's land batteries from the water. General Hoke would be attacking with 12,000 men on the 18th, and if the *Albemarle* was not on hand as planned, his army might well be chewed to pieces.

While the ironclad was not entirely complete, Cooke had agreed to put the ram in motion, hoping to finish what needed to be done on the way downriver. So they had started off around 3:00 that afternoon with forges burning on the flush decks and towing a flat boat with a portable forge and equipment behind. A few miles downstream they passed by Williamston, where bands played and the whole town lined the river to get a good look at the formidable ironclad everyone had been hearing about for months. The sky was blue, the trees close to full bloom in middle April, and even Cooke had to admit it was a marvelous sight. People cheered until the boat rounded a bend in the river and steamed slowly out of sight. The experience excited the crew. Even Cooke had waved his cap.

The crew of the *Albemarle* consisted of infantrymen on loan from General Hoke's command: lanky North Carolina farmers, trappers, and frontiersmen who could spit tobacco juice and shoot a rifle with anyone, but who knew absolutely nothing of a sailor's duties. Fortunately, as they drifted downriver they passed the steamer, *Cora,* and twenty real sailors previously promised to Cooke by Hoke were transferred aboard. Thank God. At least now he had a few men who knew port from starboard, and on those few he would have to rely heavily in the fight to come.

From Williamston, they continued down the Roanoke, with ironworkers and carpenters scurrying over the boat's frame fastening down the last of the iron plates, while below decks the gun crews drilled on loading and firing the rifles. But they didn't get far.

Around 10:00 o'clock that night several bolts that anchored the coupling to the propeller shaft sheared and, much to Cooke's disgust, the ironclad had to be moored along the riverbank until repairs could be made. It took the better part of six hours to prepare and fasten the new bolts, then almost immediately something else went wrong, and they lost control of the steering. Cooke sent his best mechanics aft to see what the problem was while he went above to attend to the rams being heaved-to along the bank of the river. Once the lines were fastened and the ironclad secured, he lit a cigar, took a few angry puffs, and glared out across the river. Then he heard the sound of quick footsteps behind him.

Cooke turned. "What?" he demanded, squinting into the darkness.

It was John Benton, Boatswain Mate. The man took a deep breath, was puffing hard. "R-rudder head, Captain," he said. "Done snapped."

"Can it be fixed?" Cooke wanted to know.

"Yes, sir, it can, but it will take awhile."

"How long?"

"Couple hours, at least," Benton replied.

Cooke frowned. "No choice," he said. "Get to it and make it fast. Fast as you can."

"Aye, aye, Captain."

Off to the east the first vague light of day was just now topping the trees. Cooke went below decks, watched the work proceed for a while then decided to grab some rest. So he repaired to his small quarters, stretched out and in minutes was sound asleep. He awoke around 9:00 that morning, sunlight streaming in above his head, and the rudder work almost complete. Once he'd judged the job satisfactory, he went topside and called for the lines to be cast off.

The morning air was clear and warm, and the boat slipped away from the shore easily on the current. With that, the CSS *Albemarle* was under power once more, albeit considerably behind schedule. Just aft of the ram the *Cotton Plant* chugged contentedly along with its compliment of Rebel infantry.

The river was high from fresh rains, running swiftly, and the ironclad made good time throughout the remainder of the day. On board, hammers rang and men scurried feverishly about their business as the last of the iron plates were fixed into place. At nearly 10:00 o'clock that evening he dropped anchor only 3 miles above Plymouth and called for a meeting of his officers.

Cooke had reliable reports that the Federals had deployed a series of obstructions across the river to impede or even snare the ram as she approached – sunken boats, chains, pilings, etc. – and he deemed it foolish to proceed until those dangers had been investigated. It was agreed that a small group should row south toward Plymouth, check the river for obstructions, and sound the waters where necessary. The men returned in just over an hour and Cooke, along with Gilbert Elliott – the ironclad's young designer – met them up on deck as they climbed aboard.

James Cooke rubbed his hands together anxiously. "Well, what have you discovered, Lieutenant Roby?"

The lieutenant frowned, shook his head forlornly. "More bad news, I'm afraid, Captain."

Cooke slumped. "What now, sir?"

"It's going to be just about impossible for us to pass over the obstructions downriver, sir."

Cooke folded his arms across his chest tightly. "You're sure?"

"Absolutely," Roby replied. "We took soundings, Captain. No more than six feet to clear as we got it."

Cooke shook his head in disgust. "Well then," he said, "there's nothing left for us to do. Bank the fires, and tell the men to turn in for some rest for the time being."

"Yes, sir," the lieutenant answered.

As the men shuffled off, Elliott grabbed hold of Cooke by the elbow. "Captain," the young man implored, "I can't for the life of me believe that. Not enough water to clear? Not even with all these rains we've had of late? The river's higher now than I've ever seen it."

"Yes, I agree," Cooke said, "but you heard the lieutenant. What are you suggesting?"

Elliott tossed his hands in the air. "I cannot imagine coming all this way for nothing," he cried. "At least let me take a few men and go see for myself. I have no doubt that the lieutenant is a fine officer, but let me at least double check. No harm in it."

Cooke smiled. "No, no harm at all," he agreed. "Go ahead, and take who you will. But be spry about it, Mister Elliott, and take good care. You'll be the second boat out this evening, and the Yanks might be a good bit curious by now."

Elliott beamed back at him. "I will, Captain."

In a few hours, Elliott was back, and this time the news was good. He had taken careful soundings and found that in the middle of the river the depth was a good ten feet above the obstructions. In some places even higher. The *Albemarle* should be able to pass with ease if they kept to the center of the river.

Cooke's heart leaped in his chest. "Now, listen, you're sure of this? Absolutely sure?"

"Oh, yes," Elliott replied. "We checked it real close. Along the banks it becomes shallow, just like Lieutenant Roby saw, but not in the middle. We're good there."

Cooke smiled. "Well then, we'll make a go of her. Lieutenant Roby!"

"Sir?"

"Let the men sleep till 2:30. Then we're going to weigh anchor and head downriver. Mister Elliott's soundings indicate a good ten feet of water over the obstructions in the middle of the channel."

"Very good, sir," Roby answered. "Glad to hear it."

Cooke grinned, winked at Elliott. "Yes, Lieutenant. See to it."

"Aye, aye, sir."

At precisely 2:30 A. M. the anchor was weighed and the ironclad began to slip downriver again. Cooke sipped from a cup of coffee and stood next to the helmsman as the ram approached the first obstruction. From time to time he gazed out the forward portal, but could see precious little. The night was dark, and a low fog swirled across the water.

"All ahead, slow," he ordered, "and keep to the middle of the channel, by God."

"Yes, Captain," came the reply. The engines hummed loudly behind them, the boat shuddered and the timbers groaned.

The ram drifted slowly down the Roanoke and passed over the first obstruction with no difficulty. About a mile outside of Plymouth, the helmsman called to Cooke, and pointed hard to starboard.

"A battery, Captain!" he said. "Off the starboard bow, on the south shore of yon island."

Cooke had a look for himself. Through the swirling fog, he could just make out the shape of the large mounds of dirt that housed the guns. His heart started to beat faster. "Well, now," he said, "I guess we're about to find out if our last few months of work have been at all worth it."

The helmsman nodded back. "That we will, Captain. Them's *big* guns, all right."

Almost immediately, the heavy thud of cannon blasts rolled over the river, the concussions rumbling through the water, shaking the lanterns below decks. Most of the crew stiffened, held their breath. The heavy shriek of naval shells arched directly overhead, fiendish sounding. But most of the Yankee shells flew high and long and missed the ram entirely, detonating harmlessly in the water a good distance away. Those few that found their mark simply ricocheted off the ship's casement with a loud "pong!" or as Gilbert Elliot put it, like "pebbles thrown against an empty barrel." After the first few shells bounced off the iron siding, most of the crew sat back and breathed easier. The ironclad was solid as a rock. If those 100 lb. shells couldn't hurt her, Cooke knew that little could.

The *Albemarle* sailed past the battery undamaged. There was no point in returning fire, as far as Cooke could see. It did not appear the Federal batteries could even dent the ram, and he'd rather save his ordnance for the real fight, perhaps no more than minutes away, as the river current stiffened and pulled the ram south at an ever increasing clip.

A few seconds later, they cleared another line of obstructions and slowly came abreast of Plymouth. Cooke could, through the darkness and fog, just dimly make out the silhouette of the village several hundred yards off to starboard. Only a few lights could be seen flickering through the darkness. The enemy, he knew, would not be far away. The crew stopped talking and joking. A grim seriousness took over below decks.

Then Cooke spotted the running lights of what appeared to be two ships closing rapidly from downriver. He stood back, took a deep breath.

"Open the gun ports!" he ordered, and the chains clanked loudly overhead as the heavy metal doors slid sideways on command. "The enemy's off our starboard bow and closing, gentlemen! I'm afraid this is general quarters!"

"General quarters, everyone!" Roby screamed. "Y'all heard the captain. General quarters!"

A taste of morning fog and the odor of musky river, humid and mildly discomforting, poured through the open gun ports as the ironclad slashed through the water. The men were all quiet now at their posts, tense, waiting for his next command.

Cooke forced a smile, tried to sound reassuring. "Steady as she goes," he told the helmsman. "We're off to their starboard now," he continued, "but on my command I want you to cut a course angling straight for their bows."

"Aye, aye, sir."

He took another deep breath, turned toward the gun crews. "Load solid shot and stand by for action."

"Solid shot!" the gunners screamed, and the crews raced around the guns. The huge shells were loaded quickly.

"Ready on number one, sir!"

"Ready on gun two, Captain!"

James Cooke had no idea at all just what General Hoke's plans or intentions were for the land assault. All he knew for sure was that the Federal navy would be waiting for him, and that they would fight with anything and everything they had to try and stop him from breaking through. He squinted through the small portal, could see the Yankee ships closing faster now, knew the man who commanded the Union boats from the old navy – a capable and experienced commander by the name of Charles Flusser.

Cooke counted slowly, waited patiently until the time was exactly right. "Helmsman!" he yelled finally.

"Sir?"

"Now!" he bellowed, and the ram lurched suddenly to starboard, slashing across the water, making steadily for the bows of the oncoming craft. "Yes! Yes, that's it!" Cooke cried.

"We're closing, Captain!"

At that moment, James Cooke noticed vaguely that the pain in his legs had disappeared entirely. His mouth hung open slightly, his throat was dry, and his heart was pounding, but beyond that he felt trim and entirely in control. The moment he had been waiting for, working for, virtually living for, for two long years had now finally arrived. He had bet everything on the *Albemarle*. Now he would see just how wise that wager had been.

"That's right!" Cooke cried. "Take her in hard now, son, and we'll bust these Yankee bastards wide open. Let's send Mister Abe Lincoln a little message from the folks of North Carolina. What do you say?"

"Aye, aye, Captain," the helmsman replied.

"Engineer!" Cooke yelled.

"Sir?"

Cooke winked, folded his arms behind his back. "Full speed ahead!"

Chapter Seven

April 19th – Early Morning

Cooke could see the Yankee vessels bearing down on him clearly now, slicing across the river, white water foaming along their bows. They were only a hundred yards off his starboard bow, the *Albemarle* closing rapidly, 376 tons of iron behemoth angling its sharpened ram dead on the bow of the lead Federal craft.

"All ahead, full!" Cooke shouted, almost willing his ironclad across the water.

Through the forward portal he could see but dimly that the two ships had been somehow lashed together with chains and hawsers, a gap left between them of some 30 to 40 feet – just enough space to accommodate another vessel. It was the strangest arrangement he had ever seen, but its utility occurred to him instantly. The intention was to trap the *Albemarle* between the two Federal boats, then pummel the ironclad at close range while perhaps boarding from both sides. It was an odd, desperate tactic, and James Cooke was not impressed in the least. The solution occurred to him almost as quickly as had the problem – he would beat them at their own little game.

The ironclad sheared across the water like a vengeful beast, engines thumping wildly, speed steadily increasing, on a collision course with both Yankee ships.

"Fifty yards and closing, Captain!"

Cooke's intention was to slash the bow of the first ship, then bore a hole through the starboard flank of the other. Desperate shouts and orders already could be heard from the Federal officers as the three ships closed on one another at a furious pace, now only 40 yards apart. The guns on the Yankee boats were firing, but their shells were simply glancing off the ram's iron plating like large hammer blows – piercing the ears, rattling the timbers, but damaging nothing. The air outside was alive with a wild, booming thunder. Jim Cooke's blood was boiling.

"Steady now, boys! All hands *down*!" Cooke yelled, as the ram closed to within mere feet of the first ship at full speed.

Then there was a sudden shudder, a slippery crunching sound along the ram's port bow. That was followed almost immediately by an enormous impact dead ahead, a thunderous collision that jarred the *Albemarle* rearward, and sent many of the crew who had not taken the last order seriously tumbling to the deck in a tangle of arms and legs.

Cooke was holding on for dear life and was able to right himself quickly. "All engines stop!" he screamed, as the ironclad drove deep into the enemy ship's belly. There was the screech of metal on metal, water spraying, men screaming. Then the bow section of the *Albemarle* began to tilt low, sinking deeper and deeper into the water of the Roanoke. This was not what Cooke had planned. He had not simply rammed the second Federal ship but had gored deep inside it.

"We're stuck!" the helmsman roared fanatically. "The damn Yankee boat is sinking, and we're stuck inside her, Captain! We're going down too!"

Cooke's mind was racing. "All astern, full!" he screamed. "Now! For God's sake, get us the hell out of here!"

Everywhere men were screaming, falling, water was pouring through the forward gun ports, cannons booming, shells ringing off the sides of the iron casement. The ironclad continued to sink. There was bedlam both inside and out.

"All astern, full!" Cooke ordered over and over again, screaming at the top of his lungs, and the engines throttled suddenly to life. The timbers that bound the craft began to heave and creak as the ironclad struggled desperately to free herself, but the *Albemarle* could not budge even an inch. They were still caught, still taking on water, still sinking.

The helmsman's eyes were bugging wildly. "We're going down, Captain! She's going to take us to the bottom with her. We can't get away!"

Cooke whirled about and screamed to the engineers, "Give her everything, God damn it! Everything you've got!"

The coal-heavers were working at a frantic pace, stoking the fires with shovelful after shovelful, and the engineers were trying to force every last bit of power out of the engines. Sweat and fear lined all their faces. As the huge engines surged and strained the timbers above and around them creaked and groaned, steam hissing from the boilers. The *Albemarle* was struggling for its life, and every man aboard knew it.

Water rushed around Cooke's feet. He gulped once, strained to concentrate. Men were splashing, slipping, falling. Steam was hissing in his ear, guns firing, the helmsman swearing at the top of his lungs. He knew they had at best only seconds before the ironclad would go down for good.

Cooke fought to maintain control, to clear his head. Every life depended on him in this one catastrophic moment, on his ability to think clearly.

"All astern, full!" he roared again, the one and only thing he could think that made any sense in all this madness. Then he looked up and saw many of the crew staring at him, near panic. "Grab some rifles and go above decks," he ordered them. "Don't let the bastards board us!"

They had just started up the ladder topside when suddenly he felt the *Albemarle* shift just slightly. His mind was racing, calculating – what was this? Then it happened again, the slightest deviation. The ironclad shifted once more, this time noticeably, and he felt the fore section start to rise.

"We're free," he said, in almost a whisper, and the answer came to him immediately. The Federal boat had sunk to the bottom, and, when it struck the mud it turned just slightly, just enough to free the ram from the gaping hole in its side. "All astern, full!" Cooke screamed again. "Let's get the hell out of here!"

The engineers understood, pushing the engines in reverse for every bit of power the twins could provide. Slowly, almost miraculously the bow continued to rise, and Cooke could feel the ram backing now, pulling away. Men were staring at him, hoping, praying ... waiting. The water below decks began leveling, washing around his feet. Then there was a surge, both back and up at the same time, and with a lurch the bow came free and broke the surface with a crash. The crew let out a wild cheer.

James Cooke took a deep breath and looked around. Then he remembered the other Yankee craft that the ram had only swiped. Dead ahead he could see only the superstructure of the boat they had rammed above water – it appeared, from what he knew of the Yank fleet, to be the *Southfield* – and far across the river he spotted the other vessel, slowly turning toward them.

"There it is!" Cooke bellowed. "Bring her about, then all ahead, full." He cupped his hands around his mouth and yelled to the forward gun crew. “She’s in range dead ahead,” he continued, pointing. “Can you get a good shot at her?”

The answer came quickly as the forward Brooke rifle exploded, the concussion booming back through the chamber – thunderous, ear-cracking – and smoke wafting across his face in small, rippling eddies.

“Was that a hit?” Cooke wanted to know, fanning the smoke aside.

“Can’t tell, Captain,” came the answer from the forward gun.

“’Fraid she’s pulling away, Captain,” the helmsman said. “The Yank is running.”

Cooke had a long look for himself. Sure enough, the second Federal vessel appeared to be making a run for it downriver. “Ha!” he laughed. “Looks like they’ve had enough of us for one day. There she goes, hobbling down river like a wounded duck. We cut her bow pretty good.”

“We won’t catch her though, Captain,” the helmsman pointed out. “She’s making good time, hobbled or not.”

“Yeah, I know,” Cooke admitted with a touch of sadness. “To hell with her, then. We have other business to attend to.”

Part of him was elated, another part dejected. While it was apparent that he’d won a fine victory, he wanted that victory to be complete, a thorough thrashing of every vessel that opposed him. James Cooke didn’t simply want to win; he wanted to run roughshod over the entire Federal Fleet. But for the time being that would have to wait.

“All ahead, full, Mr. Helmsman,” he said with a chuckle.

“Aye, aye, sir.”

“Take her down a mile or so below Plymouth, and we’ll drop anchor.”

“Yes, Captain.”

As the *Albemarle* steamed south, Cooke threw open the hatch above and went topside for a good look. Through his glass he could easily observe the Federal craft as it withdrew – now suddenly joined by two others – all three limping around a bend in the river that at last took them out of sight. The second boat he had fought was the *Miami*, he was sure; Charles Flusser's flagship, and he imagined that he had given Flusser far more than he had bargained for. The retreating Yankee boats tossed a few shells his way before disappearing, but it was apparent they wanted nothing more to do with his ironclad.

The sun was up now, its beautiful clear light pouring over the river banks, and James Cooke felt about as good as he had ever felt in his life. That was for you, Mister Lincoln, he thought to himself as the breeze came up and ruffled the flag behind him. For two long years he had been waiting for this very moment, and while the fight had lasted only minutes, he knew he would savor the joy of it for a long time to come.

They cut the engines about a mile south of town and dropped anchor not far from shore. Cooke called for both casualty and damage reports, then sent a boat with a small party off to make contact with General Hoke's land forces.

The reports were tabulated quickly. The ironclad had suffered slight damage to nine iron plates, and only one man had been killed – that being Crewman Harris, who had foolishly stuck his head out one of the gun ports to get a better view of the battle and took a Yankee bullet for his curiosity. Beyond that, the clash had been a stunning success for the Confederacy. It appeared that not a single Federal ship would be willing or capable to take on the CSS *Albemarle* anytime soon – at least on the inland waters.

Dispatches were finally received from Hoke, and that afternoon and much of the following morning the *Albemarle* moved in close to shore and pummeled the Yankee defensive positions in and around Plymouth, reducing most to rubble. On the morning of the 20th, the Federal garrison ran up the white flag, surrendering over 1500 troops and 25 pieces of artillery. Richmond rejoiced. So overmatched had the Federal squadron been by the *Albemarle* that all of the Confederacy's fondest aspirations had been accomplished with lighting swiftness. Cooke had little doubt that the shock waves of his return to Plymouth would be felt soon in Washington City, and that pleased him no end.

Later, on the evening of the 20th, Cooke steamed south again and dropped anchor just below the town. A few days later word arrived that the Confederate ironclad *Neuce* had run aground on its maiden voyage downriver and that for the foreseeable future she appeared to be hopelessly marooned. Any pending assault on New Bern would in all probability have to be spearheaded by the *Albemarle,* which Cooke welcomed as good news – it would only increase the already formidable reputation his ironclad and crew had earned, while granting him yet another splendid opportunity to further reclaim his reputation.

What's more, he also received news from Hoke's intelligence that the Federal Fleet in Albemarle Sound was now in a state of virtual disarray. Not only had the *Southfield* been sunk and the *Miami* damaged, but, according to several reliable reports, the Yankee commander had been struck and killed by an errant shell during the height of the contest.

Cooke's grudge was not against the officers of the Federal Navy, many of whom he still considered good friends, so he bowed slightly upon receipt of the news and said a short prayer for a worthy opponent. Commander Charles Flusser was dead, and he was truly sorry about that, but he did not dwell on it for long. That was a risk, after all, that they had all accepted when they signed on. Besides, he still had an ironclad to look after and a war to fight.

Chapter Eight

April 30th – Morning

Cushing put the glass to his eye again and carefully scanned the horizon – it was a beautiful, sunny morning. A fine wind had come up and the *Monticello's* engines were thumping away nicely. A crisp chop painted the blue ocean water with a thousand white bursts as the sleek vessel sliced its way across the waves. High overhead, gulls circled the ship as spray washed gently back across the deck. The sun was high and bright, the sky an almost radiant blue as the *Monticello* cut across the water with all the speed and grace of a thoroughbred dashing for the finish line. The day was warming, his crew well fed and happy; what was not to like on this, the 30th day of April?

They were sailing E. N. E. well off Frying Pan Shoals in search of any Rebel runners that might have slipped out of Wilmington the night before. Because of his exploit in Smithville, the navy had seen fit to provide him with a roving commission, and now William Barker Cushing operated well outside the general limits of the blockade. By means of a melding of logic, good seamanship and even better hunches, his task was to try and overtake any fast Confederate blockade runners that managed to slip past the fleet on their outbound trek to Bermuda. Cushing had to reckon on wind and tide, and so far his reckoning had come up short. He'd spotted only one runner, and that one he had lost when a main valve stem bent and the *Monticello* lost power.

Cushing loved the wind, the water, and the almost unrivaled speed of the *Monticello,* but in the end the blockade hadn't provided much in the way of sport. His weeks at sea had been long and boring, and while most of the crew fancied it good sailing, to Will Cushing it was nothing but dull.

He was scanning the horizon and had spotted something of interest when the call came from above – "Smoke on the horizon, dead ahead!" – and Cushing turned and focused his glass directly over the bow. It was smoke all right, but the ship appeared much too large for a runner, and it was headed straight their way.

"It's the *Cambridge*, I think," he said. "But let's keep a good eye out, just the same. If it's not, perhaps we'll be in for a little fun, and if it is, at least we'll catch up on the latest news. Mister Jones!" Cushing called.

"Sir?"

"Please keep a close eye on that vessel. I'm going below. I'll be in my cabin."

"Aye, aye, Captain."

Then Cushing stopped, winked. "And let's not run her down and sink her," he joked, referring to the incident with the *Peterhoff* that had occurred when Jones had had command of the deck.

Jones smiled, nodded. "No sir. Quite enough of that."

"Yes, quite enough."

Cushing went below, pulled out the charts and began rechecking his course. A few minutes later there was a light rapping on the cabin door. "Captain. …"

"Yes, come in."

It was Ensign Howorth. “It is the *Cambridge,* sir,” Howorth told him, “just as you suspected. They’ve signaled they have mail, orders, and some dispatches, Captain.”

“Very well, Mister Howorth,” Cushing replied. “Bring the *Monticello* about and send over a line. I should be interested to see what’s going on in the real world.”

“Aye, aye, sir.”

A half hour later he went up and watched as the *Cambridge* neared and the exchange was made. He waved to her captain, then went back to his cabin for a short rest. Spotting the *Cambridge* had been the most exciting thing he’d done in days.

Later Howorth was at his door again. “Captain.”

“Yes, yes, enter.”

Howorth came in carrying the mail and dispatches. “Where do you want them, sir?”

“There, on my desk. Thank you.”

Howorth put the papers down then backed away slowly, oddly.

“What is it, Mister Howorth?” Cushing asked curiously.

“Nothing, sir.”

“Really? Since when does *nothing* seem to unravel you so?”

“Well, sir ... I mean, I guess I just want to say ... ”

Cushing laughed. “What?”

“Well, I just want to say that I’m sorry, Captain.”

Cushing’s smile disappeared. “Sorry? For what?”

Howorth walked slowly across the cabin, picked a dispatch from the pile on the desk then handed it over. “I didn’t open it sir, but I know what it is. The news came over from the boys on the *Cambridge.*”

Will picked up the dispatch, opened it carefully and read. Cushing read, read again, then read one more time to be sure he had not gotten something wrong, some small word or letter out of place or misinterpreted. But nothing was wrong. He dropped the dispatch and slumped down on a chair.

"I am sorry, Captain. I know you were close to the commander. We're all sorry, believe me. I wanted to tell you that. We all wanted you to know. He was a good man and a fine officer."

There were no words in him anymore – no words, thoughts, or feelings. There was not even any anger. All that had vanished. There was just a great hole in the center of his being, the same terrible hole that had appeared that day in Washington when they had handed him the telegram about Alonzo. He was beyond speech, beyond reason, beyond thought. It was as if his world had utterly imploded. For a moment, he thought he might actually collapse.

"Sorry again, Captain," he vaguely heard Howorth say from what seemed a mile or two away, then the door closed softly as the ensign departed the cabin.

"... Yes, thank you," he heard himself say.

For six hours, Will Cushing did not move. He simply sat at his desk and watched the surf rolling outside. But he was not really watching at all. It was more as if he were lost, or stunned, or even unconscious. For those six hours, time did not exist. Nor was there hope, or reason, or even warmth in his veins. For those six hours, there was only the intense suffering of loss blowing through his soul like a hurricane. The gallant Flusser is dead, he kept thinking, trying somehow to comprehend the incomprehensible. Flusser is dead.

Later the cook inquired if he would be taking dinner as previously ordered, and he answered absently that he would, not actually hearing the words, not really understanding. Shortly thereafter several officers appeared for dinner – nervous, reserved, sorrowful. He let them in without speaking and the cook's mate served the wine. No one knew what to say, what to do. Finally, Howorth suggested a toast and they all raised their glasses immediately.

"To Commander Charles Flusser," Howorth said. "As fine an officer as has ever served!"

They all drank, and Cushing drank too, oddly mechanical, still not entirely aware of his own movements. Then he put the glass down and walked to the starboard portal. He stared into the darkness for a second or two, then turned and asked: "What is the name?"

" ... Sir?"

"The name ... of the Rebel ram .... What is the name?"

"Oh, yes, sir," Jones replied. "The *Albemarle*, Captain. That's the name of the ironclad. It is supposed to be a most formidable vessel."

Cushing seemed lost in thought for a moment, nodding slowly to himself. Then he turned around abruptly and faced them.

"I tell you this, Gentlemen," he said in a voice so calm yet so striking that every officer instinctively stood at attention. "As God is my witness," he continued, the words seeming to rise from some deeper part of him, from that place where only truth resides, and thus these words were cast in utter conviction and delivered with absolute certainty, "I shall never rest until I have avenged his death!"

There was a long, lingering moment of silence. No one moved or said a word. Every man in the cabin realized that what he had just heard was no idle boast, but rather a grim sentence of death, duly pronounced, awaiting only its execution.

Chapter Nine

April 30th – Night

Lincoln took off his soaked coat, trousers, and shoes, tossed them into the corner, and searched around for something dry to wear. He stood up stiffly, caught himself twice, then lost control and let out a mighty sneeze. Lincoln had stood for much of the rain swept and windy afternoon on a balcony at Willard's Hotel, watching as much of Burnside's Corps passed in review below on Pennsylvania Avenue. They were marching through Washington, bound for Grant's encampment near Culpeper Court House in Virginia, soon to take part in the greatest – and Lincoln hoped the last – campaign of the war.

"Would you like a fire, sir?" a servant asked, taking the wet clothes away.

"Yes, I think that might do fine," he answered, trying to rub the cold out of his hands. While it was late April, the rains had blown in from the west for much of the day, heavy and cold, and the last thing Abraham Lincoln needed was a foul case of pneumonia.

He cupped his hands over the first flickers of fire that crackled in the hearth, waiting for the warmth to rise. The troops had hurrahed and cheered him all afternoon as they passed in the street below. God, how he loved that! Many of the troops passing that afternoon had been the first of the newly formed black regiments, and when they spotted him up on the balcony they shouted, cheered, and tossed their hats in the air. Such was the power of freedom. Many of those men had been slaves only years or even months before, and now they were all free men marching off in the cause of emancipation. The world was changing, not slowly, not methodically, but in a cloud burst, and those not quick enough to grasp the meaning of the times might easily get swept away by the winds that were howling across the American landscape.

A few of them there on the balcony at Willard's had suggested, as the afternoon wore on, that he should get out of the rain, that he'd done more than his fair share, but he'd replied that if the men could stand the rain, then he guessed that he could stand it too. Burnside's whole corps was marching toward the train depot. From there, they'd be off on the waiting railroad cars of the Orange & Alexandria line, bound for Culpeper. There, Ulysses Grant was assembling the largest land army the republic had ever seen – by reports already over 120,000 men. To accomplish that task Grant had already called in every unit he could get his hands on; he had even stripped the Washington defenses of most of its troops. Now within days, perhaps even hours, Grant would barge across the Rapidan River in search of Lee's forces. By tomorrow or the next day many of those boys who'd cheered him that afternoon, Lincoln knew, would be dead. So, he guessed he could stand up to a little rain if they could stand up to that.

They cheered him as president, but in the end, he knew, it was far more than just his office. They had all come from big towns and small – teachers, lawyers, clerks, farmers – because they believed in what the war was about. They were all in it together, and in that sense he was no different than any one of them. They were all small links in an enormous chain, and without every last one of those links, Lincoln knew, the chain would never hold.

What they marched and fought for had meaning far beyond the hackneyed political slogans and jingles of the day, and Lincoln struggled always to make that clear, to connect with them all in some meaningful way. This was not always easy. Often words proved lacking, but words were all he had to work with. In the end,the war was about liberty, about a new way of living while preserving the rights and freedoms the revolution had created for generations more to come.

Late that afternoon, for instance, he'd wandered down amongst the last of the troops, a veteran regiment of Ohio boys, as they were marching off and many had gathered round in the cold and rain when they spotted him. The rain dripped from their caps, across their faces, down into their shirts and coats, yet none of them seemed to mind. They were cold and wet, yet still they smiled and cheered as he approached.

He stopped, smiled, put his hands on his hips. "Boys," he called out, "how is everyone doing this fine, wet, Washington afternoon?"

They all laughed.

"Well, that's good," he replied. "Glad to see you're all in good spirits."

"We're about to go whip the Johnnies, sir!" one yelled.

"Yeah let us at 'em, Mister Lincoln."

He chuckled, folded his arms behind his back. "Glad to hear you so ready on such a dreary afternoon. Does me good. Does the whole country good." Then he stopped, thought for a moment longer before continuing. "This war, you know, well, this war means a lot to us all."

"We know, sir."

He paused a moment, waited till they all quieted down. "Do you?" he asked. Then he motioned for them to come closer, to gather round so that everyone could hear him clearly.

They all formed a small circle around him, then fell silent.

"I want you boys to understand something important," Lincoln said, straining for the right words, "something you can think about while you're out at the front. See, I happen temporarily to occupy this big White House. I am a living witness that any one of your children may look to come here as my father's child has. It is in order that each of you may have equal privileges in the race of life, with all its desirable human aspirations. It is for this the struggle should be maintained, that we may not lose our birthright."

Not one man said a word.

"In that sense, boys, this war's for you, for all your sons and daughters, for your children's children yet unborn. It's for the future that we must fight this war. For the future of the world."

"We understand, sir," came the reply from the back of the group. "And we won't let you down."

"Then God bless you," he said, and stood back solemnly as they marched off to war.

Soon they would all be at the front, he knew. Soon the great offensive would begin. That thought made him both anxious and excited. For much of March and April he and Grant had discussed the coordination of the upcoming campaign in detail, Grant taking the train up from Culpeper once or twice a week to consult. The final results had been entirely to Lincoln's liking. At long last, the nation's armies would move simultaneously against joint objectives, forcing all the Rebel armies to stay put and fight rather than being able to shift men and equipment from one theater of operations to another to meet disjointed threats. The North's strengths were in men and manufacturing, and the new strategy would use those advantages to maximum effect. All Federal armies would have a piece of the action, no matter how small. As he'd told Grant, "Those not skinning can hold a leg."

The design was grand but simple. In the East, Grant would go after Lee's Army of Northern Virginia, while in the West, Sherman would burst into Georgia and capture Atlanta – a critical railroad hub. Benjamin Butler's Army of the James would move from Fortress Monroe on the Chesapeake Bay up the Virginia Peninsula and cut off the railroads leading into Richmond from the south at Petersburg. From Louisiana Banks would drive into Alabama, then join with Sherman's forces once Atlanta had fallen. If all went as planned, the Confederacy would simply be overwhelmed, and the Federal forces, once combined, would be unstoppable.

The planning was over now. The campaign was in Grant's hands from here on out, and that left Lincoln to wait and fret. He preferred work to fretting, but there was nothing he could do, and as he watched the Ohio Regiment disappear into the rain, already his nerves were beginning to fray and jangle. Everything he believed in was riding on this one campaign.

Late that afternoon he'd stopped by the War Department and sent a telegram off to Grant's headquarters as a last word of encouragement, then walked back to the White House alone. Now he had only to sit back and await the outcome – that was the agreement he'd made with Grant. All his other generals in the past had demanded that he make the big decisions. Now that he finally had a commander ready and willing to take on that task, Lincoln was glad to be done with the responsibility. While he had, out of necessity, taught himself a great deal about warfare, he much preferred to leave the fighting to professionals. So from here on out he would make the important decisions on military policy, but would leave Grant to fight the war on his own. In a day or two the greatest offensive campaign of the war – indeed, one of the greatest in history – involving four armies spread over a half continent, would commence. Nothing less than the future of democratic government on the North American continent rode on the outcome.

There was no reason Grant ought not to succeed, but not every military scenario appeared quite as rosy. A few days ago he'd met with Gideon Welles, the Secretary of the Navy, and been briefed on the situation in the Carolina sounds. There a combined Confederate land and naval force had recently retaken Plymouth, North Carolina. A few days later the Federal army had been forced to evacuate Washington, N. C., as the town was now considered indefensible. The arrival of the long awaited Rebel ironclad CSS *Albemarle* had turned the strategic situation in the area upside down, and the Union fleet was now forced to huddle together at the mouth of the Roanoke River, trembling like frightened sheep awaiting the wolf's next appearance.

Welles had received an encouraging report from Admiral Samuel Lee, the overall commander in that naval district, but no one was sure what would happen next. Two Federal vessels had tangled with the ironclad. One had been sunk outright, the other seriously damaged, and the navy had nothing that it could throw at the Confederate ram except numbers. Lee was planning a seven-ship attack against the *Albemarle* should she poke her nose into the sound – as was soon expected – and while Lee's confidence was high, Lincoln's was not.

He could still recall the day in '62 when they'd received word of the *Merrimac's* initial foray off Hampton Roads in Virginia. The Rebel ironclad changed the face of naval warfare in an instant, had gone through the wooden Federal Fleet as if playing with toys. Indeed, so one-sided had the contest been, that the next morning the Secretary of War, William Stanton, had run from room to room in the White House during a cabinet meeting, half expecting the iron monster to appear on the Potomac and begin shelling Washington City itself. Fortunately, the Union ironclad *Monitor* had made its debut the very next day, and while the two eventually fought to an essential draw, the lessons of the superiority of iron ships had not been lost on Abraham Lincoln. He fancied the *Albemarle* to be a serious problem, and instructed the navy to do everything it could to destroy her, or at least keep her bottled up.

The warmth of the fire finally began to ease the cold in his fingers, and he pulled a chair close and sat for awhile, thinking little, just letting the heat work its way into his arms, legs, and knees.

The war in the Carolinas, of course, was only a sideshow when compared to what would soon take place in Virginia. While news of the navy's failure against the *Albemarle* was hardly good for Northern morale, a failure by Grant's army in the upcoming days or weeks along the Rapidan River could spell nothing but disaster for the cause of freedom. That was something he feared even considering.

So Abraham Lincoln knew he had much to worry about on this rainy April night, and no doubt for many more nights to come. In his mind, he could almost hear the sound of the guns already – terrible, thunderous ... prophetic. But exactly which side the thunder would eventually favor remained, for him, maddeningly unclear.

Chapter Ten

May 5th – Afternoon

Cooke could make them out clearly now, three large Yankee gunboats, all well armed, all three headed straight for the *Albemarle*. There was no time to lose.

"General quarters!" Cooke yelled, then he put the glass to his eye again. Just ahead were the four small gunboats that he had been chasing for the better part of an hour, but now those too appeared to be turning and moving into line of attack. Soon all the gunboats would be on top of him – seven against one. Had the hunter suddenly become the hunted, he wondered? Had he stumbled into a trap? This, Cooke thought, was getting interesting.

"Load fore and aft with spherical shot!" he cried, carefully gauging the distance between his bow and the lead Federal boat.

"Aye, aye, Captain!"

They had departed Plymouth that afternoon, three boats in all, the *Albemarle*, *Cotton Plant*, and *Bombshell* – an old Erie Canal steamer the Yankees had used as a transport – all three bound for New Bern, North Carolina. Cooke had had the *Bombshell* resurrected from the mud of the Roanoke's bottom and refitted after the Yankees had surrendered Plymouth, and by mid-afternoon all three had made it from the mouth of the Roanoke River into the open waters of Albemarle Sound.

A scout had informed Cooke that the Yanks had somehow gotten wind of his mission to New Bern and would be waiting for him once he emerged from the Roanoke. So he had pushed his departure date up, hoping to catch the Yankees napping, and when his small squadron finally steamed into Albemarle Sound he had surprised four Federal vessels laying a line of torpedoes. They fled at once, he gave chase at once, and now, with the sudden appearance of the three larger gunboats, things definitely seemed o be heating up. While he did not fear a single one of them, he knew that taking on odds of seven to one would be no picnic, and he immediately gave orders for the *Bombshell* and *Cotton Plant* to turn about and withdraw.

Hoke's division had been recalled to northern Virginia in order to help defend against Grant's anticipated spring offensive, and in his stead General Pierre Beauregard had been placed in command in North Carolina. Beauregard planned on using the *Albemarle* to methodically destroy much of the defenses that the Yankees had constructed in and around New Bern before committing his ground troops, and James Cooke fancied this new plan quite sound.

But the journey from Plymouth to New Bern by water was a long one. They would have to travel down the Roanoke, then across the Albemarle, Croatan, and Pamlico sounds, and finally all the way up the Neuce River to New Bern. They had all started off with high hopes that afternoon, but now the Federal fleet was coming at him with everything they had. Seven boats against one probably meant 60 guns to his two, but Cooke had not the slightest intention of backing down.

The Federal ships were steaming straight toward him in two lines a half-mile apart, three vessels in one line, four in the other. The lead vessel – a heavy, double-ended gunboat that was in all probability carrying at least twelve guns – appeared to be the

Mattabesett, Captain Melancton Smith's flagship. Cooke had information that Smith had replaced Commander Flusser as head of the local Federal Fleet, and Smith reportedly had big ideas about sinking the *Albemarle.*

"Hard to starboard!" Cooke commanded, taking one long last look through his glass. It was time to abandon the casemate for the safety of the ironclad's interior. "Everyone below!"

It was a beautiful warm day, the sun high above, the view across the sound clear and unspoiled. It was a perfect afternoon for a fight – entirely unlike that morning in April when he could hardly see through the darkness and fog – and he hated to abandon his perch above decks for the cramped, stuffy space below, but necessity called.

The hatch slammed shut with a heavy, metallic clank, and as they scurried down the ladder he could feel the *Albemarle* begin to veer to starboard.

"Open gun ports!" Cooke barked, glancing out the helmsman's portal. "Let's see if we can get a few shots off against the bastards before they get in too close. But make 'em count, lads," he insisted. "Make 'em count!"

The aft Brooke was loaded and ready on the port side. Once in range it blasted away, twice striking the *Mattabesett* and causing considerable damage. The crew cheered wildly with each hit.

James Cooke grinned. "Let the damn Yankees fire away," he said. "They can't touch us. They can't hurt us, boys."

The *Albemarle* took up a course virtually parallel to the approaching Yankees, and as the first line passed, the Yanks fired an enormous broadside. Several shells struck the ironclad's casemate with ear-piercing concussions, and while none dented the iron, wood splinters flew every which way below decks. The shock and ear-splitting din were unnerving.

Cooke could see that the *Mattabesett* was now clearing his starboard bow and quickly ordered the forward gun to respond. "Roby!" he yelled, "give the Yank the bow gun now!"

At once the forward Brooke fired. The shot hit a cannon on the deck of the Yankee vessel, sending sailors flying in the air like rag dolls in a ball of smoke and fire.

Cooke cheered, threw up his arms. Then off his stern he spotted the *Bombshell* still tagging along to starboard, and he knew the *Mattabesett* was making straight for her. "Keep up a steady fire!" he demanded, as the next of the Yankee ships closed. But it was suddenly difficult to see, as thick grey smoke from the guns and smokestacks lay over the water, clouding his vision.

"I can't see anything, Captain!" Roby screamed.

Cooke was not scared of their guns, but being rammed by one of the seven was something else entirely, and if he could not see, he could not steer to avoid them. The *Albemarle* sat so low in the water that one of the Federal boats might run right over her top and sink her almost by mistake, if not by intention. Cooke strained to see when suddenly the smoke cleared for a just second.

There they were, a shaft of golden sunlight glinting off their decks and guns, a stunning, almost breathtaking sight, even in the heat of battle. The *Mattabesett* sat dead in the water off his quarter, another Yankee vessel passing just off his starboard bow, white water bristling around her, while the third heavy gunboat was spotted drifting abeam. They had him surrounded. Off his stern, the *Bombshell* looked to have been struck several times and appeared disabled; why she had not turned and fled as he had ordered, he could not say. Now the other Yankee ships were closing in on her for the kill.

Aboard the *Albemarle* both gun crews continued to fire, but only when they could see clearly enough through the smoke to get a sure hit. Around them, the heavy din of cannon fire continued unabated, and shots repeatedly struck the hull with thunderous explosions. The cannon fire seemed to be coming from every angle. Below decks the sound of the shells raining against the iron casement was beyond description, almost maddening. So deafening was the constant drumming that many members of the crew had blood running from their ears and noses. Sulfur smoke blew through the gun ports like a hot fog, burning Cooke's eyes and obscuring his vision. He was starting to think he had made a mistake, that he had let his own fiery temper get the best of him, that he had bitten off more than he could chew.

Then he caught a brief flash of motion headed toward his starboard beam – they were trying to ram him! "All ahead, full!" Cooke screamed at the top of his lungs. "Full! Now!"

The ironclad lunged forward, but far too slowly to avoid the closing Yankee ship.

Roby, eyes bulging, cupped his hands around his mouth and yelled: "Stand by with small arms and prepare to repel boarders! We're going to take a hit!"

The crew at the aft Brooke ran her out as the Yank closed and fired a shot almost point blank into her bow from only yards away. The shell blew a hole in her the size of a giant rain barrel, but there was no stopping the Yankee ship's forward motion now.

"Damn it to hell!" Cooke shouted, watching as the looming bow of the Federal vessel closed to within only feet of the ironclad. "All hands *down*!" he screamed, and then they were hit, the Yankee boat slamming into them just behind his starboard beam.

The impact was horrific. The screeching wail of iron on iron, the sounds of wood cracking and splintering, of men screaming, stumbling and falling hard to the deck filled his ears. The CSS *Albemarle* shook and shuddered as if it had struck the great Rocky

Mountains themselves at full throttle. The ironclad was wrenched hard to starboard by the collision, and water began splashing through the aft ports. James Cooke swallowed hard and for a moment had to fight with himself in order to maintain control of his emotions.

All around him, men were hollering and screaming, while others were dizzy and demoralized beyond reason. It felt as if they had been struck by a hurricane. No one had ever experienced anything like it, and Cooke realized that many of his crew had been shocked virtually senseless by the collision. So he stood up slowly, calmly tugged his coat back into place, then said in the most relaxed voice he could manage, "Stand to your guns, lads, and if we must sink let us go down like brave men."

Outside he could hear the engines from the Yank vessel churning, could feel the larger ship's momentum pushing down against the hull of the ironclad. "They're trying to drive us under," he said, but it soon became apparent that the tactic wasn't working, as both boats continued to glide along the surface, locked together in an odd, violent embrace.

His crew regained a measure of composure, and for the next ten minutes the two ships remained locked in a dance of death. Above, the Yankees were tossing grenades at the ironclad's ports and trying to get barrels of gunpowder down his smoke stack, but his own sharpshooters were holding them off. The other Federal boats sat silent, watching, realizing that the two combatants were too close together for them to open fire on the ironclad. Then slowly the competing forces of the two boat's engines turned the Yank just slightly off the *Albemarle*'s starboard bow, and Cooke sensed his opening.

"Hard to port!" he ordered. Every man waited anxiously as the engines whined, the boat bucked, then in a moment the ironclad yanked hard to port and pulled clear. Some men cheered, others sighed, but either way, the *Albemarle* was free again.

At that moment he was fully broadside to the gunboat that had rammed him, and Cooke immediately ordered the forward gun loaded as he brought the ram about for a quick shot. In seconds the forward port was opened, the gun thrust out, and the shot fired into the side of the Yank just below the foremast, instantly wreaking havoc. At once there was an enormous explosion, the violent screech of steam escaping, and the Yankee vessel suddenly listed hard to port. Within minutes she was sinking.

Cooke, furious now, his blood boiling with the fever of battle, ordered the reeling Yank gunboat boarded and seized. He would teach them a lesson, God damn it! Thirty of the crew grabbed rifles and cutlasses and assembled on the ironclad's forward deck, but word quickly came back that the Yanks were themselves waiting on deck in droves and that any attempt to board the wounded gunboat would surely prove suicidal. Reluctantly, he ordered his men down, then told the gunners to blast the Federal craft from stem to stern until there was nothing left of her but floating debris. He could make the Yank out clearly now – it was the *Secaucus* – yet despite all the damage she still managed to escape and limp slowly along toward Sandy Point and safety. "Damn!" he cursed. With the other Yankee gunboats closing, he had no time to chase her.

Dead ahead now was the *Miami*, closing slowly on his bow. "What's this?" Cooke yelled, glaring out the helmsman's port.

"Torpedo attack!" Roby called back. "I think they're trying to get on our bow, Captain, to torpedo us!"

"Like hell they will," Cooke scoffed, realizing the *Miami* would have to come in very close, then drop a long pole with a charge attached to position it under his bow. "Ahead, half," he ordered. “When they adjust to that, go full astern. Then we’ll swing her port-to-starboard, then back again. They won’t get near us. If you can get a good shot in, blow her to pieces.”

The *Miami* never came close, only bobbed in the water like a wounded duck, offering her bow and port side for target practice. After the ram’s gun crews landed a few well-placed shots, the *Miami* appeared crippled and unmanageable, spinning about, seemingly dead in the water. Two down, five to go.

Next came the *Wyalusing.* She steamed up on the *Albemarle*’s port side and unleashed a full broadside that rattled the ram’s inside like a bell chamber but did no damage. Like all the other shells, these simply bounced off the iron plating and rebounded into the water with huge, angry splashes. Slowly, carefully, the *Albemarle* responded, both guns scoring mighty hits against all the Federal boats as they maneuvered for position.

The *Wyalusing* played on the *Albemarle* for almost a half hour, firing over sixty rounds and accomplishing little, while one of her own rudders was blown away by a shot from the ironclad’s forward Brooke. Foundering now from a number of well-placed shots, out of ammunition and out of ideas, she finally gave way to the *Commodore Hull,* which took up the same tactic for another half hour, only to meet with the same lack of success.

After observing this awesome display of the *Albemarle’*s strength from his position aboard the *Mattabesett,* Captain Smith finally decided to run up the flags and order a cease-fire. His fleet was doing nothing more than wasting their ammunition while taking severe damage with every approach of the ironclad. Smith had seen enough.

Cooke was at the helmsman’s port, staring as the flags went up aboard the *Mattabesett*, a great sense of elation washing over him, when he heard Lieutenant Roby call out from the boilers, his voice trembling slightly.

"C-Captain!" Roby cried, "We have a problem here."

Cooke turned around, stared. "What?"

While the iron casemate was holding like the Rock of Gibraltar around them, the *Albemarle*'s smokestack had been so riddled with shot during the course of the fighting that her furnace was suddenly failing for a lack of draft and her boilers rapidly losing steam. If her fires weren't spiked soon, the ram wouldn't be able to move at all. What the Yankee gunboats had not been able to accomplish intentionally, Cooke now realized, they might well have accomplished by nothing more than good fortune. If he lost power he knew they would simply circle and ram him until the ironclad went under. In the blink of an eye what he had conceived as a great victory had turned into a desperate situation.

"The fire's just not *burning,* Captain!" Roby screamed, sweat pouring down his face. "And we're almost out of coal anyway. We have nothing left to feed the furnace."

"We have to get out of here," Cooke replied, trying once again to remain calm, to think it through. He turned around, placed his hands behind his back, and said in an unruffled tone, "We must get the steam up again. Now, Lieutenant!"

"But there's no draft!" Roby protested, angrily tossing his hands in the air. "The smoke stack is full of *holes* for God's sake, Captain! With no draft to speak of, we can't get any pressure up in the boilers! How the *hell* we gonna move her?"

"Throw in every last ounce of coal, and anything else we've got that will burn," Cooke shot back. "If the Yankees see us dead in the water ... well, we will be. I can promise you *that!*"

"*What* else, Captain? We have no fuel to burn but coal."

"Anything that will burn," Cooke repeated, his mind suddenly awhirl. "Furniture, bulkheads, doors .... Rip the wood from the cabins, toss in the planking. And do it quick!"

"Aye, aye, Captain."

The crew scrambled throughout the vessel, grabbing anything that might burn, tossing it into the furnace – books, papers, furniture, bulkheads ... anything. The pressure increased, but only slightly. The *Albemarle* came about ever so slowly, and started limping back toward the mouth of the Roanoke. For a second, there was hope. But then the pressure failed again, and the twin screws began to slow. Cooke could hear the sluggish, rhythmic slap of the waves decreasing against the hull. Off his stern he saw the *Commodore Hull* and the *Ceres* trailing lazily, lobbing shells whenever it pleased them. They were waiting, curious, watching like vultures.

"What are they up to, Captain?" Roby asked.

"They're just watching, for the time being," Cooke answered, glaring out the stern port. "As long as we keep moving we'll be okay."

"You know, I just thought of something, Captain," Roby went on, wiping the sweat from his face with the back of his sleeve. "We got us a whole pantry full of bacon, ham, and lard. I believe that'll burn real hot, what with the fat, grease, and all in it. Draft or no."

Cooke swung round, slapped himself on the forehead. "Damn!" he cried. Then he broke into a broad grin. "Get it out, Lieutenant. I'll be damned if you're not right! You're a genius, sir! I believe you just may have saved us!"

So the meat was tossed into the furnace, and sure enough, within minutes the fires were raging again, steam pressure rising rapidly. The twin screws began to turn slowly, then to hum. The men stood and cheered, tossing their caps in the air. The *Albemarle* was back in business.

They steamed down to the mouth of the Roanoke, where Cooke had the ironclad quickly brought about one final time to face his fainthearted pursuers. He had no intention of letting them think he was breaking off the engagement. Not James Cooke! It was the *Mattabesett,* after all, who'd called for a cease-fire, not him. He was only out of fuel, low on ammunition, and in need of a new smokestack. Cooke, still mad as a hornet, had every intention of coming back the following day to finish off the lot of them.

"Roll out the bow gun!" he yelled, and the metal chains clanked loudly overhead again as the forward portal rumbled open.

In response, both Federal vessels veered off quickly and started a run back down the sound to where the five other Yankee ships sat shot to pieces, most of them dead in the water.

"Fire!" he heard the gunner yell, and the Brook rifle thundered a few parting shots, huge shells shrieking over the water and striking the *Ceres* in her stern as she fled. The men cheered as smoke rose ominously from the *Ceres*, and the boys tossed their caps again. They had been fighting for almost four hours straight, but they were all laughing now – exhausted, relieved, yet somehow wildly elated. They may not have demolished the entire Federal Fleet, but they'd sunk two and torn the rest to pieces.

Then he ordered her about once more, and the *Albemarle* began its cruise back upriver to Plymouth, smelling for all the world like the greatest breakfast ever put afloat, but not a man on board seemed to mind.

Chapter Eleven

May 7th – 2:04 A. M.

Lincoln looked up, spotted the servant, and asked again, "Have you heard anything of the train?"

"Yes, Mister President," came the response. "The train is due in a half hour, and I've sent the carriage over already."

Lincoln nodded appreciatively, thanked the man and then went back to his pacing. He began walking across his office toward the dark window again. Around him, Gideon Welles and the rest of his cabinet sat, quietly chatting amongst themselves, waiting nervously for word from the front.

Lincoln had sent a special train down to Virginia in order to bring the reporter back to Washington. Then he left specific instructions that the man was to be admitted to the White House at whatever hour he arrived. After two long days and nights of intense worry, Abraham Lincoln had decided that he had to know *something*, so he had asked for the young reporter from the New York *Tribune,* Henry Wing, to be brought to him. Wing was bright and aggressive, and had always made it his business to travel with the fighting men of the army. If anyone would know what was going on at the front, Lincoln knew it would be Wing.

Grant's offensive had begun in earnest on the night of the 4th, and, from what little Lincoln had been able to learn, for two days now the two armies had been slugging it out somewhere near the Rapidan River in Virginia. For those two long days Lincoln had sat, patiently waiting for some sort of report on the action to be brought from the telegraph room at the War Department, but nothing had come in. At night he aimlessly wandered the corridors of the White House or stared hopelessly at the ceiling above his bed, unable to sleep, waiting for something. Anything.

During those two long days not a single report had been filed by his new commander. Not one telegram, dispatch, note, or word had arrived. Not a hiccup had come from Grant, and now Lincoln was starting to fear the worst. It had always been his experience that generals were quick to celebrate what they conceived as success, so no news from generals in the field generally did not auger well.

He had tried to relax, but the tension was eating him alive. During the day, he could at least work, but the long nights were killing him. At night he often left his useless bed, wrapped himself in a long robe, and paced the floors of the White House, fear and worry generating the worst sorts of irrational misgivings during those late hours when optimism all but vanished and horror spread through his mind like a malignant weed. He'd had so little sleep that the dark bags under his eyes looked more like fresh welts, and he often felt weak to the point of collapse. He had not been hungry at all, and what little food he managed never agreed with him anyway. His world seemed to be rapidly unraveling. What had begun with such hope and anticipation only a few days ago seemed already to be crashing down all around him. Had Grant already stumbled head first into disaster? Was the nation in peril? He had to know.

Lincoln stopped pacing for a moment, stared back across his office. On his desk sat a report from the Secretary of the Navy detailing the fleet's most recent encounter with the Confederate ram, *Albemarle*. More bad news. Lincoln shook his head, started pacing again.

While the report from the Secretary had been couched in the most favorable terms, the truth of the matter lurked just below the surface. A simple analysis of the facts, for instance, indicated that the ironclad had returned to its berth at Plymouth, appearing to have survived the contest virtually unscathed, while the navy's attack squadron – by virtue of its own official reports – had been battered almost to pieces. Almost six hundred rounds of ammunition had been hurled at the ironclad, yet virtually nothing had come of it. By contrast, the *Albemarle's* two guns had fired only twenty-two rounds, and now all seven Federal boats were in for repairs, four of them disabled.

Indeed, while celebrating this great "victory" the navy fully admitted that it had little if any idea how to deal with the *Albemarle* should it decide to make another appearance, which after the drubbing she had handed Melancton Smith's gunboats, seemed an imminent event, perhaps no more than days away. With victories like this the Union would soon be lost, he thought, so he had instructed the navy to do anything within the realm of possibility to either destroy or confine the ironclad. Two years of hard fighting and many, many lives would be undone if she were allowed to range free upon the North Carolina sounds. The Northern Copperhead press was already making hay of the disaster. Abraham Lincoln had a list of many serious problems to which the CSS *Albemarle* now had to be added.

He continued his pacing. "Mister President."

Lincoln stopped in his tracks, glanced sideways. "Yes?"

"Your guest has arrived, sir. Mister Wing is here to see you."

Lincoln nodded slowly, rubbed his face. “Yes, show him in at once. Bring him here to my office.”

The young reporter came in with Secretary Welles, took the president’s hand and shook it firmly. Wing had been with Grant’s army for the past three days and Lincoln was desperate to hear everything he had to say. There was about the man the faintest aroma of cigar smoke and whiskey. “Thank you for coming at this late hour,” Lincoln said, pointing to a chair. Wing was then introduced to the various cabinet members who had waited all evening for some word as to the outcome of General Grant’s first encounter with Robert E. Lee’s Army of Northern Virginia.

Wing smiled. “My pleasure, sir. I am honored, of course.”

“Please, have a seat, and tell me all that you have seen of this battle in the Wilderness,” Lincoln said. “We are all *most* anxious.”

So Henry Wing sat across from Abraham Lincoln and told them all everything he could recall. They talked for over an hour, Lincoln and the cabinet members asking question after probing question.

It seemed there had been a great clash on the first day, and Lee had come very close to slicing the Federal army in two. Grant recovered and counterattacked, but that attack fizzled in the heavy undergrowth of the Virginia Wilderness, and Lee in turn counterattacked him. The Wilderness itself, Wing went on, a region of tight, twisted trees and impassable undergrowth where in places men could hardly see ten feet in front of their faces, was as much an adversary for both sides as were the contesting armies. Infantry units simply broke apart in the woods, cohesion became difficult, coordination over any distance at all close to impossible. It was perhaps the worst place imaginable to conduct such a battle, but it appeared that Lee had struck Grant there deliberately in order to even the odds. On the second day, the Rebels had gotten on Grant’s flank and chaos ensued, but then that attack also ran afoul of the impossible terrain, and eventually ran out of steam. Since then there had been only some sporadic firing.

Lincoln rocked back and forth, measuring every word Wing had to say. “So,” Lincoln asked finally, “who, would you say, had the upper hand when you left?”

Wing frowned. “Neither side, as I saw it,” the reporter answered. “When I departed, the contest seemed more or less a draw, but a very bloody draw, indeed.”

“A draw?” Lincoln asked.

“Yes, sir.”

“I see.”

After that the cabinet members rose to leave, but Wing remained behind and then asked for a brief, private meeting with the president. “Of course,” Lincoln said, and then slumped down in his chair across from the reporter.

When it was clear that everyone else had departed, Wing smiled thinly and began a brief, confidential report. “I know that General Grant will not back away from this fight,” Wing said emphatically. “He told me so.”

“He did?” Lincoln said, sitting up stiffly. “Please, tell me more.”

“Well, sir,” Wing continued, shifting slightly on his chair, “when it became clear I was leaving the front, I saw the general and he told me something that he wished me to report. But only to you, and only in private. That’s the way he put it.”

Lincoln’s heart began to beat quicker. He leaned forward. “And ... what was that?”

“He said, ‘If you do see the president, Wing, see him alone, and tell him that General Grant says there will be no turning back.’”

Abraham Lincoln closed his eyes momentarily, the words ringing in his ears joyously – at least this general would *fight.* He opened his eyes, nodded appreciatively. “So he won’t be retreating?”

“No, sir. At least that’s what he said to tell you.”

Abraham Lincoln stood, walked over to the young reporter who slouched before him, yanked him from his chair and gave him a hug. Lincoln felt enormously relieved. If this battle was not to be a clear-cut victory, at least it would not be a clear-cut defeat. And if Grant kept on pushing, then perhaps ... tomorrow? “Will the fighting be renewed?” Lincoln asked.

Wing shook his head miserably. “Perhaps, sir, but it is an awful place to fight, sir, this Wilderness. It is. And it has been a desperate battle, of that I can assure you. But our boys fought very hard, sir. Very hard.”

“I am sure of it,” Lincoln replied. “They always do. The men, I mean. And casualties? Does anyone have any idea, any estimate of what our losses are so far?”

Wing grimaced. “Nothing from Grant’s headquarters, if that’s what you mean. No, I haven’t heard anything official. But from the men I’ve been talking to, and from what they tell me of the fighting, I would hazard, sir, that our casualties might already be well in excess of twenty thousand.”

Lincoln jerked back as if struck in the face. “*Twenty thousand!* ... In just *two days?*”

Wing nodded.“It was hard fighting, sir. Very, very, hard.”

Lincoln leaned forward, cupped his hands tightly over his forehead. “Twenty thousand men,” he repeated. “What will I tell the people?”

"And we may never really know the casualty count for sure," Wing added. Then he gulped, looked sideways. "It ... it was that sort of a fight."

Lincoln looked up, stared at him. "Why? What do you mean? What sort of a fight?"

"Well, sir, the ground, the brush, you see, is quite dry in the Wilderness these days," Wing tried to explain, suddenly having difficulty with his own thoughts. "Last night much of it caught fire from all the artillery shells bursting about in the trees, you see." Wing looked away, took a few deep breaths, struggled to continue. "These fires, sir, well ... these fires spread rapidly, feasting on the cartridge boxes of the dead and wounded. Most of the wounded still lay unattended in the woods and brush. No one could get to them, you see. These boys had nowhere to go; most of the seriously wounded could not move, you see, could not get *away*, and well ... "

Lincoln closed his eyes. He could hardly believe his ears and fought back a wave of almost uncontrollable remorse. He tried to speak, to give voice to his grief, but no words could capture the depth of his feelings, so he simply sat and faced the young reporter, mute as a stone, the image of his soldiers screaming hideously, burning to death in the woods, forever seared into his brain. Twenty thousand men gone, many of them boys; consumed by flames, unable to run, unable to avoid the hell that was fast approaching. And he had sent them there ...

"I'm sorry, Mister President," he heard Wing say. "It is an ugly place, this Wilderness. Believe me. It is not something I would care to see again. You see, you see ... some of the men, I mean ... "

"What?"

"I'm not sure I should ... "

"Say it ... please."

"Well, sir, some of the men ... " Wing continued hesitantly, "took up their muskets and ... shot their own comrades rather than see them burned alive in the flames. Believe me, it was a most difficult thing to see, but far more difficult to do!"

Abraham Lincoln felt his body go numb. "Please, sir, go on."

Wing looked away, swallowing hard; he was having difficulty controlling his thoughts and emotions. "I … I saw a man shoot his own brother from a distance of about fifty yards through the flames, sir, then stand up, pull a pistol from his belt, and shoot himself in the head."

Lincoln nodded, felt a pain almost beyond description descend upon him. "Thank you, Henry," he said finally. "I think I have heard quite enough now. You have been most helpful. I cannot thank you enough. Is there any way by which I might repay your help? I know it was a long and dangerous trip for you up from the front."

"My horse, sir," Wing said. "I had to leave my horse Jesse behind, and I'm fearful the Rebels might snatch him away from me."

"No sir," Lincoln responded, "that shall not happen." Lincoln thought for a moment. "I will order up a special military train to take you back directly to where you left your horse. Will that do?"

"It will indeed, sir," Wing responded happily. "Me and that horse, well, we're mighty close."

"Then it is done," Lincoln said. "And do not be a stranger, Mr. Wing. I stand in your debt."

Wing stood, shook hands again, and left the room.

The hour grew late, but there was nothing for Lincoln to do now but resume his pacing. So he walked the halls, wrapped in a robe of grief, pacing away the hours until the first rays of daylight finally broke the eastern horizon. Twenty thousand men in only two days! What would he tell the country, he fretted; the people, all those wives, friends, children, and parents? What would he say? When would it end? Yes, Grant would fight, and that at least was *something*, but how long would it go on?

He hovered by a window for a moment when suddenly an odd, terrible thought struck him. Suppose Grant was finally able to take Richmond, but there was not a soul left to celebrate? Suppose they were all dead by then, killed off in this awful war? Suppose that when it was, at long last, over, he had no country left to administer, no nation at all, but only a vast, silent graveyard stretching from Maine to California? Was the nation now paying in blood for the errors of the past, and if so, just how much would God demand? What, exactly, might balance the scale?

He shuddered, could hardly get the thought out of his head. Then, as the sun crested the horizon, he slowly dragged himself back upstairs, put on fresh clothes, and tried to prepare for another day. In the end, that was all he could really manage. The greater issues, he knew, were all in the hands of God, but still those issues begged a frightening question: Was the nation now struggling to grow as he hoped, or dying as he feared; striving for a better tomorrow, or being torn apart in an orgy of blood, smoke and fire in a wayward place called hauntingly, almost prophetically, the Wilderness?

Chapter Twelve

June 18th–Afternoon

Cooke read the dispatch twice, folded it over, then set it aside on his desk. It broke his heart, but under the circumstances he really had no other choice.

For weeks now he had tried to pretend that the pain wasn't so bad, but there was no pretending anymore. Ever since the *Albemarle* had returned to Plymouth after its clash with the Yank gunboats on the sound, his health had been in steady decline, and now he could barely hobble around. As a favor to both himself and his service, he had written to the Secretary of the Navy a few weeks ago asking to be temporarily relieved of duty and given time to recuperate. The lingering case of what he called biliousness that had been dogging him for years had mushroomed into something unmanageable, and Cooke knew from experience that only time and rest would mollify it. He was in no way up to taking the ironclad out on the water for combat again in his condition and, truth be known, another battle like the one they had recently experienced might well kill him outright, as fragile as he now felt. So he had written to Steven Mallory, and today the answer had finally come. He picked it up, read again ...

Sir:

On the reporting of your successor, Commander Maffitt, you will consider yourself relieved of the command of the C. S. *Albemarle.* You will report by the 22d instant, or as soon thereafter as practicable.

By command of the Secretary of the Navy.

So, it was done. His temporary loss of command did not come without consolations, however. To begin with, his actions against the Federal fleet had earned him the appointment to Captain in the Provisional Navy of the Confederate States, a rank he was proud to have achieved. Secondly, since his demonstration of the ironclad's prowess, the CSS *Albemarle* was now deemed so valuable an asset by the authorities in Richmond that she could not be risked again, at least until complimented by a sister ship of equal or greater power. So for the near future at least, he did not think the ram would be leaving the Roanoke, and thus, while he would be off to recuperate for a few weeks, he doubted he would be missing much of anything in the way of action.

The thinking in Richmond now was that another victory over the Federal Fleet by the *Albemarle* would be of only limited tactical value to the Confederacy, while the potential loss of the ironclad – in all likelihood by repeated rammings – would be an outright disaster. If the ironclad were to be lost, the Yankees would immediately storm back through Washington and Plymouth, and both sides would be right back where they had started in early April. But Cooke knew the Yankees would *never* try to come up the Roanoke as long as the *Albemarle* was berthed at Plymouth, so berthed in Plymouth she would remain. All indications were that the Yankees were content to just sit at the mouth of the Roanoke; and until another ironclad could be built to augment her, it did not appear the *Albemarle* would be going anywhere either. For the time being it was a stalemate.

While the reaction across most of the South to the *Albemarle's* success had been nothing short of euphoric, and the ironclad's praises trumpeted far and wide, Cooke realized the truth of the matter to be something less favorable. Indeed, to his mind, her two shakedown engagements had proven unequivocally that the boat had any number of design flaws that were critical, if not potentially fatal.

To begin with, the ram drew far too much water and lacked proper buoyancy. She sat too low in the water, which made her far too easy to ram. More importantly, the design of the gun swivels – while certainly innovative – had proved impractical in battle. What had looked good on the drawing board did not pan out on the water. Quite often, by the time the guns were swung around into proper position, loaded and then run out, the target they had been preparing to fire upon had moved off. Then the crew had to go through the routine once more, only to crank open another gun port and discover that the enemy had once again shifted position.

Moreover, Cooke had discovered that two guns alone were insufficient for a clash with a squadron of well-armed gunboats. While the Federal boats had gotten off hundreds of shots against the *Albemarle*, his crew had managed only slightly more than twenty, and while those shots had proved extremely effective, he could not help but wonder what might have happened if he'd had four more guns to employ. A superior design, he'd concluded, would be to put two additional guns on each broadside, while keeping the same two Brooke positions fore and aft. That sort of arrangement could address targets at any point on the compass in the most efficient manner. There was absolutely no doubt in Cooke's mind that, had he been in command of such an ironclad on the 5th of May, he would have sunk every boat that faced him, and that was precisely the design he had recommended to the navy for the *Albemarle*'s sister ship, which he hoped soon to help build.

Unfortunately, the *Albemarle* could never be reconfigured to meet those new modifications. What was needed was an entirely new vessel built from scratch. Fortunately, Steven Mallory, the Secretary of the Navy, and Commodore Robert Pinkney, the commander of his naval district, were completely in favor of the new modifications and construction he had suggested, and Pinkney had already requested permission to procure some four hundred tons of railroad iron for the job. If the iron could be located, construction could begin almost at once, and Cooke fully expected to be appointed superintendent of the project once he recovered his health – who better in North Carolina could speak to the strengths and weaknesses of ironclads than he? And this much he knew: an ironclad with six guns, as he conceived it, would rule the sounds for some time to come.

Iron, of course, was the problem, as iron had always been the problem. Indeed, one of the best reasons for not fighting the *Albemarle* again was that she had lost a few iron plates during the recent engagement and they had yet to be replaced. In that sense, one good, lucky, or just stray shot might blow her to pieces and end her domination of the Roanoke.

In all likelihood an enforced period of inactivity would not sit too well, Cooke realized, with her new commanding officer, Commander John Newland Maffitt. Cooke knew Maffitt from the old navy, and Maffitt's reputation had only grown in leaps and bounds since the outbreak of Civil War. Maffitt had captained the CSS *Florida* sailing from her homeport in Mobile Bay, preying on Federal commerce across the wide Atlantic, and in time he'd become almost as famous as Raphael Semmes, captain of the infamous blockade-runner, CSS *Alabama.* Failing health had forced Maffitt to leave the *Florida*, but he was recovered now, and

Cooke was sure Maffitt would bring with him high expectations of combat on the open waters of the sounds. Until the new ironclad was fitted-out, however, he would have to be satisfied with champing at the bit, no matter how tempting a target the Federal Fleet appeared from afar.

"Ready, Captain?"

Cooke looked up – it was Lieutenant Roby. "Yes, Lieutenant. I want to thank you for your assistance. 'Fraid I'm not quite so spry as of late."

"You just need a little rest, Captain. You worked so hard getting the ironclad ready. It takes a toll on a soul, I'm sure."

"Well, you may be right."

Roby took up a few of Cooke's packed cases. "I'll have your bags brought out to the carriage. Least it's a nice day to move."

Cooke stood up slowly, wobbly, and walked carefully across the cabin. He stopped and tapped the bulkhead with his knuckles. "You'll take good care of her now, I hope?"

Roby laughed."Of course, sir," he replied. "Only the best. After all, she's the pride of the Confederate Navy now."

Cooke grinned, patted Roby lightly on the shoulder. "She is," he agreed, "and we made her that, you and I, Lieutenant. And Elliott of course. Mustn't forget Elliott."

"No, sir."

Outside the sun was beginning to dip but the day was still hot, and the heat lay over the river like an uncomfortable blanket. Cooke ducked away for a moment, the heat and bright sun disorienting him just slightly. Roby took him by the sleeve, helped him slowly toward the carriage. They finally made it to the carriage and Cooke steadied himself, then smiled weakly again. "I'll be back, you know. There's no getting rid of me."

"I know, Captain. We all know. We wouldn't have it any other way."

A few of the crew stopped and saluted as Cooke passed, but there was no ceremony to it, nothing official. He didn't want that, wanted only to be off for a while, then just as quickly back again. Just a sick leave – nothing more. And he wanted them to remember him as he had been that day out on the sound, not weak and nearly disabled as he felt now. So he returned the salutes quickly then swung himself up into the carriage.

"Commander Maffitt should be here in a few days," Cooke said, taking a long look around. "I will rest in my quarters until he arrives to replace me."

"That should help you some, Captain," Roby said, tossing his bags into the back. "It's much cooler off the river and out of the sun. It will do you good."

He turned back and stared at the CSS *Albemarle* one last time. She sat high and regal in the water now, glistening in the sunlight like an armored knight. All the repairs that they had the supplies and equipment for had been accomplished, and the smokestack from the *Southfield* removed and substituted for the shell-riddled affair with which they'd limped back into Plymouth. Trim, sleek, and powerful, she had done everything he had asked of her – that and more.

In just a few weeks he hoped to be starting construction on the new ironclad up at Edward's Ferry. She would be a bit more refined, of course, and certainly more powerful than the *Albemarle*, but no matter how fast or formidable, the new boat would never replace her in his heart. He had labored to build her, and like Don Quixote of old, they had sallied forth together to slay dragons. Unlike Don Quixote, however, the enemies they found and defeated were very real, and he and the *Albemarle* had returned together as heroes. He had breathed life into her, and in return the

Albemarle had given him back his reputation. He could not have asked for more.

Chapter Thirteen

June 23rd – Dusk

Cushing turned, stared off into the darkness, listened ...

"Boat ahoy!" came the cry from the riverbank, and Cushing knew at once that they'd been spotted.

"What do we do, Captain?" Howorth whispered under his breath.

"Hold still," Cushing replied.

They all sat breathless, waiting, the cutter bobbing gently in the water. Then the clouds overhead tumbled beyond the full moon, and moonlight exploded across the water, illuminating the river as if it were day.

"Boat ahoy!"

"Boat ahoy!" came the report again from shore, the cry now echoing up and down the length of the riverbank.

"They're on to us!" Howorth hissed.

Suddenly, signal fires flared up and down the bank, and the crack of musketry rang out. Bullets began to plunk in the water around the cutter.

Howorth stared at him.

William Cushing took a few deep breaths, felt the great calm of battle descend upon him: a clarity of mind that he experienced nowhere else. In the pale light of the moon, he could see the muffled oars hanging just above the water, numerous new signal fires bursting to life along the bank, the anxious faces of his men staring, waiting for his next order. He glanced across the water, mind awhirl, then the idea suddenly blossomed. He pointed hard to port. "Row to that moonlit patch of water over there," he whispered.

Howorth rubbed his chin nervously. "They'll see us there for sure, Captain."

"Row," Cushing repeated.

The sleek cutter lunged across the water toward the dancing patch of whiteness as bullets continued to slap the water around them. The boat moved smoothly, quickly, until fully engulfed in the radiant light, now a perfect target to anyone on shore. Once he was sure the Rebels could see them in the clear light of the moon, Cushing turned and pointed downriver toward Smithville. "Now, boys," he yelled, "turn on your oars, turn her down-stream. We're getting the hell out of here!"

The cutter leaped again, every man pulling as hard as he could, the oars slicing the water in perfect rhythm. Along the shore shouts and orders from the Confederates could be heard, drums beating, rifles firing. The long shadows of men running along the shore came bouncing out over the black river toward them as the cutter sped away. Rebel bullets continued to hiss overhead and lash the water, but none hit the boat, and soon the cutter struck the current rushing east and their speed increased considerably.

They rowed hard for about two minutes. The moon finally disappeared behind a bank of heavy clouds, and Cushing held up his hand. "Bring her around, boys," he ordered in a low voice. "But keep it quiet. Very quiet."

The cutter hung in the water motionless, soundless, the long oars dripping just slightly, until Cushing was sure the Confederates did not know where they were. Then he pointed back upriver. "Let's go."

Howorth studied him, startled by the command. "Upriver, Captain?"

Cushing smiled. "You'll see."

The muffled oars struck the water again, and they rowed back up the Cape Fear toward Wilmington, right back the way they had just come down. Moonlight shimmered suddenly across the water then disappeared just as quickly again behind a tumbling bank of clouds. The signal flares continued to leap to life along the bank, and shots rang out, but they were no longer so close, and soon they left all the excitement and activity behind. The Confederates had seen them turn and race downriver and presumed, of course, that the Yankee boat was sprinting for safety at the mouth of the river; so now all the picket stations downstream were being alerted to be on the lookout. But he was moving in the opposite direction. Will Cushing had fooled them again.

Suddenly Cushing sensed an odd feeling on the back of his neck, powerful, prickly. He turned swiftly, caught Howorth staring at him, smiling. Howorth saluted. "I should have known better, Captain," he said, shaking his head. "I should have *known* by now." The ensign saluted.

Cushing laughed and returned the salute.

They had shoved off from the *Monticello* about 8:00 that evening – Jones, Howorth, Cushing, and fifteen handpicked sailors – on a mission to reconnoiter the Wilmington defenses. The Confederate ironclad *Raleigh* was his ultimate goal, but before he could sink her he had to find her, and before he could find her he had to understand the array of defenses the Rebels had constructed along the inner river.

Several weeks earlier the *Raleigh* had steamed out of Wilmington and run off the entire blockading fleet, allowing several sleek blockade-runners to slip away unmolested. Cushing, off on his roving commission at the time, had heard of the debacle and immediately set sail for the mouth of the Cape Fear River, fully intending to take on the ironclad as soon as she appeared. But it had not come out again, so rather than wait, Cushing had decided to go in and find her himself. If the mountain would not come to Mohammed ...

Once again, Captain Sands had balked at his request, but Cushing immediately went over his head and secured permission for his escapade from the highest authorities in Washington. His idea had been approved from the Secretary of the Navy on down, and his plan was to board the ironclad with a handpicked crew and capture the gun deck, which would in turn provide access to both the magazine and engine room. With that, the boat would be his, and he would either scuttle her on the spot or steam off for the open sea, depending on conditions. But he needed to find the *Raleigh* before he could seize her, and that meant another midnight excursion up the Cape Fear River.

The cutter slipped easily around a long bend in the river, the men rowing hard, as Cushing kept an eye out over the stern. Far behind, the orange glow of the signal fires began to fade above the treetops, and the reports from the muskets grew faint. Another mile or so upriver the sound of shots disappeared altogether, leaving only the darkness, the sound of the river lapping gently against the cutter's prow, and the heavy, ripe odor of the Carolina low country. The oars struck the water with a steady cadence, the boys passed a canteen among them, and the cutter glided steadily closer to Wilmington with every stroke.

They rowed on silently, peacefully, until the first rays of sunlight began to glow in the east, and the air above the river started to brighten. Along the riverbank, birds began to stir and chirp. Day was approaching rapidly and with it, Cushing knew, heavy traffic on the river would commence again. Here the river was still wide, with low marsh thick along its edges, so they located a good spot along a bend, hid the boat, and settled in for the day. They would rest and pass the daylight hours while carefully observing the traffic that passed on the river. Cushing spread the men in a thin skirmish line in the trees along the river's edge just in case anyone might approach. The boats were hauled up into the thick grass and hidden carefully. They had covered about fifteen miles overnight, and he estimated that they were no more than five or six more from Wilmington. They had brought along two days rations of hardtack and salt horse. He saw that it was distributed fairly and then curled up under a long branch to watch the boats pass on the Cape Fear. It was just after 6 o'clock in the morning.

The sun rose and the day warmed uncomfortably. Out on the river there was considerably more traffic than he had anticipated, but no one came close to spotting them, and the day passed uneventfully. The men dozed from time to time in the heat, as Cushing studied the channel. Many boats came and went, Cushing made notes on all the naval traffic, but he saw no sign of the *Raleigh.*

Then, near sundown, two boats suddenly appeared around the western bend of the river and began closing directly on their position. Cushing, immediately sensing an attack, sent word down the line for his men to be ready, then inched out toward the river, pulling a pistol from his belt. He could not imagine just how they had spotted his position, but this was no time for speculation. He cocked the hammer calmly and waited.

The boats came on as if they were entirely aware of the small Yankee party hiding in the bushes, heading straight for them, and William Cushing began hatching a plan as to how his small group might fend off seventy to a hundred Rebel infantrymen. The boats came in, closer and closer. Behind ample cover on the bank his men took dead aim, and he was about to give the order to fire, when at the last second he realized they were not a group of soldiers at all, merely fisherman drifting on the current. Cushing waved for his men to back off, then stepped out of the trees into the water in front of the boats.

"Ahoy there!" he called, cupping his hands around his mouth.

One of the boats backed away slightly while the other bobbed idly behind. Then they started to come in closer.

"They're coming in, Captain," Howorth observed from behind a bush.

"Yes, I see," Cushing replied, waving to the fisherman. "When I give the word I want ten men to jump out and corral them with me."

"Just give the order," Howorth whispered as the boats neared.

Cushing continued to wave as the boats bobbed in closer, then whispered "Now!" and ten sailors burst from underneath the bushes, stormed into the river, and leveled their guns at the unsuspecting fisherman. It was over in a flash.

Cushing smiled, waved again. "Good afternoon, gentlemen," he said. "So good of you to join us."

"What in the *hell!*" he heard one of the fishermen exclaim. "They're God damn *Yankees!*"

Cushing nodded toward Howorth. "Reel them in, if you would."

The boats were pulled close to the shore, the startled fisherman offering no resistance.

Cushing put his pistol back under his belt, smiled, stepped closer. "We mean no harm, gentlemen," he told them. "We'd just like a little information." One of the fishermen held up his arms.

"Whatever you want, Yank. Just don't shoot us. We got's us women folk and chillun's at home. We ain't no fighting men."

"Well, you see, I have an invitation to come aboard and visit the crew of the ironclad *Raleigh*," Cushing said, "but I can't seem to find her." He scratched his head. "Must've got lost on the river last night. I thought that perhaps you gentlemen might steer me in the right direction."

"She done run aground at high tide weeks ago," came the response, "downriver a piece. Then when the tide went out the weight of her own iron crushed her, Mister. 'Fraid she's dead in the water and won't be goin' nowhere anytime soon. Sorry about your invite. Truly."

Cushing beamed at them. "Is that so?" he said, not knowing whether to believe the report or not. He waved them all out of the boats. "Come ashore and let's chat a bit," he said, and the fishermen reluctantly tumbled overboard and waded up the bank.

They seemed perfectly willing to tell him anything he wanted to know. They sat in a small circle and told him where he would find the remains of the *Raleigh* and gave him detailed information about the Confederate defenses upriver near Wilmington. Cushing decided to keep them as pilots and had their boats hidden safely away in the brush. His intention was to shove off for Wilmington once the sun was down.

"How would you gentlemen like to take a little cruise with us, all at the expense of the United States government?" Cushing asked, stepping into the cutter.

"We got a choice?" one of the fishermen asked, tobacco juice running down his chin.

"No," Cushing answered.

"Then I guess I'm all fer goin'."

Once the sun was down they piled into the cutter. A few miles below the city they observed the first of three lines of obstructions the fishermen had warned them about. This was a string of logs, chains, and pilings: just enough of a mess to foul any boat trying to run upstream. In the center of the obstruction was a narrow passage about forty yards wide, directly under the heavy naval guns of a Confederate battery. That particular margin of error was too narrow even for William Cushing, so he had the cutter beached, then started upstream with nine men along the bank of the river. Sure enough, not far ahead he encountered two more lines of obstructions, both of which were also under the daunting muzzles of large naval rifles. The route into Wilmington harbor was obviously well defended. It would be impossible to run.

"What do you think, Captain?" Howorth asked, kneeling beside him on the bank. "It's just as the fishermen told us. Three lines of obstructions guarded by plenty of guns. Maybe they were telling us the truth about the *Raleigh.*"

"Yes, maybe," Cushing agreed.

Jones glanced upriver nervously, then back at Cushing. "Captain, you're not thinking of ... "

Cushing smiled. "No," he replied. "Not through that gauntlet of guns. Unless, of course, you would like to lead us, Ensign?"

Jones broke into a grin. "No, no, Captain. I've seen quite enough."

"What then, Captain?" Howorth asked.

"We'll take the cutter downstream to that creek we passed a few miles back," Cushing said. "It leads into the swamp behind the city. We'll go that way and see what we can find."

They located the stream in the dark with no trouble, turned and rowed their way up the creek a few miles until it turned into swamp. Here the water was so shallow that they had to pole the boat slowly forward. Finally, they came upon a road that appeared to bisect the swamp, and which cut off further passage by water. It seemed to be nothing more than a logging road, and Cushing took seven men, one of them a fisherman, and headed off to reconnoiter. About two miles through the darkness they stumbled onto another road. This, the fisherman identified as the main road running from Fort Fisher into the city. Overhead ran a single telegraph wire, undoubtedly the only line of communications in the area. Cushing smiled – what a wonderful spot to raise havoc.

"Ensign Jones," Cushing called.

"Sir?"

"I want you to take this man back to the cutter," he said, pointing to the fisherman, "and tell the boys that Ensign Howorth and the rest of us are going to stay here and see who comes past during the day. Who knows, we just may catch us a general."

The sun was rising slowly, and Cushing had his men disperse just off the main road in the trees. Soon a hunter came by, and he was quickly captured and detained at gunpoint. While he had no intelligence as to the Rebel defenses in the area, he turned out to be the proprietor of a general store a mile or so down the main road, and this information Cushing filed away should they need to restock their provisions.

Shortly thereafter a horse was heard clopping down the road, and Cushing had his men dash off into the woods to lay in wait. The horseman proved to be a Rebel soldier with a mailbag slung over his shoulder, and Cushing thought them both an interesting catch.

Will stepped out into the road in front of the horseman, hands folded calmly behind his back. "Hello there!"

The soldier stopped, stared at Cushing. "What in the world? A Yank?"

"I'll be taking that mailbag now," Cushing said with a polite smile. "Oh, and feel free to dismount. You'll be staying right here for awhile."

The Rebel glared at Cushing as if he were crazy and had just started for the pistol at his side when four sailors leaped from the trees, rifles cocked and aimed at the Confederate mail carrier.

"I'm sorry," Cushing said, "you were saying ... ?"

"What the devil!" the mail carrier exclaimed, turning in the saddle. "This is official mail, you know. It's not to be … well …"

Cushing nodded. "I'll be glad to sign for it and I take full responsibility for any delays. Now, drop the bag on the road and dismount, please. Perhaps we can avoid further unpleasantness."

The Rebel, staring down the barrels of four rifles, realized he had little choice.

"A fine decision," Cushing said as they escorted him off. "Howorth!"

"Sir?"

"Take a good long look through that mailbag. There might be some official documents."

"Yes, Captain."

As the day wore on, numerous people passed on the road, and quite a few were detained. Those that were stopped were captured with great care – Cushing knew he could not afford to have anyone escape and sound the alarm. A small group of prisoners slowly expanded into a larger group, and by late afternoon they had some twenty-six civilians under guard. From conversation alone, Cushing was able to determine that a military courier would pass on the road sometime around five that afternoon, and he decided to wait and intercept him before leaving. Then they would head back to the cutter and slip downriver overnight to the ocean. That was the plan.

Meanwhile, Howorth exchanged uniforms with the Confederate mail courier they had stopped earlier, and headed off for the general store to secure more food. They had discovered numerous letters in the mailbag that clearly detailed the garrisons of the local forts, amounts of artillery along the river, and provisions stored nearby. It was all information that Cushing knew the Secretary of the Navy would love to see. Fortunately, they'd also found enough Rebel currency in the mailbag to purchase a small feast, but Cushing warned Howorth to be careful, lest he be captured and possibly hung as a spy.

"Shoot, Captain," Howorth protested, "my Reb vernacular is as good as anyone's."

Cushing smiled. "Don't overdue it," he said. "You're supposed to be nothing more than a Reb mailman, not *Hamlet* with a drawl."

Howorth removed his Confederate cap, bowed deeply, then tossed his hands in the air dramatically. "Tah bay, oh not tah bay, nah that thar's tha question ... ah reckon."

Cushing laughed. "Go now. And please confine yourself to purchasing food."

As Howorth started off, Cushing sent all the captured civilians back to the cutter under guard, and then started placing the rest of his men along the road to spring the trap on the Rebel courier as he approached. In short order Howorth returned, a supply of chicken and milk in hand which, when augmented with local blueberries, provided a fine meal for all concerned. When the men were finally finished with dinner, Will pulled out his watch and had a look – almost 5 o'clock. He walked deliberately up the road and stopped.

"Here," Cushing said to one sailor, then pointed to the other side of the road. "You two over there."

"Yes, sir," one of the sailors responded, but just as they started toward the trees two riders in grey uniforms galloped suddenly around the bend and stopped in a burst of dust no more than fifty yards distant. Cushing was still standing in the center of the road with several of his men nearby, and the Rebels spotted them at once. Yankee sailors armed with carbines – not the usual scenery near Wilmington. In an instant, the Rebel riders turned and galloped off in a fury of flying dirt.

"Damn!" Cushing shouted. They'd been spotted! This spelled disaster.

He dashed into the woods and grabbed the reins of the mail carrier's horse, leaped into the saddle, and slapped the horse's haunch. The horse bounded from the trees onto the road, and for a minute or two ran well. But almost immediately the steed began to slow. Cushing knew he could not let the riders get away and sound the alarm. If that happened the whole river would be alive with Rebel pickets looking for them, batteries of artillery primed and waiting, from Wilmington, clear out to the Atlantic – a distance of nearly twenty miles. So he chased the couriers hard for almost two miles, but he could not catch up. His horse simply wasn't up to the task, and the farther he fell behind, the more valuable time he knew he was losing. Finally, he gave up. Will pulled the horse up and started back.

"*Captain!*" Howorth cried, jumping onto the road from his hiding place in the underbrush. "Did you catch them? The couriers?"

Cushing wiped the sweat from his face. "No, damn it. They got away."

Howorth's eyes sprang open wide. "Every Rebel gun from here to Fort Caswell will be waiting for us, Captain," he said, "and every boat they have will be out on the water searching. We're way behind enemy lines, over twenty miles, I'd bet! Now they're onto us. We got big trouble here, I think."

Cushing rubbed his face, frowned. He dismounted in a leap and threw the reins aside angrily. "Yes," he agreed. "For once, William, I think you're right.... *Trouble* is what we've got, all right. Big as it gets!"

Chapter Fourteen

June 25th – 6:00 PM

Cushing pushed the horse aside and pointed at the telegraph wire running directly overhead. "Cut it!" he yelled at the sailors nearby. "Quick!"

Two men came running, jumped, clambered up the poles like monkeys. They cut two lengths of wire and tossed them to the ground. Three other sailors quickly grabbed up the wire, rolled it, and tucked it away in a haversack for safekeeping. If the Rebels were going to repair the line, at least they would have to bring their own wire.

"What do you think we should do now, Captain?" Howorth was asking, worriedly dogging along next to him as the men shinnied back down the poles.

Cushing stopped dead in his tracks. "I think we need to get the *hell* out of here, Ensign!" he replied. "That's what I think."

"Yes, sir," Howorth affirmed. "That's just what I was thinking."

The men quickly gathered up their rifles and gear and fell into line. There was no time to waste.

"Follow me," Cushing ordered, and they all started off on the trot down the logging road. In ten minutes they'd caught up with the rest of the prisoners, and from there they all hustled back to the cutter. Fortunately, Ensign Jones had thought ahead and gathered up a number of canoes from the locals. Most of the prisoners were placed in these, the canoes then lashed to the stern of the cutter, and they all shoved off. By 7 o'clock they were back out on the creek headed for the Cape Fear. By dusk, they were on the river.

Howorth made his way forward in the cutter and took a seat next to Cushing. "We can't take all these prisoners with us out to sea, Captain. But then I guess you know that."

"I know."

"What are you thinking? May I ask?"

"I'm not sure," Cushing replied. "Got any ideas?"

"We could make 'em all walk the plank," Howorth joked.

Cushing laughed. "That's a bit inhospitable, don't you think? Jeff Davis would never forgive us."

"I suppose," Howorth agreed. "But we can't just put 'em ashore. We do that and they'll alert every Reb between here and Fort Fisher."

"Yes, I know," Cushing admitted. "Here's what I'm thinking. Downriver a bit there's an island in the middle of the channel, if I recall. We'll put them off there. That way no one will get hurt, and the Reb search parties will be sure to find them come morning."

Howorth nodded agreeably.

The island was spotted within five minutes and the cutter made haste for the nearest point. They had just slipped into the marsh grass along the shore when a rumbling sound from behind caught everyone's attention. Cushing turned and spotted a large steamer coming around the nearest bend in the river behind them. Then it made a slight turn and headed straight toward the island.

"Rebels!" Jones yelled.

"Damn!" Cushing hissed. "Pull the cutter back into the grass," he ordered. "Everyone out. *Fast!*"

The prisoners were pushed and the crew dove into the water. Quickly his men pulled the cutter into the thickest part of the marsh grass, then yanked the canoes in behind. The bow of the steamer, now only 200 yards distant, was bearing down directly on them in the fading light of day, coming fast.

"Do they see us?" Jones asked.

"Don't know," Cushing answered hurriedly. Then he turned to his crew. "Everyone go under water when I go," he said. Then he leaned over the tops of the canoes. "Get down low, now," he commanded the prisoners. "I promise, it's a bullet for anyone who makes even a noise."

He could hear the paddle of the steamer thrashing the water harder and harder, and small waves from the bow were starting to rise through the marsh grass and lap up around his mouth. The boat was no more than forty feet away now. He nodded toward everyone, took a deep breath, went under.

Under water, the steady thump of the paddle wheel sounded as if it were going to come right over top of them. He opened his eyes to see the splash and bubbles of the paddle no more than ten feet from his nose, watched as it passed, listened as the sound slowly diminished. Cushing waited until the sound of the paddle had moved off a bit downstream then raised his head slightly above water. He took a deep breath, let it out slowly. Cushing could make out the name on the steamer's stern as it churned by – *Virginia* – clearly, and could still hear the men on her deck talking and laughing. A close call, he thought. Yes, as close as it gets.

Will waited until the steamer had disappeared downriver, then crawled back into the cutter. "Okay, everyone up," he ordered. Then he grabbed Jones by the sleeve. "Take all the paddles and sails out of the canoes."

Cushing stood, dripping wet, and leaned over the side of the cutter toward the canoes.

"Listen up, all my good friends from Seceshia," he said. "Fraid we're going to have to part company now. So sorry. Of course, I would like to book you all into the finest hotel in Wilmington for the night, but I'm afraid there's just not time enough for that – war and all. Perhaps next time. So I'm going to take your paddles and sails and set you adrift. You'll all be fine: no doubt discovered within an hour or so by your fine river patrols who will be out by the droves looking for us. By then, we will be well on our way, and soon you will be safely back in your homes entirely unharmed. I apologize for any inconvenience we may have caused you."

He retained one of the fishermen, however, a known river pilot, and with him they set out downriver for the site of the *Raleigh's* grounding. They finally found the Rebel ironclad just after midnight on a small spit that loomed out from the shore into the channel. Cushing had the cutter beached and he, Jones, and Howorth quickly jumped out and had a look for themselves. It was just as the fisherman had claimed earlier, the boat's iron had collapsed her frame and the ram was a complete wreck. She would never sail again.

"A formidable craft if ever there was one, aye Captain?" Jones said with a cackle.

Howorth laughed. "It would be better if they did not make them from toothpicks. You'd think they would learn."

Cushing smiled. "Indeed," he said. "Pity though. I would love to have taken her."

"There will be plenty more where this one came from, Captain," Howorth said. "Your chance will come soon enough. I'd bet on it. No sense tempting fate."

They all piled back into the cutter and pushed off on the current again. It was dark and misty and the musty smell of marsh grass filled the night air. They were all wet, tired, and uncomfortable, and the most dangerous part of the trip loomed just ahead now, trying to pass the Confederate forts and works near New Inlet. There was little question in Cushing's mind that the Rebels would be waiting, and he really had no set plan as to how he would deal with them. He decided he would simply judge what was best once he got there.

A few miles short of Fort Fisher, the cutter came upon on a small boat sporting four Confederate sailors accompanied by two lady friends. The crew quickly overtook them, and the occupants were taken into the cutter without a fight. From the sailors it was learned that several boats were waiting dead ahead, guarding New Inlet; in particular a large sailboat with seventy-five soldiers on board whose only mission was to find and capture Cushing and his small command. This was not good news. The odds were becoming more discouraging by the minute.

As the cutter continued on her way Howorth again took a seat next to Cushing and began rubbing his face anxiously. "I do not doubt you for a moment, Captain," he said with a big grin. "I hope you know that by now."

"Of course."

"But I was *wondering*," Howorth went on, "if I might have just an inkling of your next plan before we actually run afoul of the Rebs, who are, I'm guessing, waiting no more than a mile or two ahead of us now?"

"Certainly," Cushing answered, sitting comfortably cross-legged, penning a note by the light of a match. "In fact, I've just decided on something."

"Oh really? What, Captain?"

"We're going to go straight at the Rebel sailboat, board her and subdue her crew with pistols and cutlasses," Cushing replied. "Then we'll row off her starboard side as we pass the fort, using the sailboat as cover. The Rebels won't dare fire at their own people, I'm guessing. Then out to sea we'll abandon the cutter and sail back to the *Monticello* in the Rebel boat." Cushing offered all of this with a completely straight face while composing his note.

Howorth took a long, deep breath, then let it out slowly. "I see," he said finally. "As you see it then, Captain, the eighteen of us will simply jump aboard the Rebel schooner or whatever, subdue the seventy-five or so armed Rebels, then coast on out to sea past the fort."

"Yes. That's about the size of it," Will agreed.

Howorth slapped his knee and laughed out loud. "Lieutenant Cushing," he exclaimed, "if that plan had been put to me by any other officer in this navy I would have thought to have the man arrested. But from you it sounds like music. How is that, sir?"

"Because you know it will work."

Howorth grinned from ear to ear. "How many of the Rebels on board this sailboat would you have me personally capture, Captain?"

Cushing looked up from his writing, thought for a moment. "Twenty sounds like a good round number."

"*Twenty*?"

"Listen," Cushing said, suddenly dead serious, "they're not sailors or veteran troops. They're nothing but militia, and they've probably never even been in a fight. They're far more scared of us than we are of them. If we go at them hard they might just surrender without firing a shot. Or more probably panic and run away. Wait and see."

Howorth nodded, smiled."And one more thing, Captain ... "

"Go on."

"Just who, may I ask, are you writing to at a time like this?"

Cushing grinned. "Remember their Colonel Jones from Smithville?" he asked. "Remember how he claimed that we better not try any stunts on his river again?"

"Yes, I do," Howorth said.

"Yes, well so do I. So I'm just writing a short note to tell him how sorry we were to miss him during our little three-day junket up and down his Cape Fear River. Told him I'd try and stop by for a nice, long visit the next time we come around."

Howorth doubled over laughing. "And where are you going to leave it?"

"On the last buoy before Fort Fisher. I'll leave it well marked."

Within two minutes, they'd found the buoy bobbing in the channel and left Cushing's wry note properly attached. Almost immediately afterward they spotted what appeared to be a large guard boat, running just off of Federal Point. Cushing judged it to be the well-manned Rebel sailboat they'd been told about. "All right," he said, "let's go straight in after them."

The men bent their backs, and the oars ripped the water as the cutter lurched forward.

Cushing leaped to the prow of the boat. "Revolvers and cutlasses, everyone!" he ordered. "We're going to ram the boat and take her!" Then he turned and smiled at his prisoners. "Best keep your heads down folks. It could get a little hot around here in a minute or two."

The moon broke through the clouds then, flooding the river with a clear, white light, and the wind came up suddenly out of the southwest, sending clouds roiling overhead in the night sky like great, grey tumbleweeds. Cushing looked up, saw the trees bending along the river's edge, the clouds fuming above. A storm, he realized at once, was brewing out at sea.

They were closing hard on the sailboat now, and the Rebels could be seen running around on the deck in confusion. Everything looked good for ramming, and they had closed to within only fifty yards when Jones yelled out – "Off starboard, Captain! Off port, too! And look now, they're behind us!"

Cushing whirled around, took it all in at a glance. Now there were three more boats rowing out toward him from his left, at least five more on his right, and the lone sailboat was angling off on his stern. Every avenue of escape had been cut off. They'd been surrounded, trapped. His mind was suddenly awhirl, racing, calculating.

Cushing leaped to the helm, sheered the cutter hard to port, then spotted the sailboat filled with sailors moving just off on his right. They had him dead in the moon's glow and were tight off his stern, not giving an inch. He couldn't possibly fight all the boats, yet there was no place to run. Howorth was staring at him again. Cushing could feel his heart thumping in his chest.

Then in an extraordinary burst of comprehension it all came clear to him. The cutter was at the exact point of divergence of the two channels that led from the river out to sea, one leading more or less south out to Fort Caswell – the way they had come in – the other east through New Inlet. The tide was rising in New Inlet, but from the strength of the wind Cushing realized instantly that a storm was moving ashore, and that the sea would be far too rough near Fort Caswell for the cutter to break through the surf. Sensing that his pursuers were not experienced sailors, but more probably militiamen in rowboats, he guessed they just might be ripe for a good bluff. But the Rebels were closing fast. There wasn't a moment to spare.

"Hard to starboard!" Cushing ordered, and the cutter sheered hard to the right this time, rushing forward on the strength of the tide, cutting directly behind the sailboat then moving quickly out of the dancing light of the moon. They rowed hard toward the southern channel for a minute or two then brought the cutter about in the heavy wash, bobbing low in the waves. There they waited, sweating ... watching. Seconds seemed like hours.

"There, Captain," Howorth whispered into his ear finally, pointing off the cutter's port bow. "Do you see them?"

Passing in front of them in the darkness were all nine Rebel rowboats, making hard for the southern channel. They could hear the oars slapping the water wildly, the officers shouting.

"Beautiful," Cushing whispered back. He put up a hand. "Steady now."

They sat quietly in the cutter until all nine boats had moved well off to starboard. The channel through New Inlet to the sea now lay essentially undefended, only the sailboat off to their port beam presented a problem, and it was clearly visible in the moonlight.

"Now!" Cushing ordered, dropping his arm, "Hard to port! Take her straight in on the sailboat. We're going to board her!"

"Aye, aye, Captain."

"Once again, gentlemen," Cushing said, staring straight ahead as the cutter rushed toward the Rebel boat, "it will be revolvers and cutlasses."

The men gathered once more in the front of the cutter as she came out of the darkness, dead on the starboard side of the sailboat. The startled Confederates did not see them until the last moment, then desperately tried to avoid a collision by tacking, but in all the furor and confusion they lost the stays, and the sailboat drifted off helplessly on the tide.

"Forget her!" Cushing screamed! "Keep going!" he laughed as the cutter shot by the sailboat, the weary crew rowing harder now than they had ever rowed in their lives. But now there was nothing between them and the New Inlet channel except a dark stretch of water.

"Row, boys, *row!*" Cushing yelled as the cutter bounced high over the waves.

"Captain!" Howorth yelled, "the other boats have spotted us, and they're coming about."

Cushing glanced back. "Let them," he replied. He stuck his nose up, enjoyed the salty spray from the approaching surf on his face. "They're a hundred and fifty yards behind us," he went on, "and not getting any closer. They'll never catch us now."

The cutter leaped through the channel as the crew strained at the oars, then slammed head on into the heavy surf off Caroline Shoals. Striking the waves at exactly the right angle, the boat was over the first line of breakers in the blink of an eye, and well out beyond the surf in only seconds. It had all happened so quickly that the guns at Fort Fisher had not gotten off a single shot.

The cutter headed straight out to sea through a heavy surf, but no one seemed to mind anymore. Everyone smiled, laughed, and joked. Soon they hailed the *Cherokee* lying directly off New Inlet. The crew gladly tossed a line to the cutter, and promptly began towing them back toward the mouth of the southern channel where the *Monticello* waited at anchor.

Will Cushing had picked up a lot of valuable letters and information, but even more importantly, he had gotten first hand knowledge of all of the defensive arrangements on the waters around Wilmington – intelligence for which both the army and navy were desperate. Now that General Grant's overland offensive had managed to push Lee's army back from the Wilderness near the Rapidan River clear to the outer defenses of Richmond around Petersburg, a large-scale operation to take the city of Wilmington was in the offing. His little excursion had proved a stunning success: the intelligence he'd secured for that pending operation would be invaluable.

Around 1 o'clock in the afternoon, under a hot and glowing sun, they finally rendezvoused with the *Monticello.* The crew scrambled out of the cutter, up the rope ladder to the deck, then off below decks to their bunks. Most of them had been up for over sixty-eight hours with nothing more to keep them going than a few short naps. Cushing had not slept at all.

The officer of the deck stood at attention then saluted stiffly as they came aboard. "Welcome back, Captain," he said. "I was starting to worry. We all were. Was it ... tight, sir?"

Cushing smiled, returned the salute then patted the officer on the shoulder. "Tight?" he said. "Hardly tight. It was rather ... *dull*, actually."

For sixty-eight wonderful hours William Cushing had been utterly alive, his every nerve, muscle, and fiber exploding with the most intense concentration of thought and energy he had ever known. Now, sadly, it was over, but what a beautiful adventure it had been. *This,* he realized, was what God had created him for.

He went to his cabin, closed the door, and finally began to relax. He removed his coat, sat on the edge of his bed, and ever so slowly untied his shoes. Cushing's eyes began to close, then he fell backward in a daze, sound asleep before his head hit the pillow.

Chapter Fifteen

July 2nd – Late Afternoon

Cooke pushed the pillows aside, sat up slowly, and felt along the side of the bed for his cane. He found it leaning against the chair, stood very carefully, balanced himself precariously alongside the bed before trying to walk.

James Cooke was still weak and infirm. His head often felt light, his legs painful, but at least things seemed to be getting slowly better. Just the day before he'd been out for a good walk, and while it had been both difficult and painful, it did not hurt so much as before. Today he'd slept and wasted away much of the day in bed, but he had no intention of staying on his back forever.

He'd just heard the front door close and knew that Mary was back from town with food, a few odds and ends, and hopefully the mail. So it was time to get up. Besides, he wanted to read the paper in his favorite chair.

"Oh, you're up, Jim," she said as he maneuvered his way out the bedroom door. "Are you sure you should be…?"

"I'm just fine," he said, stabbing the floor awkwardly with his cane. "Legs are much better now."

"Still, I'm not sure ... " she went on.

"I'm not headed to China now, Mary," he said, trying to smile. "Just over to the chair," he insisted stubbornly, pointing with the cane.

She fretted, tried to take him by the arm. "Let me help ... "

"I'm under a full head of steam now," he objected, "and making a steady course for my rocker. Grab me by the arm and I'm liable to sheer hard to port, Mary, and ram the wall at full steam ahead."

She laughed. "You know, you're almost impossible to take care of, Jim."

He made it to the rocker, smiled, and turned around. "Yes, I know that," he said. "Been in the navy since I was a pup. Not much for convalescing."

"Yes, but that's exactly what you need, and you know it."

"No man appreciates his wife more than I do you, Mary," he replied. "You know *that*. I will admit I am difficult, but I'm coming along. Were the newspapers in the mail? Haven't been able to keep up with a thing."

"Thank goodness yes," she answered, tossing her hands in the air. "Thank the Lord we won't have to go another day without a newspaper for you, James. They're old, but they're here."

He smiled, rubbed his hands together anxiously. They had moved from their home in Portsmouth to Warrenton, North Carolina, at least for the duration of the war. There they found a pleasant cottage to rent, but the truth was it was never really home, never felt quite right.

"It's hard, Mary, being a captain in the navy," Cooke said. "In the middle of everything one day, then all of a sudden outside looking in the next. What papers have you brought me? Is there any news of the *Albemarle*? Anything at all?"

"I've got the Washington and Wilmington papers," she replied, tossing them onto his lap. "Jonas Thomas says he has the most recent Richmond paper at home, and he will be glad to share it with you tomorrow, once he's had a chance to read it thoroughly himself."

"Now, you say you have the Washington paper, aye," Cooke said. "I fancy that will be interesting. Haven't seen a Yankee paper in a week or two, Mary. Wonder what they're saying up at the North?"

"I wouldn't know, Jim."

"And the *Albemarle*?"

"I saw nothing, but you can look for yourself while I'm getting dinner around. Where are the boys?"

"Oh, off playing somewhere," he replied vaguely, eagerly thumbing through the first few pages of the Washington paper. There were numerous stories of Grant's recent siege of Petersburg – most of them uncomplimentary, he was pleased to see – but not many naval articles.

"What do the Yankee writers have to say, Jim?" Mary asked from the kitchen.

"Just some talk of Grant taking Petersburg," he answered.

She came through the door slowly, hesitantly. Then she stopped. "What do you think, Jim?"

"About what, Mary?"

"The war, of course. Our chances."

He hesitated. "I think our chances are still good, Mary," he replied after a noticeable pause.

"Do you really?" she asked. "I pray you are right. From here, I fear it does not look as good as all that."

"And from where is that?" Cooke asked. "Where is here?"

Mary pointed to her face. "From these two eyes," she said.

"Look," he answered quickly, "it is true Grant has pushed Lee back to Petersburg, but in one month Grant has lost three major battles – the Wilderness, Spotsylvania Court House, and Cold Harbor – and is no closer to besting Lee than he was when he crossed the Rapidan in May. The Yankees have lost over 54,000 men in just over one month, Mary. That's *54,000 men!* The Northern papers are screaming, and not just the Copperheads, castigating both Grant and Lincoln daily and bitterly. The Yanks cannot go on like this forever. It would be impossible. You should read their papers."

She looked away. "54,000 *boys*, Jim," she said, staring out the side window. "Like our boys. All of them someone's son, father, or friend. You know, we knew many of those boys before we left Virginia – before this horrible war started. That's why I cannot read the papers anymore. The articles sicken me, Jim. They *sicken* me. And do you know what else, Jim?" she went on, upset now. "I may not be a military expert like you, but I can surely see that Lee's army, once fighting far away in Northern Virginia, is now struggling to keep Grant from overwhelming Richmond. Tell me, how many more great victories like these you describe can the Confederacy survive? Oh yes, I hear the people shouting about these great *victories*. Sometimes I wonder if we haven't all lost our minds."

Cooke glanced up at her for a moment, then dropped his head and stared at his slippers. He felt suddenly miserable, uncomfortable. "Yes, I know," he said, but barely above a whisper. "I understand, Mary. It is not easy, this war, but you know I did not want this fight. I was not one of the hotheads screaming for secession."

She shook her head forcefully. "No, neither of us were."

"I will tell you truly, Mary," he said, shaking his head mournfully. "Don't repeat this to anyone, but I still get chills sometimes when I see the old flag."

She smiled. "Do you?"

"Yes," he admitted freely. "I sailed under that flag for many, many years, Mary. I'm not ashamed to say I loved it. To see the stars and stripes flapping in a brilliant sky above the deep blue sea, well, it was a sight, I will admit." Then Cooke wrung his hands together in his lap, tried to make sense of something he had never really been able to make sense of. "But what were we to do, Mary?" he asked forlornly, almost hopelessly. "I ... I could not turn and fight against my own people, my friends … my kin. You know that. We are *Virginians*, Mary!"

She shook her head. "I do not blame *you*, Jim," she said. "It's true, we had no other choice. But the war just goes on and on, thousands of boys perishing every month. Soon ... "

"Soon what, my dear?" he asked.

"Jim, we have three young boys ourselves .... Are you blind?"

He shook his head violently. "No Mary, they are *much* too young!"

"There are fourteen year olds dying for the Confederacy in Petersburg right *now*, Jim. If the war continues ... well, you tell me; who will Jefferson Davis call for next? Ten year olds?"

"I am a full *captain* now Mary," he reminded her. "Should it ever come to that, the boys will come with me and I will watch over them. You have my word. Rank still has its privileges."

She hesitated for a moment, then turned and stared him straight in the eye. "Yes, Jim, if you are still here to do so."

He laughed nervously. "What do you mean? Why, I have the finest boat in the world, Mary. The Yanks cannot touch me."

"The papers, Jim," she objected, "said the *Albemarle* had been seriously rammed. I forced myself to read them all – every last one. They said it had taken on a great deal of water, that ... " She stopped, staring at him anxiously.

He frowned. "Well, the papers always exaggerate," he offered lamely.

"Not always."

"Yes, always."

"Then why do you bother to read them?" she demanded.

He looked away, bested again. "Listen to me, Mary," he implored finally, "I have written to the Secretary and we will soon have permission to begin construction of a new ironclad. You see, I have made some very important modifications to the original design. I promise you, this new one will be unstoppable, and once built she and the *Albemarle* will take back *all* the sounds from the Yankees. That's why we must be absolutely certain no harm befalls the *Albemarle* before the new ironclad is ready, Mary. That would be a *disaster*."

"I see," she said, listening intently.

"Then, Mary," he continued excitedly, "with all the lush low country of Eastern North Carolina back in our hands we will be able to feed, not only Richmond, but most of Virginia, including General Lee's army at Petersburg – and feed them until hell freezes over. With ample food and supplies Lee will be able to hold Grant off forever, and then it will only be a matter of a few more months until the people of the North grow weary of having their sons hurled at Confederate earthworks and slaughtered for no reason at all, like pigs by the butcher. Lincoln will lose the coming fall election, and then, with a new administration in place, their great General Grant will soon be out of a job. I am convinced of it!"

"How can you be so sure Lincoln will lose?" she asked.

"Oh Mary," he replied, "his *own* party does not want him anymore. Their objections are the same as your objections, and here is the thing – you're both right! Grant cannot beat Lee, the Northern war effort has been entirely mismanaged, and, come November, Lincoln will *lose* because of it!" He shook the newspaper in his hand. "It's all in their papers!"

"Well, I hope you are right, Jim," she said. "The whole world is weary of this war, of boys coming home without arms and legs, or worse; not coming home at all."

"Yes," he replied softly, "I know .... I know."

She tried to smile. "Well, let me get back to dinner."

Cooke took up his newspaper again, rifled the pages for a while when suddenly a small headline on the front page caught his eye:

Captain Cushing's Exploits in the Cape Fear River

"What's this?" he asked absently.

"What?" Mary called from the kitchen.

"Nothing," he answered, then started to read. Cooke read the entire article, read it again, then laughed out loud.

"What's so funny?" she asked, setting the table in the dining room.

"Oh my," he said.

"What?"

"This *damn* Cushing ... "

"Watch yourself, please, James. You're not out on your ironclad with your salty crew just now, you know."

Cooke frowned, nodded, then began all over again. "This young *Federal lieutenant* has made the Wilmington command look like a pack of nitwits again, Mary. *Again!* It's not the first time he's done this, you see."

"Tell me," she said.

He shook his head mournfully. "Three days up and down the Cape Fear he sailed, Mary, right under their noses. Then they finally surrounded him with ten boats – ten boats! – and still he managed to get away. It's sad. Very sad. Are these sailors we have working the boats near Wilmington? I think not. It looks like we've got nothing more than a crew of donkeys or circus clowns working the river down there. Can you *imagine*?"

She finished with the silverware then put her hands on her hips. "You know, I did hear something about that the other day, Jim. Laura Mosby was talking about it. I overheard that General Whiting became quite upset."

Cooke folded the paper, put it aside. "Upset?" He laughed. "He should be a bit more than a little upset, if you ask me. This lieutenant is nothing more than a boy, Mary. Twenty-one years old he is, and he's got Whiting's entire command going around in circles like some kind of carnival trick. And it's not the first time. I'm sure Whiting has got to answer to Richmond for all this, but what in the world can he say for himself? ... 'Oops'?"

She smiled. "This Cushing seems quite intrepid."

Cooke leaned back in the rocker, chuckling to himself.

"Why are you laughing?" Mary asked.

"Because, my dear, I'm glad he's Whiting's problem and not mine."

"Well, what would you do, Jim, if he *were* your problem?"

"Send our three young boys out after him on their wooden raft, I suppose," he said with a wry smile. "They'd probably have a better chance finding this young Cushing than Whiting's misbegotten fleet of rowboats."

Mary laughed. "And knowing our boys, Jim, they'd just bring him home for Sunday dinner! What would you do *then*?"

He stood, took up his cane. Then he hobbled into the dining room and gave her a hug. “In all honesty, Mary,” he told her, “I’d say ‘Come in, my boy, have a seat at my table, and tell me how in the *hell* you managed all that!’ That’s exactly what I’d do.”

She laughed and hugged him back.

Cooke smiled, kissed her gently on the cheek. “And while we’re speaking of such life and death topics,” he said, “what, may I inquire, have you fixed us for dinner?”

Chapter Sixteen

July 5th – Late Afternoon

Cushing returned the salute smartly then stepped toward the officer on deck. “Lieutenant William Cushing to see Admiral Lee,” he announced.

“Yes, welcome aboard, Lieutenant. The admiral is waiting for you in his cabin. You are to go right down.”

Cushing moved quickly through the afternoon sun and descended into the dimly lit bowels of the USS *Minnesota,* Admiral Lee’s flagship. Cushing had gotten word a few days earlier that Lee had read the report of his recent excursion on the Cape Fear River, and now the admiral was suddenly anxious to see him about leading an important new mission. It had taken William Cushing four days to sail from Wilmington to Norfolk once he had received the dispatch, and now he moved through the long, dark corridor barely able to conceal his excitement. Twice he stopped and had to be redirected in the right direction toward Lee’s cabin. He knocked politely, straightened his coat, then stood back and waited. This, Cushing sensed, was going to be a defining moment in his career.

“Yes, what is it?”

“Lieutenant Cushing, sir. As requested.”

“Cushing? Yes, come in.”

He opened the door gingerly, stepped through and spotted the admiral behind his desk. Cushing saluted smartly.

Lee – a lean, handsome man with thick, sandy hair and a trim grey beard – returned his salute, smiled, then stood and shook his hand. “Thank you for responding so promptly, Lieutenant,” the admiral said, pointing toward a chair.

“My pleasure, sir.”

Lee smiled again. “I’ve read your report regarding your activities around Wilmington last month. Most impressive.”

“Thank you, Admiral.”

“I can tell you Secretary Welles is also pleased with your success.”

“Well, I’m certainly gratified to hear that, sir.”

Lee sat again, leaned back and crossed his legs. “I’m not going to beat around the bush,” he said. “Frankly, there’s no *time* for that. The department has an extremely important mission on its hands. It is critical yet difficult, and, to say the least, hazardous. Very hazardous. It will require an officer who is both intelligent and daring. And it will take *guts*. After reading your report, well, I thought of you. Interested?”

“Of course, sir,” Cushing replied, having a hard time remaining seated in his chair. “And I should say I feel quite flattered. I want to thank you for even considering me, sir. Now, may I inquire, sir, just what this mission entails?”

Lee studied him for a moment then nodded slowly. “Yes, you may. Some way, somehow, the Confederate ironclad *Albemarle* must be destroyed. That’s the mission. It *must* be accomplished. This, of course, is coming from the highest levels in Washington.”

William Cushing felt a bolt of pure excitement flash through his chest. “I have prayed many times for just this opportunity,

Admiral," he said, hardly able to contain himself. "My good friend, Commander Flusser ... "

Lee frowned. "Yes, I know about all of that."

"Do you want me to lead a flotilla of gunboats upriver against the ram?" Cushing asked, his mind suddenly awhirl with possibilities. "I suspect ramming her –"

"No," the admiral interrupted. "We have decided not to risk any more wooden ships. It seems rather pointless to repeat endlessly what we know won't work. Rather I thought we might try some new tactic that just might succeed."

"I see," Cushing said.

"By the way," Lee continued, "we have received information that for health reasons Captain James Cooke has temporarily resigned as commander of the ram. He has been replaced by Commander John Maffitt."

Cushing's ears perked. "Maffitt," he repeated. "You mean the captain of the Rebel raider *Florida*?"

"Yes, *that* Maffitt," Lee replied. "Naturally, the department is fearful – what with Maffitt's reputation – that he will soon be up to no good. Maffitt is known to be a wily and aggressive officer, not one to be taken lightly. The *Albemarle* represents enough of a problem as is. With Maffitt on board now…"

"Is the ram still berthed at Plymouth, sir?" Cushing asked.

"As far as we know," Lee answered. "We should have some patrols out soon to pinpoint her location, and hopefully, at least the defensive arrangements the Rebels have made surrounding it. But I must warn you, Lieutenant, all the information we have developed so far indicates the ram is heavily defended. Very heavily."

Cushing crossed his legs. "Then I will lead an expedition upriver to destroy her," he said confidently. "I will need eighty men – good men."

"You shall have your eighty men, Mister Cushing," Lee replied without the slightest hesitation.

Cushing smiled, leaned forward over the admiral's desk, and began to put his thoughts on paper. Admiral Lee watched and listened intently as Cushing wrote, the admiral's chin perched on the back of his hands, eyes clear and focused.

Cushing's first idea was to take India rubber boats through the swamp adjacent to Plymouth, then launch them across the Roanoke toward the ram. If done quickly, he might be able to overwhelm the small local guard and crew, cut the ironclad out, then – with everyone safe from hostile fire inside – steam back down river to the fleet. His second idea was to take several small, fast, steam-driven cutters outfitted with torpedoes upriver and try to sink the *Albemarle* in her berth.

"Which do you consider the most practical?" Lee asked.

Cushing thought for a moment. "In all probability, the torpedo attack."

Lee nodded. "I agree," he said. "The simpler the plan, the fewer moving parts so to speak, the less chance of error. And any small error in a scheme such as this could lead to disaster. But for now what I want you to do is take some time and think all this through carefully. Then, once you've had time to consider all the various elements and obstacles, put your mature view down on paper and send it to me. If I like what you propose, I will forward it up the chain of command immediately to Washington with my recommendation."

"Of course, sir," Cushing said. "And again, thank you, sir."

Lee leaned gravely across his desk. "No matter how well planned and executed, Lieutenant, this mission will be extremely hazardous. I cannot emphasize that enough. The Rebels have the river picketed from the mouth of Albemarle Sound clear up to Plymouth. The ram's crew is on watch, and there is an infantry detail assigned there for the sole purpose of defending the ironclad. This will be no picnic, I promise you that. You had better think this over very seriously."

"I understand, sir," Cushing replied. "But I believe all those obstacles can be overcome. I'm confident of it."

Lee sat silent for a moment, gauging, it seemed; measuring the young man seated before him. "Very well, then," he said finally. "Of course, everything we have discussed here must remain absolutely secret. The destruction of the ram will be difficult enough as is. If word of a mission to destroy her leaks out, well … I fear the mission will become suicidal."

"I understand," Cushing said.

"Then good day, Lieutenant," Lee said, standing again and taking his hand. "Get your thoughts back to me as soon as possible. This must be done soon."

For two days William Cushing thought of virtually nothing other than the attack on the *Albemarle*, and on the third he put his best idea down carefully on paper. He had decided upon a torpedo attack utilizing at least two small boats – preferably three – the first, the torpedo boat, to slash in and detonate its charge while covered from behind by the other two. All three craft would be specially outfitted with small howitzers in order to fire canister in the hopes of subduing any defenders or crew determined to fight it out. Once the torpedo had been detonated, the two additional boats would serve to cover the withdrawal, or stand by to pick up survivors. If done quickly, silently, and professionally the assault would work. He was certain of it.

Cushing was pleased with his plan and considered it entirely achievable. With all the detail in mind, he sat down at his desk aboard the *Monticello* and began to write:

> Deeming the capture or destruction of the rebel ram *Albemarle* feasible, I beg to state that I am acquainted with the waters held by her, and am willing to undertake the task.

He finished the proposal late that night, changed a few small details, then had it delivered to Admiral Lee the following day. Shortly thereafter Cushing received a response indicating the admiral had already approved Cushing's plan and had sent it on to Secretary Welles for prompt consideration. In the meantime, Lee was going to search for someone to replace Cushing on board the *Monticello* while he was detailed off on his new mission.

Late that evening, Will Cushing poured himself a glass of port and sat alone at his desk. The magnitude of the mission that he had agreed to take on was finally beginning to dawn on him. The fact that the navy had turned to him for such an important endeavor pleased him enormously. Now, as well, he would be given the opportunity to make good on his pledge to avenge Charles Flusser's death and to deliver a lasting blow for his brother, Alonzo.

Commingled with the elation of the moment, however, came a growing, almost gnawing sense of concern. For late that night he had come to the stark but sobering realization that – based on the formidable odds he would be facing – any mission to destroy the *Albemarle* would be far more difficult than anything he had ever attempted before.

Chapter Seventeen

July 11th – Afternoon

Lincoln walked slowly up the steps toward the battlements and paused. On the top step Lincoln hesitated for just a moment, took a long, deep breath and then moved off to a vacant spot along the parapet overlooking the open fields to the north. He pulled his hat down a notch to shield his eyes from the glaring, afternoon sun. Then he set his jaw firmly; he felt anxious and excited and desperate all at once. The war had come marching swiftly all the way to Washington in search of Abraham Lincoln, and he was not about to shy away from a single Rebel bullet. He had fought them from afar, had heard all the tales of their invincible leaders, of their hard-marching "foot cavalry," of the dreaded Rebel yell. Now he was about to see them with his own eyes.

For two months now his armies had been stymied on almost every front, progress nearly negligible, yet the casualty lists had swelled to an appalling level. In Georgia Sherman's massive army had been harassed and hindered every step of the way by a Confederate force under Joe Johnston, and Lincoln had no idea if Sherman would ever even see Atlanta, much less take the city.

In the East, Grant, traveling with the Army of the Potomac, had not fared much better. Fought to a bloody stalemate in the Wilderness in early May, Grant had three times attempted to sidestep Lee's army to the south and east to get around him toward

Richmond, only to discover Lee waiting across his path each time in freshly dug earthworks.

The fighting had been horrific at Spotsylvania Court House, then again along the North Anna River, and worst of all at Cold Harbor, where Grant lost almost 13,000 men in the first week of June alone, 6,000 of those in only twenty minutes. The butcher's bill for the spring campaign had already topped 54,000 men, yet Lee appeared no closer to defeat than when Grant's cavalry first splashed across the Rapidan in early May. Now Grant's army had fumbled and stumbled its way into a siege of Petersburg with no end in sight, and the people of the North were beginning to stir uncomfortably. The spring was rapidly becoming a season of bitter disappointments, but none more bitter or more disappointing than what Abraham Lincoln faced now as he gazed out over the open fields just north of Washington.

Through the smoke and spiraling dust, Lincoln could clearly make out the grey-clad skirmish lines moving forward, as batteries of Confederate artillery were unlimbered nearby and rolled into place. For days, the Northern papers had been screaming dire warnings as the Rebels marched through Maryland, and now Jubal Early's Confederate army had finally arrived on the very outskirts of Washington. Recently detached from Lee's Army of Northern Virginia, Early's command – according to some newspaper accounts numbering as high as 20,000 or even 30,000 men – seemed, like a summer thunderstorm, to have materialized out of thin air just days ago in Maryland. How a movement of such scope could have evaded the attention of his top generals was simply beyond him, but the problem now ranged far beyond one of mere professional competence. Washington City, the capital of the nation, the very heartbeat of freedom in a world still very much in chains, was in danger of being seized, perhaps even sacked, and there was precious little Lincoln could do but watch, wait, and worry.

On the previous day Lincoln had wired Grant at Petersburg, strongly suggesting that he come north with enough troops to crush Early as soon as possible. Grant instantly agreed as far as the troops were concerned, but thought it best that he remain behind. Now two full Federal corps were en route by way of naval transports up the Chesapeake Bay. But those troops had yet to arrive, while the advanced elements of Early's long columns were already forming lines of battle in the heat and swirling dust right before the president's eyes. In a war known for its military fiascos, none seemed more desperate or ill-timed than this. Despite an enormous inferiority in men and material, somehow the Rebels had managed to swiftly move a strong force to the very gates of Washington. How could this be?

Jubal Early had marched up the length of the Shenandoah Valley, taken Winchester and Harper's Ferry before moving into Maryland, where he then held and ransomed both Hagerstown and Frederick City. From there he moved south, burning mills and factories, and tearing up railroads as he marched. General Lew Wallace had taken his small force out of Baltimore and valiantly fought a pitched battle on the banks of the Monocacy River near Frederick against Early, but Wallace was so outnumbered he could accomplish little except delay the Rebel advance for the better part of a day before being routed from the field.

For days, the governors of bordering states had been begging Lincoln for protection and troops, but that morning the begging had ended abruptly – the telegraph lines feeding the capital had been cut. Now, Washington sat alone and essentially undefended, Confederate troops deploying leisurely within sight of the President of the United States as the local commanders fretted over how to oppose them. Grant had stripped the Washington defenses of almost all usable troops for his spring campaign, leaving behind only militia and convalescents to man the battlements – hardly a match in numbers or ability for Early's veterans. It was a nightmare come true. Lincoln had not been able to justify either Sherman's or Grant's ineffective spring campaigns to the people. How in the world was he supposed to explain this? If Washington were taken for even a day, and the White House and government buildings put to the torch by the Rebels, Lincoln knew the nation would never forgive him. Yet that was not the worst of it. Downtown, in the Treasury Building, sat the gold reserve. If the Rebels got their hands on even a portion of that…

"Mister President, I do not believe that it is safe for you up here," an officer nearby suggested politely, but Lincoln paid him no mind.

If Washington was going to fall, then he would be on the battlements when it fell, for if Early's troops gained the capital, set the city ablaze, and helped themselves to the nation's gold reserve, then all was surely lost anyway. The people would never stand for such a debacle, and rightly so. So he would remain on the battlements, defying the Rebels in whatever way he could. If the war was to be lost on the afternoon of July 11, 1864, then he would go down too. If the nation was to perish, of what possible use were either he or his policies?

"Mister President," the officer continued, "the Rebels may be forming for an attack on our front. It may be very hot up here soon. I would suggest that perhaps ... "

"What's that?" Lincoln interrupted, turning and staring at a contingent of troops forming below.

"Cavalry, sir," came the reply from General McCook, the commander of the local defenses. "It's the 7th Michigan, sent up from Petersburg a few days ago by General Grant. Dismounted now, of course. They left all their horses in Virginia."

"Well, I hope they didn't leave their rifles and ammunition behind too," Lincoln remarked.

"Oh, no, sir," McCook replied.

"Very good," Lincoln said. "What are they about?"

"I'm sending them out to bolster our skirmish line, sir," McCook explained. "They're only about six hundred men, but they're good solid veterans, and they know how to fight."

Lincoln nodded, watching as the men prepared to file out.

"As I have it, Mister President," McCook continued, "the vanguard of the Sixth Corps has already landed in Washington and is on the march here now."

"Yes," Lincoln replied, "I saw them myself this morning down at the dock. But they are still a good few hours march from here, General..." Lincoln replied. He turned and pointed to the Confederate skirmishers moving over the distant hills, "...while the Rebels are here *now*."

Just then the pop of musketry broke out across the entire Confederate line as the Federal skirmish line moved out at the double-quick against the Rebels. Smoke began to swirl and cloud, the red flashes of rifle fire becoming more and more obscure as the blue troops formed into a line and began inching forward. Lincoln stuffed his hands into his pockets, watching intently. Here and there bullets thumped into the wood nearby or twittered overhead. He paid them no mind.

Earlier that day, the first of Grant's reinforcements had debarked their transports along the Potomac River and he and his son Tad had been there to greet them. As the troops formed into units and began marching off into town, many of the soldiers spotted him standing on the embankment there with Tad and began cheering, hollering, and hurrahing, even tossing their caps in the air. Lincoln waved as they passed, their energy and enthusiasm proving infectious, and for an hour or two he had felt strong again.

Lincoln was immediately reminded of the trip he had taken just a few weeks prior. He had traveled by water down the Chesapeake to Grant's headquarters at City Point in Virginia, and when he rode with the General and his staff through the camps of the XVIII Corps, many of the newly enlisted black soldiers gathered round to see him. It was a moving moment. They reached out, called his name, and fought to simply touch his horse or bridle. They waved their hands and shouted and cried as if he, Abraham Lincoln, was The Almighty himself, and the pure emotion of the moment was almost overwhelming. As Lincoln rode off he had had tears in his eyes.

Often it was the soldiers, these men who had offered up their lives for the cause of liberty and abolition, who reminded him of the essential correctness of his beliefs and motives. That the men who had voted with their lives for Union always voted overwhelmingly for him told Abraham Lincoln everything he really had to know, and if they would stand by him now in this hour of need, then he would never abandon them. They had come to fight this day in Washington and, quite frankly, so had he. That's why the bullets hissing in the air nearby were not a bother.

"We appear to be pushing them, sir."

"What?" Lincoln asked absently, lost for a moment in his own thoughts.

"The Rebels, Mister President," McCook pointed out. "Our boys appear to have pushed them back a good piece."

Lincoln strained to see through the swirling, grayish yellow smoke. "Yes, yes," he answered, not entirely sure just what he was witnessing.

The competing lines of skirmishers had blasted away at one another now for almost a half hour, the Confederates giving way slowly, before digging in their heels a few thousand yards or so out. There both contingents appeared to have settled into a more stubborn but less heated affair, neither side willing to give ground, but neither side advancing. What was now transpiring was not entirely clear to anyone up on the battlements, the smoke of battle and the intervening distance combining to limit everyone's view of the situation. Before it had appeared as if the Rebels were preparing for an imminent assault; now it was not clear at all what their intentions might be.

Lincoln turned to McCook, who was carefully studying the situation through his field glasses. "What can you tell?"

The general frowned. "Nothing for sure, Mister President," he answered, shaking his head. "It does appear we have driven them back a few hundred yards, but the situation remains very unstable. Many Rebel units have been coming up all afternoon, and, sir, their sharpshooters are very good. You should not remain up here much longer."

"You are up here."

"Yes, sir," McCook replied, "but this is my job."

"Yes, well, this is my job too," Lincoln reminded his general. He was, after all, the Commander in Chief, the civilian head of all military forces, and ultimately the one person responsible for the prosecution of the war. Besides, the view from atop the fortress was engrossing, a riveting diversion from the usual affairs of state and political tomfoolery that awaited him back at the White House, much of which had turned just as sour that spring as had the military outlook across the country. So anything at all that could provide him even a few minutes distraction from his usual grim fare was very much appreciated.

That spring he had managed to secure his party's presidential nomination for the coming fall election, but it had not come without a scrap. The convention met in Baltimore in early June, and while Lincoln finally emerged as the unanimous selection with a vote of 506-0, it had taken some arm-twisting on the part of his people, and still, not everyone was satisfied. The Democratic convention was scheduled for late summer in Chicago, and from the looks of it – what with the failure of almost all of the spring's military campaigns – they would in all probability nominate a peace candidate, perhaps even his old general, George McClellan. Daily now there were reports and editorials demanding – despite his unanimous nomination – that Lincoln step aside, or calling upon this or that other person to consider running, and the prospects of his reelection seemed to be diminishing daily. And that was not even the bad news.

The convention in Baltimore had championed a plank calling for an immediate congressional endorsement of a constitutional amendment prohibiting slavery, but only a week after the convention the House took up the issue and failed to gather the necessary two-thirds majority – a graphic illustration of the nation's small but unbending resistance to abolition, and of the fight that was ultimately waiting for Lincoln concerning this issue. Almost daily now he had disputes on his hands as to how the Southern states would be reconstructed once the war ended, and late in June Lincoln and Chase became embroiled again in yet another squabble over Treasury appointees. Chase resigned once more, and this time Lincoln accepted, noting simply the differences between them, and in late June he was forced to suspend the writ of habeas corpus in Kentucky. All of these issues had generated firestorms of angry debate and criticism. Daily, it seemed, new catastrophic problems emerged to torment him, like ghouls summoned from the underworld, all bound and determined to undermine or derail his fondest aspirations.

Lincoln felt a light tap on his shoulder.

"Behind us, sir!" McCook said, pointing.

Lincoln turned around. "What's that?"

The general was surveying the area behind the fort through his field glasses and continued pointing south. “Dust in the air,” he said, “moving this way. Do you see it?”

Lincoln cupped his hand over his eyes; he could clearly see the low-hanging cloud now over the road leading north from the city. “Yes, I do,” Lincoln replied.... Reinforcements?”

“I should think so, sir,” the general replied, the unmistakable pitch of relief in his voice. “First of the XI Corps boys moving this way, up from the city.”

A moment later the rear gate to Fort Stevens swung open and General Horatio Wright, accompanied by most of his staff, rode onto the quadrangle below in a swirl of dust. They tossed their reins to awaiting orderlies and quickly dismounted. Lincoln felt a surge of deliverance as McCook excused himself and hurried off to greet them. In seconds they were scrambling up the steps to the battlements for a look at the Confederate dispositions, and Lincoln moved off slightly and let them go about their business. While only a few officers had yet arrived, the vanguard of the corps could not be far behind, he knew, and soon there would be strength enough to match the Rebels – or so, at least, he hoped. Perhaps the capital city would be saved after all.

For some reason the Rebels did not attack, and late that afternoon the first brigade of Yankee infantry finally arrived, surely hot and clearly fatigued from the long day’s march, but present and accounted for nevertheless. They were quickly deployed along the works, and the battlements began to bristle with Union strength. So Lincoln slipped back down the steps to where Tad was waiting patiently in the shade. The Confederate sharpshooters were good, after all, and maybe, he reasoned, it wasn’t the wisest thing he could do, after all, to stand out on the battlements in his dark suit and top hat like a deliberate target.

The skirmish fire had died down, at least for the moment, fresh Federal infantry were on their way, and Tad was becoming hungry. It was time to go. Abraham Lincoln returned to his carriage for the ride back into the city, where a desk full of paper and problems awaited. He watched as another brigade came up on the double-quick, red-faced and sweating, and poured like a long, blue ribbon into the fort.

Lincoln had no idea what would ultimately come of the Confederate deployment just beyond the gates, but, if good fortune held, it appeared for the moment that the republic might survive. In a season of very slim pickings, he could at least thank God for that.

Chapter Eighteen

July 12th – Afternoon

Lincoln stood atop the battlements once again, just as he had the day before, watching intently as the big guns were loaded, then wheeled into position. All across the ramparts, men were running, officers shouting, flags flapping on the breeze. The defiant Springfield rifles of the VI Corps now bristled out toward the Rebels like an infant forest for as far as Lincoln could see, and the sight gave him strength.

The Federal infantry had continued to land and march throughout the long night, and now the fort and all its approaches were brimming with troops, regimental flags, and supply wagons brought up from the city. It required no elaborate military training to grasp the simple fact that the position had changed overnight from one that had been entirely vulnerable to one of considerable strength. Yesterday afternoon the Rebels could have stormed over the battlements without so much as a fight, but today it would be a different story. Why the Confederates had not attacked was a mystery, but a mystery that no longer interested him. He knew only that they had not, and that as the first rays of the sun splashed warm and golden on the streets of Washington, the federal government, his government, remained intact.

Abraham Lincoln had finally fallen asleep on the couch in his office early that morning after fretting the late hours away, worried the Rebels would launch a night attack and come barreling into the city in the early hours of darkness, setting buildings afire, headed straight for the treasury building. He had visions of a city in flames, of grey clad cavalrymen trotting down the streets with torches in hand, women and children screaming as the last, desperate hopes of a united nation went up in flames. It was not a pleasant vision.

He could easily imagine the Confederates racing in and out of the treasury, loading a portion of the nation's gold reserve into their train of wagons, and making off for Richmond. Lincoln could not get that nightmarish thought out of his head. Of course, he had left firm instructions to send immediate word of any troubling developments, but instructions, he knew, could be forgotten, especially in the heat of battle. So he had worried and worried, pacing the halls nervously, staring out into the darkness, looking for the first sign of trouble. Occasionally he stopped by the window to listen, for a moment or two, for the ominous sound of artillery in the distance or Rebels at the gates, while agonizing over how best to get an amendment passed to the Constitution that would prohibit slavery. It had been another long, hard, exhausting night.

He awoke early that morning to the first glimmers of sunlight that slanted through the window, saw that the city was still standing, the long avenues beautifully draped in the first rays of light, and thankfully empty of Rebel horsemen. That realization had given him such a rush of relief that he stretched out comfortably again and slept soundly for two full hours, the first true rest he'd had in days. Then, after his morning cabinet meeting, Lincoln, Tad, and Mary all rode out to Fort Stevens again to see for themselves just what had become of the fearsome Rebels.

On their way out of town they passed many infantry brigades still trudging their way north, and the soldiers cheered and hurrahed as he went by. Lincoln doffed his hat and waved it overhead, and the spirit of the men gave him an enormous lift. Once inside the fort, Mary and Tad remained below, but Lincoln – despite repeated warnings from numerous officers not to place himself again in the line of fire – had mounted the battlements in full view of the enemy, just as on the day before. He had to see for himself. No secondhand report would do.

Now the heavy guns were loaded in preparation of a push out against the Confederate lines still clearly visible north and west of the city. Two full brigades of veteran infantry were forming below, gaunt, hard looking men who clearly knew their business, and it was apparent something important was soon to commence. Lincoln's heart began to quicken. The war, that odd reality that they often discussed and debated at length in cabinet meetings like some far off fantasy, had marched itself to his very doorstep. It was here at long last, and he would face it head-on.

Somewhere down the line an order was shouted. The cannons suddenly erupted, rippling flashes cascading along the crest of the battlements accompanied by claps of thunder, then a vast blanket of white smoke drifted out and over the parapets on the breeze like a fog over the forecastle of a clipper ship. It was a powerful, compelling moment, and Lincoln stood virtually transfixed as the smoke whirled up and around him, then cleared on the wind like a curtain being drawn. Off to the north he could see the last of the enormous shells exploding now over the Rebel positions, scarlet bursts followed by short, smoky plumes. Even at this distance the ground still shook and windows rattled and the whole thing had the feel of enormous power. He'd felt it from his toes to his top hat, and it was a sensation he would not soon forget.

Then Generals Wright and McCook were suddenly at his side, asking for his permission to push the infantry out to the homes on the far ridge where Confederate sharpshooters had taken up positions. Without a concerted effort, it was explained, the Rebels would continue peppering the Federal line with shots. The area had to be cleared, so Lincoln signed the order at once, then stood back and watched as the gates were thrown open and the infantry marched out and formed on the open plain in front of the fort.

The sound of flying lead increased overhead, the slashing, whirring of musket balls slicing past. Many of the leaden projectiles exploded in the wood and dirt nearby, and their volume intensified noticeably along the line. Abraham Lincoln tried to pay them no mind and would not be moved; his boys were going in, and by golly he would be there to support them.

He was a six-foot-four target garbed entirely in black, with a top hat that only increased his silhouette, but none of that mattered just then. Compared to the issues at stake, his personal safety seemed utterly insignificant. Besides, he knew in his heart that his death had already been fated, the time and place the only real issue, so what really was he playing with? His life and death were not in the hands of the Rebel sharpshooters, as Wright so grimly feared, but rather in God's, and God, he knew, had written the script long before his birth. What would be would be.

Then not ten feet from where he stood he heard the horrible "thump" of metal entering flesh. He turned, saw a man buckle and fall, a ball in his stomach, a strange, confused look on his face. Lincoln saw blood pooling in the man's hands, then on the dirt, running freely across the battlements. He was an army surgeon, and men were running, scrambling to get to him, and he was quickly carried off to the hospital below.

Now Wright was at his side again, this time red-faced and nervous. "Mister President," he almost begged, "surely you can see for yourself the danger you are in. I cannot guarantee your safety here on the works."

Lincoln ignored the warning. "What brigade is that?" he asked.

"Wheaton's, sir," Wright answered finally, at a loss for words.

Lincoln nodded. He knew Wheaton as a solid officer.

There were shouted orders below on the plains now, flags first lofted then lowered. The infantry stepped off smartly, marching north at a vigorous clip. The Rebels responded with a flash of musketry, and men toppled from the ranks. The big guns on the battlements responded again, shells shrieking north and west, howling like hideous, disembodied demons before bursting over the Rebel skirmishers. The red flash of rifles splattered across the plain, guns boomed, the ground shook, and smoke roiled across the scene in spiraling waves. It was an unnerving moment – shocking, exciting, dreadful, yet somehow uplifting all at once. It was the awful face of war, his war, the conflict he believed in more than anything, and he found himself utterly absorbed in the spectacle, almost glued to the ground like a statue.

Then he heard it: "Get down, you damn *fool*, before you get shot!"

Lincoln turned about curiously, glanced down into the quadrangle. There he spotted a young officer with his hands still cupped around his mouth. Their eyes met briefly, and the color quickly drained from the young officer's face. Then the boy saluted, did a smart about face, and marched off into a gathering of soldiers on the far side of the fort.

Lincoln smiled – the officer had obviously meant no disrespect – but the young man's warming hung over him like a thunderclap. Men rarely spoke to him with that sort of precision in Washington, and the obvious fact that the young man did not know exactly who he was addressing only added weight to his words. Lincoln paused. If he appeared nothing more than a fool to a twenty-year-old officer, perhaps it was because that was exactly how he was acting – not at all like the Commander in Chief, as he envisioned, but only like a *fool*.

While Lincoln's dreams and visions consistently seemed to suggest that he would not survive the war, that fate could still surely be tempted, he knew; circumstances contrived to collapse uncertainty into certainty, so to speak. It was, after all, one thing to feel fated, another to hurl oneself in front of a locomotive and expect anything less than death. Was putting a gun to the side of his head and pulling the trigger a consequence of fate or an act of free will? Often he felt that the universe spoke to him through his dreams, but he had never really considered the possibility of it shouting at him through the mouth of a young officer because he had entirely misinterpreted those other warnings. But that certainly felt like what had just happened.

He backed away from the battlements, turned, and headed toward the steps. Perhaps, he thought, the nation deserved better than a president who did not know the difference between prudence and irresponsibility, bravery and indiscretion. He hesitated on the top step for a moment again, searched vainly for the young officer who had shouted the caution, but could not spot him anywhere. Too bad, he thought. He would have liked to have thanked him.

For the remainder of the afternoon he sat in the grass below and followed the fight outside by the sounds of battle alone, and by late that day he could tell the Rebels had been pushed back considerably. Soon reports started to filter in that the Confederate supply train had been spotted rolling over the ridges north and west of town; a sure sign of their withdrawal, some thought. Lincoln did not know what the Rebels intended to do next, cared only that the capital had survived, spared surely by the slimmest of margins, but spared nevertheless. Already, word had reached him that the financial markets in New York had gone into a state of collapse, and no doubt there would be severe political fallout as a result of

Early's foray north, but at least Washington, the nation's capital, had survived.

Once it was clear that the capital was no longer in critical danger, he wandered over to the hospital to chat with the wounded before leaving. There he went from bed to bed and spoke gently with the boys, thanking them all for everything they had given. Then it was time to leave.

The carriage ride back to the White House was slow and melancholy, and here was the thing that bothered him the most: deep down inside he had always been a fatalist, the notion that life had been long ago determined having taken hold in his younger days. But if life was scripted by an all-knowing deity, then it seemed only logical that all lives and all events had to be a part of that script, and free will, therefore, an illusion.

Lincoln was entirely familiar with thinkers such as Emerson, Carlyle, and Parker, as well as the subtleties of their transcendental thought: the notion that the spiritual aspect of existence transcended the physical, and that both history and humankind were steadily progressing toward an ideal, spiritual reality. He had come to accept the transcendental conception as an ontological fact, had even lectured on it in the past, and that philosophy had formed the basis of his address delivered at Gettysburg the preceding fall, when he had called for a "new birth of freedom" – something only possible if freedom was, in fact, progressing in scope.

But it suddenly came to him that if humankind and human thought were evolving, and freedom and democratic government simply the most recent social and political expressions of that growth, then free will – the capacity to make genuine decisions that could in a sense change the direction of the script – had to be an emergent phenomena as well. After all, it was only men and women who had the capacity to make free choices; not bees, flies, or monkeys, as far as he could see. Thus, free will might not be an illusion at all, but rather a budding capacity yet to be fully realized. Like freedom itself, free will might simply be in its infancy, and thus the question was not one of fatalism versus free will – no longer of mutually exclusive ideas – but rather of how both concepts could inhabit a more sophisticated, evolving mix.

In that sense, the young infantry officer may well have saved Lincoln's life, not because he had been scripted by Providence to do so, but because he had cared enough to do so. Lincoln stared out into the trees, lost in thought as the carriage jostled along the dusty 7th Street Road.

The swirling currents he was trying to navigate seemed to be running deeper and deeper with each passing day, and while that made the future just that much more extraordinary to contemplate, it also made the burden he bore seem all that much heavier. The issues colliding in the heated vortex of Civil War at times seemed so vast that often Abraham Lincoln felt literally lost and overwhelmed. And while he had managed to barely avoid disaster over the past few days, he knew that Jubal Early's failure to take Washington would never be confused with real success for the Union. Unless the downward spiral of military blunders and stalemates was soon reversed, he feared his chance of winning the fall election would diminish to near zero, and with that would go the last real chance of reuniting the country. No one else, he knew, would see the war through. The election was scheduled for the first week of November. Abraham Lincoln needed help, and he needed it soon.

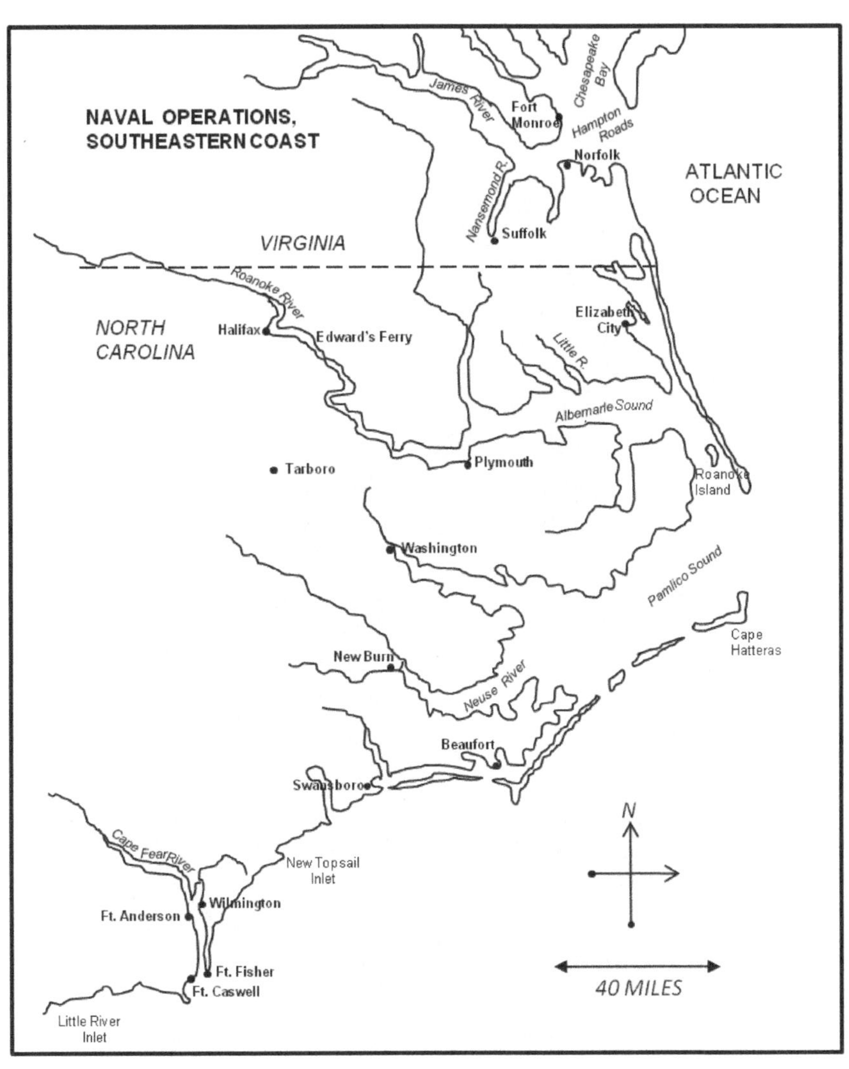
NAVAL OPERATIONS,
SOUTHEASTERN COAST
James River
Fort
Monroe
Chesapeake
Bay
Hampton
Roads
Norfolk
ATLANTIC
OCEAN
Nansemond R.
Suffolk
VIRGINIA
Roanoke River
NORTH
CAROLINA
Halifax
Edward's Ferry
Elizabeth
City
Little R.
Albemarle Sound
Tarboro
Plymouth
Roanoke
Island
Washington
Pamlico Sound
Cape
Hatteras
New Burn
Neuse River
Beaufort
Swansboro
Cape Fear River
New Topsail
Inlet
Wilmington
Ft. Anderson
Ft. Fisher
Ft. Caswell
Little River
Inlet
N
40 MILES

Photo # NH 51748 Lt. William B. Cushing, 1864

LIEUTENANT CUSHING IN 1864

Photo # NH 63719 Cdr. James W. Cooke, CSN

COMMANDER JAMES W. COOKE, C. S. N.

Alonzo Cushing (second from right) in staff with General Burnside , near Fredericksburg, VA

Photo # NH 1673 "Wood Versus Iron", CSS Albemarle in action, 5 May 1864

Photo # NH 76384 General plan of CSS Albemarle

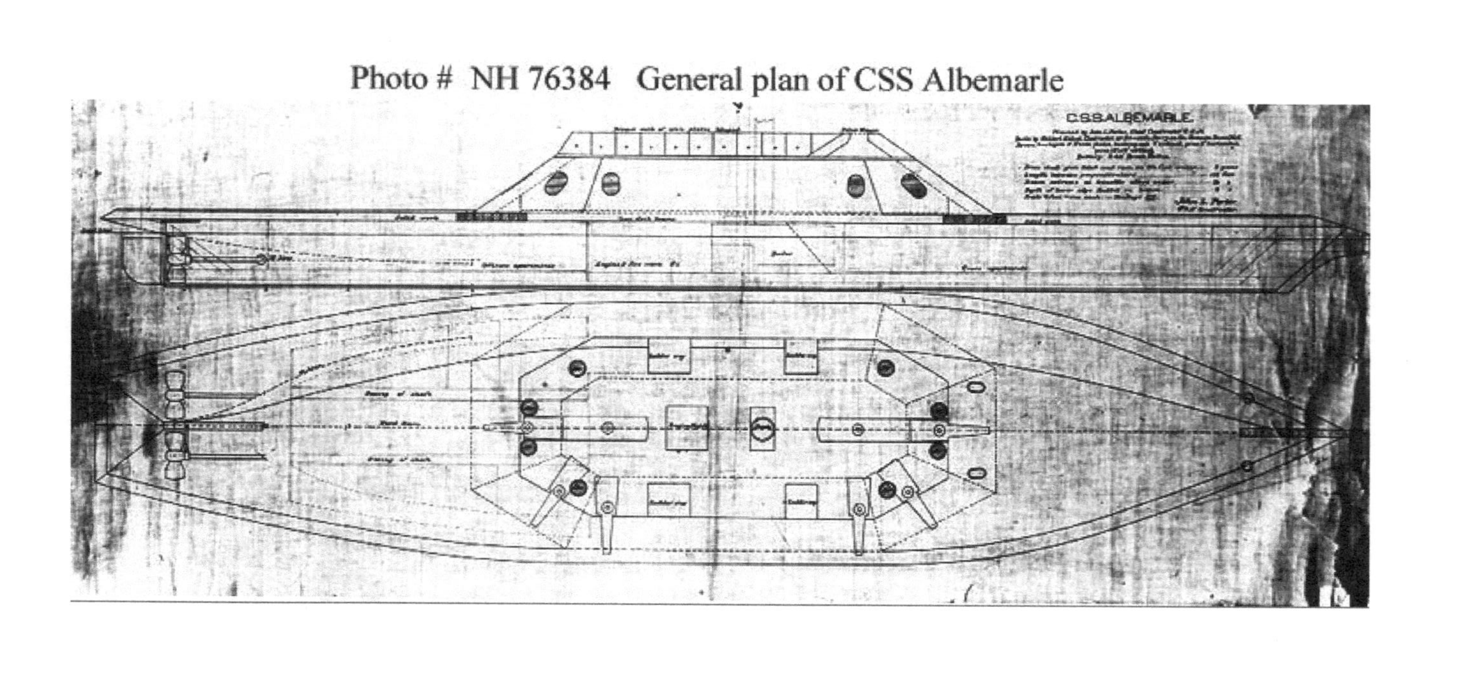

The *Albemarle* as it is rammed by the *Sassacus*

Photo # NH 79932 "Cushings's Daring and Successful Exploit"

CUSHINGS DARING AND SUCCESSFUL EXPLOIT.

Photo # NH 42220 "Lieut. Cushing's Torpedo Boat Sinking the Albemarle on Roanoke River, N.C."

LIEUT. CUSHING'S TORPEDO BOAT SINKING THE ALBEMARLE ON ROANOKE RIVER, N. C.

Photo # NH 50468-KN Bombardment of Fort Fisher, N.C., 15 January 1865. Watercolor by John W. Grattan

The Federal Fleet bombards Fort Fisher prior to the infantry assault

Chapter Nineteen

July 27th – Early Afternoon

Cushing leaned back on his chair and tried hard to project a sense of complete self-assurance. It was a hot, humid Washington afternoon, and William Cushing had the sudden urge to tug strenuously at his collar. But he fought it off and listened intently instead. He had been deep in discussion for over a half hour, and so far the discussion had not been going well.

"Quite frankly, Mister Cushing, after looking over your proposal, I would have to rate your chance of success as very, very low. Admiral's Lee's reconnaissance indicates the defenses surrounding the *Albemarle* appear virtually impregnable. You've read it, I'm sure."

William Cushing smiled brightly, trying the best he could to radiate a bulletproof sense of confidence. He was dressed in his best uniform, washed and ironed twice, checked thoroughly just that morning for even the slightest trace of lint. His shoes were freshly shined and his hair carefully combed. He was, he thought, the very picture of the professional naval officer. But so far none of that seemed to have counted for so much as a fig. His proposal for the destruction of the *Albemarle* had met with nothing short of profound skepticism on the part of the naval hierarchy.

Cushing shook his head in disagreement. "Yes I've read the reports, sir," he replied. "That's *exactly* why they will never expect it. For months the ram's crew, pickets, and the surrounding garrison have been doing nothing but sitting on their hands. They're scared of nothing. Yet over time idleness breeds over-confidence, and over-confidence, complacency, sir, and it is just that sense of complacency I intend to use to my benefit. Their elaborate precautions will prove their downfall."

"Hmm. Well ... perhaps."

Cushing had arrived in Washington under orders from Admiral Lee. He was to go over his plan for the destruction of the *Albemarle* with the highest authorities in the navy, and now he was meeting with Gus Fox, the Assistant Secretary.

Gus Fox was one of the most energetic, knowledgeable, and intelligent officers the navy had ever produced. Retired from the old navy before the war, he had returned to service after Fort Sumter had been fired upon, and soon took over virtual command of the everyday administration of the department. It had been Gus Fox who, only a week or so before, as Jubal Early's Confederate army approached the gates of Washington, had made arrangements – against the President's wishes – for a swift boat to stand by on the Potomac to ferry Abraham Lincoln to safety should the Rebels gain entrance to the city. He was a man of confidence, knowledge, and decisiveness. Indeed, so trusted was he that President Lincoln, in order to get straight to the nub of things, often came directly to Fox with his problems rather than bothering Secretary Welles; Cushing knew that if Fox was not in favor of his plan, there would be no attack on the *Albemarle*. He had to convince Gus Fox that his plan had merit, but so far Fox remained far from impressed.

"I have thought the details through thoroughly," Cushing assured Fox, leaning forward over the Secretary's desk. "It may appear rash, but there is really nothing rash about it."

Fox folded his hands together, shook his head pessimistically. "Do you really grasp, Lieutenant, just how dangerous this mission is?"

"I understand the defensive measures employed by the enemy, if that's what you mean."

Gus Fox frowned. "Look, Lieutenant," he continued, rubbing his face anxiously, "I certainly appreciate your enthusiasm. No one wants this damned ironclad destroyed more than I do. Believe me. But all the enthusiasm in the world is not going to breach those defenses." Fox tossed a hand up in the air to emphasize his point, pointing vaguely south toward North Carolina. "No, sir, not *those* defenses."

"I believe that I can penetrate the Rebel measures, sir."

Fox slapped the top of his desk with both hands. "Mr. Cushing," he said, "the Roanoke River is picketed by the Confederates from Albemarle Sound clear up to Plymouth. There is now infantry, perhaps as much as an entire brigade, encamped near the *Albemarle* with no purpose other than to defend the ram from attempts just like the one you are contemplating. All approaches, as we have it from our intelligence reports, are now swept by artillery. No doubt they have every range on the river pre-calculated. Should you even get within a few hundred yards of the ram you'll be eating double charges of canister for breakfast, sir! *That* is what you will be up against."

Cushing leaned back stiffly in his chair, thought for a moment. "Is there a better plan, sir?" he asked finally.

Fox frowned, rubbed his face nervously again. "No, there is no *better* plan," he admitted. "Indeed, there is no *other* plan at all."

"Mine *will* work, sir. I'm confident of it." Cushing held up two fingers. "Two boats, sir, that's all I will need."

Fox rolled his eyes. "I'm not quite as confident as you, Lieutenant," he replied. "But we are under great pressure here to do *something*. The president ... damn it, the *country* needs this damn boat sunk! But I am not in the habit of sending men out on missions I'm confident they will not return from, no matter the situation. That is not something I care to do. Not in this navy."

"Sir," Cushing went on, "both boats will be soundproofed and armed with torpedoes and howitzers. If the first boat fails, the second boat won't. We'll catch them napping. I'm confident of it."

"What makes you think you will get within five miles of the *Albemarle*?"

"I know the waters and I know the Rebs, sir," Cushing answered. "I have had some, well, successes recently ... "

Fox nodded, leaned back. "Yes, yes, I have read all the reports. Impressive successes, I will admit, Lieutenant. That's exactly why I hesitate to approve this plan. Your record has made you a valuable member of the navy. Your service, indeed your life, sir, is not something I care to toss away foolishly. What you are suggesting will be far different than what you have already succeeded in doing. Far different."

"Not really, sir," Cushing objected politely. "Nighttime raid up a North Carolina river to surprise an unsuspecting enemy. It's really the same thing as I've been doing all along. It's not so much different than my excursion into Smithville, I think."

"Smithville was hardly even guarded," Fox replied.

"No, sir," Cushing objected. "Smithville was very *well* garrisoned. They just weren't expecting us, and once we got there they really didn't know what to do about us. That's the key as I see it – surprise. Like I said, the Rebels at Plymouth are by now so overconfident, I doubt they really think that anyone would ever try to test them. And that's why they are vulnerable despite all their men and precautions, sir."

Gus Fox rubbed his face again; he was becoming mildly agitated. He stood, walked stiffly to the window, stared out into the hot afternoon. He watched birds flutter in a nearby maple for a few seconds.

"I *don't* want to authorize this raid," Fox said finally, almost angrily, "but the ram must be destroyed! And soon, damn it! If the *Albemarle* breaks free into the sounds again and ravages the fleet ... *again* ... well, it will put our war effort back considerably, and I don't have to tell you that that may finish the president's chances for reelection come this fall. I really don't want to even think about any of that."

"Shall I try it then, sir?" Cushing pleaded. "It will work. I'll do my best."

"I know you will, Mister Cushing," Fox said, staring at him from across the room. "I just fear your best will not be good enough. And I value you, sir. We have good officers here and there, you know, but no one else who has made the Johnnies look like such *fools*. I love to see the Johnnies made to look like fools. So does the president. I don't want to lose you, Mr. Cushing."

"You won't, sir."

"How old are you, Lieutenant?"

" ... Sir?" Cushing asked.

" Old ... how old are you?"

"Oh. Well, I'm twenty-one, sir. But soon to be twenty-two."

Fox closed his eyes, kneaded his forehead with the tips of his fingers for a second or two. "What in God's name am I doing?" he asked himself softly.

"My plan will work, sir," Cushing insisted. "Trust me. You will see. Besides, there is no other. No other plan, sir. You said so yourself."

"No," Fox admitted, folding his arms behind his back forlornly, "there is no other plan."

Cushing smiled.

"Well, all right then," Fox said. "I will write the order. I suppose in the final analysis I really have no choice."

"You won't regret it, sir. I promise."

"Yes, very good," Fox replied. He moved to his desk, penned the order then handed it over to William Cushing. "You are to report to Admiral Gregory in New York. I've told him to provide you with whatever craft, material, and supplies you may need. Anything at all. I don't care how many boats you need, or men for that matter. Just make it work. Plan it well, Lieutenant. I've also told Gregory that you have the full confidence of the department, and that he should cooperate in every way. Of course, the mission can be discussed with no one. Absolutely no one."

"Thank you, sir," Cushing replied, taking the order and hurriedly stuffing it into his coat pocket. Then he stood and saluted smartly.

Fox returned the salute, nodded grimly, then looked away quickly. "Good day, Lieutenant," he said, "and God go with you."

Cushing smiled, started for the door, then turned back to thank Fox one last time.

But, thinking Cushing long gone, Gus Fox now had his head in his hands, and was staring glumly at the top of his desk. Then he closed his eyes and shook his head sadly. "God forgive me for what I have just done," he whispered to what he thought was an empty room. "God forgive me."

Taken back, Will Cushing paused for a moment. The smile disappeared from his face. He slipped out of the office and closed the door quietly behind. So, it was done. William Cushing was now on a collision course with the mighty *Albemarle,* the ram he had taken an oath to destroy. Only one of them, he knew, would survive.

Chapter Twenty

August 20th – Late Afternoon

Cooke took the letters, smiled and bowed just slightly.

"Good to see you up and about, Captain," the postal clerk remarked.

"Good to *be* up and about," Cooke answered with a wink.

"Soon you'll be back giving the Yanks hell, I'm sure."

Cooke chuckled. "Well, I'm glad at least someone is sure, sir. You wouldn't hear that if you asked my wife, you know."

The clerk smiled back. "I can see the health in your face now, Captain. It won't be long at all till you're back on the water, fit as a fiddle. God knows we need you. The damned Yankees are tightening the blockade down tight as a drum. Can't hardly find a good pair of socks or a bottle of brandy to speak of anymore. But once you're back, things will change, I know. You'll take that fine ironclad *Albemarle* out again and whip the Yanks but good. That's what I've been telling everyone."

"Well, ... thank you, sir," Cooke said. "I appreciate your confidence."

The clerk smiled warmly, found a few more envelopes behind the desk, and handed the lot over.

James Cooke waved a quick salute, took the last of his mail, and headed back out into the heat of the August afternoon. Close to one hundred degrees, someone had remarked, and Cooke was not about to argue. The heat seemed to almost rise right up out of the ground in shimmering waves, laying low and heavy in the lanes and back alleys; hot as a furnace, thick as a blanket. Wretchedly steamy, it seemed as though he could almost part it with his hands. But it felt so good to be up and moving again that he didn't really mind the heat, and he had found that if he moved slowly it wasn't so much of a problem.

James Cooke was almost his old self again. He felt the strength welling up in his body like steam rising in a ship's boilers, and the trick now, he knew, was not to overdo it. He was desperate to get right back into the thick of things – or he feared that he would be forgotten and left behind – but Mary had warned him against it and, of course, Mary was right. Cooke would have to ease his way back into his work and then eventually back into command. While his mind was more than ready for the leap, his body was still far behind, and it had always been the body that betrayed him. So he'd promised Mary that he'd take it slow, and he always tried to keep his promises.

On the other hand, that had not stopped him from getting the ball rolling, so to speak. The week before, he had enjoyed his 52nd birthday, and after Mary and the boys had regaled him with a chorus of "Happy Birthday" he had slipped off to his desk and written a letter to the Secretary of the Navy requesting reinstatement, hopefully as superintendent of the Halifax Yard. Cooke was sure he felt well enough now to begin the process, knowing all the while that it would take at least a few weeks to work everything out. He was confident that by the time the new orders were issued, he would be entirely healthy once more.

James Cooke strolled across the street and quickly found a spot in the shade. He pulled out a handkerchief, wiped the perspiration from his face, and lifted his nose to catch even the slightest trace of a breeze. In the shade below the oaks, he found a nice spot on a bench, sat, and quickly surveyed the envelopes he'd just picked up. Sure enough, the third one was a telegram addressed from the Office of Orders and Detail – a response to his inquiry, no doubt. He fumbled nervously with it for a moment or two but he was nothing but thumbs, so he simply tore the damned thing apart and yanked out its contents. The telegram read:

> Captain R. F. Pinkney Commanding Naval Defenses in that section of North Carolina including Kinston and Plymouth was directed on the 10th inst. to make his headquarters at Halifax with special reference to the superintendency of the Naval Works at that point.
>
> There is no place for you at present but you will be placed on duty as soon as possible.

Cooke folded the telegram over twice and stuffed it into his hip pocket – it was hardly the news he had been hoping for. He had hoped to be approved for the position at Halifax but, for the time being at least, that appeared an impossibility. Pinkney outranked him, and rank was everything in the new Confederate Navy that it had been in the old Federal service.

What other work they might have in store for him he did not know, and frankly was not terribly interested to discover. He wanted to supervise the construction of the new ironclad, a boat conceived without all the design flaws that the *Albemarle* had demonstrated during combat; a vessel he was sure would be virtually invincible on the sounds. The whole thing had been his idea, his design, and he had hoped to make it work, but now, well, who knew what would come of it. Exactly what, he thought bitterly, did Pinkney know of constructing ironclads? Nothing!

He shook his head angrily, pushed himself up onto his feet, then started shuffling off down the lane toward home, disappointed and unsettled by the telegram from Richmond. Then a second posting protruding from his hand caught his eye. It was a letter from Gilbert Elliott, the *Albemarle*'s designer, and the one who would in all probability be contracted by the Confederate government to build the new ram. Cooke stopped, felt a sudden surge of optimism. He peeled the letter open carefully and read:

> I am now making arrangements to commence hauling the iron on the Atlantic & North Carolina railroad, and will start the work in a few days. After the contract is made for hauling the iron I do not see how Sec. Mallory can avoid contracting the ram. The molasses I promised you was sent to Mr. McMahon's Express office some time ago, but I learn today that it had not been shipped.
>
> I will endeavor to get it off and hope you will receive it in a few days.

Jim Cooke felt better. There was no contract yet for the new ironclad, but if Elliott's ploy worked one would probably be granted within the upcoming weeks.

It had been his work and steady influence that had finally made the *Albemarle* a successful project – indeed, a fearful weapon – and he was now confident the Navy understood all of that. And if Mallory didn't, he was sure that Elliott would set him straight. So, for the time being, he would just have to wait and see. But the letter made had him feel good, and he couldn't help but notice that as he walked the rest of the way home he whistled all the while – heat, dust, and all.

And God only knew, he was looking forward to that molasses.

Chapter Twenty-One

August 22nd – Noon

Cushing stood at the bow of the open launch, fashionably styled by the navy as picket boat *No. 1,* as it cut a course across the Hudson River, bouncing on a light chop under a bright, clear sky. He brought the boat about, sheering sharply toward the target he had earlier selected – a large boulder protruding from the water – tucked away tightly under the towering palisades. It was now a comfortable day, puffy clouds floating high overhead, the air dry and vibrant. The New York afternoon was cool, hence the river a pleasant duty, and for William Cushing the boulder represented an interesting target.

Cushing had been at it for two days now, practicing with the spar torpedo designed by the naval engineer, John Lay. He had discovered that the contraption had many defects, but it was the best the navy had to offer, and the only thing he had to work with. What he'd found was that the lanyard and trigger lines had to be pulled at precisely the right time or else the charge would detonate too late or too early, or the torpedo might rise up short of the target. So far he'd managed only one successful test out of three, but he was starting to get the hang of it.

"Now!" Cushing ordered, and Howorth extended the long spar pole under water.

The engines were cut, and as the launch drifted slowly toward the target, Cushing stood with the torpedo release line in his right hand and the trigger line in his left. The charge was constructed so that once he pulled the trigger pin, a small ball would drop, striking a cap and detonating the torpedo. But first the torpedo had to be brought properly into position, then released to float up under the target before exploding. The process was tricky and exceedingly delicate and the slightest mishap spelled ruin.

As the boulder approached he tugged the release line, freeing the torpedo. Then he timed the torpedo's ascent with a short count to five, and yanked the trigger line. There was a sudden, spectacular explosion directly opposite the boulder, exactly where he had been aiming. A plume of water shot high into the sky.

"Yes, Captain!" Howorth cried, leaping in the air as a shower of foam sprayed back over the boat. "Right on target!"

Cushing smiled. "I'm starting to get a feel for it," he replied, wiping the water from his face.

"It's a tricky business," Howorth agreed, hands on hips, smiling ear-to-ear.

"Timing," Cushing answered. "That seems to be the whole of it. If I can just keep the two lines working together, we should be all right."

Howorth smiled again and clapped his hands together joyously. "The *Albemarle* doesn't stand a chance, Captain," he said.

Cushing nodded his agreement. "Yes, but the torpedo is still the last ditch as far as I'm concerned. I'll only use it if I have to."

"Still have plans on cutting the ram out, do you, Captain?"

Cushing grinned. "Wouldn't that be lovely?" he said. "To come in so quietly and with such surprise that we might overwhelm the crew and steam the ironclad off entirely intact. I know the small town of Plymouth," he went on, "and if we put in upriver, I'm convinced we can slip through town and surprise the guard."

Howorth tossed his head back with a laugh.

"Then we'll run up our own colors," Cushing went on, "and sail her out to the fleet in the sound, the stars and stripes flapping in the breeze overhead. I'd love to do that. My God, how I'd love to do that. Could you imagine the look on Admiral Lee's face?"

"That would, I believe," Howorth said, "make quite a lasting impression."

It was Cushing's turn to grin.

They had arrived at the Brooklyn Navy Yard weeks ago, but getting everything together had proved a far more difficult task than William Cushing had anticipated. To begin with, there were no India rubber boats available that met his requirements, so he had to pick from a number of picket boats that were under construction. He finally chose two open launches, about thirty feet long, driven by small engines and propelled by a screw: picket boat *No. 1* and picket boat *No. 2. S*o far they had managed to get a boom rigged-out on one, but were awaiting the second boom, which was due in any day now. Twelve-pound howitzers were also to be mounted on the bow of each to fire canister if need be, and while the guns had been requisitioned weeks ago, they were still in transit. God only knew where they really were. It seemed that very few things worked smoothly in the navy.

But he had made progress: he understood now how to use the torpedo effectively, and once both boats were completely fitted-out he'd be ready to move the operation south. But in all probability, Cushing knew, that meant at least a few more weeks.

"When do you think we'll be able to pack and leave for North Carolina, Captain?" Howorth asked as they brought the launch about and started back down river toward the navy yard.

Cushing rolled his shoulders. "I hope to start out no later than the second week of September," he answered.

Howorth frowned.

"What?" Cushing queried.

"Have you seen the New York papers? They are surely drumming the president."

"You mean the *Tribune*?" Cushing asked.

"Yes, the *Tribune* in particular, but almost any of them will do. It seems the president does not have a friend in the whole country anymore."

"He damn well has *us*!" Cushing shot back.

"You know what I mean, Captain."

Will Cushing rolled his eyes. "That damn Horace Greeley and his pack of hounds," he almost spat. "They are traitors, if you ask me, every last one of them."

"It is no secret that Greeley and many other Republican politicians have turned their back on Mister Lincoln," Howorth agreed. "Greeley has already called the president 'unelectable' and there is talk all over town that they will call for a new convention in late September, after the Democrats have chosen their man, and try to dump the president in favor of a peace candidate."

"Do you think there is any real chance of that?" Cushing asked.

"Yes, I do," Howorth replied. "Unless there are some dramatic successes soon in the war, I do. And both Grant and Sherman appear stalled with no immediate prospect of a breakthrough. That leaves us, as I see it."

Cushing frowned, shook his head in agreement. "Yes, I've thought of that. Gus Fox said essentially the same thing when I met with him in Washington, and I know it's on Secretary Welles' mind too. The destruction of the *Albemarle* would give the president a much-needed boost. I know that, believe me William. And I would love to give him that boost."

Howorth offered up a thin smile. "The Democratic convention is in early September, and soon after that Greeley and his cabal will make their move, if there is a move to be made. Then the election is in November."

Cushing rolled his eyes again. "I know all of that, William," he said. "But I can't change the damned calendar, and I sure can't seem to make the navy move any faster than it wants."

"I'm just saying that the sooner we move ... "

"The better," Cushing agreed, finishing Howorth's sentence for him.

"Well, that's right, Captain. The sooner, the better. I think we have an opportunity here to do something for the country," Howorth went on, "but if we dally, well, we just might not have a country to do it for once we're finally ready. That *could* happen."

Cushing felt an almost uncontrollable bolt of anger rise up through his chest. He smashed his balled fist into the palm of his other hand. "We will take that ram out before the election, so help me God!" he shouted. "You have my solemn word on that, William," Cushing continued, waving an arm angrily overhead. "For Flusser, Allie, Lincoln and the Union I will do it, and nothing … *nothing* will stop me!"

Howorth stared at him for a long moment, stunned speechless by the vehemence of Cushing's declaration.

Will Cushing turned and glared at Howorth. "*Nothing!*" he shouted again.

Then Cushing set picket boat *No. 1* on a hard course across the harbor, bound now for the East River, the Brooklyn Navy Yard, and a violent rendezvous with history.

Chapter Twenty-Two

August 23rd – Early Morning

Lincoln sat glumly at his desk, picked up the pen, and hesitated.

It had come to him late the night before that the coming election was already lost, and that he should prepare for that eventuality now, while he could still think clearly and thus avoid the embarrassments and faux pas of an emotional defeat. So he'd decided to put his thoughts down on paper, to carefully pledge his support to the new president and administration while pointing out the fact that the Union would have to be saved before the inauguration, for surely his opponent would have won on a platform dedicated to complete and immediate reconciliation. But despite all his best efforts, he found it hard to actually begin to address in such a formal manner his own defeat, and more so the loss in vain of so many, many lives.

It seemed to Abraham Lincoln that the simple elements of chance alone would have by now provided him with at least a small victory or meager success on the field of battle. But all that long summer the news had been bad, and if he had not believed firmly in the correctness of his cause, he would, of necessity, have had to have attributed his stunning lack of success to a disapproving Providence, so consistent, discouraging, and inexplicable had it been.

But to believe that God should favor slavery over freedom was for Abraham Lincoln to believe up had suddenly become down, and when the leading members of his own party had come to him and demanded he drop emancipation as a condition for peace, he'd told them straight out that he'd "be damned in time & eternity," if he did, and he had meant every word of it. He could not – just like that! – turn his back on everything that he believed, as if what he had been fighting for had been nothing more than empty political talk: easily altered, just as easily forgotten.

But fine convictions alone did not win wars, he knew, and now it seemed that he had come to the end of the road. Jubal Early's army had been allowed to escape across the Potomac after its bold raid on Washington and was now rampaging up and down the Shenandoah Valley, endlessly threatening the Northern states, and evoking a steady chorus of discontent.

While Sherman still appeared no closer to taking Atlanta than he had in May, in late July, Early had sent a detachment of cavalry across the Maryland border into Pennsylvania, where they burned the small town of Chambersburg to the ground. The Rebels seemed somehow capable of going anywhere they wanted to go and doing just about anything that they cared to do. That raid had brought howls of consternation and claims of incompetence down on Lincoln's head, and all that he had to respond with was more dogged determination. The cupboard was empty of military success to offer the nation, yet it was *only* military success, he knew, that might save his administration.

Ultimately Grant – who still remained hopelessly bogged down at Petersburg – had dispatched Sheridan north to the Shenandoah with a strong contingent of men to defeat Early, but so far nothing had come of it, and Jubal Early's small army still seemed just as game and footloose as they had in early July. Thousands upon thousands of men had died, yet still Lincoln had nothing to show for it, and the nation, he knew, was growing weary of war.

In response to this unending string of military setbacks and the fact that many of the army's enlistments would soon be up, Lincoln had been forced to call up another 500,000 men to serve the country's needs. This too had set off a howl of protest, a storm of negative editorials, and Horace Greeley had written personally to Lincoln begging him to end the bloodshed at any price. Lincoln was well aware that Greeley and much of the Republican Party hierarchy were plotting seriously against him and that few if any of the Washington insiders considered him electable anymore. It had been forty-four bleak months since he had taken the oath of office, but this month of August '64 seemed surely the bleakest of all.

He stared at the blank paper on his desk, thought for a moment, then slowly began to write. It was the last thing in the world he cared to do, but now it had to be done. The most likely candidate to displace him was George McClellan, he thought, so he wrote with that thought in mind:

> *Executive Mansion*
> *Washington, Aug. 23, 1864*
>
> This morning, as for some days past, it seems exceedingly probable that this administration will not be re-elected. Then it will be my duty to so co-operate with the President-elect, as to save the Union between the election and the inauguration; as he will have secured his election on such ground that he cannot possibly save it afterwards.
>
> General, the election has demonstrated that you are stronger and have more influence with the American people than I. Now let us together, you with your influence, and I with all the executive power of the Government, try to save the country. You raise as many troops as you possibly can

for this final trial, and I will devote all my energies to assisting you and finishing the war.

A. Lincoln

He read it over twice, sealed it then tucked it away in his pocket.

That afternoon, at his cabinet meeting, Lincoln took it privately to each member and had them sign the back of the memorandum, while giving no hint of its contents. Later that evening he put the envelope away in a drawer, then laid his head down briefly on his desk. It felt as though life was rapidly leaking away from his body and soul. Never before had things looked so bleak; never before had he felt so defeated. The people, his party, even his friends seemed to have abandoned him. Could God be far behind?

Chapter Twenty-Three

September 13th – Evening

Cooke took a long sip of ice water from his glass then placed it down squarely on the blanket. He frowned, looked sideways at Mary. "It is not so bad as all that," he said, trying to sound convincing.

"Yes, it is," Mary objected, rummaging through the picnic basket. "Would you like a piece of chicken, Jim?"

"Yes, indeed," he replied, stuffing a napkin into his shirt. "This looks wonderful, Mary. A mighty fine job, and a good idea." It seemed a perfect night for a picnic.

She smiled. "I thought you would like it, now that the heat has finally broken. Nice to get outside again. What a pleasant night."

Cooke looked around, enjoyed the dryness of the air, the first coolness of the coming fall that had filtered south over the past few days. "It is that," he agreed.

"Where are the boys?" she asked.

"Off hunting Yankees down along the creek," he answered. "Let's hope they don't find any."

She laughed. "Well," she went on, "I hate to sound the pessimist, but I think things have changed for the worse."

He rolled his eyes. "It's one defeat, Mary," he objected. "Just one. We can't win everywhere, all the time."

"No," she said, "but it is Atlanta, Jim, queen city of the South, and a most vital railroad hub. I've heard it all over town. Oh, but you know all that ... "

"Yes, Atlanta has fallen to Sherman," he agreed, "and I will admit that is bad news. In fact, very bad news. But it is still only *one* defeat."

"Then please enumerate for me, if you would, James Cooke, our latest *victories*?"

"Have you forgotten so quickly, Mary? How about The Wilderness, Spotsylvania Court House, Cold Harbor, just to name a few."

"Those were months ago," she pointed out, "and you know it. Would you like some of these cold potatoes?"

"Yes, absolutely," he replied, clearing room on his plate. "But here is the thing, Mary," Cooke went on as she spooned out an ample helping, "we don't have to have victories. We only need to avoid defeats. We don't have to beat them to win the war; we need only survive. But they surely must beat us to claim victory. That's the difference, and a big difference it is."

"Well, Atlanta was a disaster by any standard, if you ask me, Jim."

"Okay, Mary, I will give you Atlanta. But as far as I am concerned it also showed just how weak Lincoln really is, and he is the key to the war. Not Sherman or Atlanta, or even Grant. It's *Lincoln*, Mary, and Lincoln is very weak. I know that now for sure."

"How so?" She asked. "Where are the boys, by the way? They're going to miss dinner! And they love fried chicken."

"All they do is eat, Mary. I've never in my life seen so much food disappear so fast as those three boys eat it, and I've been in the navy watching grown men eat for over forty years. What in God's name are you worried about?"

"Oh, I don't know," she answered. "Anyway, what were you saying?"

"I was saying that the fall of Atlanta showed me just how weak Lincoln is with the people at the North. Did you see what he did?"

"No."

"He ordered two-hundred gun salutes fired off in almost every major city in the Union. Can you imagine that? Two-hundred gun salutes! Just because Atlanta fell to Sherman. Washington, New York, Baltimore, New Orleans, Philadelphia: boom, boom, boom! My goodness, Mary, you would have thought Sherman had taken Europe, South America, and Australia for good measure. Old Honest Abe knows he is beaten, Mary, and it now appears he'll do anything to pump up his name. Anything!"

"Perhaps you're right, Jim."

"The Federal election is only a month and a half away now, and every Yankee paper I've read says the same thing – Lincoln can't win. The Democrats have nominated McClellan and McClellan is a peace man. The North is tired of war, Mary. They will vote McClellan in. And then the war will end, and it will end on *our* terms."

"But they say McClellan has pledged to fight for Union, just not for slavery. So the war will go on, Jim."

"Ahh, that's just election talk," Cooke insisted. "I don't think McClellan will really fight for *anything*. McClellan will run from the war just as he ran from our General Lee during the Seven Days. He's got no stomach for the fight. Once elected, he will be happy to sue for peace at any price. You wait and see."

Suddenly, there was a commotion as their three boys came racing down an embankment into the small glade and tossed a passel of letters onto the blanket. "Got the mail, Pa!" one of them yelped, then all three sped off again along a path that led back to the creek.

Mary sat up quickly on her knees and cupped her hands around her mouth. “Boys! Boys!” she hollered. “Dinner!” But they were out of sight before the words were out of her mouth, and not one of them had turned to listen. She put her hands on her hips. “My goodness,” she said. “And here I’ve brought all this food.”

Cooke laughed, glancing at the letters. “In a moment,” he said, “their stomachs will be empty and they will be back here to eat us out of house and home once again, and then you will be sorry you even said such a thing.”

She laughed then picked up one of the letters. “From Richmond.”

“What’s that?” he asked.

“A telegram from the Office of Orders and Detail,” she answered. “Your new assignment, Jim?”

He sat up straight. “Please, let me see.”

Cooke took the telegram, tore it open excitedly, read:

> Proceed to Halifax, N. C. without delay and relieve Captain Robert F. Pinkney Provisional Navy C. S. of his present duty commanding naval defenses etc. By command of the Secretary of the Navy.

Cooke’s eyes almost popped out of his head. He began shaking the telegram.

“I’ve got it!” he almost shouted, waving the telegram over his head like a flag. “I’ve got it!”

“Got what, Jim?” Mary demanded. “What have you got? Do you mean the Halifax Yard?”

“Yes! Yes, the Yard, by damn!”

She clapped. “Oh, my word! Let me see.”

He handed over the telegram, heart thumping. What an unexpected surprise. "I felt in my bones I would get it, Mary. I said so. Do you remember? I said so."

"Shhh," she admonished, reading intently.

"Pinkney is a good man, Mary, don't get me wrong. But what does he know of building ironclads? Nothing, that's what he knows. I knew the navy would come to its senses. By damn, but this is good news."

"Watch your mouth, please."

"Oh, yes, sorry," Cooke replied with a grin. "By damn, this is *great* news!"

She laughed.

In the pile of letters tossed onto the blanket Cooke spotted one that appeared to be from J. J. Roberson, a procurement officer and naval inspector from Wilmington. Roberson generally traveled a circuit between Wilmington, Kinston, Halifax, and Tarboro, procuring coal, oil, iron and other oddities for the navy, as well as making the necessary inspections of work in progress. He knew a great deal about what was going on. Cooke had hoisted a few bottles of ale with Roberson, had always gotten along well with him, and was curious as to what he might have to say. He opened the letter quickly and began to read.

"What's that, now?" Mary wanted to know, putting the telegram down.

"Just a short note from J. J. Roberson – you know, the naval inspector. Seems John Maffitt has been replaced as captain of the *Albemarle.*"

"No! Truly?" Mary said. "That comes as a surprise."

Cooke shook his head. "No, not really. Maffitt is a man of action, Mary, and while his reputation alone may well have given the Federals pause, being skipper of the *Albemarle* right now is strictly a do-nothing job. Maffitt was probably bored to tears. They won't let him go any further south than the mouth of the Roanoke, and from what I understand they're so short of coal down at Plymouth that he can hardly get around to even that. The navy could surely better utilize Maffitt's talents elsewhere. They're wasting him in Plymouth."

"What will they do with him? Does it say?"

"J. J. says Maffitt has been reassigned as skipper of the *Owl*, a swift blockade runner, an assignment he will probably fancy to be heaven after being cooped up on the steamy Roanoke all summer at Plymouth. He's been replaced by Alexander Warley."

"Do you know Warley, Jim?"

"Not personally, no, but he has a fine reputation. Oh, and listen here ... "

"What?"

"Roberson says the contract for the new ironclad I designed was awarded to Gilbert Elliott on August the 29th. Work should start soon."

Mary beamed at him. Now she knew that he would not be far from home and, for the time being at least, would be well out of harm's way. "Could you have possibly asked for more, Jim?"

"Only to be made an admiral, Mary, and have my pay tripled. That would have been nice too, now that you mention it."

"Well, did you check your other letters?"

Cooke chuckled. "No, Mary I haven't, but now that I think of it, that could be pressing my luck just a bit. I'm happy as is. Yes, very happy. We'll have the same veteran crew together again to start on the new ironclad, and for once it will be a priority with the navy brass. The new boat won't take us too long to complete. Then we'll see how the new Yankee president, McClellan, likes having his fleet blasted to pieces."

Cooke started picking up the dishes. His mind was awhirl, and he felt suddenly in a hurry. “I suppose we should start clearing up here now,” he said.

“We’ll get you packed up and on your way by morning,” Mary replied confidently.

The three boys suddenly materialized at the edge of the blanket then, sweaty, dirty, grass in their hair. “We’re hungry!”

James Cooke laughed, slapped his leg, and sat back down. “Goodness gracious, Mary,” he said with a wink. “If I have to wait for our boys to fill their stomachs I may as well retire now. I won’t see the Halifax Yard for months. Maybe years.”

“Shush,” Mary said. “Sit and eat, boys. Your father’s in a hurry.”

Chapter Twenty-Four

September 30th – Evening

Cushing walked slowly, the rain falling harder now, carriages sloshing water up and over the sidewalk as they splashed through the puddles nearby, soaking his pants, filling his shoes. But he didn't notice the water, and he really didn't care. He had no idea how long he had been walking, how many miles he'd covered, or even where he was, anymore. Will Cushing was soaked, cold, and miserable, but none of that seemed to matter. He felt numb, fearful, lost.

He had boarded the train in Fredonia that morning, bound for New York City. That afternoon the wind had come up, not long after that a heavy rain, and the train had been delayed several hours because of the bad weather. Once he got to the station he had simply debarked and begun walking, entirely lost in his own thoughts and fears. The wind didn't bother him. He hardly noticed the rain.

By the middle of September they had finally gotten both launches fitted out with howitzers and torpedoes at the navy yard, and Cushing started them both off for Virginia on the 22nd, with Howorth in charge of picket boat *No. 1* and Andrew Stockholm piloting *No. 2*. They were all to rendezvous at Fortress Monroe in Virginia in early October. Cushing had wired Gus Fox that he would return to Virginia by a different route and, once he'd gotten

Fox's okay, he'd snuck away by train to Fredonia for a few days of rest. It was his first trip home in quite some time, and he knew full well that it might be his last.

The train ride north from the city had been spectacular. The air was clear and cool, the trees already gone over with bright fall colors, and he had spent the few days available in Fredonia in nothing more than fun and hijinks. He'd flirted with as many ladies as he could find, seen most of his old friends, and spoken with the editor of the local paper, all the while mindful of the secret fact that he might never see any of them again. On his last day home he finally made up his mind that he had to explain the mission to his mother. There was no one on earth he loved or respected more. Cushing knew that Fox had given him strict orders to tell no one, but his mother could keep a secret, and he felt that he had to let her know.

Overnight the sky had changed from crystal blue to a metallic grey, and a steady wind had begun blowing across the border from Canada, bringing with it cold air and the first real feel of winter. Will had risen early that day, but could not think of the best way to tell his mother, so he spent the morning in a state of confused anxiety. He paced back and forth through the living room and ate almost nothing as his mother watched nervously from the kitchen.

He finally decided to take her out of town in the carriage, to a spot where no one could possibly overhear their conversation, and explain the details of the mission as best he could. It was the only solution he could come up with. So he hurriedly harnessed the horses to the rig, told her with sudden urgency to grab her hat and coat, and they started out on the road toward Arkwright Hills, his mother holding onto her hat tightly as the wind whipped and gusted around them. At the highest point on the road, well out of town, he pulled the carriage off onto the grass. There Cushing helped his mother down and found a spot for her to sit behind a tree out of the wind. As he kneeled in the grass in front of her, Will could tell she was nervous and upset. So was he. She looked away as he cleared his throat, then leaned forward on his knees.

"Mother," he said, "I have very important news. I've been selected by the Secretary of the Navy to lead an extremely important mission."

She glanced back his way, saying nothing, but her face took on a look of great sadness.

"For the past few weeks I have been in New York City at the Navy Yard, getting everything together and practicing," he continued. "The boats and equipment are now ready, and I've sent them back down to Fort Monroe. I'm to meet up with them there in a few days."

She stared at him with a steady gaze, but he could see that her breathing had already become troubled.

"We are going to go in after the Confederate ram, *Albemarle,* Mother," he said. "It has to be done. The ironclad must be either taken or destroyed."

His mother blinked, swallowed once, then looked away.

So he explained his entire plan, every last twist and small particular, laying it all out step by step, including even the most minor details. He told her of the *Albemarle*'s enormous strength and record of destruction, the picket posts all the way upriver, and the infantry garrison guarding the ram's berth at Plymouth.

Dry leaves – amber, gold, orange – tumbled and piled slowly around his legs as he spoke. Occasionally the breeze tossed her hair. Lastly he told her he was convinced the ram was vulnerable and that he was sure he could do the job and return safely. Then he immediately tempered that statement with an admission of Gus Fox's misgivings. That accomplished, he sat back and waited for her response.

She said nothing for a long while, simply looked off over the windblown hills, considering everything he had told her. Then she finally spoke, and when she did her voice was sharp, almost angry in its tone. “I don’t see how you can possibly succeed, Will,” she said, shaking her head in dismay. “If this ship is so strong that a thousand men and nine ships could not destroy it, how can they expect one man to do it with two little wooden boats?”

“They attacked its strengths,” he explained. “I intend to attack its weakness.”

She shook her head again. “This cannot succeed, Will. I will lose you just as I lost Allie.”

“I will succeed, Mama,” he replied softly, “or you will not have any Will Cushing, that is true.”

She looked away, wiping the sudden tears from her eyes.

Will rested his hand on her arm.

“I do not understand any of this,” she sobbed. “Why you? You’re only a boy.”

“The navy has no one else.”

“But why?” she cried. “What’s so important?”

“For the president,” he tried to explain. “For the country ... ”

“How? Why?”

“The secretary is fearful the Confederates will employ the ram just prior to the election in an attempt to further spoil Lincoln’s chances. If that happens ... well, it simply must be destroyed. And if I can destroy it, then I’m sure it will give the president a substantial boost with the voters. Just like Sherman’s victory at Atlanta.”

“The *country*?” she repeated incredulously. “The *president*, the *voters,* Will? How about you? What about me?”

He took her hands in his. “I had hoped you would pray with me, Mama,” he told her. “Please, pray with me. Pray *for* me.”

Slowly she sat up on her knees and as she did he moved next to her in the grass. They bowed their heads together and prayed.

"God, have mercy on my son," she prayed. "Please Lord, he's so young. And let this awful war end. Soon."

Then they repeated the Lord's Prayer together, and when they were done she rose and walked straight back to the carriage and got in without saying another word. They rode back to town in stony silence. The next morning he got up, hugged her once, and left.

Now he was walking alone, lost somewhere in New York City, drifting aimlessly through a torrent of rain and wind, like a zombie. All day his mind had been numb, his body unfeeling, the awful reality of the task he had taken on truly beginning to dawn on him for perhaps the very first time. The prospect of his own death slowly began to settle upon him then like a great darkness, a heavy, frightening sensation that he could no longer shake off, avoid, or escape.

So he walked for hours, drenched from head to foot, shivering almost uncontrollably until he spotted an intersection he somehow recognized, and realized that his cousin, George White – a procurement officer living in the city – had a place not far away. Cushing quickly hailed a horse cab and moments later was knocking at the front door.

The door swung wide. Will tried to smile, wiping the rain from his face with the back of a soggy sleeve. "Hello, George."

"What in God's name? ... Will, is that you? It is! What the hell are you doing?"

"Just out for a little walk. Got lost ... "

"My God, man," White said, "come in, come in. Look at you, Will; you're absolutely soaked and shivering. Your lips are blue, Will. You look frozen."

"It was a long walk."

"Come by the fire and take off those wet clothes," George said. "My goodness, Will, but this is crazy. I'll fetch you a nice brandy, something warm to eat, and a dry set of clothes. What in the world – ?"

The next morning the rain stopped, the sun came out, and Cushing did not feel quite so awful anymore. He didn't at first know why. Will ate a hearty breakfast, thanked his cousin, then bid him good-bye.

"Cousin George," Will said, "I am going to have either a vote of thanks from Congress or six feet of pine box by the time you hear from me again." Cushing smiled brightly, then shook George's hand and bounced down the steps. An hour later he was on a train bound for Baltimore.

In a strange, almost morbid way, he realized, something deep inside had come to accept his own death now as almost inevitable, and that awful comprehension had produced in him an odd, and entirely unpredictable effect. Rather than feeling numb and lost and desolate, as he had the day before, Will Cushing actually felt rather light and carefree. In a sense he had dismissed the prospect of living just as one might toss aside an old coat; but lost with the prospect of life extended had also gone overboard all his hopes for the future. And since fears are born of hope just as night gives life to day, he found himself suddenly, strangely, even startlingly fearless. Now he felt only an odd, almost breathtaking sense of abandon. And the reason for that sense of abandon was really quite simple. Dead men, Will Cushing had just come to realize, have nothing to lose.

Chapter Twenty-Five

October 12th – Morning

Cooke stepped from the launch onto the small dock at Edwards Ferry, the sound of hammers and saws in the fields nearby rising in the air like music to his ears. James Cooke smiled and put out his hand. "Well, Mister Elliott," he said, "it is good to see you again after all this time."

Gilbert Elliott rubbed his hands down along the sides of his trousers to clean them off, then took Cooke's hand and shook it vigorously. "It is mighty good to see you, too, Captain," he replied. "I am entirely convinced that you are the only man in the navy who could have managed all this. The only one."

Cooke laughed with a whoop. "Well, I don't know about all *that*, but I will tell you, Gilbert, I am pleased with how you are moving along here. Very pleased! By the way, you know, I approved a partial payment for you weeks ago – fifteen thousand dollars it was. Did you receive it?"

"Yes, Captain," Elliott answered, a smile winding its way across his face. "And I can assure you that it is being put to good use. And did you receive the molasses I sent you?"

"I did, sir, and I can assure you that my wife and sons appreciated it greatly. Wonderful molasses. Worked wonders with a batch of cookies Mary baked just last week."

"Glad to hear it," Elliott said with a wink. "And I must say I am glad to see that you're feeling better, Captain. We can't do this job without you."

"I'm fine," he insisted. "Just needed a little rest was all."

Elliott grinned, pointed toward the ironclad. "Well then, Captain, would you care to see what we've accomplished so far?"

Cooke's eyes sparkled. "Absolutely!"

The new ironclad was laid out in the cornfield near where they had built the *Albemarle,* its ribs and timbers seemingly rising up out of the ground like some extraordinary prehistoric behemoth. If everything went as planned, it would be finished and delivered to the navy by late February. Even from a distance Cooke liked what he saw.

"Yes, yes," he said as he walked closer, "I see what you've done here now, Gilbert, and I must say it looks fine. She must draw no more than six and a half feet of water, though. You know that, right?"

"We've planned for that, Captain. Just as you specified."

"Good," Cooke replied, rubbing his hands together. "I have word that some of her machinery and the boilers are almost completed in Richmond. They'll be shipped down by rail in just a few weeks."

"Very good," Elliott said. "I understand that the iron will be rolled and the guns cast at the Tredegar Works soon, as well. Things seem to be going much more smoothly this time around."

Cooke nodded his agreement. "They understand in Richmond now, Gilbert," he said. "They saw what the *Albemarle* could do. But this boat will be superior, and the two combined will be virtually unstoppable. That's why this ram is a priority. Too bad we couldn't finish her up a bit earlier than February."

Elliott frowned. "I could push everything up, Captain," he said, "but without the iron, what difference would it make?"

"Yes, I suppose you're right," Cooke agreed, studying the flank of the craft. "I'd just like to help the war effort along."

"I understand," Elliott replied. "Do you suspect Sheridan's recent defeat of our General Early in the Shenandoah will hurt us terribly?"

Cooke shook his head no. "No, not terribly," he said, knowing all the while that he was polishing the truth. "Early was a sideshow at best. But still, it can't help, I suppose. The fall of Atlanta hurt too. Now all the Union efforts can be concentrated on General Lee's army at Petersburg. That's unfortunate."

Gilbert Elliott rubbed his chin. "Well, if I knew the iron was coming, I could probably push up the date for completion. As well you know, Captain, getting the iron and then getting it on her is the hard part. Framing her out, well, that's not so difficult."

Cooke smiled. "Yes, indeed, Gilbert," he said. "I know that."

Elliott folded his arms across his chest, thought for a moment. "Any chance Lieutenant Warley will take the *Albemarle* downriver before the election and put a whipping on the Federal fleet? That might surely help our cause."

"Not a chance," Cooke answered emphatically.

"Why, Captain?"

"Well, it's just too risky," Cooke answered. "You see, I agree with you, Gilbert, that it would be a feather in our cap if we could damage their fleet again, but just suppose something went wrong, and the *Albemarle* were severely damaged, or even rammed and sunk? That could happen, you know."

"Yeah, I see what you're saying, Captain," Elliott said, rubbing his chin thoughtfully. "Suddenly we would be helping Mister Lincoln's chances of reelection rather than hurting."

"Yes, exactly," Cooke agreed. "But even more so, if the *Albemarle* were to be lost now, there would be nothing to stop the Yanks from immediately regaining all of eastern North Carolina, not to mention steaming all the way up the Roanoke River. What would stop them? Plymouth would fall in the blink of an eye, and soon there would be Federal gunboats sitting off the Halifax Yard with their cannons trained on my office. Should that happen you and I would be out of business before you could snap your fingers, Gilbert."

" I would not care to see that, Captain.""

"That's why the *Albemarle* must stay put for the time being," Cooke went on soberly, "and why we must complete this ram as soon as possible. Once this boat is done we will be able to sweep the Yankees right out of the sounds, regain all of eastern North Carolina, and help feed Lee's army for God only knows how long. But not until this boat is done."

"Well, you know I'll move just as fast as I can," Elliott said. "You get me that iron, and I'll get her done."

Cooke grinned. "Now, you know I called for two layers of one-inch iron this time, rather than the one layer of two-inch."

"Yes, and I agree; that is a good idea," Elliott replied.

James Cooke nodded vigorously. "The one inch plates seem to be rolled much more compactly, and in combat I believe they will bend from a shot that would crack the two inch iron. If we do it right, this boat will be virtually impervious to the enemy's fire at almost any range. Absolutely impervious."

"Oh, we'll do her right. You can count on that, Captain."

"And with the additional guns ..." Cooke said, then stopped in mid-sentence. "Well, you can well imagine for yourself what we would have done to the Federal fleet in the sound, had we had guns broadside as well as fore and aft."

Elliott smiled. "We'd be shucking oysters on Roanoke Island right now, Captain, eating corn off the cob, and thinking on more pleasant things, I suspect."

Cooke's eyes danced. "That we would."

"Well, Captain Cooke," Elliott said, "the guns aren't the problem, nor the boat's draft, nor her engines, for that matter. Iron's the problem. So if you can get me *that*, then I will build you this boat just as you want her, and then I reckon it will be open season on the Yanks."

"I will do everything in my power to get whatever you need," Cooke promised. "And you must do everything in yours to move along quickly." Cooke broke into a broad grin. "Do we have a deal, Mister Elliott?"

Gilbert Elliott stroked his chin one last time, then extended his hand. "You got yourself a deal, Captain Cooke."

Chapter Twenty-Six

October 24th – Late Afternoon

Cushing waited patiently on the afterdeck of the *Shamrock* for the men to be assembled. The afternoon was warm and pleasant, a light breeze having blown up off the land earlier that day, and Will Cushing felt completely calm and in control for the first time in many days. Earlier that afternoon he had reported to Commander William Macomb on his flagship at the mouth of the Roanoke River. Macomb was now in charge of the Federal blockading squadron on Albemarle Sound, and Cushing presented the commander with his orders from Gus Fox. It was agreed Cushing would need a few more men to join his expedition, and Macomb immediately sent out word to all his commanders to query their crews for volunteers for a very hazardous mission – only the best men were to be considered.

It had been a long, trying, arduous three weeks for Will Cushing since leaving his home in Fredonia. On October 10 he had arrived at Fort Monroe on Hampton Roads, only to discover to his dismay that one of his two motor launches had not yet arrived. Howorth and Stockholm had somehow gotten separated somewhere on the Chesapeake Bay, and now Stockholm and picket boat *No. 2* were nowhere to be found. Cushing waited two days for Stockholm to show, only then to find out that Admiral Lee had been replaced by a new man, Admiral David D. Porter.

While Lee had been fond of Will Cushing and generally impressed with his deeds, Will quickly discovered that Admiral Porter did not share those sympathies at all, and the lost motor launch became an immediate issue. Cushing could hardly explain the disappearance, dared not reveal the fact that he had been off essentially on a lark home at the time, and subsequently was left with no explanation at all. So Cushing was promptly ordered back out on an army tug in search of Stockholm, but that expedition proved entirely fruitless. When he returned, Porter was ready to cancel the mission against the *Albemarle* outright, and only an impassioned plea on Cushing's part convinced Porter to finally let the mission go forward as planned – but with only one launch.

That accomplished, Will quickly packed up and headed off for the North Carolina waters on October 20 by way of the Chesapeake and Albemarle Canal. Besides Howorth and himself, Will had five other volunteers from the *Monticello* with him, good men all, and while they had all been briefed on the mission's hazards, none beyond Howorth had been told of the actual objective.

The trek through the canal proved hot, tiring, and tedious. Once they ran aground, and they had to borrow a flatboat at gunpoint from a local farmer in order to raise the launch and gain deep water again. They finally arrived at Roanoke Island on the 23rd, only to be advised that a good thirty miles of their trip had been through unprotected Confederate territory. The officers on Roanoke Island were amazed they had made it through at all. Will and his crew shared a laugh, and a good laugh it was – after the fact, of course.

Unfortunately, worse news was waiting at Roanoke Island. There Cushing was shown an article from a Northern newspaper outlining a plot to destroy the *Albemarle*. While the article was incorrect in terms of its details, it was still likely to put the Confederates on alert, for it was well known that they perused the

Northern papers just as Grant's agents regularly read the Richmond, Savannah, and Charleston publications. While the breach in security bothered him, it was not unforeseen; both sides foolishly allowed their movements and intentions to be endlessly reported in the papers. The natural counterstroke was to plant false or misleading stories such that neither side could bank on newsprint for accurate information. But a story about the *Albemarle,* he knew, was bound to raise suspicions, and thus heighten the already tight security around the ram.

The other bit of unfortunate news was that, unbeknownst to him, a torpedo raid had already been launched and failed against the ironclad in May. In that instance, five enlisted men attempted to swim close to the boat and attach torpedoes, but they were spotted in the water and promptly driven off in a hail of gunfire before they could set the charges. The problem, again, was that now the Rebels had already been alerted to the probability of a torpedo attack, and had in all likelihood taken extensive precautions against that possibility. Just what those precautions might consist of remained unclear, and might well remain unclear until he made his way up the Roanoke River all the way to Plymouth – requiring last minute, perhaps even split second, adjustments to his plan.

But Will had his orders, and that was good enough for him. The bad news did not bother him. Whatever additional defensive measures the Confederates may have employed were bound to be meager in comparison to the odds he was up against to begin with, he felt, so what did they really matter?

On the night of the 24th they shoved off again from Roanoke Island. To confuse any local Rebel spies – and there were bound to be many of them in any occupied territory – Cushing announced his destination as Beaufort, and even headed off in that direction for a few miles, before turning around and heading down the sound toward the mouth of the Roanoke.

Now he stood on the afterdeck of the *Shamrock,* waiting patiently to fill out his crew. As the men gathered slowly on the deck before him, Howorth came close and whispered in his ear.

"These are all good men, Captain," he said. "Word of your arrival has already spread through the fleet, and I tell you we will have our pick of the very best. Seems many a lad would love to sail with the famous Lieutenant Cushing."

Will smiled, folded his arms across his chest. "Is that so?"

"It is, Captain," Howorth replied. "As I have it, not a man approached refused the duty, and some even offered a month's pay to be taken along."

"Well, William, that is good to hear," Cushing agreed. "But if the whole fleet knows we are here, then there's a good chance the Rebels know it too. And that's not so good."

Howorth rolled his shoulders. "What can be done to contain news like this, Captain?" he asked."The lads respect you. You're a legend in the navy already, if you didn't know it. Word has spread like wildfire."

"Form a line there, boys," Cushing called out. "That's it." Then he turned back to Howorth. "Tell me about the new men."

Howorth cupped a hand around his mouth. "Good tough bastards, all of them," he insisted. "They're all the best. The absolute best. John Woodman there is a master's mate off the *Commodore Hull*; Charles Steever is an engineer from the *Ostego.* At the end of the line there is Richard Hamilton, coal heaver on the *Shamrock* – look at the arms on him, Captain – and Seamen Houghton, Harley, and Smith are all from the *Chicopee.* You know the rest, of course. I'm told they're all good with knife, carbine and cutlass."

Cushing nodded, smiled, then stepped forward. “At ease, gentlemen,” he said.

The small group relaxed momentarily, then fell silent. Will could see they were eyeing him closely, measuring, perhaps, the man against the reputation.

“I want to personally thank you all for coming today,” Cushing went on. “I’m impressed that you all volunteered for a hazardous mission. Now I’m going to tell you exactly what you have volunteered for.”

There was a short burst of laughter.

Cushing smiled, letting the laughter trail off naturally. “The mission is to either capture or destroy the *Albemarle*.”

Not one man batted an eye.

Cushing hesitated for a few seconds, allowing the weight of his statement to sink in. When no one balked, he continued.

“My priority is to cut her out and return downriver to the fleet with the ram intact. If we can take them by surprise and overpower the crew, I think that’s our best bet. Once inside the ram we will be fundamentally bullet proof. But, of course, that may not work. In that event, I have come with a motorized launch specially equipped with a spar torpedo. If we have to, we’ll go in and take her down with that.” He stopped, glanced slowly from face to face. “Any questions so far?”

No one said a word.

“Very good then.” Cushing said. “Of course,” he continued, “I must tell you, gentlemen, this will be no picnic. I’ve had a long talk with Commander Macomb and Ensign Sommers. Sommers has just completed a few reconnaissance missions inland and has the latest intelligence on the *Albemarle* and her defenses. He reports the garrison at somewhere between three and four thousand men, so if it comes down to a straight shoot out, it appears the fourteen of us might be, well, slightly overmatched.”

They all laughed.

Cushing smiled, crossed his hands behind his back and continued. “Let’s hope we can avoid that. The river is picketed from its mouth clear to Plymouth, so the entire mission will have to be done in absolute silence. We might be observed anywhere between here and there. Additionally, I’m now told the Rebs have unlimbered several batteries of artillery along the riverbank, covering all the approaches to the ironclad. Both of the ram’s Brooke rifles are also trained out over the water. Obviously, if we are detected, it could get *very* hot. Questions?”

“When do you plan on going, Captain?” one man asked.

“Soon,” Cushing replied. “No more than a day or two from now at the latest. Other questions?” he asked.

They all shook their heads.

“Very well,” Cushing said. “For those of you who elect to go, not only must you not expect, but you must not even hope to return. I can promise you only glory, death, or, perhaps, promotion. But one way or another, we will certainly have the satisfaction of getting a good lick in at the Rebels. Now,” he continued, “any man who is no longer interested in the mission will be absolutely free to leave, and nothing further will be said of the matter, I can promise you that. This will be a very difficult task, and anyone who has even the slightest doubt should not risk going.” He waited then, allowing each man to carefully consider his decision. “Okay then,” Cushing went on finally,” I would ask simply that those men still interested take one step forward.”

All twelve men stepped forward as one.

Cushing broke into a broad grin. “I’m not surprised,” he said. “You are the finest men I have ever been around. I want you all to know that. Now, we will have a day or so to go over every detail of the mission. Listen closely. All of our lives will depend on each one of us doing our jobs flawlessly. Obviously, gentlemen, on an undertaking such as this there can be no room for mistakes. No room at all. Ensign Howorth!"

"Sir!"

"Brief the men."

Chapter Twenty-Seven

October 27th – Early Afternoon

Cushing leaned back in dismay, then stared across the table at Howorth.

William Howorth rubbed his face, frowned miserably, and began tapping the tabletop nervously. "This is not good news, Captain."

"No," Cushing agreed. "This is not good news."

Just that morning three runaway slaves had been picked up in the water, swimming out toward the fleet. They had just escaped from a plantation near Plymouth and had come in with detailed information about the *Albemarle* and the Rebel defenses surrounding her. When this was combined with the intelligence previously provided by Ensign Sommers, a new and even more disturbing picture had emerged of the Rebel defenses.

"All right, let's go over it again," Commander Macomb suggested, rubbing his eyes with the tips of his fingers.

Howorth frowned, then took up his notes. "Okay, according to the runaways, the wreck of the *Southfield* still sits in the center of the channel, submerged up to the hurricane deck. The Rebels have converted this into a picket post of sorts right in the middle of the river, and there may be at least one naval gun mounted on her, commanding the channel, perhaps more. As if that weren't enough, the Confederates now have a schooner anchored not far off the *Southfield* manned by an officer and at least twenty-five infantrymen. The schooner is also armed with at least one artillery piece – how large we can't say. Oh, by the way, both the schooner and the *Southfield* are equipped with signal rockets and are on standing orders to warn the garrison surrounding the ram of anything that looks even remotely suspicious."

Macomb grimaced. "Gentlemen," he said, "this mission is sounding more and more suicidal by the minute. I don't know; I have half a mind to call the whole thing off."

Cushing tried hard to smile. "Commander," he said politely, "my orders come directly from Gus Fox in Washington. With all due respect, sir, I believe only Assistant Secretary Fox can countermand them."

Macomb nodded. "I'm in no mood to argue orders, Lieutenant," he said. "I'm in command in this area, and I'm just trying to point out the obvious. The chances of success for this mission have been reduced to near zero. How in the world do you expect to get past both the pickets on the *Southfield* and this new schooner without them alerting the garrison at Plymouth? Seems impossible! I hate to see good men die for nothing."

"Agreed," Cushing replied. "But the more heavily defended the ram is, the less likely will the Rebels be to actually expect an attack. Crazy as it sounds, I believe these most recent Confederate efforts might actually aid us in gaining the element of surprise."

Macomb rubbed his chin, rolled his eyes. "One in a hundred," he said. "Those are the odds as I see it, and that's being damn generous."

"If they spot us, yes," Cushing agreed. "But if we can slip past their pickets ... "

Macomb shifted on his chair, tossed a hand up wearily. “I’ll ask again, how do you plan on getting past the *Southfield* and this schooner anchored in mid-channel?”

“I have an idea,” Will Cushing answered.

Macomb frowned. “Go on. I’m all ears, Lieutenant.”

“We’ll tow a cutter behind the launch with ten or fifteen men inside. Then we’ll cast the cutter off near the *Southfield,* if need be, and the men will float up and overwhelm the pickets there. Of course, these men must be very good, especially with knife and cutlass.”

Macomb rubbed his cheeks, then looked away. “I don’t know,” he said. “That seems far-fetched. But maybe …. Maybe.”

Cushing looked across the table at Howorth. “Ensign?”

“I think it just might work,” Howorth replied. “It’s both novel and quiet. The Rebels would never suspect such a thing.”

Macomb listened quietly, then turned to his own Lieutenant Duer, who was seated to his right. “Mister Duer,” he said, “do you have an opinion on any of this?”

Duer sat up straight. “Honestly, Commander, I think it’s an excellent idea. I’m with Ensign Howorth. I think Lieutenant Cushing’s idea will work. In the dark they might well be able to gain the *Southfield* and subdue the pickets without a shot being fired.”

Macomb nodded, rubbed his eyes, and thought it all over again. “Well, okay then. Do you think we have fifteen good, tough men who will volunteer for this mission?” he asked.

Duer could hardly contain a grin. “Commander,” he said, “I don’t believe there is a man aboard the *Shamrock* who would not volunteer to accompany Lieutenant Cushing on any mission we propose. Not one man.”

"Well," Macomb answered, "we shall see soon see about *that*." He turned back to Cushing. "Have you fixed the problems that spoiled your attempt last night?"

"Yes, sir," Cushing replied.

The night before they had set off in the launch determined to go after the *Albemarle,* but they had misjudged the tides and ran aground almost immediately at the mouth of the river. Cushing was furious. They were not able to free the boat until two in the morning, and even then, despite the late hour, Cushing decided to try and push on to Plymouth. But the launch had not traveled more than a few hundred yards further when they were hailed by a Federal picket boat that had heard the sound of their engines. Cushing immediately identified himself and was able to avoid any further complications, but the mission had to be put off for the time being.

At first Will considered the misfortunes terrible luck, but soon came to his senses and realized they had, in fact, been visited by a stroke of good fortune, for if the Federal picket boat had been able to pick out the sound of their engines so easily, surely the Rebels would do so as well. So the previous night's problems had given them the opportunity to make a few corrections that might save both the mission and their lives. When next they left bound for the Roanoke he would be sure to go with the proper tide, and with the engine now far better soundproofed.

"The Confederate pickets won't hear you?" Macomb asked. "You're sure?"

"Yes, Commander," Cushing answered. "The fleet's carpenter has done a most admirable job, I assure you. We won't be bothered with that problem again."

Macomb stood. "Very well, then," he said."Let's see to those extra men you will be needing." The commander wheeled around. "Lieutenant Duer!"

"Sir."

"Have the entire company of the *Shamrock* formed in the ship's waist," Macomb ordered. "Let's go see just how many of them have an appetite for adventure."

So they all stepped out into the afternoon sun as the entire ship's company – two hundred and seventy-five men – gathered hurriedly in the center of the boat. Cushing and Howorth stood at the rail above with Commander Macomb as Duer prepared to address the men. Cushing could hardly help but notice that the eyes of the crew members drifted his way. Many of them nudged one another and pointed. Then Lieutenant Duer cleared his throat, and everyone fell silent.

"I need eleven men and two officers," Duer called out, "to accompany Lieutenant Cushing on a dangerous expedition, from which probably none will return." Duer hesitated then, looking out over the assembled mass of men, giving them all time to carefully consider what he was saying. "None but young men," he went on, "without encumbrances will be accepted." Duer paused again, glanced over at Cushing momentarily, then continued. "Those who wish to volunteer please step over to this side of the ship."

The ship's entire company – all two hundred and seventy-five men – stepped quickly to their left.

Cushing felt his heart take a small leap in his chest; he knew he had just witnessed a sight, a remarkable vote of confidence, that not many men ever have the fortune to experience.

Macomb smiled and nodded happily. "I thought as much," he said. "Impressive. Now, pick your men, Lieutenant Duer, and pick them with care." Then Macomb turned abruptly toward Cushing. "You shall have your crew soon enough, Lieutenant Cushing," he said. "So tell me, when do you plan on striking out again?"

Will Cushing glanced up at the clouding sky, the flags flapping lightly in the breeze. He realized that the longer he waited the more likely it was that the Confederates would get wind of his presence. He nodded solemnly, rolled his shoulders. “Tonight.”

Chapter Twenty-Eight

October 27th – Late Afternoon

Cooke opened the newspaper to the third page and laid it gently across his desk. "This is the most recent Yankee paper I have come across," Cooke said. "Have you seen it?"

"No, Captain," Colonel Whitford replied.

Whitford had just taken over command of the infantry garrison at Plymouth, and Cooke wanted to be sure that every conceivable precaution had been taken to defend the *Albemarle*. "Look here," Cooke continued, pointing out a particular article. "This is a description of a Yankee plot to attack the ram."

Whitford picked up the newspaper and began reading. "Hmm, very interesting."

"It's probably nothing more than something meant to mislead us," Cooke continued, "but still, we must be prepared. I know you're new here, so I thought it would be good if we could get together for a talk. Was the boat I sent adequate, Colonel? Comfortable?"

Whitford smiled. "Wonderful, actually," he answered. "The ride upriver was a pleasure, Captain. We're not used to such pleasantries in the infantry."

"Good," Cooke said. "It is always good to talk face-to-face, I think."

"Yes, of course," Whitford agreed, scanning the article with interest.

"You see, the *Albemarle* is the key right now to the entire region's defense," Cooke went on, trying to impress upon the colonel the importance of his new assignment. "The task of the garrison is to guard the boat, but in reality, for the past few months the boat has been guarding the garrison. The Federal navy seems content at this point to simply keep her bottled up in Plymouth, and that is fine with me for the time being. You see, we have now under construction at Edward's Ferry a new ironclad that will be even more formidable than the *Albemarle.* Once it is complete, I plan on using them together to open all the sounds. The Yanks have nothing that can stop that combination, but we must hold Plymouth until the new ironclad is complete. Without the *Albemarle* that would be impossible. I wanted to make absolutely sure that you understood that, Colonel. The *Albemarle* cannot be lost. Every precaution must be taken to defend the ram."

"Yes, and I appreciate your explanation, Captain. It certainly makes things a bit clearer. Often in the infantry we get orders, but rarely explanations."

"Good," Cooke replied. "This is why the *Albemarle* is so important to us right now, Colonel, and why we must be prepared for anything. I'm convinced the Yanks will not come up the Roanoke with their wooden fleet, but they might well try something else. Maybe *anything* else to get at the ram. It would be an enormous feather in their caps to take her out, and nothing short of a disaster for us should they succeed. Now, the artillery ... ?"

"Unlimbered at the river's edge, Captain," Whitford responded. "Several batteries covering every quadrant and approach to the ironclad. Believe me, once we open up, a child's toy boat could not last more than a few seconds out there. I've discussed the arrangement with Captain Lee and I'm satisfied the artillery will destroy any single craft or small group of boats that might approach long before they reach the ram. The gunners have all the ranges prefigured."

Cooke rubbed his hands together. "Good, good. As you know, I now have a schooner anchored off the wreck of the *Southfield* and a picket post on the remains of the ship. Nothing should be able to get past them, day or night, but if they fire a signal rocket ... "

Whitford smiled, shook his head knowingly. "We will immediately light the illumination fires all along the waterfront and stand to the guns. Everyone has their orders. Believe me, Captain, I would hate to be in the Yankees' shoes should that happen. For us, it will be like shooting ducks in a pond."

Cooke nodded, feeling better. "Well, that's good to hear. Now," he went on excitedly, "we have people working for us at the Yankees' Roanoke Island base and also observing their fleet in the sound. Should you get a report from any one of them that you don't understand, just forward it on to me for further analysis."

"Well, I'm glad you brought that up, Captain. A short report did come in just yesterday, and I wasn't entirely sure what to make of it."

"Go on. "

"Seems a motor launch with a spar rig on the front has been spotted at the mouth of the river within the last day or so. Newly arrived, as I have it."

"A spar rig," Cooke repeated curiously. "You mean rigged out for a torpedo?"

"Well, that's what I'm guessing, yes," Whitford answered.

Cooke shook his head. "A boat like that can only be meant for one thing – a torpedo attack on the *Albemarle*."

"Well, whatever," Whitford said confidently, crossing his legs. "I'm not really all that worried, Captain. We'll be ready."

"You know the Yanks tried to torpedo the ram months ago," Cooke said. "That's why I had the floating log apron built and laid down all around her. It's an extra measure for safety's sake. Should they get that close – and they won't, of course! – but should they, the Yanks will be greatly upset to discover they can't get near enough to the ram's hull to detonate their charges. Ha! Any trip to Plymouth for them will be a wasted trip."

"Well, I can see you've thought of everything, Captain," Whitford said.

"I've tried, Colonel. Believe me, I've tried."

"And we will be ready on our end," Whitford assured him. "I will admit I'm not much for boats, but I believe I can handle men and artillery as well as anyone."

"Wonderful," Cooke said. "Listen, if you have time I'd love to show you the new ram under construction over at Edward's Ferry. We're all very proud here of what we've got going. Would you like to make the ride over with me, Colonel?"

"Of course," Whitford replied. "I'd love to see what it looks like."

Both men stood to leave and Cooke had gestured toward the door when Whitford suddenly hesitated. "Oh, and one other thing ... "

Cooke smiled. "Yes, what's that?"

"Just ... a name."

"A name?" Cooke asked. "How do you mean, a name?"

"Well, there was another short report with a name, but I can't quiet recall .... A lieutenant, if I remember correctly."

Cooke stopped dead in his tracks. "What do you mean, a lieutenant, Colonel? Do you mean along with the report of the Yankee motor launch came the name of a lieutenant? A Federal lieutenant?"

"Yes, exactly. Of course, the name meant nothing to me. Just some lieutenant."

Cooke stared at him, could feel the muscles in the back of his neck begin to tense. "Think Colonel, please. The name?"

"Well, I just can't recall right now, but I'm sure it will come to me soon. Sorry, should have written it down."

Cooke tapped his foot on the floor nervously. "Was this name perhaps ... Cushing?"

"*Yes*," that's it exactly, Captain. Cushing. Meant nothing to me, of course. But you seem to know ... "

James Cooke took a long, deep breath, then let it out slowly. He turned and pointed back toward his desk. "Please, have a seat, Colonel," he said. "I'm afraid we have a problem."

"A problem you say, Captain?"

"Yes, Colonel. A big problem."

"How is that?"

"Cushing," Cooke said, rubbing his chin nervously. "He will come for the ram."

"Well, we will be ready for this Federal lieutenant. I promise you that, Captain. Besides," the colonel went on, "the weather is terrible and only getting worse. No worry about an attack tonight, I should think."

Cooke glanced out the window and saw drops of rain beginning to splatter on the dirt nearby. He frowned. "No," he said, "you don't understand."

"Understand?"

"This is exactly when he *will* come, Colonel. He will not do what you expect. And he will come soon, not wait around for us to spot him and his boat and figure what he is up to. No, he will come very soon, perhaps even tonight. Now, is the usual guard posted?"

"Absolutely, Captain," Whitford replied.

“Then I have an idea,” Cooke said. “Double it.”

“*Double?* Double the guard?”

James Cooke nodded his head. “Yes, double the guard at once. In fact, I will send a telegram to Lt. Warley telling him to double his guard on the ram immediately.”

“Immediately?” Whitford asked, taken aback by the sudden concern.

“Tonight! Yes, Colonel, tonight.”

Colonel Whitford stared across the desk at Cooke, dumbfounded. “All this for some young Federal lieutenant, Captain? I don’t understand.”

Jim Cooke tapped the desk rhythmically for a few seconds. “Oh, you will, Colonel,” he said finally. “Believe me, you will.”

Chapter Twenty-Nine

October 27th – Early Evening

Lincoln picked up his pen and began tinkering with the numbers again, shifting states and electoral votes from one column to the other. By late October, most of his staff had come to agree that the looming presidential election seemed to be leaning ever so slightly in his favor – something that would have been unthinkable just two months ago – but Abraham Lincoln was not so sure, and hardly ready to claim victory. He had been hounded, reviled, accused, accursed, and written off for so long that that sort of presumption seemed to him at least an absurdity if not an outright sin.

So he took his time, carefully placing each state into a column, those he thought would go for McClellan in one, those that would probably vote for him in the other, and each time the result was the same – a dead heat. No matter how he sliced it, according to his methodology the election appeared too close to call.

Of course, in many ways the fact that he even had an election to tinker with seemed nothing short of miraculous. In late August, his prospects had appeared so dismal that few would have bet a penny on his chances, but then the steady headwind of misfortune that he had been bucking since March seemed suddenly to shift, even if ever so slightly. Atlanta fell to Sherman in early September, and Jubal Early was beaten in the Shenandoah Valley twice by Sheridan, first at Winchester and then later routed at Cedar Creek.

Suddenly the overall climate favoring a Federal victory in the war seemed to improve, and Lincoln's political stock rose – as did his spirits – right along with it. He still had the concession letter he had written to McClellan back in August tucked away in his desk, of course, but now he had at least some plausible reason to believe he might never have to use it.

In late August, as predicted, the Democrats selected George McClellan as their candidate, and that choice – along with the most recent Federal victories – helped Lincoln as much as anything. The talk in his own party of dumping him for another candidate began to fade as the rank and file came finally to comprehend just what they would have on their hands if McClellan were to defeat Lincoln in the general election: a debacle due in large measure to their own intriguing.

General McClellan made no bones about the fact that he would not continue the war for emancipation, and suddenly the abolitionist wing of Lincoln's Republican Party came face-to-face with the potential grim consequences of their own clamorous discontent. In short, standing next to McClellan, Lincoln looked pretty darn good to most Republicans, and within a few weeks most of the rabble-rousers, Horace Greeley and his incendiary crowd included, had closed ranks once again behind him. Indeed, so disturbing was the prospect of a McClellan presidency that Greeley boldly announced in the pages of the New York *Tribune* that from that day forward his paper would "fly the banner of Abraham Lincoln for President."

Not that Lincoln had sat idly by as events developed. While he declined to campaign overtly, behind the scenes he had played every card in his hand to nudge his chances along. Most of the speculation of someone replacing him, for instance, had centered on General John Fremont, who in May had formed an independent third party. While that party had not gathered much steam or many supporters, its platform generally reflected the abolitionist wing of the Republican Party, and therefore Fremont was considered a darling by many of those previously dissatisfied with Lincoln. If Fremont ran he would garner many votes that would otherwise go to Lincoln. So in mid-September, as the 'dump Lincoln' ardor began to fade, he cut a deal by which Fremont was to drop out of the race and come out in support of Lincoln if the president would drop his Postmaster, Montgomery Blair – an outspoken critic of the emancipation movement – from his cabinet, in favor of someone more attuned to Fremont's sensibilities. Blair, who had always been a thorn in Lincoln's side anyway, was promptly replaced with William Dennison, and a significant problem swept out the door.

That fall a battle erupted in all of the state legislatures concerning the votes of the soldiers in the field. Most of the states immediately passed legislation allowing the men to vote while away on duty, but a few – driven by the McClellan/Copperhead vote – declined. Indiana narrowly defeated the legislation, and on that governor's request, Lincoln promptly had six widely respected officers returned home on leave from Sherman's army to campaign in the Republican interest. It had been punch and counter-punch all fall. McClellan was backed by the powerful railroad and banking industries. Lincoln countered by ordering all Federal employees to vote Republican or lose their jobs. Both sides were pulling out all the stops in an election that, as the gap between the candidates narrowed, was becoming increasingly contentious.

Lincoln put down his pen. On his list he had placed Pennsylvania and New York in McClellan's column, Ohio in his own. Those three states held the largest block of electoral votes and thus to a great extent the election would hinge on them. By all reasonable estimates, the race was close in all three, but a breakthrough in either New York or Pennsylvania seemed essential if he was to win. But that breakthrough, he knew, would never be gained through political manipulation. That sort of voter movement could only be accomplished through the one instrument that had power enough to sway the national mood to begin with – success on the battlefield against the Rebels. But Early had been defeated and scattered by Sheridan, and Sherman now marched essentially unopposed, so only Grant, it appeared, could add that missing element. But Grant remained bogged down at Petersburg with no prospect of a breakthrough in sight.

The door opened and a servant brought him a cup of coffee and set it on his desk. Lincoln smiled. "Thank you."

The servant adjusted the lamp, returned the smile, excused himself.

He was feeling better now, a modicum of vigor returning, rebounding right along with his hopes of political success. While the dreams still came at night, and those nights were still haunted by visions of dying boys and charred and burning battlefields, he was at least able to sleep and eat enough to maintain his strength. That in turn affected his mood, and his mood for the first time in many months could be characterized as elevated.

But good moods, he knew, would no more win the election than would fine aspirations, and the election was now only days away. On November 8, the nation would make its choice. He was close to overtaking McClellan – he could feel it in his bones – but close alone would never do. Lincoln was painfully aware, after all, that in politics close was simply another word for defeat.

Lincoln circled New York and Pennsylvania on his list and tried in vain to think of what he might do to further influence the vote in those states. There were still a few offices he could dole out, and to further curry the soldier vote he had offered James Gordon Bennett, editor of the influential New York *Herald,* the position of Minister to France, should Lincoln, that is, be fortunate enough to win the election, and therefore be in a position to make good on such a promise. Still, by his own calculations, he lagged behind.

In the end, he doubted that political influence of that sort could carry the day, anyway. He needed something more than clever musings from newspaper writers to influence the people on issues such as war and peace, life and death, the very future of the republic. He needed help from the battlefield, a success that would galvanize the electorate.

Lincoln had no idea from where that help might come, but he had little doubt that that was what he needed. Still, he refused to fret. Abraham Lincoln sensed that in his life, in the war, even in the times in which he was living, the invisible but guiding hand of an all-knowing Providence was hard at work. Deep waters were flowing, molding, shaping the future of the entire world, and already those currents had brought him back from the virtual exile of political irrelevance to the very threshold of victory. If his cause was right, he had no doubt those waters would carry him over the top, that even now events were conspiring to that purpose, and that soon they would make themselves known.

Chapter Thirty

October 27th – 11:28 pm

Cushing wiped the rain from his eyes with the back of his hand then checked his watch one last time. Picket boat *No. 1* had just reached the mouth of Roanoke River, right on schedule.

They were moving slowly now through darkness and rain, fifteen men in the launch, another thirteen towed behind in the cutter. They had all been carefully instructed that there could be no talk, whispers, or coughing, not a sound from either of the boats. The launch was chugging along slowly but steadily, the engine covered by a wooden box wrapped in a tarpaulin to muffle the noise as much as possible. A light, cold rain was falling, pelting the trees and river, deadening the sound of their approach that much more. The weather was cold and miserable for sure, but a bit of good luck nevertheless. They would be hard to hear on this wet, wretched night, harder yet to spot.

Will Cushing was as calm as he had ever been in his life. There was no past or future for him, no worries of failure, no recollections of Alonzo, Flusser or thoughts of death to upset him. His mind was entirely focused on the mission now, the moment at hand, that and nothing more. If he could keep it to just that, he knew he'd be fine.

Cushing stood in the forward section of the motor launch with the rest of the officers. Howorth stood just ahead, manning the howitzer. Ensign William Gay was up on the bow near the boom. Everyone was in their proper position, already prepared for action.

Cushing was connected forward to Howorth and Gay by cords, rearward to Stotesbury at the engine in the same manner. Will had worked out a series of pulls and tugs in order to communicate with each man without the necessity of speech, and he held each of those lines firmly in his right hand. In his left he held the two lines that would work the torpedo, and through constantly imagining the use of each line in his mind he had been able to gain a full command of the arrangement. He was confident that, even under a galling fire, he would not make a mistake. Much would depend on it.

The launch moved slowly under the overhanging branches along the south bank of the Roanoke. The rain was falling harder now, the wind beginning to whip across the surface of the water, causing the boats to bob and sway. Visibility was awful, but that, Cushing knew, figured to his advantage; the less the Rebels could see the better. The crew huddled together in the boats, wet and shivering, but in good spirits despite the weather – they were good, tough men, these. From the mouth of the Roanoke to Plymouth was roughly nine miles, and he expected to encounter the wreck of the *Southfield* sometime near two in the morning. So far, everything had gone as planned, but all that could change, he knew, with a single shout or crack of a branch along the riverbank.

Focused entirely on the mission as he was, for Cushing his time on the river seemed neither short nor long, strained nor carefree. It just was, and he stood entirely at ease in the boat, prepared to be spotted and hailed by a picket post along the shore, ready to leap into action, but so far that had not happened. For the others it seemed not so easy, and he could sense the building tension.

Several times he wiped the rain from his face, and he could feel, from the constant jangle of the line in his hand, that Stotesbury was busy working the launch's engine to the maximum. Stotesbury knew his job. They all knew their jobs.

Time passed slowly on the rainy, silent Roanoke.

Just around 2:00 AM they rounded a narrow bend in the river and Cushing sensed that they would soon be closing on the remains of the *Southfield.* He pulled a white handkerchief from his pocket and waved it back toward the cutter – a prearranged signal for the men behind to take their positions at the oars and have their weapons in hand. At first he was not even sure they had seen him, but then he heard the faint creak of oars twisting into oarlocks, and he knew they had moved to their posts.

Then he felt a sudden tug from Ensign Gay up forward near the boom – it could only mean one thing. Cushing took a step forward and squinted hard into the misty night. The rain had let up slightly now, and through the gloom he could just make out the dark outline of a patrolling schooner lying virtually dead ahead across their bow. Cushing quickly reached for the wheel and gave it a slight turn toward the riverbank. Almost immediately the rest of the men spotted the schooner as well, now less than a hundred yards straight ahead. They all froze in place, ready to leap aboard and kill or capture anyone who spotted them.

As the launch motored slowly upriver, the water slapped gently against the bow, the engine puffing away softly in its muffled compartment. Cushing had a hard time believing they had not already been detected. While his mind remained calm, his every sense began to ache, almost throb, in anticipation of some noise, yell, or gunshot. He was ready for anything. Never before had he felt so utterly alive. He strained to see, and his eyes ached from the effort.

Every eye was glued to the black silhouette ahead, hearts racing, muscles tense. Then Cushing saw the shadowy form of the *Southfield* emerge from the mist and rain like some unearthly phantom, suddenly looming larger and larger, further off their starboard bow. But they were much too close to the schooner now to change course and head for the middle of the channel. Will realized immediately that they had no choice but to make for the narrow water between the bank and the schooner, and if they held their course they would pass within no more than a few yards of her stern. It would be very, very close, but it had all happened so quickly, he had no other choice. Every man stood as still as death itself. Even in the rain he could smell their sweat.

The launch closed on the schooner: 50 … 30 … now only 10 yards away. Faint voices suddenly became audible, muffled by the light rain, then laughter and a few footsteps. Suddenly a match flared on the schooner's deck and Cushing reached for his pistol, felt the ivory handle in his hand like piece of carved ice. He could hear his own heart thumping gently in his ears. In his other hand he held the line firmly that led to Stotesbury. If he yanked hard three times, Stotesbury was to drop the line to the cutter, but it was not time for that yet. Cushing held on calmly, patiently ... waiting. Then he understood – someone had just lit a cigarette. Nothing more than that, no alarm, no signal. He watched as the flame died away, as the sentry turned, and he could hear the voices fading, then laughter again, but now weaker, much weaker. Then they were past the schooner.

They all held their breath, watched closely astern as the launch continued on its way, the cutter still in tow. Then the launch finally rounded a bend in the river and the schooner and *Southfield* slowly disappeared from view. Every man took a deep breath. Cushing could almost feel their smiles through the darkness, their relief. He would have never guessed they would have gotten past the picket boats without being spotted and hailed. Amazing! Now it was only a few minutes more, he knew, until the hulking silhouette of the *Albemarle* would emerge from the darkness. So far the mission had passed like a dream.

Ten minutes later they rounded another short bend and off the port bow he spotted her, at first murky and indistinct, more a dark blur than a ship, but much too large and imposing to be anything else – unmistakably, it was the *Albemarle.* He nudged Howorth, pointed, and Howorth saw it too. For the first time that night his heart began to quicken.

Cushing cut the wheel sharply and the launch veered toward the bank. He strained to see through the darkness and mist, looked for pickets, for the artillery emplacements, for a dock where he might put in. Then he spotted a wharf jutting out into the water just past the length of the ironclad, and he steered straight toward it. If they could get to the dock undetected, they would all pile out and try to overwhelm the crew and then cut the ram out. Cushing's plan was working. Up almost nine miles of guarded river and past two picket boats and no one had spotted them yet. It was almost too good to be true. Inside his coat Cushing had even stuffed away a flag to raise over the *Albemarle* once he had cut her out. It was his fondest dream to steam out amongst the Federal Fleet with the stars and stripes flapping in the wind high above the ironclad.

They came in slowly toward the wharf, the cutter still in tow – he would need every last man once they hit land. Howorth looked back at him, nodded. Cushing nodded in return. Feeling calmer than ever now, he kept the launch on a wide course for the far side of the wharf, away from any pickets that might be stationed on the ram. Then he held up his pistol, and everyone readied their guns and cutlasses, crouching low in the boat, ready to leap as soon as they neared the dock. No longer did he sense fear or tension in the crew. Now he sensed excitement.

On the rear of the ram, a sentry stood suddenly, awakened by something out on the dark river, some sound or movement. The sentry gazed out over the black water toward Will Cushing. He raised his rifle just slightly. "Who ... who goes there?" the sentry called.

Cushing turned, stared at the guard … waited.

"*Who goes there!*" the sentry called again, much louder this time.

Then another voice joined the chorus, nervous, high-pitched. "Who's there? Identify yourself!"

"Who goes there?"

Now there was movement along the bank, sentries standing, moving into position, men running here and there.

Cushing had thought it all through a hundred times, every last possibility, and this one was simple enough. The opportunity to seize the ram was gone, and he dismissed it at once without a second thought. Now he could only go in and use the torpedo, so he tugged hard three times on the engineer's line for Stotesbury to release the cutter. They had already been spotted, so there was no longer any need for quiet or secrecy. From here on out everything would depend upon speed, guts, and cunning.

Will turned and hollered to the men in the cutter. "Cast off, Peterkin!" he screamed, "Go back and get those men on the schooner!" Then Cushing yanked the wheel hard and pointed the bow of the launch straight for the *Albemarle.* He was going in.

All along the river bank the Rebels were running and screaming now, stunned and confused. "Identify yourself!" one kept yelling, fear rising in his voice. "Identify yourself!"

Suddenly, lights mushroomed across the horizon, several preset illumination fires going up in bright, leaping flames, and the light spilled out over the water like a dazzling spray. On the shore the sound of a warning rattle filled the air, high pitched and hostile, and already the first crack of muskets could be heard. Bullets began thumping in the water nearby and cracking off the launch's smokestack.

As the cutter drifted back and away into the darkness, the launch, relieved of the cutter's mass, jerked ahead, quickly picking up speed as they closed on the ironclad. The launch's bow was no more than fifty feet off the *Albemarle's* stern when he spotted something floating in the water dead ahead, and Cushing turned the wheel slightly and cut the engines to get a better look – a circle of logs surrounding the ram. Damn! He had not planned for this. But his mind was still clear and calm and he instantly began to calculate.

A musket ball snapped at his coat, another ricocheted off the stack with hollow a ponggg! Suddenly the water was alive with the small plumes of bullets, the air around them hissing with lead. Cushing leaned over the side of the launch, studied the logs carefully then yelled back to Stotesbury, "Full speed ahead!"

Will turned the wheel hard, took the launch back out into the dark water away from the ram in a long wide circle, and as he did a shotgun blast blew the entire back of his coat away, while a bullet tore off the sole of one shoe. Cushing ignored both. "More!" he yelled at Stotesbury. "I need everything you can get! Full speed, damn it!"

Stotesbury nodded calmly, leaning patiently over the engine, trying to coax every last bit of power he could manage from the thumping pistons.

Cushing thought, *These are good men. Yes, we are going to do this!*

Now the launch was fairly flying, almost skimming across the water, and Will Cushing knew exactly what he had to do. He would come in straight on the logs, and if he hit between two of them just right the bow of the launch would skip up and over the log apron, and he would slide right in on his target – the ram's port quarter. Once inside the ring of logs, of course, they would never be able to get back out, but escape was no longer a consideration. He had come for the *Albemarle* and, one way or another, he was going to take the *Albemarle* tonight.

He yanked the wheel again and the launch began its last hard turn toward the ram. The air around them was humming with lead, the water rippling with shots. In the white light that surrounded the ironclad like a gleaming halo he could clearly see, dead ahead, the red sparks of musket shots, men kneeling, running, yelling. Others were pointing, loading rifles.

As they closed on the target, a bullet whistled past his ear while another tore through his coat pocket as it was flapping in the breeze. Cushing paid them no mind, keeping his eye dead on the black silhouette of the ram, now clearly outlined against the raging bonfires on shore. Behind him not a word was spoken, every last man ready to do his job, whatever the price.

Only twenty yards away now, spray in his face, bullets humming, Cushing could see the logs clearly again. He angled the launch to strike directly between two, hoping to hit them perfectly and slide the bow up and over.

"What boat is that?" came the frantic cry from the ram as the launch barreled in on the docked ironclad.

Cushing laughed. "We'll soon let you know!" he shouted back. Then he looked over at Ensign Gay. "Swing the boom out!" he ordered.

As Gay pulled on the boom, Cushing yanked the lanyard from the howitzer and a double shot of canister rocked the ram and all those around it, the blast rattling off the iron casement like a hail of lead.

Bullets were snapping and cracking and hissing everywhere around them as they struck the log apron at full speed. The impact was enormous, sending water splashing and many of his men lurching. The hollow groan of wood cleaving wood filled the air for a second or two. Then the launch stopped, hanging precariously atop of the logs, rocking slightly, before finally slipping forward into the pen with the ram. They'd done it!

The impact had knocked Will Cushing forward against the bow, but he quickly regained his footing and leaped up onto the deck with Gay. The launch was now shielded by the *Albemarle* from some of the gunfire and blanketed in dark shadow, yet Cushing could see well enough to make out the ram's iron casement and, just below that, the water line. He nodded, seeing that Gay had the boom in the water. He could hear clearly the metallic clank of the winch sliding the torpedo ahead toward the ram. As bullets ricocheted off the stack and thudded against the ram like hail on a barn roof, Cushing moved on the deck gingerly, watching only the length of the boom as the torpedo neared its position of explosion. In his right hand he held the control line, in his left the line to the trigger.

"Load solid shot! Now!" he heard the order come from inside the ram.

Cushing glanced up and spotted the enormous Brooke rifle emerging from the ironclad's port. It was glaring straight at him, the gaping muzzle not twenty feet from his face.

But fear was useless here – there was no time for fear. A shot took his cap off, another sliced through his collar while a third stung his hand. Two more bullets passed through his coat, a sixth cut his sleeve. Blood was trickling down his neck now, soaking his coat, but he ignored it all. Behind him his men were screaming, falling, but he would have to deal with that later. When he was confident the torpedo was in position Cushing pulled on the right hand cord, detaching the torpedo from the boom. Then he began a slow count to five, allowing the charge to float up directly under the ram's hull. It was just as he had practiced.

"Bring it down one more tick!" he heard the Confederate gunner scream from inside the ram, "then blow the Yanks to hell!"

Will glanced up, saw the mouth of the giant Brooke continue to pivot down, zeroing in, heard the clank of its breech slam shut. Cushing knew he had at best seconds before the gun would blow them all to pieces.

But for Will Cushing time seemed to be moving in slow motion, and in the smallest fraction of a second he was able to recall his practice runs out on the Hudson River, the giant boulder, the wide, blue sky, that perfect detonation.... Three, four ...

"Aim!"

Ever so gently William Cushing pulled the trigger line, mindful that it could not be yanked too hard or else the cord would snap. Then he said it out loud – "five"– and when he felt the cord go taut he gave the line a last … gentle ... tug.

Chapter Thirty-One

October 28th – 3:11 A. M.

Cushing was hurled backward by the enormous concussion, then bounced to his knees as the force of the explosion slammed the nose of the launch under water like a child's toy.

The heat and sheer concussive violence of the massive naval gun's eruption had passed just over their heads, and the magnitude of both explosions had forced picket boat *No. 1* underwater, swamping the small craft. The Brooke rifle and the torpedo had fired at almost the same instant, and for a moment or two Cushing and his men lay prostrate in the bottom of the launch, stunned. It appeared the Rebel gunners had not been able to lower the naval rifle enough to strike Cushing or his crew, but the force of the Brooke's explosion – passing just over their heads – was immediately followed by a massive column of water unleashed by the torpedo's detonation which, after rising well above the ram, collapsed upon the motor launch like a thunderclap, sweeping many of the sailors into the cold Roanoke. Immediately after the explosions an eerie silence enveloped the scene, both sides simply shocked beyond thought or action, but that condition did not hold for long.

"Surrender!" came the cry from the guards kneeling onshore near the *Albemarle*.

Cushing stumbled to his feet, refusing to reply, and glanced back toward his crew.

"Surrender or we will blow you out of the water!" the Rebel yelled again, this time in a far more angry, desperate tone.

"Never!" Cushing shouted back, and immediately bullets started to thump and whack again against the sides and deck of the launch.

The mission had been completed, the launch now sat swamped and entirely unserviceable. There was nothing left to do but run. There was no time to gather the crew, so it would have to be every man for himself. Cushing whipped around, motioning to what remained of the crew behind him in the launch. "Men!" he yelled, "Save yourselves!"

With that he tossed aside his sword and pistol, yanked away what was left of his bullet-riddled coat, and pulled off what remained of his shoes. Will took one quick jump to the stern of the launch and dove headfirst into the river as whistling bullets searched for him in the darkness. The water struck him like a cold shock, and initially the chill cleared the hazy confusion of the explosion from his head, but it was not long before the bitter cold began to wear away his strength.

For the first few yards, he remained under water. Then – as he swam away from the light near the ram – he surfaced and began swimming for the far bank of the Roanoke as hard as he could. Despite his slender build, Cushing was a strong swimmer, and it was not long before he had gained the middle of the channel. Here and there bullets still zipped in the water around him, but for the most part the firing had ended.

He stopped and treaded water, spotted men with torches running along the opposite bank, and then saw a boat in the water behind him. It was headed his way. Cushing dove under and held his breath until the boat passed overhead. Then he surfaced quickly, drew a few deep breaths, and started swimming downriver with the current in the middle of the channel. He reasoned that they would be looking for him at the nearest points along the riverbank, so he struck out for the longest course he could think of – south, downriver toward the sound.

"Cushing! Cushing!" The Rebs were running along the shore, shouting his name.

He could hear them calling from the boat now too, and each time they neared, he slipped back underwater and waited until they passed overhead. But the cold and exertion were beginning to take a serious toll on his stamina, and he knew he could not last in the frigid water for long. He had to get downriver and out of the water somewhere along the bank at a spot that was unguarded. Cushing had no idea what had happened to the rest of his men, could only hope that they too had escaped unharmed.

"Cushing! Give yourself up!"

He turned, swam hard, the current sweeping him south toward the wreck of the *Southfield,* and in a few minutes the shouts of the Rebels faded away, darkness and silence enveloping him again. Here there was only the sound of the water rippling, his strokes slapping the water, his own labored breathing. The bullet wound in his hand was beginning to throb, getting worse the further along he swam, but he tried to ignore it, tried to think of nothing but each successive stroke. Cushing swam mechanically, his mind compelling every stroke, his body responding to fear and necessity, and he swam unthinking until he heard thrashing in the water not far away.

"Cushing! Please, ... help."

He stopped, treaded water for a few seconds, listened. It was one of his crew.

Will turned, began swimming back up stream, forcing himself through the strong current until he finally located the man, struggling frantically in the water, near exhaustion. It was John Woodman.

"Can you make it?" Cushing asked, circling Woodman, water lapping into his mouth as he spoke.

"Can't swim ... anymore," Woodman gasped, so exhausted he could barely move.

"Here," Will said, reaching for Woodman and pulling him to his side. "Hold on to me!"

Cushing took hold of Woodman, then began swimming slowly, awkwardly, painfully with one arm, holding Woodman loosely with the other. He began working his way toward the bank, but the current was strong and land seemed a mile away.

Cushing could not fathom how long he and Woodman struggled in the river together. Time had lost all measure and meaning; it could have been five minutes; it could have been five hours. He swam and worked beyond anything he had ever done before, beyond anything he could ever have imagined, but the current was strong, and no matter how hard he worked he could not gain the shore. He became very, very cold, his breathing labored. Will battled the river until the pain in his hand went numb, until his arms and legs felt so cold and heavy they would no longer do as he wished. He swam until he could not swim anymore, until his body began to give out, until the feeling in his limbs disappeared entirely. Death, he realized grimly at that moment, was rapidly closing on both him and Woodman.

Will Cushing stopped in midstream, began to choke on small waves of river water, to snort and scuffle. He fought desperately against going under. He struggled to hold onto Woodman's increasingly heavy body, to keep them both above the incessant, slapping waves. He fought until he could no longer feel his hands or fingers, until his breath became short, until his own thoughts became muddled and unclear.

Then suddenly Woodman was gone. What! What! Woodman had slipped away from Will's frozen grasp, lost behind somewhere in the cold water. Woodman! Woodman, he thought, where…

Cushing thrashed about madly in the river, frantically trying to locate Woodman in the dark, muddy water, but there was nothing there, no body, no John Woodman to grab hold of anymore. Woodman was gone, Cushing realized with a shock. Woodman was dead.

Now Cushing could hardly think, much less move. Woodman was gone, swept away by the cold Roanoke River, and the sudden, frightening thought came to him that unless he moved soon the river would take him too. That stark comprehension sent a shock of fear through his numb body, and suddenly there was a small burst of energy, a rush of clarity, and his arms – almost miraculously – began to move again.

He did not so much swim then as flail, scrambling, slapping, and clawing his way through the cold river, fighting to gain the bank – fighting for his life. More than once he went completely under, only to struggle again to the surface, coughing and spitting, but never giving up. He could feel nothing. The effort was entirely beyond his body now, his mind it seemed, somehow animating his arms and legs, willpower alone supplying the means of propulsion.

And then even his willpower gave out. Cushing was done – numb, frozen, exhausted – and he began to sink slowly for what he sensed would be the last time. His mind struggled, but his body would no longer respond, and he began to drift downward into the depths of the river, so dark, quiet, and eternal. As he did, something deep inside of him began to scream out that he did not want to die, that it was all wrong, but none of that seemed to matter; and then he reached out and felt something in his hand – mud.

Will Cushing realized he had struck the lower portion of the riverbank. He reached forward frantically, grabbed another handful of mud, yanked hard, then felt himself rise and break the surface. He took one great, wonderful breath of lovely air, then floundered in the shallow water, pulling himself forward, rolling and flailing his way through the thick, slippery muck up onto the bank. In about three inches of water Cushing finally managed to struggle to his feet, took two steps forward, then collapsed face first onto the muddy riverbank ... unconscious.

Chapter Thirty-Two

October 28th – 5:11 A. M.

Cooke tossed the covers aside, slid from his bed, and began pacing the floor of his quarters again, just as he had done on-and-off all night long. He stopped short by the window.

Outside the rain had ended, the wind had settled, and there was only a fine, cold mist hanging over the boatyard. Cooke could just make out the last of a few stars blinking above the fog, and it appeared the weather was clearing. In another hour or so the sun would be up, the morning would slowly warm, and he guessed that by mid-day it would be pleasant out on the river again.

Cooke had been able to sleep but fitfully. The news delivered earlier that evening by Colonel Whitford that Cushing and a torpedo rigged motor launch had arrived at the Federal Fleet in the sound had robbed him of his peace of mind. Suddenly the prospect of having to deal with the intrepid Cushing – something Mary had teased him about only weeks before – had become fact, and it was a reality he did not treasure. He had pushed hard for the position at Halifax, and with it came the responsibility for the defense of North Carolina's inland waters. Employing defensive measures that would confound and thwart the Federal Navy's usual strategies and tactics was one thing – he had, after all, decades of service and know-how to draw upon. But stopping a brash young officer, whose entire career had been built upon taking enormous risks while bypassing the conventional wisdom of the service, was something else again. Suddenly all the preventative measures he had installed to defend the *Albemarle* seemed questionable, even inadequate.

What would Cushing do? That was the question that had been rattling through his brain all night long, and it was not an easy problem to solve. Jim Cooke was a tough customer and a fine naval tactician, but he was not a young man anymore, and he knew he did not think like this Lieutenant William B. Cushing. Cushing, he knew, was at best only twenty-one years old, far too young to understand the real risks of the ventures he was undertaking, and much too inexperienced to realize that these operations of his bordered on the tactically suicidal. Because of this Cushing might well try anything, and James Cooke had not the time, manpower nor resources to defend against every potential. So the same question kept rolling through his mind – what would Cushing *do?*

Off to the east he could see the first white trace of light on the horizon, and he knew the sun could not be far behind. That brought with it at least a measure of relief. For some reason, things always seemed to look much worse late at night than they ever really were, and he knew he had constructed a sound defense. He went over the list again in his mind and with each added level of security – the multiple pickets, the schooner and *Southfield,* the artillery emplacements, etc., etc. – Cushing's prospects for success seemed to dwindle geometrically. But that, of course, was simply his conventional mind at work, and since there was nothing conventional about Cushing, where exactly did that get him? Nowhere. He had even instructed the guard to be doubled, but would that make a difference?

In the end, Cooke realized, he had employed the strongest measures against Cushing, no matter how unconventional, bold, or ingenious a plan the young Federal lieutenant might devise. The log apron was now complete around the ironclad, strung out a good thirty feet from its hull, and no torpedo launch would ever be able to penetrate it. The log apron was impassable, and that one fact trumped all else.

"Thank God," Cooke whispered to himself, looking vacantly out over the dark river, tapping the window nervously with the tip of his finger.

The light was increasing now, bringing with it the smallest measure of warmth, and Cooke suddenly felt tired again. The long night was finally over. He would get a few good hours sleep and then go over to his office. There would be coffee – at least something hot that they all now pretended was coffee – and biscuits, and he would be able to laugh off his anxiety, perhaps even tell a joke or two.

Poor Cushing, he thought. Perhaps the boy was already dead, wounded, or captured. Or perhaps not. But even if Cushing somehow managed to make it all the way upriver clear to the log apron, he would only be stranded along its edges and then cut to pieces by the artillery and the thousand or so muskets waiting for him.

"I am sorry, Mister Cushing," he mumbled to himself, pulling the covers up over his shoulder. "But this is war, and I did not invite you up the Roanoke to attack my boat. You will find that this is neither Smithville nor Wilmington. No, not so easy as all that."

Reassured, he laid his head down again and closed his eyes. He would try for at least a few hours of restful sleep, and then deal with the long day ahead. Cooke had come very close to convincing himself that Cushing had absolutely no chance of success, and he felt better for it. Much better, in fact. So he closed his eyes, began to snore, then awoke with a sudden start. Why was that? he wondered, but then he understood: he felt better, but better was not good enough.

Chapter Thirty-Three

October 28th – 6:02 A. M.

Cushing licked his lips, tried to move his legs, but realized ever so slowly that his entire body seemed frozen. When he finally, but vaguely, came to his senses, he had no idea just how long he had been face first in the mud, but as the sun rose higher and higher it slowly came to him that it was now early morning and that somehow he had survived the night. The meager heat of the October sun slowly warmed his back, bringing him gradually to life, and after an hour or so he tried to move his arm; something he finally managed to accomplish, but only with great effort and pain.

Cushing braced himself on his left elbow and gently raised his head. He glanced about, grasping in a foggy way that he was still on the Plymouth side of the river, but not nearly as far downstream as he had anticipated. Indeed, as he turned and looked back upriver, he realized that he had hardly made it beyond the town, that he was, in fact, in the swamp on the southern edge, lying less than fifty feet from a Rebel fortification. On a parapet only twenty yards away was a Confederate sentry with a slouch hat, brown eyes, and a few days growth of beard gazing north out over the river. The only reason Cushing had not been spotted, he realized, was that he was now entirely covered in a garment of brown mud, weeds, and muck so that he blended in with the bank almost perfectly. For the time being it appeared that he was safe where he lay, but he could hardly lie there forever.

Ever so gradually the heat from the sun brought back his strength, and he watched the day as it dawned slowly in the town below. In Plymouth he could see many soldiers and officers buzzing about angrily, and he could only conclude it was in response to his mission. Just how successful he had been remained an open question. Had he sunk or only damaged the *Albemarle*? That he would like to know, but for the time being his first objective was to get himself off the riverbank and into the rushes that bordered the cypress swamp nearby. That, unfortunately, would require a trek over forty feet of open bank while directly under the nose of the Rebel sentry. Lying still undiscovered was one thing, moving, he knew, would be quite another, but dogs were nearby running lively and free and soon, he realized, one of them would find him and alert the sentry to his position.

Cushing carefully timed the sentry as he walked his tour, then lurched to his feet and made a rush for the heavy swamp ahead. He'd made it almost halfway when the sentry turned abruptly, and Cushing dove for cover near a short path that wound its way up toward the village. Breathing heavily, his legs aching painfully, he lay as flat as he could and tried desperately not to move a single muscle.

There he remained, quietly observing the sentry, when suddenly four men appeared on the nearby path walking directly toward him. He held his breath; he had no time to react, no place to go. So Cushing simply lay motionless as the four neared his location, no more than a few feet from the edge of the path. The men came on, talking excitedly, and continued directly past him, so close that one almost stepped on his arm, but somehow, almost miraculously, they did not see him.

"Have you seen the ram?" he heard one ask.

Cushing's ears perked.

"Yes," was the response. "How in the world was it done?"

"No one is sure, but ... "

The four walked on gabbing about the raid, but as they moved away he could no longer make out their conversation. But that didn't matter anymore. He had to move or surely be detected soon, and he had come too far to fall into Confederate hands. His determination had always been his principal weapon, and his determination was beginning to boil anew.

For almost an hour Cushing crawled slowly across the open ground toward the rushes, slithering carefully on his stomach whenever the sentry turned away, then lying absolutely motionless each time he turned back. It was frustratingly slow work, but he could not afford to alert the sentry. Finally he gained the edge of the swamp, rolled into the high grass, at long last clear of the sentry's field of vision. It was a beautiful feeling.

But the dense marsh held its own, peculiar hazards. The cypress swamp, Cushing soon discovered, was nothing but a welter of thorns, stickers, and thick briar bushes interlaced with rolling creeks and soft pockets of deep muck. As he scrambled inland his bare feet were torn to shreds by the sharp, razor-like thorns, and his arms and hands snagged and ripped by stickers.

For hours he stumbled through the swamp, trying to keep the sun over his shoulder, pitching forward into mud holes, tearing his feet to bloody shreds. Occasionally he found some high dry land where he was able to rest for a moment or two, but by and large the trek was another exhausting struggle with the elements. Once he spotted a Rebel work party sinking a series of boats in the river to form an obstruction, and he had to slip away quietly, deeper into the marsh, for fear of being spotted.

At last he gained the far edge of the cypress swamp where he emerged near an expansive cornfield, the corn now dry and crackling in the late October sun. He found a furrow and followed along it to a small grove of trees, dodging a group of Confederate soldiers on the way. In the trees it was dry and cool and Cushing collapsed with his back up against a tall maple to rest, breathing hard, his legs aching clear up to his knees from the pain in his feet. He was a bloody, tattered, muddy mess, but at least he was alive and away from the garrison. The sun was almost directly overhead, and he judged the hour near noon. He was very hungry.

Cushing closed his eyes for just a moment, allowing himself a short rest, knowing all the while he could not risk falling asleep only to be spotted by a Rebel farmer, or sniffed out by dogs, and turned over to the numerous patrols that were combing the area. He thought of his mother then, of Alonzo and Flusser, and he smiled to think of them, but he knew he still had a long way to go before he could truly hope of getting out alive. When Will opened his eyes again a black man – old, tall, and thin – was standing directly in front of him, a look of complete shock on his face.

Cushing rose to his knees, ready to spring if the man called out.

But the man said nothing, took a few steps back, appearing more frightened than dangerous.

Cushing held out his hands to calm the man. "I am a Federal officer," he said slowly, "and if you give away my position, I can tell you, sir, that Abraham Lincoln will personally come down here and take care of your business. So I wouldn't do that if I were you."

The man stared at him sternly for a moment then smiled. Then he shook his head, and Cushing understood – he had no intention of giving Will up.

Cushing leaned back against the trunk of the tree, relaxed. He smiled up at the man. "You took me by surprise," he said.

The man nodded, still saying nothing.

Will thought for a moment then reached for his billfold. “The government of the United States could use your help,” he said with a grin. “And the Federal government pays well.”

“What you need?” the old man asked.

“I want you to go into Plymouth and find out if the *Albemarle* is sunk,” Cushing told him.

The man stared at him with a blank face. “The *Ala ... what?*” he replied.

“The *Albemarle*,” Cushing repeated. “You know, the big iron boat with the two monster cannons that was moored at the wharf there on the river. I want to know if she is still afloat, or sunk to the bottom.” Cushing dug through his billfold, pulled out a small raft of muddy, soaked bills. “Here,” Will went on, “almost twenty dollars in good Federal greenbacks,” he said. “Go ahead, take 'em. You go on into town and find out for me. But don’t dare tell a soul I’m here, you understand?”

The man nodded slowly, took the money. “I got you, Suh,” he said. “I won’t give you up, no how.”

“Good enough,” Will said. “Come back as fast as you can, and don’t bring anyone else.”

The old man disappeared through the trees, and Cushing closed his eyes again and rested. In less than an hour the old man was back. He came in a hurry and kneeled excitedly in the grass in front of Will.

“Dat boat is dead gone sunk to the bottom,” he said with a bright smile. The old man’s eyes glowed with admiration. “But I tell you, day will hang you if day’s catch you,” he continued. “All dem’s white men’s got’s da most awful case of da consternation now, you see.”

Cushing smiled. “I’ll bet they do,” he said.

He put out his hand, shook the old man's firmly. "I thank you for your help," Will said. "Now, you didn't tell anyone about me did you?"

"No, suh," the old man protested. "Not a soul. I know you's got's to get away."

"How do I get back to the sound?" Cushing asked.

The old man thought for a moment, rubbed his chin. "Go back dat way," he said, pointing through the swamp, "an hour or so. Stay right in dat direction, see. You will hit da road out dat way. Road take you down to da river far up. Maybe you finds a boat dere, see?"

Cushing stood. "That way?" he asked, pointing.

The man nodded his head. "Dat's da best," he agreed.

"What's your name?" Cushing asked, putting his hand out again.

The old man took it, pumped it hard. "Ol' Jim dey call me," he said.

Cushing patted him on the shoulder. "I am in your debt, Jim," he said. Then he turned and started back down into the swamp.

For another hour he hiked and crawled and struggled through the marsh, then finally scrambled up the grassy bank of a small stream. Low and behold, Will Cushing stumbled out of the bristles onto a dusty dirt road right where the old man had said it would be. He stopped, put his hands on his hips, and grinned from ear-to-ear.

"Thank you, Ol' Jim," Cushing said under his breath, as pleased as he had ever been in his life. He was worn far beyond exhaustion now, but mere exhaustion would not stop him. He had to keep moving no matter what, and at least now he had a road to walk on. It may have been nothing more than some old dirt farm road, but compared to the cypress swamp, it seemed like heaven. Will Cushing checked the position of the sun once more, then began hobbling toward the river, blood from his feet tracking the road behind.

Chapter Thirty-Four

October 28th – 2:14 P. M.

Cooke walked into his office, shut the door, and stared again at the telegram on his desk. In a way he had almost thought it would not be there when he came back this time around; like a bad dream, he would soon awake and the telegram would be gone, his desk clean and empty, just as he had left it the night before. But none of that was so. The telegram was still there, its terrible ramifications seeming to hang in the air above his desk like a noxious miasma.

Cooke had made it in to work just after eight that morning, cheered by the clear sky and bright weather, feeling refreshed after just a few hours rest. He immediately noticed, however, an odd sort of tension in the yard, a reluctance it seemed, on the part of a few of his subordinates to speak, but he dismissed most of that out of hand as nothing more than his own glum imagination – the wages of worry. Then he saw the telegram sitting on his desk, and even from a distance he could sense it contained bad news, and he had approached the stark, white memorandum that morning with a unique sense of trepidation. James Wallace Cooke had attacked seven Federal gunboats without even so much as a second thought, but this single sheet of white paper supine on his desk had scared him to death.

He circled the desk slowly, took the note up gingerly, noticed then that it was from Lieutenant Warley, the new commander of the

Albemarle. His heart quickened and his palms began to sweat. Why would Warley send him a telegram?

Cooke read the dispatch slowly from start to finish, then read it again and again until the truth finally began to sink into the pit of his brain. The *Albemarle* was gone. Somehow, through some inconceivable method and incomprehensible means, Cushing had gotten to the ironclad. How was that even possible? Cooke was sure he had thought of everything, every possible defensive measure to guard the ram. Yet in the end none of that had mattered. The *Albemarle* was gone.

His first reaction was calm, restrained, and professional. The Roanoke River had to be blocked at any number of points, and he quickly fired off a telegram to Warley instructing him to sink every boat and obstacle he could get his hands on in the river below Plymouth before the Yankees got wind of Cushing's success and came steaming upriver with everything they had. Then he began looking at charts to determine the best places to lay other obstructions above Plymouth to keep the Yanks away from his yard at Halifax – the new ironclad under construction at Edward's Ferry had to be protected even more, now that the old one was gone.

But now all that was done; it was the middle of the afternoon, and a sense of anger, even desperation was beginning to boom through his thoughts. Everything he had been working for was now in jeopardy, indeed, close to ruin. Cooke approached the desk slowly and noticed that a second correspondence had now arrived. It was a letter directed to the Secretary of the Navy, a copy having arrived at his office that afternoon by steamer from Lieutenant Warley at Plymoth. He began to read:

> Plymouth, N. C., *October 28, 1864,*
>
> Sir: The night of the 27th instant, a dark, rainy night, I had the watch doubled and took extra precautions. At or

about 3 o'clock a. m. on the 28th, the officer of the deck discovered a small steamer in the river, hailed her, received an unsatisfactory answer, rang the alarm bell, and opened fire on her with the watch.

The officers and men were at their quarters in as quick time as was possible, but the vessel was so near that we could not bring our guns to bear, and the shot fired from the after gun, loaded with grape, failed to take effect. The boat, running obliquely, struck us under the port bow, running over the boom, exploded a torpedo, and smashed a large hole in us just under the water line, all the while withstanding a heavy fire of musketry.

The boat surrendered, and I sent Lieutenant Roberts to take charge of her. I manned the pumps and gave the order to fire up, so as to use the donkey engine. The water rose so fast that all exertions were fruitless, and the vessel went down in a few moments, merely leaving her shield and smokestack out. In justice to myself I must say the pickets below gave no notice of her approach, and the artillery which was stationed by the vessel for a protection gave us no assistance, manning only one piece, and that at too late a time to be of any service.

Having condensed this report as much as I could, I respectfully request a court of enquiry, to establish on whose shoulders rests the blame of the loss of the *Albemarle.*

I am, respectfully, your obedient servant, A. F. Warley,
Lieutenant, Commanding, C. S. Navy
Hon. S. R. Mallory,
Secretary of the Navy

Jim Cooke removed his reading glasses, leaned back and rubbed his face. At that moment, he wanted to punch a hole right through the side wall of his office.

Just what was to come from a court of enquiry was anyone's good guess, but, in the end, would it really matter? Plymouth was obviously lost – the Federal reoccupation would only be a matter of time – and the Halifax Yard now in imminent danger. Worse yet, all the land retaken that spring would be handed back to the Yanks, and with it would go the Confederacy's ability to easily feed and supply Lee's army at Petersburg. In short, the *Albemarle*'s demise constituted an unmitigated disaster.

Cooke stared at Warley's report for a long while, then balled it up in the palm of his hand and hurled it across his office in disgust. It bounced once off the far wall then rattled to rest on the floor not far from his feet. He could toss it again, of course, but what was the point? He could heave it a hundred times, he knew, set it ablaze, even cut it into a thousand pieces, but it would never go away.

Chapter Thirty-Five

October 28th – 4:51 P. M.

Cushing ducked away from the road into the dark, shifting shadows of the woods. He moved slowly now, like a fox, from tree to tree, inching closer until there was finally a clear view. He was hungry, tired and cold, but somehow he was able to force his mind to remain clear and focused, and suddenly he liked what he saw.

After hours of painful hiking Will Cushing had at long last reached the Roanoke River again, now far downstream from Plymouth. Through a gap in the trees he'd spotted a Rebel picket post: seven men it appeared from a distance. Just below them he noticed a small skiff tied to a tree in a creek that led out to the river. He quickly ducked behind a bush, lay flat and still on the cold ground, watching. He wanted that skiff.

Cushing had been walking for the better part of the afternoon, and now the sun was starting to dip in the western sky. He guessed it was getting close to 5:00 o'clock. Just beyond him the skiff was dancing lightly on the end of a rope that was tied loosely to a cypress tree on the opposite bank of the creek – an inviting target. On a small knoll further downstream, two of the Confederate pickets had kindled a small fire for supper. Cushing decided to wait. If they all went back to eat their meal together – and if he was very quiet and careful – he reasoned he just might be able to slip down into the water and make off with the skiff unseen.

So Will lay quietly below his bush for another twenty minutes, watching the pickets come and go, counting them all again and again. The possibility they were being observed never seemed to occur to them. The delicious aroma of frying bacon wafted across the creek to him on the breeze, causing his stomach to grind, and he had to force himself to think of something else. It had been over twenty-four hours since he'd had anything to eat, and his body was becoming mutinous.

He heard one of the pickets up by the fire call out to the rest, and gradually the others headed for the path. He watched intently, counted each man as they moved on, then counted them all again as they gathered round the fire. Cushing waited until he heard the distinctive clank that accompanied coffee being poured from a pot into tin cups before sliding out from under the bush. Then he crawled slowly down to the creek and slipped into the water up to his waist. The stream was not deep and he managed to walk across with ease, always mindful to keep the large cypress tree lined up between the pickets and himself to block their view.

Cushing glanced inside the skiff, spotted two paddles, then began to untie the rope attached to the rear of the boat. He was surprised at just how nimbly his fingers moved, pleased by his own self-composure. He made not a sound. In a few seconds he had the knot untied, and he let the line drop gently into the water, all the while careful to remain hidden from view behind the large tree. Then he knelt deeper into the water and began pushing the skiff ahead of him out toward the end of the creek. The pickets never looked back, and he managed to get the boat down the length of the stream without being noticed. Will gained the Roanoke, pushed gingerly around the first bend in the river – a good thirty yards – then rolled into the boat and took up a paddle. For the first time in fifteen hours, he had real hope of returning to the fleet alive.

Soaked and cold to the bone, his spirits soared nevertheless, fed by nothing more than sheer determination.

Cushing began to work the paddle, smoothly slicing the water with each stroke. He moved out to the center of the channel, pleased that dusk was closing like a dark curtain, a low blanket of mist already beginning to form just over the tops of the trees. Soon he would be virtually invisible to pickets on either bank, and then his only worry would be his flagging strength and the desperate sense of exhaustion that was beginning to grip his body. Determination was a wonderful thing, but even Will Cushing realized that determination alone could take him only so far.

Dusk gradually gave way to darkness, and Cushing paddled on into the night, stroke after painful stroke, never stopping to rest. As he traveled downriver his body seemed to fall asleep around him, no longer willing or able to remain aware of the seemingly endless, painful exertion. Only his mind and arms remained alert, working somehow in unison, unwilling to give in to the rigors of fatigue. His mind seemed to expand then, to glow, become luminous, like a bright light over the river, fueling his depleted body by desire alone. Have to remember this, he thought absently – the mind can work miracles.

Around 9:00 o'clock he finally gained the mouth of the Roanoke and paddled his way out into the sound. Normally he would have had great difficulty in such a small craft, but fortunately tonight the skies were clear, winds dormant, and the water was calm. Cushing kept paddling, never stopping, never resting, guiding off two stars toward the location where he hoped to locate the fleet. Finally – and now near delirium – he spotted what appeared to be the running lights of a ship off in the distance.

Another hard half hour of paddling brought Cushing within hailing distance of the lights. Once he was sure he was well within range, he dropped the paddle, cupped his hands around his mouth, and yelled with every last bit of energy he could muster, "Ship ahoy!" Then he collapsed into the bottom of the skiff, insensible.

The next thing Will Cushing knew was the feel of his back slapping hard against the fitted planking of a ship's deck, the closeness and scuffle of men all around him. Cushing opened his eyes, saw what seemed like a hundred faces he did not recognize, smelled the faint, mingled aromas of grog and tobacco smoke circling nearby.

Then he heard a voice call out from somewhere near, "This is what I found in the skiff, Captain. Hell of a mess. Hard to say it's even a man, but I think it is. As much mud as it is man, if you ask me. You might have a look."

"Move aside," came the response, then "Move aside, I say," and Cushing saw the crowd split apart and an officer's face appear, a bushy beard with a pipe sticking out, black eyes narrow and curious. The face hovered above him, came closer, a look of recognition suddenly gleaming in those dark, curious eyes. The officer dropped to his knees. "Oh my God," he said. "Cushing, ... Cushing, is this you?"

Will recognized the officer now as Acting Master Brooks and realized he must have paddled his way back to the *Valley City*. Cushing's eyes were open wide, and he tried to respond, but while he could form the words clearly in his mind, his lips could not bring them to life.

Brooks leaned even closer, stared hard into his eyes. "Cushing," he asked again, the entire crew around him now deathly silent, "is this you?"

Will moved his fingers, blinked, fought to speak. "I ... I … "

"Yes, take your time," Brooks said softly.

"It is I," Will finally managed, then closed his eyes.

Brooks rubbed his whiskers furiously, eyes bulging. "Get *blankets!*" he yelled. "And water, boys. Bring water. And someone call the surgeon. Now! This is *Cushing*, lads, back from the dead. My God, it's *Cushing*!"

They were covering him with blankets now, shoving them under his head and arms, and Brooks was still leaning close. "Lieutenant Cushing," Brooks said, watching approvingly as they wrapped him in warm blankets, "we have all heard. The crew of the cutter came back and reported, but they could not say if your assault was successful. Do you know, Lieutenant? What I'm asking," Brooks went on, "is the *Albemarle*, the ironclad, ... is it sunk? Do you know, was the job ... done?"

Cushing looked up, nodded slowly, felt a smile cross his face. "It is done."

Brooks leaped to his feet, clapped his hands together once with a mighty whack! then whirled about to face his men. He threw one arm in the air triumphantly. "It is *done*!" he bellowed, and the whole crew erupted with an enormous cheer, tossing their caps in the air.

"Lads," Brooks commanded, "I want Lieutenant Cushing taken below to the surgeon's table with the utmost care. Tell the surgeon I will be down in a minute. The lieutenant will need a bath, a good, hot bath, some brandy, and of course some fresh clothes."

Will felt his body being lifted then, a host of men around him, smiling, holding him gently, moving ever so carefully. "We got you, Lieutenant," one said. "Don't you worry now."

Brooks called out to the officer of the deck. "Mister Williams!"

"Sir?"

"I want a message signaled immediately to Commander Macomb aboard the *Shamrock*."

"Yes, sir," Williams replied. "Your message, sir?"

Will put his hand out, wanting to hear, and the men carrying him stopped for a moment.

Brooks turned solemnly, glanced at Will, bowed toward him just slightly. “Tell him ... well, tell him Lieutenant Cushing appears to have returned from the depths of hell ... and the *Albemarle* is no more.”

Chapter Thirty-Six

October 28th – 10:49 P. M.

Cushing stood on the aft deck of the flagship *Shamrock* with Commander Macomb as loud cheers swept across the sound and rockets hissed skyward, exploding in the air above the fleet. It was an extraordinary, spontaneous celebration of pure joy, and one Will Cushing knew he would never forget. Flares and rockets by the score rose in the air from every ship in the squadron, popping and thumping and exploding overhead like a new galaxy of stars, all in response to Cushing's return and the sinking of the Confederate ram. The good news had been signaled and spread like wildfire from ship to ship, touching off new rounds of rejoicing with each passage – Goliath had been slain; the *Albemarle* was no more.

Will had been hurried below decks of the *Valley City* where he had been treated like a visiting noble. After a quick examination by the surgeon, he had bathed, had his feet and hand bandaged, and was then nourished with small amounts of bread and brandy. A new uniform was located, warm sweaters donated, an overcoat hung around his shoulders, and feeling entirely invigorated, he was soon helped on board a small cutter bound for Macomb's flagship. The men who rowed him over, he was told, considered it an honor.

There, as he stepped aboard he was greeted with wild cheers from the same crew that had volunteered to a man to accompany him on his mission two days before. He had destroyed the

Albemarle, been wounded, his uniform virtually blasted from his body, wandered through the jungle-like swamps of North Carolina, only to steal a Rebel skiff and make his way back to the fleet. His story seemed epic, almost beyond belief, and it was already making the rounds. On the deck of the *Shamrock* men stared at him as if in awe, but the truth of it was, Will felt no great pride in what he had accomplished, only relief. Most of all, he simply looked forward to seeing his mother again.

Macomb smiled as the rockets streaked and boomed overhead. "Lieutenant," he said, "tomorrow we are going to go back up the Roanoke and retake Plymouth."

Cushing smiled. "Yes, sir."

"But I want to go over your mission first thing in the morning and get off a report to Admiral Porter. Navy command needs to know what you've accomplished. I want you to get some rest tonight; we'll be at it first thing in the morning."

"Very well, Commander."

"And I'll need to know about those artillery emplacements around Plymouth, along with all the fortifications you saw."

"Of course. But I must say, sir, the Rebel artillery fire was most ineffective. I don't think they even fired at the torpedo launch at all. Not until I was in the water myself did I hear the sound of artillery, and that was very brief and entirely misdirected."

Macomb grinned at him. "Good," he said. "The less capable the Rebels, the better it will be for us."

Cushing laughed. "I'm looking forward to tomorrow."

"Yes, well, you've had quite enough activity for the time being, Lieutenant," Macomb replied with a chuckle. "I'm going to send you back up to Norfolk on the *Valley City.* You're a hero, Lieutenant, whether you know it or not, and I'm not about to risk having you shot before you can enjoy it, or at least file a full report. Gus Fox would have my head and my stripes, not to mention my rear end, if I lost you now."

Will shook his head. "I don't feel a hero, Commander."

Macomb smiled. " Well, you sure as hell *are*, so you'd best get used to it. What you accomplished was, well, remarkable."

"Thank you, sir."

Macomb shook his hand, stepped back, returned Cushing's salute then bid him goodnight.

But the rockets kept soaring, and the men kept cheering, and despite the awful pounding his body had taken, Will was not yet ready for sleep. At that moment, life had become for Will Cushing about as marvelous as he had ever conceived it could be. Only a few hours before he had been struggling just to keep his limbs moving, and more than once he had wondered if he would survive for even another two minutes. No more. As the rockets burst brilliantly in the sky above, as the men hurrahed and the crew stared at him in wonder, William Cushing wondered honestly if it was in any way possible for a human being to feel better than he did at that moment.

Chapter Thirty-Seven

October 30th – Afternoon

Cooke lowered his head and turned away.

"It was not your fault," Mary insisted again, and while he knew she meant well, they were really just words; and no matter how well intentioned, words, he knew, could not alter facts.

"It was my job to prevent such a thing," he said.

"Nonsense!" she said emphatically. "You are a captain, Jim, a commander of an entire department. You give orders, instructions, but others must carry them out. It is not your job to place the cannons, stand guard along the river, or pull the trigger on the musket."

At Mary's suggestion, they had taken a boat up to Edwards Ferry to inspect the new ironclad and get a breath of fresh air – to get away from the Halifax Yard and all the disappointment it seemed now to harbor. But for all the hope that the new ram represented, Cooke's thoughts remained firmly riveted in the past.

"I cannot help it, Mary," he continued, staring out over the tumbling river. "I feel responsible. So many of our hopes rode with the *Albemarle*."

"And now it is gone, so it is time to conjure new hopes, Jim," she told him. "And if I recall, this is the boat that not so long ago represented the future to you. I don't see how that has changed. This boat is still here. The future is *here*."

He nodded, turned and glanced at the wooden frame of the new ram. "Yes, well, I guess that's true," he agreed.

She smiled. "The *Albemarle* was important only for defense, to buy time until the new boat was ready. Am I right? Now look, Jim, the new ram is coming along splendidly."

He folded his arms across his chest. "Yes, Elliott is doing a bang up job," Cooke answered. "He's ahead of schedule."

"Well ahead of schedule, it appears," Mary said.

"Yes."

"So you see, there is still hope."

Cooke frowned. "Yes and no," he replied. "It's true Elliott is well ahead of schedule, but as you can see, all of his work is wood. The ship's framing and wood casement are coming along nicely, but there is still no word on the iron. First we hear one thing, then another. One day it's this, the next day it's that. The iron is supposed to be coming by rail in a few more weeks, but I don't believe it, Mary. What they tell us changes almost daily, and it's not that anyone is lying. They just don't know, or they are told something different every day just as we are. And without the iron the wood boat is utterly useless. I don't know ... "

"You're just gloomy, Jim," she said. "I understand, of course, but you'll get over it."

"I'm not so sure," he protested. "With no iron to cover the boat we are wasting our time here. We work and plan, but I have to wonder, Mary. It's gotten to the point that I feel at times as if we are being asked to spin castles out of cotton."

"Was it not that from the beginning, Jim?" she asked. "And I don't mean the boat."

"Yes, possibly," he agreed. "Things do not look good at all for the Confederacy these days, but never before have I let things affect me so much personally. The loss of the *Albemarle* has changed all of that."

"Because the *Albemarle* was as much your boat as it was Elliott's. It was your sweat and toil as much as anyone's. And it was *that* boat in which you earned your redemption."

"That's true, he agreed."

"But this one is yours too, Jim," she insisted. "It's your design, and Elliot is building it. You and Elliott again. And it will be even more powerful than the *Albemarle*."

"If it ever tastes water, that is."

"Why wouldn't it?" she asked.

"The Yanks have already retaken Plymouth, Mary," he explained. "They know what we are up to here at Edwards Ferry. They will come soon for the ironclad. They cannot afford to let us sit around here unmolested and complete it. And they won't."

"But haven't you fortified the river?"

"Yes, of course," Cooke said. "We're putting in an eighteen gun battery at Rainbow Bluff, and a torpedo nest some three miles below that at Poplar Point. Torpedoes are also being placed at Shad Island Bend and along the shore near Jamesville. And Fort Branch, of course, remains a formidable obstacle."

"So, you see?" Mary said. "You have every right to presume the ironclad will remain safe and sound and delivered on schedule."

"Yes, that's true.... If the iron comes."

She smiled, took his arm in hers. "Face it, you can only do your part, Jim. That's all. Just do your job and hope that others will do theirs. What else can you do?"

He nodded. "I suppose you are right."

"It was not your fault," she told him again.

"I suppose."

"It was just one of those things, Jim."

He frowned, shook his head in protest. "No Mary, it was *not* just one of those things. I still don't know how he did it – how Cushing got through, I mean. It was not just one of those things at all. It was a *hell* of a thing!"

"Does all that really matter anymore?" she demanded. "The *Albemarle* is sunk, and it may be the Confederacy will not be far behind, Jim. I hate to say that, but it's true, I think."

He stared out over the river for a while, thinking it over. "Perhaps," he answered finally. "If Lincoln wins the election then, yes, perhaps. But if McClellan wins ... "

"What do the Yankee papers say?" she asked.

He shrugged. "The election is very close now. Very close."

"Do you think the sinking of the *Albemarle* will help Lincoln?"

"It cannot but help Lincoln. Perhaps a great deal."

"And Cushing?" she asked.

He shook his head forlornly. "I know nothing of Cushing," he replied. "He was not among the list of those captured, and his body was not located by our troops. Two bodies were found. His was not one of them. I suspect he was either killed in the explosion, shot, or perhaps drowned afterward."

She stared at him for a moment then looked away. "It was a very courageous thing, I think. What he did, I mean."

"It was a hell of a courageous thing he did, Mary," Cooke replied. "A most remarkable thing, in fact."

Mary looked him squarely in the face. "Do you hate him for it?" she wanted to know.

"Hate him?" he repeated, surprised by the question. "Hardly, Mary. I admire him for it," he went on. "A great deal, in fact. I have no doubt it will go down as one of the most heroic missions ever conducted by the navy. I would just like to know how the hell he did it."

"Have the papers said anything about him?"

"They only report that he was in charge of the raid. What happened to him, of that there has been no mention. At least so far as I know."

"Do you think there's a chance he ...?"

Cooke smiled. "Survived?"

"Yes."

"Very little, Mary. But there is always ... "

"At least a chance?"

"Yes," Cooke said. "Always a chance. He seems, after all, a most energetic officer. Perhaps ... "

"I hope he got away, Jim," Mary said. "He was just a boy."

He smiled, patted her hand then leaned close to her ear. "I will tell you something very private, very personal, if you promise not to repeat it to anyone."

"You know I don't spill your secrets. Have I ever?"

"No," Cooke admitted.

"What then?"

"Well, last evening after the reports were all in from Plymouth I went down to the river for some time to think by myself. To clear my head, so to speak. I thought about the destruction of the ram, what it meant for the future, then too of Cushing. And just as you said, it occurred to me there might be a chance that he had survived, so I decided to pray."

"You? *Pray?*"

"Yes, Mary," Cooke said. "I will admit, as well you know, that my communications with God Almighty have been somewhat strained and infrequent over the years. I have been at sea since I was a pup, Mary, and there was never much time for all of that. So God and I have never been on familiar terms, so to speak."

"That is to say the least, Jim, but do go on," she said.

"This Lieutenant Cushing and I, Mary, we are both navy men, you see. Same ocean, same water, same ships, same ... risks. What he did, well, ... I understood, admired it actually."

"Yes?"

Well," he continued, looking over his shoulder to be sure no one was near enough to overhear, "I am not sure that praying for the Yankees is exactly a treasonable offense here in the Confederacy, Mary, but if it is, then last night I'm afraid I committed treason."

She smiled into his eyes, took his hand in hers and held it tightly. "You are a fine man and an excellent officer, Jim Cooke," she said. "And I am sure in my heart that if God were to listen to anyone, He would most certainly listen to you. This has become a very bitter war, and few men honestly pray for their enemies anymore."

Cooke smiled, rubbed her fingers gently. "You don't understand entirely," he said.

"What?"

"The boy, Cushing," Cooke replied. "He's never been the enemy, Mary. Not really."

Chapter Thirty-Eight

November 3rd – Afternoon

Lincoln had seen the story in all the papers but had not yet received the official report. So while Nicolay was off on an errand somewhere in the White House, Lincoln leaned over his secretary's desk, grabbed the newspaper, and took a closer look.

The sinking of the *Albemarle* had splashed across headlines from Baltimore to Bangor, and for Abraham Lincoln it could not have come at a better time. From both a military and political perspective – unless Robert E. Lee were to throw down his sword and surrender his army en masse – he could not have asked for more. Not only was the incessant threat of the Confederate ram now removed, but the navy's success rang as yet another clanging bell in the changing fortunes of war – further proof that his administration was firmly set on the right course, and that that course was paying dividends.

In New York, where Cushing's family resided, the lieutenant had been hailed as no less than a conquering hero, and people could not get enough of his escapades. The *Times, Herald, World,* and *Tribune* had all run prominent articles on this latest exploit; Cushing's picture had suddenly become almost as popular as Sherman's. Indeed the headline splashed across the front page of the New York *Times* read **A Bold, Daring and Romantic Feat,** and Cushing was the talk of the town.

William Cushing's courageous assault on the *Albemarle* had captured the nation's fancy, Lincoln's included, and it was easy to understand why. While the North had its share of heroes, few had ever displayed the audacity or dash that many Rebel officers like J. E. B. Stuart or John Mosby had routinely exhibited in the past. The Rebels had men who seemed to thumb their noses at both fear and their Federal adversaries while performing stunning feats of valor. Twice Stuart had ridden his command around the Yankee army – much to McClellan's ire – and Mosby once ambled into a Federal camp near Fairfax, Virginia, and under the nose of the entire encampment had kidnapped the Union general from his bed at gunpoint and ridden off entirely unmolested.

But here was a young Yankee lieutenant whose name alone now sent chills down the backs of every Confederate garrison along the southeastern coast, and whose latest mission was considered by many respected military experts to be one of the most daring ever conceived. Stacked on top of his previous exploits, Cushing was fast becoming one of the most fascinating and romantic figures of the entire war.

On the previous day, Gideon Welles had informed Lincoln that Cushing had in fact survived the assault on the *Albemarle* and somehow managed to make his way back to the Federal Fleet in the sound. The Navy Secretary pointed out that the young lieutenant had been promised a jump of two grades if he were successful in his attempt on the ironclad, but a promotion of that magnitude was something that required presidential approval. To that Lincoln promptly replied that he would gladly jump Cushing twelve grades if the navy would only put the request in front of him, and he meant every word of it.

Lincoln adjusted his glasses, began scanning the article, thinking it interesting that Cushing's exploits had struck such a deep and emotional chord across the whole North. Praise was coming in from every quarter. Politicians, editorial writers, business and civic organizations along with private citizens were all voicing their admiration of Cushing's triumph. In New York and Pennsylvania the cheers were particularly vociferous, and since those states were both considered strong McClellan territory Lincoln immediately took heart. In New York City, the Chamber of Commerce had authorized a resounding testimonial to Cushing, while the Union League of Philadelphia had publicly lauded the lieutenant as a true national hero. Far beyond the usual or traditional rhetoric the press minted at times, Cushing's success seemed to have touched off a genuine national celebration.

The destruction of the *Albemarle* had suddenly galvanized the nation like a bolt of lightning out of the blue, instantly rousing enormous emotion and support. Just how deep those sentiments really ran or would ultimately affect the electorate was hard to gauge, but the final test was fast approaching. In just six days, Lincoln knew, the election would provide his answer.

Chapter Thirty-Nine

November 6th – Evening

Cushing stepped from the train onto the empty platform at Fredonia depot, walking gingerly, his feet still bandaged and painful, his back aching.

The evening already had a chill about it; he noticed a light breeze puffing out of the north. Dry leaves came spinning and swirling across the platform, and he yanked his collar close around his neck. Fall seemed to have already given over to early winter in upstate New York. He even spotted a few light snowflakes tumbling across the road nearby. But then the breeze trailed off just as suddenly as it had come up, the leaves settled, and for a moment the night felt comfortable again. Cushing took a long, deep breath – it was good to be home. In fact, it was good to be alive. Just a few days before, Will Cushing recalled, he had not expected to be either.

Cushing had departed Albemarle Sound on October 30 aboard the *Valley City*, bound for Hampton Roads and a meeting with Admiral Porter. Torpedo launch *No. 2* – the lost picket boat Porter had been furious over days before – was now long forgotten, and Cushing received a hero's welcome. Porter showed him a rough draft of a general order he intended to have read before every officer and sailor in the fleet, heartily commending Will for his effort in sinking the *Albemarle.* And while that was extremely gratifying, the respect in Porter's eyes was more gratifying still.

After making the usual rounds, shaking many, many hands, and being once again checked over by navy surgeons, Will telegraphed his mother from Norfolk. "Mrs. Cushing," he wrote, "Have destroyed Rebel ram *Albemarle.* Am all right. Thanks of Congress, promotion, and fifty thousand (50,000) prize money. W. B. Cushing U. S. N."

After his meeting with Admiral Porter, Cushing had been granted a substantial leave to recover from his wounds. So he had packed his bags and started back up to Fredonia the same way he had come down, with stopovers in Washington, Baltimore, Philadelphia, and New York. Little did he realize just how much of an impact his mission had had on the country until he stepped off the train in Philadelphia.

While walking just outside the train station on Broad Street, Cushing was promptly recognized by a passerby – his picture had been displayed in the local newspapers almost daily – who begged to shake his hand, then turned and began calling to everyone within earshot. In no time at all, Will found himself in the center of an admiring mob; people were pumping his hand, cheering, slapping him on the back. That episode proved to be just the beginning.

All the way up the coast he was recognized, stopped, praised and honored. Women hugged him. Men shook his hand. Crowds gathered to applaud whenever he stopped to eat or take a walk in the street. On a tram in New York City, the passengers all stood and cheered "Hurrah!" on the count of three. Old ladies handed him flowers, young ladies kissed his cheek, and for Will Cushing – just back from the thorny cypress swamps of North Carolina – it had been truly heady stuff.

On the train ride north from New York the acclaim seemed to decrease in almost direct proportion to his distance from the city, until at last he sat in the bumpy car alone as it rumbled to a stop at Fredonia Depot. And that was just fine with Will Cushing. Acclaim, he had discovered, could be just as unnerving as it was inspiring, exhausting as it was invigorating, and since he was not by nature either a vain or public person, he was perfectly content to leave it behind.

He took up his bags and walked slowly down the street toward home, the roads and alleys that first night back seeming somehow as fresh and new to him as if they had just been cast by the hand of God. No small detail escaped his attention, from the branches bouncing overhead in the maples that lined the streets, to the children's wagons left unattended on neighbor's lawns. There were piles of leaves left for burning everywhere, and he breathed in the comforting aroma of wood smoke hanging over the town like an invisible mist. He was home. By God, he was home.

As he walked by one of the yards, Will recalled Alonzo years ago literally pulling him out of a fight by both legs as he scrapped with all three Petersen brothers. Passing another, he remembered chasing a snake through Mrs. White's spring garden when he was no more than ten. Those recollections seemed so fresh and vibrant that they easily could have occurred just yesterday, he thought, and for the first time in his memory they appeared as pleasant thoughts. And that was an odd notion, for Will Cushing had spent so much of his youth in Fredonia throwing fists, that often he had felt like little more than an unwanted intruder in his own hometown.

He turned the corner, spotted his mother's house, and his heart began to beat a bit quicker under his shirt. Will had envisioned the scene in his mind a hundred times already, walking through the door slowly, quietly, then surprising his mother in the kitchen. There had been no time to send a telegram saying when he would be arriving home, and he could only hope his unexpected appearance would not be awkward.

Cushing stopped on the front walk, pulled his jacket down snugly, and set his hat straight on his head. He dusted himself off carefully, then went quickly up the stairs and slid open the door. Will stepped inside. He saw the fire burning low and smoky off to his right, the lamps flickering down the long hallway straight ahead. He smiled, made his way quietly down the hall then, gently pushed open the door to the kitchen. “Surprise!” he yelled.

But no one answered. Will frowned, had a look around, then walked back out of the kitchen into the center hall. “Hello!” he shouted again, but no answer came. Odd, he thought.

Cushing brought his things upstairs to his old room – the one he had shared with Allie for all those wonderful years. Then he took a look throughout the entire house but found no one around. Back in the kitchen he discovered a fresh baked apple pie on the counter, sliced himself a piece, and enjoyed it immensely with a glass of well water from the pitcher his mother always kept handy. He decided to have a look outside.

The town seemed unusually still that night, so he walked along the street, enjoying the sounds and smells of home, He rounded a few corners, then ducked into Mr. Whitaker’s small store. The bell overhead jangled lightly as he closed the door. He walked to the counter.

“Hello,” Cushing called out, “anyone around?”

There came the sudden sound of shuffling from the back room and Whitaker appeared in the narrow hall, walking toward him then, but much smaller and older in appearance than Will recalled. Cushing smiled, nodded pleasantly. “Mister Whitaker,” he said. “You probably don’t recall me, but ... ”

Whitaker stared at him blankly for a moment or two, then the bright flame of recollection danced in his eyes. “Willie?” he asked.

Cushing smiled.

"Oh, Willie," Whitaker said. Then he threw his hands up in the air. "No, no," he went on, correcting himself immediately, "Will, I mean! It's not Willie anymore. And look at you. So tall and polished. An *officer*." Whitaker came out from behind the counter, grabbed Will by both shoulders. "We've all heard," he went on, beaming up at Cushing. "The whole town has heard, Will. What a thing it was you did, sinking that big iron boat like that. All of Fredonia is proud of you, boy. You're a real hero!"

"Well, thank you," Will answered. "Where is everyone, by the way? Seems like the whole town has disappeared."

"Oh, up at the war meeting," Whitaker answered. "Over at the Concert Hall. Once or twice a month now. Lots of talk and news and angry arguing." Whitaker laughed, winked. "I stopped going, but I'm one of the few. Most everyone goes religiously."

"I'm looking for my mother," Will explained.

"Oh, I'm sure you'll find her there, especially what with all the good news coming in lately about you. She's a bit of a celebrity around here now, you know."

Will chuckled. "I'm glad," he said. "She deserves it."

Whitaker patted him on the shoulders again. "You go over to the Concert Hall, Willie, and you'll find her for sure. Just look around. The whole town is there. But listen now, you come back here tomorrow, 'cause I'm gonna have something special for you. A gift. From me to you, from my heart."

"That's kind, Mr. Whitaker," Will protested, "but you really ought not – "

"No, I want to. Something special. Please."

Will nodded slowly. "Sure, all right. Thank you."

The door closed gently behind him and he heard the bell jingle again from within, muffled, as he made his way out into the night. Cushing smiled. He had enjoyed his visit with Whitaker, but he was looking forward to seeing his mother now more than ever. His pace quickened and he cut across a few backyards and up an alley toward the concert hall, forgetting entirely the discomfort of his feet and the sharp pain in his lower back. The doors to the hall were all closed tight as he neared, and the building appeared packed. Outside a few young boys were tossing a ball on the yard. Snowflakes swirled, then settled gently on the grass.

Cushing made his way up the front walk and the boys stopped their game of catch, then watched closely as he approached. Cushing smiled, nodded politely. "Good evening," he said.

To Will's astonishment, the first boy jumped to attention and saluted him, then all the others followed suit.

Will laughed, returned the salute, then bounced up the remaining stairs to the front door.

Inside the hall was both warm and quiet. Straight ahead a man was speaking on stage, urging unity and fortitude and perseverance in an effort to bring the war to a successful conclusion. Will removed his hat, dodged a few onlookers at the rear of the building, then began quietly making his way up the center aisle, searching for his mother.

He had taken no more than ten steps when the speaker stopped in mid-sentence, staring curiously over the top of his bifocals as Will continued toward him. Cushing hesitated, looking left to right, then back again.

Will heard murmurs, followed in turn by the sound of people shifting and moving, low whispers, heads turning toward him. He continued moving slowly toward the stage. Suddenly the speaker – alone and impulsively – began to clap. That was followed by a smattering of applause, then a thunderous ovation, as people turned and recognized just who had entered the hall.

Cushing stopped dead in his tracks, stunned by the commotion. The applause grew, blossomed, bounced and reverberated off the walls and ceiling, rocking the small concert hall like a hard north wind. Then there were whistles, cheers, and foot stomping added to the ruckus, people calling his name, pounding their chairs on the floor. Everyone was standing now, applauding. The noise became almost deafening.

Will stood in the center of this unexpected explosion, truly startled, caught entirely by surprise as a thunderclap of admiration erupted inside the little building like a sudden storm. He had no idea what to say or do, so he simply stood by quietly and said nothing.

Then he spotted his mother at the far end of a near row, her eyes glued to him, hands on her cheeks, tears already streaming down her face. He smiled, fought to control his own emotions, then raised his hat toward her, and with that, the ovation grew even louder.

The applause mushroomed, booming in his ears, drowning out every other sound, thought or emotion, reaching a crescendo of intensity he had not thought possible. No sage or scribe could have conceived a better welcome. It was the most extraordinary moment in his life, and Cushing realized then just what it meant to return from the realm of the dead to the pounding, pulsating, world of the living. He waved his hat toward his mother, then out toward the cheering crowd, and for the first time in his life he felt an enormous sense of affection for them all.

Chapter Forty

November 10th – Evening

Lincoln closed the door, went to his desk, and began examining the election returns one last time.

Lincoln had taken the election from McClellan convincingly – a landslide, many were already calling it – and the final numbers from across the country were certainly received in the White House with an enormous sense of relief. McClellan had managed to carry only three states – Delaware, Kentucky, and New Jersey – resulting in an overwhelming electoral victory of 212 for Lincoln while his opponent managed to garner only 21. Lincoln's staff, the army, and most of the Republican Party promptly hailed the election results a sure-fire mandate for Abraham Lincoln and his policies, but the truth, he knew, lay not too far below all the impressive tallies.

Lincoln leaned back, put his feet up on the corner of his desk, and began studying the numbers. The truth of the matter was, the election had actually been far, far closer than the Electoral College suggested, and while he had taken almost all of the states, most of those contests had in themselves been hotly contested. Indeed, while Lincoln had defeated McClellan handily in the electoral vote, the popular contest – the votes of the people – was not so nearly lopsided. In the end, Lincoln's margin of victory in the popular vote was only some 400,000, 2,203,831 voting for

Lincoln, while a whopping 1,797,019 had gone for McClellan. By any reasonable analysis, those were sobering numbers. Almost half the electorate had voted against him.

Of course, even as late as early September Abraham Lincoln had appeared unelectable, and had the election been held in August rather than November, those victorious election results would no doubt have been reversed. It was military success, plain and simple, that had gotten him back in the game. Those military triumphs had given him the final, narrow margin of victory.

On the night of the election he and Hay had walked over to the telegraph room in the War Department around 7:00 o'clock to begin mulling over the returns. The weather had turned cold and foul earlier that day, a hard rain drumming out of the west, turning all the roads and pathways to mud, and the initial mood in the room had been somber.

The storm continued to play havoc with the telegraph lines for most of the evening, but finally by midnight the results were such that it was safe to assume the election won. The room was very tense throughout the long evening, so Lincoln returned again and again to one of his favorite satirical writers, the famous Petroleum V. Nasby. For hours he regaled the gathering with story after story – although, typically, Stanton found the readings undignified – until the election results were finally solid enough to be trusted.

It was humor that kept him sane, laughter the only medicine capable of driving the darkness and suffering away at times long enough for Lincoln to catch his breath. He loved Nasby, and while some considered his satire to be uncultured drivel, Lincoln often laughed until his stomach ached, and it was that laughter that always changed his frame of mind. God bless Petroleum V. Nasby. Without him he would surely have gone to pieces long ago.

But with the election seemingly won, he put Petroleum away and relaxed, and later that night he spooned out a late night dinner of fried oysters and potatoes for everyone who had stayed up to see the thing through. Lincoln fancied it as fine a victory dinner as he had ever tasted. Then he walked calmly back to the White House to announce the election results to Mary, who had seemed far more nervous over the outcome than he.

Now he had another four years as president to attend to, a desk still covered with papers, and a great deal of work to accomplish. First and foremost, of course, would be the conclusion of the war and the battle over reconstruction. But right along with those two issues would be a fight for an amendment banning slavery from all states and territories. Without that the war might just as well have been fought for nothing, for nothing had really changed the legal status of slaves throughout the country.

In September of 1862, Abraham Lincoln had issued the preliminary proclamation that later became the *Emancipation Proclamation,* a document that changed the nature of the war from a sort of a family squabble into a moral crusade. But predicated as it was on his war powers as Commander in Chief, once the war was over the *Emancipation Proclamation's* legal standing would cease to exist. Indeed, the proclamation had been carefully crafted to take advantage of the well-established authority of the president to confiscate property – friendly or hostile – during a time of crisis in those areas deemed in harm's way. By sticking to the wording of the infamous *Dred Scott* decision of 1857 in which Chief Justice Taney had held that all slaves remained property anywhere in the country, Lincoln was able to use that decision to justify the confiscation of slaves anywhere their existence and activities benefited the Confederate cause – which was in all the *seceded* states. But *only* in those seceded states, Lincoln realized, would the proclamation stand up to judicial scrutiny.

Lincoln knew he had absolutely no legal authority to seize slaves in any of the border or free states – where there was no current insurrection – and thus his proclamation applied only to those jurisdictions that were in active rebellion, and where naturally enough – and for the time being, at least – he had no power to enforce it. But it was at least a start, and in just that manner the *Emancipation Proclamation* served to change the very nature of the conflict.

But no matter how immediately effective or ineffective, the proclamation remained nothing more than a temporary measure. Only an amendment to the constitution could change the legal status of slaves. Lincoln knew it would take a lot of arm-twisting, back room dealing, compromise, and wrangling to yank a sensible amendment out of congress and have it accepted by all the states. Yet without that the future of black Americans would remain legally clouded, perhaps for decades. Lincoln was desperate for abolition, but he wanted it firmly founded on a strong legal framework so that it would never be challenged again. The *Declaration of Independence* had declared that all men were created equal, but for the first eighty years of the republic that "all" had really only meant "white." That was an injustice that tens of thousands of men had now given their lives to change, and it was his intention – as he had stated at Gettysburg the previous November – that those lives would not have been given in vain.

Lincoln flipped to the next page, continued reading. Here he noted that the three crucial states of Ohio, Pennsylvania, and New York had somehow – and remarkably – wound up in his column; those three had provided him a whopping eighty electoral votes. Just days ago he had thought New York lost for sure, and Pennsylvania teetering on the brink, but events had somehow conspired to provide him narrow victories in each.

He had carried New York, for instance, with barely 50.47% of the popular vote, and a close analysis of the three states combined showed that he had managed to secure all those eighty electoral votes with only 52.43% of the popular vote. Those three states had catapulted him to victory, but it was also clear that a very late shift by a very small percentage of the electorate had carried the day in both New York and Pennsylvania. Without that late movement, Lincoln knew he might well have had to deliver the concession note he had written to McClellan in late August, despite the "landslide" his staff was so eager to claim. As the final analysis showed, it had been that close.

But in the end all that really did not matter. The presidency was his again: four more years to resolve the war and bind the nation's wounds.

Jubal Early was now defeated and his army scattered by Phil Sheridan in the Shenandoah Valley, Sherman was marching for the Atlantic coast through Georgia, and Grant still had Lee pinned down at Petersburg. In North Carolina, the *Albemarle* had been destroyed, and now there was talk of a combined operation to take Wilmington, the South's only remaining open port. In the coming months both Sherman's and Sheridan's forces would converge on Lee, and against such odds even the great Rebel commander would not be able to prevail. Surely, Lee would fight on to the bitter end, but now the writing was on the wall for all to see, and that end was rapidly approaching. The Southern government and her armies could last at best another six months, and that was a fact he attributed, not to his own efforts and policies, but to the selfless efforts of a million or so men in uniform. For the first time in the history of the world, a free and democratic people, – given two clear choices – had *voted* to continue a bloody, destructive war, and soon, God willing, it would be concluded.

Earlier that evening a crowd had come up and gathered round the White House, many carrying candles, waving banners, and chanting his name. It was an inspirational scene, and when they called for him, Lincoln went out and gave them a speech that he had recently prepared. He talked of many things, but the one thing that he tried to emphasize, above all else, was the lesson that he had learned over the last four years. "Humanity will not change," he told them. "In any future great national trial, compared with the men of this, we shall have as weak, and as strong; as silly and as wise; as bad and good ... Gold is good in its place; but living, brave, patriotic men, are better than gold." And so it was. And soon, he knew, those good, patriotic men would whip the insurgent Confederate government once and for all.

Then the truly great work would begin. No longer war, but peace. No longer fear, hate, and anger, but compassion. No longer enemies, but countrymen again. Lincoln closed his eyes and whispered a short prayer. How he looked forward to that day.

Chapter Forty-One

December 15th – Afternoon

Lincoln slowly worked his way through two thick stacks of paper, one awaiting his approval for promotions, the other his consideration on pardons. As always, the pardons were the hardest to get through, each case often representing a life and death decision that required all his power of concentration, lest he miss a minor point somewhere and make a terrible mistake, perhaps sending a decent man off to an indecent death. So he generally attended to those first, in the morning when he was fresh and his mind clear, then moved on to the promotions later in the afternoon.

The work never ended, and his exhaustion appeared to be deepening by the day. His first four years in office seemed to have taken a toll on him from which he might never recover. In October, Chief Justice Taney had passed away, and for months now Lincoln had been receiving delegations, pleadings, suggestions, and encouragement concerning who should be named as his replacement. Lincoln had made his choice early in the process, but had played that choice very close to his vest. He had decided upon Salmon Chase, the very man he had dispatched from his cabinet just months before, and on December 6 he finally made the announcement – much to the surprise and delight of the party faithful.

Lincoln bore Chase no animosity – life was far too short, he reasoned, for grudges. Yes, Chase was ambitious, but if ambition was a vice then Lincoln was himself nothing less than evil. Most intelligent men were also enterprising, he knew, and Chase's appointment only underscored his belief that men ought to be used in accordance with their qualifications regardless of their personal feelings toward him, or vice versa. Chase was extremely bright, motivated, and a solid backer of emancipation, and thus a good man to lead the high court once the war ended and litigation concerning slavery began rattling courthouse doors across the land.

Outside, Lincoln noticed a light snow beginning to fall, slowly covering the White House lawn, and – despite all his high hopes – he knew that conditions were not conducive to a final victory during the cold, muddy months of winter. Come spring, however, things would change dramatically, and hopefully the war would then be resolved once and for all.

Sherman was still marching through Georgia, and he had not been heard from in weeks, having disappeared off the map on his way across country toward Savannah. Many local and foreign writers were despairing of Sherman's silence, being of the opinion that it was proof positive of disaster, but Lincoln had faith that his general would soon appear on the east coast, then turn north toward South Carolina. That would surely signify the beginning of the end of the Southern Confederacy. With Sherman gutting the Carolinas while moving north toward Lee, and Sheridan marching south through the Shenandoah toward Richmond, Lee's Army of Northern Virginia would soon be swamped by massive Federal forces arriving from every direction. If, of course, some dreadful disaster had not befallen Sherman and his army traversing the backwoods of Georgia; that would be a debacle that would change everything. Yes, it was something else to worry about.

Lincoln watched absently as the snow collected gently on the sill nearby. A sudden recollection came to him of the winter storms he'd ridden through so many years ago while on circuit in Illinois, wind-driven and much colder, it seemed to him, than these mostly mild Eastern winters. He could almost feel the wind whipping against his face, the snow blowing up under his coat, snaking down his collar. Abraham Lincoln closed his eyes, shivered once, and then just as suddenly the wind and snow disappeared entirely from his thoughts, and his mind drifted back to more pleasant times.

Lincoln recalled with captivating clarity spring dances, pretty girls, that first night he'd met Mary; and it all returned to him so vividly that for a moment it seemed that, if he were to just hold out his hand, he might touch the lace on her dress again. He hung there in the past for a few moments more, recalling the sounds, tastes, and aromas of it all, and in one way those events seemed to Lincoln just like yesterday, yet, in another, so long ago that they could have occurred in a different lifetime – an odd thing, the past. He opened his eyes then and shook his head. Where had all that gone? His past seemed to be becoming hazier by the day. Time, he realized, was slipping away.

Lincoln suddenly felt sad – he hardly saw Mary anymore. If time permitted, he stopped by and spoke to her briefly at night before turning in, but time rarely permitted much of that these days, and their relationship had grown distant. He still loved her, but she was becoming more flighty and irrational by the day and he could no longer trust her to remain silent about important matters. So he had to be even more careful with her than with the others, and their time together had become more of a strain than the satisfaction of it was worth. And that was sad.

More than anything, however, it was simply the work that kept him away, twenty-hour days, day after day, and only the end of the war might bring an end to that. If he survived both the war and his second term, he would make it up to her, he thought. Maybe they'd buy a farm along a wide, slow river somewhere – the Wabash, Mississippi, or Illinois – and he'd take up farming and practice law again. Then he would come home early and they would laugh and sit and have dinner together like those days so long ago. That would be nice – if he survived, that was. He sighed, tried to forget the sadness. Then he turned away from the snow and spotted the other stack of papers on his desk.

Promotions, like birthdays or weddings, were far more pleasant work than pardons, and he always enjoyed dealing with the accomplishments of the troops. While many of the requests that came across his desk were political in nature, many were not, the latter often representing truly remarkable achievements of his officers and men. Those were the promotions he particularly enjoyed bestowing, and for days now he had been looking for one in particular.

Lincoln picked up the top file, flipped the folder open and looked it over quickly. This one was for a Captain named Johnson in Hancock's corps who had captured six Rebels at Cold Harbor, and while Lincoln was sure Johnson was a fine officer, he laid the file aside for the moment and began digging deeper. He thumbed through four or five, then spotted a request from the Secretary of the Navy that appeared more promising. Lincoln yanked it out for closer inspection, saw the name he had been looking for all along, and smiled. Cushing, yes; this was it.

He read the request carefully, picked up his pen and began to write, when an odd thought suddenly struck him. He put the pen back down again.

Lincoln tried to remember what the boy had looked like so many years ago. He knew he had met him, but no matter how hard he focused, he could not bring back the image. He closed his eyes, rubbed his face, tried to force the memory from the depths of his brain, but no amount of concentration seemed to work. If he had not seen Cushing's picture in the paper recently he would have drawn a complete blank, and now every time he tried to conjure the young lieutenant's face, it was the picture in the paper he saw, not the young man who had sat in front of him years before. Perhaps it was just fatigue, he thought. There were so many meetings these days, appointments ... faces.

Just days prior to the election Cushing had completed one of the most stunning and newsworthy missions of the war. His success had made headlines all across the country, and there was no telling just how much of an impact the destruction of the ironclad had had on the voting. As close as the election had been, every last vote counted, and there was little doubt the sinking of the *Albemarle* had turned more than a few heads – and votes. Yes, this promotion would be a pleasure. Abraham Lincoln took up the pen again, wrote –

> *To the Senate and House of Representatives:*
>
> In conformity to the law of the 16th July, 1862, I most cordially recommend that Lieutenant William B. Cushing, U. S. Navy, receive a vote of thanks from Congress for his important, gallant, and perilous achievement in destroying the rebel ironclad steamer *Albemarle* on the night of the 27th October, 1864, at Plymouth, N. C. The destruction of so formidable a vessel, which had resisted the continued attacks of a number of our vessels on former occasions, is an important event touching our future naval and military operations, and would reflect honor on any officer, and redounds to the credit of this young officer and the few brave comrades who assisted in this successful and daring undertaking.

This recommendation is specially made in order to comply with the requirements of the ninth section of the aforesaid act, which is in the following words, viz: That any line officer of the Navy or Marine Corps may be advanced one grade, if, upon recommendation of the President by name, he received the thanks of Congress for highly distinguished conduct in conflict with the enemy, or, for extraordinary heroism in the line of his profession.

ABRAHAM LINCOLN.
WASHINGTON CITY, *December 15, 1864*

He read it over twice and was about to place it in his outgoing mail when there was a sharp rap on the door. Lincoln looked up. "Yes."

The door cracked open slightly. "General Halleck is here with an important message, sir," Hay explained.

Lincoln nodded, waved. "Well then, send him in."

Halleck entered, clearly excited, telegram in hand. He was virtually beaming from ear to ear, and Lincoln thought that very odd for the dowdy, impersonal Halleck. "I thought you would want to know immediately," the general said.

"Know what?" Lincoln replied.

Halleck grinned, he could hardly contain himself. "It's from General Howard, sir, with Sherman's advance."

Lincoln felt his heart quicken, put out his hand, took the telegram. Was it news from Sherman? He stared up at Halleck. "Good news, I trust?"

"Good news, Mister President," Halleck affirmed. "Yes, very good news. You will see that the telegram is dated the 10th, sent from just outside Savannah."

"Savannah?" Lincoln repeated.

"Yes."

Lincoln adjusted his glasses, read.

> We have met with perfect success thus far. Troops in fine spirit and General Sherman nearby.
>
> Gen. O. O. Howard.

So, it was done. For over thirty days, and across 300 miles of hostile, enemy country, Sherman had marched his army with no supplies or provisions except for what he could strip from the land, and now he had reappeared on the Atlantic Coast like a rabbit popping from a magician's hat. This extraordinary success could not be overstated. The meaning to Lincoln was crystal clear. Soon Sherman, with his 90,000-man army, would march toward Lee from the south. Then the Confederate commander could either surrender or be crushed, and there could be no logical outcome to that scenario other than victory for the North, for union, and, yes, for emancipation.

All the years of work, blood, and tragedy finally appeared to be resolving toward a favorable conclusion. Soon the war would end, the country be reunited, and emancipation made a reality. And he owed it all, he knew, to the heroism and perseverance of the officers and men of the army and navy, who had never backed away from the task, and who had supported his candidacy – not with windy speeches or the empty talk of the political class – but with their fortunes, blood, and lives.

Lincoln put the telegram down, recalled suddenly the request in his other hand, and stood up abruptly.

"Can I help you with something, sir?" Halleck asked.

Lincoln smiled. "No," he answered, "I'm going to see to this myself."

He walked out of his office and handed Cushing's folder over to John Hay. "I want you to personally see that this gets delivered to Congress," Lincoln said. "Personally."

"Of course, sir."

Then Lincoln turned, nodded toward Henry Halleck, and walked back into his office, closing the door gently behind him. There he went to the window, watched as the snow gradually accumulated on the lawn, and a smile slowly wound its way across his face.

Sherman was now outside Savannah – what marvelous news! For the first time that he could recall, the weight on his shoulders seemed to have actually decreased. The smile on his face grew, and for a moment a sense of almost ungoverned joy rose in his chest. The feeling was so sudden and unexpected that it caught him by surprise. Lincoln clapped his hands together once joyfully and laughed out loud. Then he noticed that his reflection in the window had tears running down the cheeks, that those tears just kept falling, and the picture really made no sense to him because he felt so light and joyous. But jangled up with all that joy, he knew, was so much grief that the two were now inseparable, and the tears just kept falling, rolling down and across that silly smile of his, and for a few, awkward minutes Abraham Lincoln could do nothing more than stand back and watch himself cry like some strange, immaterial witness to his own tortured existence.

So he stood by the window for a few minutes more, watching the tears wash across that sad face in the glass as white snowflakes fell and collected on the ledge outside, all as silent as the distant moon. For the first time in four long years Abraham Lincoln let slip away the smallest piece of that awful pain that consumed him, and he would have loved to have ridded himself of it all, but soon he broke away and walked back to his desk. To free himself of all that misery was, Lincoln knew, an impossible task. No, there were not enough hours in the year, nor tears in the infinite heavens, to purge all that misery from his soul.

Chapter Forty-Two

December 25th – Afternoon

Cushing sat calmly in the stern of the boat as shell after shell exploded in the river nearby, sending angry spouts of water towering high in the air and crashing down on the cutter.

"Hard to starboard!" Cushing called out, and the men strained at the oars again, jerking the small craft around one more time as another round of shells came screaming through the air like disembodied fiends. This time the huge shells flew wide, missing the mark, detonating in the water some forty yards off their stern in great, watery plumes. The spray washed back over them like a hard rain, but the men continued rowing, and the guns kept booming, and Will Cushing sat in the stern of the boat, legs crossed comfortably. This was not war. This was fun.

After almost a month at home on leave, Cushing had returned to duty with the new rank of lieutenant commander, and he was promptly placed in charge of Admiral Porter's flagship, the *Malvern,* on an expedition to seize Wilmington, N. C. He had received the Thanks of Congress – made official on the 20th of December – and the promise of $50,000 in prize money, and while his back was still hurting from the explosion of the *Albemarle,* his feet had recovered nicely. But ferrying the admiral around was not exactly to Cushing's taste, and when volunteers were asked to undertake a dangerous mission on the channel immediately below the daunting guns of Fort Fisher outside of Wilmington, Will immediately applied.

Fort Fisher was one of the keys to gaining open access to Wilmington's inner harbor defenses, but the initial combined ground and naval assault had become bogged down early on Christmas Day, after an enormous naval bombardment had failed to even dent the fort's massive walls. General Benjamin Butler – in charge of the Federal infantry forces – asked Admiral Porter if the navy could slip a few boats past the fort and begin a bombardment from the rear, but the original channel had become so clogged with sunken wrecks that it was virtually impassable, and a new channel had to be sounded, charted, and marked before the mission could even be considered. Such a task required a laborious trek across the channel while in clear range of the fort's guns, a job that was hazardous to the extreme, but one that sounded curiously interesting to William Cushing.

At 1 o'clock that afternoon they had shoved off from the *Malvern* and for over two hours now he had been sitting in the rear of the cutter as shells whooshed, banged, and exploded all around him. While the artillery rounds had sprayed volumes of water into the small craft, so far there had been no direct hits, and no one in his cutter had been injured. Cushing had directed his oarsmen to row in a sort of crazy, haphazard pattern that kept the Confederate gunners from getting the cutter square in their sites, and while one of the assisting boats had been struck – and one sailor killed – Will's boat only required bailing out from time to time in order to keep up the work.

Cushing had selected the cutter earlier that morning, quickly had it fitted out with lead lines, buoys, and grappling irons, then had the blue and white pennant of a commanding officer raised high overhead. Will put on his finest uniform along with every piece of gold braid his new rank entitled him to wear. Then, sitting coolly astern like Lord Nelson at Trafalgar, and with a sailor in the bow tossing out the sounding lead and calling back the various depths, Cushing headed straight for the waters below the fort. For over ten minutes not a gun responded, the Rebels apparently stunned inert by this brazen act of daring unfolding right below their very noses. But then the gunners finally came to their senses, and the big guns began to roar.

By maintaining the haphazard, zigzag course that followed no particular pattern, Will had been able so far to utterly confound the Rebel marksmen while sounding a narrow course through the channel and marking it clearly with buoys. The guns on the walls above had kept up a steady thunder all afternoon – it was apparent that the Confederates were infuriated by his impertinence – but he paid them no mind and kept the cutter moving closer and closer to the thick walls of the fort.

Cushing smiled mischievously, crossed then re-crossed his legs. "Hard to port!" he ordered, "and row straight for the walls!"

The helmsman jerked about and stared at Will curiously. "How close, Commander?" he asked, wiping the foamy water from his face with the back of his hand.

"I'll tell you when to stop," Will replied.

"Aye, aye, Commander."

The men pulled hard on the oars, and the cutter made its way quickly toward the towering walls of the fort, a monstrous edifice built in a configuration somewhat like a giant number 7. The short, or top, portion of the seven was some 480 yards long, while the lower section stretched out over 1300 yards. The walls were 25 feet thick and 32 feet high in places, and all were amply appointed with large naval guns that commanded all approaches. Fisher was one of the most imposing fortifications in the Confederacy, and as he approached the bastion Will considered this an opportune moment to make a good, close inspection of the defenses.

So when the cutter got near enough to the shore that they could virtually spit and hit the walls, Cushing finally ordered the oarsmen to cease rowing. Around the boat, shells continued to rain, howling overhead or bursting in the water nearby, but the cutter was now so near the walls of the fort that the guns above them could not be depressed to an angle low enough to bring the cutter in range. So the shells flew high and wide, drenching the cutter from time to time in waves and torrents of water, but causing no real harm.

As the men eased off the oars Cushing stood in the stern of the craft, hands on hips, making a careful inspection of the fort's defenses, taking it all in coolly from a distance close enough that the Confederates could have thrown rocks or shoes or spoons to hit him. High above, the frantic gun crews hurled round after round in his direction, and while the boat had to be bailed out twice, in the end all the Rebel efforts proved futile. Unhurried and unfazed by the thunderous shelling, Cushing floated under the fort's guns for almost thirty minutes, eyeing every angle and crevice of the structure. Once Will was finally satisfied with his reconnaissance, he sat back down and ordered the crew to begin anew the zigzag course that led them back out across the channel.

And so it went. For a full six hours Will Cushing sat under the guns of Fort Fischer, calmly sounding, charting, and marking the new channel as frustrated Confederate gunners repeatedly fired at and missed his every move. With the channel fully marked by buoys and the sun long gone below the horizon, he finally ordered his crew back to the *Malvern* for their evening meal. They were all soaked and exhausted, but not one man on the cutter had been hurt. For those sailors who had volunteered to go with him, it had been the experience of a lifetime, and as Will Cushing waved goodbye to the irate Rebel gunners above, the cutter slowly headed back out the New Inlet channel toward the Atlantic.

As Cushing climbed back aboard the flagship, he ran head first into Admiral Porter, waiting curiously for him by the rail. The admiral said nothing at all, just stood and stared at Will with a look of absolute wonder on his face, a rarity for an officer as tough and experienced as Porter.

Will smiled, then saluted smartly. "I've got your channel all marked out and sounded, Admiral," he said. "But I'm afraid what little there is of it is awfully shallow."

"Yes, very good," Porter replied, the strained look of disbelief still etched across his features. The admiral shook his head, searching, it appeared, for the right words with which to convey his amazement. "Commander Cushing," he started finally, "it has been six hours for you and your crew directly under the fort's guns. I watched almost all of it. Well done, I must say. Was it, perhaps, a bit ... ah, hot for you out there today?"

"Hot?" Cushing replied. "No, not really, Admiral. "Pity though ... "

"Pity? Yes, yes, why's that?" Porter demanded.

"Well, I will admit I'm somewhat put out with the Rebel gunners," Cushing said.

"Put out? I see, go on."

"You see, Admiral," Cushing explained, holding up his arm as an exhibit, "I must admit they're far better shots than I initially gave them credit for. They actually got me wet, and I wasn't planning on that at all."

"*Wet?*"

"Yes," Will replied, "and now I'll have to change. So if you're planning a full-scale invasion of the place, I have but one suggestion."

Porter eyed him curiously."And that would be?"

"Tell the lads to pack an extra pair of socks," Will said. "They just might come in handy."

Porter broke into a grin – a not entirely admiral-like thing to do – then fought it off, and returned for the moment to his usual somber pose. "Thank you, Commander," he said. "I will most certainly take your suggestion into consideration."

"My pleasure, sir," Cushing said, then turned and headed below decks as the officers and crew of the *Malvern* stared in wonder.

Chapter Forty-Three

December 30th – Morning

Cooke briefly scanned the report one last time, then balled it up and threw it across the room.

"He did *what!*" Cooke screamed at the top of his lungs. "O'Malley, are you telling me this report is correct?"

Lieutenant O'Malley appeared at his office door. "That's all we have right now, Captain," the lieutenant answered sheepishly. "I don't know what else you want me to say. I knew you wouldn't be pleased."

Cooke kicked a chair halfway across the room. "Pleased?" he bellowed. "I want you to tell me this didn't *happen*!"

"I believe, sir ... it did."

Cooke tossed his hands in the air. "Wilmington is the last open port we have, and it is absolutely essential for our survival. If Wilmington falls, the Confederacy will not be far behind. Fort Fisher is supposed to be *the* citadel that guards Wilmington harbor, a fortress absolutely impervious to attack, armed to withstand a full-scale Federal assault. And now I am told that Cushing simply had himself rowed out across the channel to a location only *yards* away from the outer walls, stood up in the stern of his boat, and *studied* our defenses for the better part of an hour!"

"Yes, that's about the size of it, Captain."

"God damn it!" Cooke cried. "How could that *happen*?"

"I don't know, sir," the lieutenant replied. "Perhaps you should ... "

But Cooke wasn't interested in any half-baked suggestions. "Well, doesn't that bring into question the effectiveness of our defenses, Lieutenant?" he demanded. "I mean, for years now we have been telling ourselves that Wilmington was invulnerable, but if a single Federal officer can simply have himself rowed unmolested across the very waters that are supposed to be *death* to anything that enters, then does it not follow logically that the entire Federal fleet might just up and do exactly the same thing?"

"Yes, Captain," O'Malley replied, "I believe that would be an entirely reasonable conclusion."

Cooke rolled his eyes. "Tell me, Lieutenant, did you read the entire report?"

"I did, sir."

Cooke yanked the bifocals from his nose and glared up at the young officer. "Then correct me if I am wrong, but did it not say that he simply stood in his boat as shells from our guns repeatedly missed his craft and took down *notes* about our defenses?"

"Yes, yes, it did, sir."

"I see," Cooke said. "And that for over six hours Cushing and his small crew marked a channel through New Inlet, and that not *once* – not even *once*!" – were our vaunted artillery crews able to strike his craft during that entire six hour period, even though the Yankees were close enough to shore that a child with a *sling-shot* could have played havoc with them?"

"Yes, Captain, those are essentially the facts."

Cooke shook his head, rubbed his face. "My God," he moaned. "Then tell me this, Lieutenant, did the report go on to say anything to the effect that while Lieutenant Cushing – wait, I'm sorry, it's now *Commander* Cushing – was under our lethal fire that he, perhaps, had himself rowed close enough to the structure so that he could actually *relieve* himself on the walls of Fort Fisher while our shells were bursting in the water around him?"

"No, sir. I don't recall such a report as that."

"No?"

"No, sir," the lieutenant reaffirmed.

"But he may as well have done it?" Cooke offered disgustedly. "Aye?"

O'Malley smiled. "Yes, I suppose he may as well have."

Cooke looked up and smiled himself. "Yes. Yes, he may just as well have pissed on the walls of our impregnable fort, if you ask me, while our jolly defenders hooted and scratched themselves like a pack of silly monkeys. What in the hell is going on here?"

The lieutenant rolled his shoulders hopelessly. "I don't know, Captain."

Cooke fixed his head between his two hands as if in a vice and frowned miserably. "Do you grasp just how incompetent we appear in all this, Lieutenant?"

"Perfectly, sir," came the response.

Cooke chuckled. "All I can say is thank God the fort's garrisons are not under my jurisdiction or command. I have no idea what I would tell Richmond if all this were my responsibility. Thank God for that!"

"Yes, sir."

Jim Cooke laughed. "Cushing has made us look once again like a bunch of ... "

"Jackasses, sir?" O'Malley suggested.

Cooke thought that over a moment then shook his head. "No, I don't think so," he replied. "You see, Lieutenant, I believe that in *six* hours even a few crews of half-trained *jackasses* could have hit that boat at least *once*. No, it's worse than that. Much worse! In fact," Cooke continued, "I believe your inference, while obviously meaning no harm, might well be taken as an unfair slander on jackasses everywhere in the world."

The lieutenant laughed out loud. "Sir," he said, "I can assure you, I meant no insult to any man or beast. It's just that my vocabulary does not range beyond jackass as a noun capable of embracing such utter ineptitude as has been here demonstrated."

"Yes," Cooke agreed, mulling the problem over. "I agree. But you see now, Lieutenant, your vocabulary may soon be in for an abrupt expansion."

"How's that, Captain?"

"We may have unwittingly coined a new synonym for gross incompetence, Lieutenant. You see, in the future, when words like jackass simply fail us, when terms such as blockhead, nitwit or imbecile no longer capture the essence of our dismay, the phrase 'Confederate gun crew' might now be inserted into any derogatory sentence or disparaging exclamation, with absolute satisfaction and what we might call descriptive precision."

The lieutenant chuckled. "Well, I pray it's not really so bad as all that," he said.

Cooke looked up. "Six hours?"

Lieutenant O'Malley frowned. "Yes, well, but not everyone knows about all that, Captain."

Jim Cooke thought that over. "True," he agreed finally. "You make a good point, Lieutenant. And let's keep it that way. The less said the better."

"I agree entirely, sir. You may rest assured, my lips are sealed."

Cooke leaned back in his chair as the lieutenant made for the door, and considered again just how rapidly the situation for the Confederacy had deteriorated. It was time to take stock.

On December 9, a combined land and water effort to open the upper Roanoke had begun, the Federal fleet moving north from Plymouth, while a land force marched in concert from Williamston to Hamilton. The Yankee infantry had been driven back, while the naval force ran afoul of the torpedo nests Cooke had ordered in place after the sinking of the *Albemarle.* So, for the time being at least, the Halifax Yard remained intact, but everyone knew the Yankees would try again soon.

Far worse, Cooke knew, was the news that Sherman had marched his army across Georgia all the way to the Atlantic coast. From there, Sherman could immediately establish a new waterborne supply line and then begin pushing north. In North Carolina, Confederate forces were already stretched extremely thin, and it would be impossible for them to oppose both Sherman and an assault on Wilmington simultaneously. While the initial Federal assault on Wilmington had failed through a lack of cohesion on the part of the combined Union forces, Cooke knew that Wilmington was far too important a port for the Yankees to ignore for long. They would be back in an attempt to close it for good. But if they were strenuously opposed at Wilmington, then Sherman would move through the center of the state unopposed, while if enough force was marshaled to resist Sherman, then Wilmington would fall in mere days.

So as the last few days of 1864 dwindled away, James Cooke realized that the calendar was running out for the Confederacy as well. The ram at Edward's Ferry was well on its way to completion, but no iron had yet arrived for the casement, and, even if it came in tomorrow, that job would still require weeks to complete. Soon the Yankees would send another land force that could not be resisted by the scant troops available for the job, and then the ram would be destroyed, and all hope of reclaiming the sounds would go up in smoke right along with it. Like being checked in a game of chess, every potential move still open to the Confederacy appeared already covered by two or three converging Federal pieces, the ultimate outcome all too grimly apparent – checkmate.

The Confederacy had survived on hope and pluck and dash for almost three years, but now Robert E. Lee was at best clinging to his lines around Petersburg by his fingernails while Johnston's army in Tennessee was but a shadow of its former self. Hope was fading daily, daring a thing of the past, and all that pluck buried in sad, shallow graves somewhere between the Susquehanna and the James.

Cooke had already made up his mind. When the end came he would fire the new ironclad himself, then grab Mary and the boys and move inland as far as he could from Federal control. How the men and officers of the Confederacy would be treated by Lincoln's government was anyone's good guess, but if push came to shove, he was prepared to flee overseas. Such, he knew, were the wages of failed rebellions.

Cooke went and poured himself another cup of what today passed for coffee in the Confederacy, stood by the window, and watched as the men outside cut and hammered and sawed. Sad, he thought. He had really enjoyed his time at the Halifax Yard, loved watching the boats come together, emerging from nothing more than thin air, it seemed at times; forms crafted from the creative alchemy of wood, labor, and mind. But he could see now it was not to be. Perhaps Mary had been right all along, he thought. All they had been doing was trying to spin castles from cotton, and in the end those sorts of enterprises always seemed to fail, fated to collapse from nothing more substantial than their own critical lack of substance.

No, he had not been one of the hotheads who had screamed for secession so many springs before, but now by force of fate and character he would have to follow that bitter cause to its own bloody end. But then again, he'd had the opportunity to captain the CSS *Albemarle,* and in a strange way that seemed to have made it all worthwhile. Many, he knew, would stew for years over the looming Confederate defeat, but he would not be numbered among them.

Still, he was an officer and a fighter, and he would see the rebellion through to its inevitable, mournful conclusion. Outside in the yard there was still much work to be done. So James Cooke put the cup down and went back to his small, dusty office. This work was a rare pleasure, yet one that all too soon, he knew, would be lost to him forever.

Chapter Forty-Four

February 21st – Late Afternoon

Cushing walked down the street toward the Naval Department in Washington City with an armful of dispatches to deliver personally to the Secretary of the Navy.

He had left the *Monticello* behind in Norfolk, to be specially outfitted with a torpedo at the request of Admiral Porter, and then headed north to Washington with word of the fall of Fort Anderson, the last critical bastion guarding Wilmington harbor. After Will Cushing's expedition under the guns of Fort Fisher, Porter had promptly decided that Will's talents were being wasted as commander of the admiral's flagship, and with reports that another Rebel ironclad – the *Stonewall* – had left Bordeaux, France bound for the Caribbean, Cushing was immediately chosen as the preferred weapon of interdiction. So Will was once again given command of the *Monticello*, and handed a passel of dispatches Porter wanted hand delivered to Secretary Welles while the ship was being refitted.

It had been an interesting few months. When the initial assault on Fort Fisher failed, Admiral Porter had withdrawn his fleet a short distance, then pleaded with General Grant for additional support. On January 8, that support had arrived in the person of General Alfred Terry – in place of the incompetent General Benjamin Butler whom Lincoln had finally sacked – and some

8,000 fresh infantrymen with orders to press the matter to a conclusion. On January 13, the fleet began an all day bombardment of the fort, knocking out virtually every gun except one, breaching the walls, and wrecking the minefield below the edifice – inflicting more damage than any preceding bombardment in the history of naval warfare. An initial wave of over 200 boats ferried the infantry ashore, and by day's end the fall of Fort Fisher appeared imminent.

Porter, however, apparently wanting a share of the laurels, abruptly mustered a 2,000-man force of marines and sailors that was landed on the seaward side of the citadel with orders to assault the main walls. Cushing had wangled himself a position with the first wave and went ashore with the marines, but almost immediately the assault became pinned down on the beach. During the assault, Will was everywhere, leading men forward, pulling out the wounded, rallying sailors over and over again. But the marine sharpshooters were unable to subdue the Confederate gunners on the walls and parapets, and the sailors – armed only with pistols and cutlasses – were no match for the Confederate marksmen. Suffering almost 300 dead and wounded, the landing force was cut to pieces, but did at least succeed in creating enough of a diversion to allow the infantry to breach the fort's defenses from the other side. Fort Fisher surrendered on January 15.

Fort Anderson, situated on the southern bank of the Cape Fear River, posed a different problem entirely. While it was smaller and less daunting than Fisher, by the time Admiral Porter was ready to move on it much of his fleet had been dispersed to other theaters, and he did not consider his forces sufficiently powerful to take the position by storm. Not wishing to repeat the debacle he had initiated at Fort Fisher, other means were deemed necessary, and William Cushing was happy to supply those means.

Will had suggested a mock monitor: a fake ironclad constructed on the body of a flatboat, utilizing barrel staves floating a canvas cover to make the boat appear genuine from a distance. Indeed, when finally completed, from a range of some two hundred yards Cushing thought it impossible to discern the fake monitor from the real thing. If the canvas monitor could then be floated upstream on the tide, past the fort, the Confederates might consider Anderson no longer defendable, because if a real monitor were to gain the waters above them, the Rebel's water route to Wilmington would be cut off. Additionally, the mere appearance of a Federal ironclad on the Cape Fear would no doubt be interpreted as only the initial phase of an impending large-scale assault, something the Rebels would certainly want to avoid.

The plan worked flawlessly. On February 18, Will took a specially picked crew from the *Monticello* and towed the fake monitor into position, a few hundred yards below the obstructions at Fort Anderson. Then they let it float off on the tide, and the monitor glided in front of the fort as if steaming ahead under its own power. The Rebels opened up with everything they had, but those few shots that struck the monitor simply cut through the canvass and did no damage. The Confederates also fired off a dozen or so torpedoes, but all those missed. The canvas monitor eventually floated around a bend in the river and ultimately beached itself far beyond the fort's observation towers, exactly as Cushing had predicted – a perfect performance!

That evening, assuming that the fort was now cut off from Wilmington by water and a large Yankee force was likely to strike at any moment, the Rebels hastily abandoned Fort Anderson, not even taking time to spike the large naval guns that gazed out over the water. The Confederates swore like pirates when they discovered Cushing's ruse, but by then it was far too late. The next day Federal forces marched unopposed into Fort Anderson, and on

February 21, Wilmington – the last open Rebel port on over 3549 miles of Confederate coastline – finally fell. At long last the blockade was complete and the Southern shoreline sealed down tight as a drum. With Richmond now cut off from its last significant source of supply, and Sherman's army moving up through the Carolinas, Will Cushing realized that the end of the war could not be far away. In some ways the thought of that made him almost euphoric, in others it made him sad.

"Well, well, look what the cat's drug in. No telling what sort of riffraff will show up around here anymore."

Will looked up, spotted the secretary walking across the street, now smiling from ear-to-ear. He saluted. "Good afternoon, sir," Cushing said, returning the smile. "I'm sorry, but I didn't notice you until you addressed me."

"Lost in thought, no doubt," Welles offered. The secretary extended his hand and Cushing shook it firmly. "Good to see you again, sir," Will said.

Welles grinned at Cushing. "It has been a while now, hasn't it, Commander?" he replied. "Yet you are never far from my thoughts. I want you to know that your sinking of the *Albemarle* has made you a virtual legend around here. Yes, a legend."

Cushing blushed. "Thank you, sir."

"So," Welles continued, "what brings you to Washington?"

Will held up the satchel of dispatches. "Admiral Porter asked that I hand deliver these. I'm to tell you as well that Fort Anderson fell on the 19th and that on the 21st our forces marched into Wilmington."

"Wilmington is *ours?*"

"It is."

Welles clapped his hands together. "My, but that is *marvelous* news. Absolutely marvelous. We got telegrams yesterday, but it is good to have them confirmed."

"I thought you would be pleased to hear it," Cushing said.

"Pleased! Oh my!"

Cushing laughed.

"Let me tell you something," Welles went on. "There is an admirer of yours not too far from here that I'm absolutely sure would love to hear that news straight from you."

"Who might that be?" Cushing asked.

"Well, I'll tell you," the secretary continued, "I was just on my way over for a meeting with him. So why don't you come along? I'm sure he'd be happy to see you."

"Of course," Cushing answered. "But who, may I ask, sir, might this admirer be?"

"Why, Commander, ... it's the President, of course."

Chapter Forty-Five

February 22nd – Late Afternoon

Lincoln watched the pattern of light and shadow play itself out on the hills across the river and was reminded that yet another year had slipped away. Yes, victory seemed imminent now, but then, victory had seemed more or less imminent a year ago, too. He looked away, shivered. His hands and feet felt terribly cold, and Lincoln imagined that he should be in bed, but there was much too much to do, and so little time to do it.

Across from him, Secretary of State Seward sat chatting amiably with General Joe Hooker, and Lincoln listened absently as Hooker regaled them both with first hand accounts of Sherman's victories in the West. Hooker had disappointed Lincoln as a commander in the East, and Seward was a man of vast conceit and ambition, but he liked them both personally and was always eager to consider their views. Seward was a schemer, Hooker a blowhard, but both men had qualities that went well beyond their faults, and it was those qualities Lincoln had always tried to draw on and nourish. They were talking now about Sherman's assault on Atlanta, and while Lincoln enjoyed Hooker's account, his mind continued to drift away to other things.

The last few months had been both productive and exhausting. In January, the great fight over emancipation had finally come to a head, and on the 31st the House voted on his proposed amendment.

The galleries and corridors of the Capital were reportedly overflowing that day in anticipation of a vote that might literally change the fundamental structure of the nation. Lincoln remained in the White House, slogging through reams of paperwork, later switching over to the writings of Petroleum V. Nasby when the tension simply became too much. Then he got the results, 119 yay, 58 nay – the 13th Amendment had passed.

An enormous celebration rocked the halls of Congress when the final results were read, and that celebration continued rolling on across the country for days. The great blemish had been removed. All men created equal now meant just that, and soon the amendment would go out to the states for ratification, and those results were virtually preordained in its favor. If he had lived his entire life for one cause and one day, Lincoln had often thought since, it would have been that one cause and that one day.

But still the war raged on, and daily men on both sides lost their lives in what was increasingly becoming a forgone conclusion. The South, he'd decided, had at best a hundred days of life left. So, in early February, Lincoln had traveled to Hampton Roads to take part in a peace conference with chosen representatives of the Confederacy. Nothing came of it; Jefferson Davis was still spouting victory and independence and Lincoln would have none of it. He was initially pummeled from all quarters once news of this failed mission got out, but peace, he reasoned, was always worth at least a discussion. And once he'd sent over all his personal papers and documentation of the terms that had been discussed at Hampton Roads to the House of Representatives – which were read aloud before a rapt, hushed audience – all the foolish furor had died away.

Now only the terms of the coming peace and reconstruction remained to be sorted out. At Hampton Roads, he had offered the Southern states payments in exchange for their emancipated slaves, and he still considered that the fairest, most equitable, and most practical course of action. The South lay in ruins; its economy destroyed; its means of labor now transcended, and only cash on the barrelhead would allow a sensible and rapid reconfiguration of the Southern economy.

But many in the extreme wing of the Republican Party would not hear of it; they wanted the South severely punished, as if the Southern states were a foreign belligerent that required the whip, not a wayward faction of their own country. The planter class that had brought on the war to begin with was already in ruin, so someone had to forget the past and look ahead to the future. Since no one else seemed ready to take on the job, that someone appeared to be Abraham Lincoln.

Lincoln had already completed his speech for the coming inaugural in March, and in it he stressed a merciful reconciliation, hardly the fire and brimstone that some in the North yearned for, not in the least the eye-for-an-eye retaliation the radical Republicans favored. In the last paragraph he tried to make it clear, to lay the groundwork for a thoughtful, compassionate peace. He had worked on it long and hard, and even as Joe Hooker talked and gestured and bragged on the other side of his desk, Lincoln could see the words clearly in his own mind.

> *With malice toward none; with charity for all; with firmness in the right, as God gives us to see the right, let us strive on to finish the work we are in; to bind up the nation's wounds; to care for him who shall have borne the battle, and for his widow, and his orphan – to do all which may achieve and cherish a just, and a lasting peace, among ourselves, and with all nations.*

A sympathetic peace, emancipation, civil rights for the freed black population; all these would be met by outrage from many quarters, Lincoln knew, but all were necessary, and all hung logically together. Many in his administration were fearful that Lincoln's life would be placed in peril by championing such controversial remedies, but the moral course was not necessarily the easy course; and besides, his life had been routinely threatened for years. It was not that he did not take these threats seriously, more the rather obvious fact that anyone bent on killing him could do so no matter how much protection surrounded him or how circumspect his movements. So he dismissed the prospect of his own assassination, not because it was a foolish concern, but because in the end there was really nothing he could do about it, and it seemed pointless to worry about things he could do nothing about.

" ... and then the city went up entirely in flames, and I knew we had them whipped for sure, Mister President," Hooker was saying.

Lincoln nodded. "We have recent reports that Columbia, South Carolina was burned to the ground in similar fashion on the 17th," he said.

Hooker nodded his head. "Yes, I've read all about it," he offered with a grin. "South Carolina," he continued, "the very birthplace of the rebellion. Glad I lived to see the day. The Rebels cannot hope to stop Sherman. The war will be over in a few weeks."

"Perhaps," Lincoln replied.

The door to his office cracked ajar, and Hay stuck his head in. "Secretary Welles to see you, sir."

Lincoln nodded."Yes, of course."

Welles entered the room with another man trailing behind, a naval officer it appeared, and at first Lincoln could not make out the officer in the shadows. Both Seward and Hooker turned, spotted the officer, and for some reason appeared mildly surprised. When the officer stepped from the shadows into the light, Lincoln recognized him at once, and a smile lit Lincoln's face. The president stood and walked around his desk to greet both men.

"I thought you wouldn't mind if I brought along a certain young officer," Welles said.

Lincoln stopped in his tracks, beaming at the young man. "Not at all, Mister Welles," he replied.

The officer was clean-shaven and stood so straight and looked so young that he could easily have been mistaken for nothing more than a midshipman at the academy. Seward and Hooker seemed concurrently baffled and put out that Welles would be presumptuous enough to drag so young an officer into the office of the President. Lincoln also knew that Welles and Seward had a running mistrust of one another, were painfully adept at self-promotion, and rarely missed an opportunity to nurse any sort of suspicion into a full-fledged gripe. But Lincoln was determined that this would not be such an occasion.

Lincoln put out his hands. "Welcome, welcome," he said. "My, but it is good to see you well, Commander. And I want to congratulate you on all your most recent successes."

Then Lincoln turned to Seward and Hooker, who appeared more confused than ever, and gestured toward the young officer. "Gentlemen," he said, "it is not every day we have the honor of a true hero making a visit here at the White House. This, I assure you, is a very special occasion."

Hooker and Seward were staring at him, utterly confounded.

Lincoln grinned, enjoying their bewilderment, then pointed toward the young man knowingly. "It appears obvious to me that neither of you two gentlemen are at all familiar with one of the most famous men in our country these days. So, allow me to introduce Commander William Cushing."

Seward's eyes – previously pooled with disdain – popped open wide, and the imperious, silver-haired man virtually jumped to his feet. The startled Hooker, who had actually met Cushing years earlier, was at Seward's heels.

"Cushing!" Seward cried, almost tripping over himself as he lunged toward the officer with his hand extended. "This is certainly a delight! My, my. I have read so much of your adventures, I honestly feel that I already know you."

Hooker also put out a hand. "My pleasure, Commander Cushing, believe me," Hooker said. "Your escapades have become the stuff of legend. My staff officers thrilled over your mission on the Cape Fear River last year. And the *Albemarle!* ... Well, my goodness. And now I recall that I met you years ago on the Virginia Peninsula."

Cushing, seeming genuinely embarrassed by all the fuss, shook hands with the two and then gladly took a seat along with Welles once Lincoln made the offer.

"Your mission against the *Albemarle*," Lincoln told him, returning to his desk, "was a stunning success. Surely one of the greatest of the war."

"Thank you, sir," Cushing replied. "Many other men deserve credit for that success."

"Yes, of course," Lincoln said, "and they have been commended too. Now, tell me, what brings you to Washington? Do you plan on paddling a canoe up the James River and single-handedly taking Richmond?"

Seward laughed and slapped his knee. "Never thought of *that*," he said with a wink. "Perhaps you should run that plan by General Grant, Mister President. He's getting nowhere awfully slowly. Maybe we should turn the whole thing over to Commander Cushing."

Lincoln smiled, enjoying himself immensely.

"No, sir," Cushing replied. "No plans to take Richmond just yet. I'm delivering dispatches while my ship, the *Monticello*, is at Hampton Roads being refitted."

"Pity," Hooker said. "I rather like your idea, Mister Seward. Might just shorten the war considerably. Considerably!"

"I understand," Lincoln went on, "that you were involved in the campaign to take Wilmington, Commander."

"Yes, sir," Cushing replied.

"Just how much involved?"

So Will Cushing sat back and told them of his idea to fake the Rebels out of their position at Fort Anderson with a canvas monitor, and as he told the story Hooker and Seward roared with delight. Lincoln leaned back, crossed his legs, and laughed out loud. Encouraged by his reception, Cushing loosened up and continued, regaling them all with tales of his most recent exploits.

He told them of a night mission to the foot of Fort Anderson, for instance, where upon hearing some distant singing, he grabbed a carbine from the bottom of the boat, then leaped from piling to piling across the water, right up to one of the fort's lowest gun ports. There he observed a town meeting of sorts taking place with shouts and cries of victory, and the fort's commander urging persistence upon the assembled group of soldiers and citizens. Then they all sang a chorus of "Dixie," but this was too much for Cushing, who promptly aimed his carbine carefully over their heads and fired off a shot. When the singing stopped abruptly, Cushing shouted, "Why don't all you damn Rebels pack your bags and go to a place a bit warmer than your beloved Dixie! And when you get there, tell the devil that Will Cushing sent you!"

"Cushing!" they all screamed. Then the startled Confederates ran about in horrified circles and fired off a few wild volleys. But these hit nothing at all, and Cushing slipped silently away, retracing his steps across the pilings out to his cutter. He was rowed back down the channel before the fort's big guns began to thunder foolishly and frantically and meaninglessly into the black, empty night, hitting nothing.

Seward roared with delight as Cushing finished his story. Hooker had to rub tears of laughter from his eyes, and Lincoln slapped the top of his desk with glee at the mere thought of the befuddled Rebels running in circles as this brash, young officer simply skipped his way back to his boat. Better than even Petroleum V. Nasby, Cushing's stories were not only funny, they were extraordinary, and Lincoln could not recall laughing so hard in recent memory. They were a tonic.

So he leaned back comfortably and listened as the young officer went on, recalling a January return mission to Smithville, where he ceremoniously accepted the surrender of the town from the mayor, then reigned as "Military Governor" for a week, living in the very house he had snuck into in search of the commanding Confederate general the year before.

Then there was the story of how he had lured the blockade-runner *Charlotte* into a trap on the Cape Fear River by forcing captured Rebel pilots to display their usual signals at night. After the *Charlotte* pulled up and anchored directly next to the *Monticello,* the British captain and passengers made for Cushing's wardroom for a champagne dinner to celebrate their arrival in Dixie, only to find a young Federal commander already standing at the head of their table, who immediately ordered up another case of champagne, then offered the following toast to the astonished British travelers: "Gentlemen, we will drink to the success of those who succeed." One of the English passengers stumbled forward, studied Cushing for a moment or two, then turned and cried, "Beastly luck!" to his dumbstruck compatriots.

"Beastly luck!" Seward repeated, almost choking, laughing so hard he had to hold his sides.

And so it went, story after story, until the hour grew late, the shadows began to fade on the walls, and the young officer and the naval secretary had to move on. Noting the late hour, both Hooker and Seward also made for the door, both chuckling as they went, and Lincoln made Cushing promise to return soon for another round of stories.

Then suddenly, Lincoln was alone again, with the darkness of another February evening beginning to close over the rooftops of Washington. But now he felt different, relaxed and – for the moment, at least – entirely at ease. Even his feet felt better, and he knew it had been the laughter that had done it. Few things could hold his attention and make him laugh like that, and he certainly admired young Cushing for all his pluck and good humor. His visit had been a delight.

Lincoln went to the window, watched as the light faded over the city, and laughed a while longer over Cushing's amusing anecdotes. Then he thought again of the war, and his humor changed.

The worst of it was over now, he thought, and at least he could thank God for that. Surely there were still mountains to move, but those mountains would be moved with negotiations and ballots, not bullets and canister. Tomorrow's casualties would consist of bruised egos, no longer lost lives, and if the price was simply egos, then they could take his and do with it as they pleased.

Lincoln took a long, deep breath. The odd dreams that haunted his nights were more frequent and vivid now; the ship moving faster, it seemed, through the fog-shrouded night, the voices louder, his ultimate destination closing rapidly. Abraham Lincoln was nothing if not the soul of rationality, but he knew his dreams meant something, that they connected him in some odd way to something far greater than himself. Those dreams seemed to be telling him with increasing urgency that the end was coming soon. One hundred days – three months, give or take a day or two – was how he saw it, and then the Confederacy would be in tatters. Then hopefully – if sanity prevailed – the tearing down would be over, and the building up would begin anew.

His job had been to hold the thing together, to keep the budding democratic experiment from collapsing under the weight of its own internal contradictions, and then to put that venture sensibly back on track. Lincoln conceived it to be the most important thing that he could accomplish on earth: God's business, truth be told. Where, ultimately, that endeavor was headed, or how it would continue to unfold was anyone's good guess, but just as he had suggested during his speech at Gettysburg, with slavery now a thing of the past, the "new birth of freedom" he envisioned could not be far away. Now the war was almost won and – with the passage of the 13th Amendment – the historic cancer that had crippled the democratic enterprise since its inception, finally excised.

Some, he knew, would stumble on in their crude confusions, thinking the task complete, life static, freedom now entirely repaired, and thus nothing of substance left to accomplish except to get on with the business at hand. But that was wrong, and the day would come, he knew full well, when some future historian – perhaps from a different country, or far distant century – would have the patience to delve deeply into the book of time and, page by painful page, come finally to appreciate just how much had been sacrificed by so many to make it so. And if that prospective historian happened to come upon names such as Grant or Cushing or Sherman or even Lincoln somewhere far back at the beginning of the saga, well, he could only hope they would all be remembered well; that when democracy stumbled to its bloody knees on the American continent, he and thousands of his countrymen had been there to help pick it up. For Abraham

Lincoln knew only too well that freedom's long, troubled journey out of the dark night of tribalism, monarchy, and tyranny was far, far from over. The truth was – it had just begun.

The End

Epilogue

The end would come rapidly for the Southern Confederacy. On April 2, 1865, only a few weeks after Abraham Lincoln's last meeting with William Cushing, the Confederate defensive position at Petersburg, Virginia imploded, and Lee was forced to abandon the Confederate capital at Richmond. The Federal army moved rapidly, cutting off Lee's westward march at Appomattox Court House, Virginia. There, after a brief clash of arms, Robert E. Lee came to the conclusion that further armed resistance would be fruitless. On April 9, 1865 Lee surrendered to Grant, effectively ending the Civil War.

Abraham Lincoln: In Washington City, Abraham Lincoln thrilled to the news of the Confederate surrender, but would have only a few days to savor it. On April 14, Abraham Lincoln was assassinated by John Wilkes Booth at Ford's Theatre in Washington, D. C. After lying in state in the Federal capital, Lincoln's body was transported by rail to Springfield, Illinois, where he was laid to rest. Today Abraham Lincoln is fondly regarded as one of the finest presidents in American history.

Gideon Welles: The man who resurrected William Cushing's naval career in 1861 stayed on after Lincoln's assassination and served as Secretary of the Navy under the new president, Andrew Johnson. Welles finally left the cabinet in March 1869 and returned to Connecticut where he wrote a number of books. He passed away at the age of seventy-five in February 1877 and was buried in Cedar Hill Cemetery, Hartford, Connecticut.

Oliver Wendell Holmes: While Abraham Lincoln would not survive the carnage of war, the young infantry captain who, legend has it, called out the warning while Lincoln stood atop the battlements outside of Washington as Jubal Early's Confederate troops deployed north of the city, would. Oliver Wendell Holmes Jr. would return to Harvard University, practice law, and eventually be appointed to the United States Supreme Court. Today he is remembered as one of the most influential jurists in American history.

Henry E. Wing: The young reporter who delivered Grant's message to Abraham Lincoln after the battle in the Wilderness was a Connecticut native. Serving in the infantry with the Army of the Potomac, Wing was seriously wounded at the Battle of Fredericksburg in 1862 and had to return home to recuperate. After recovering, Wing took a position as a reporter, first with the Hartford *Evening Press,* then later with the New York *Tribune.* It was as a reporter for the *Tribune* that Wing made the long and perilous trip back from the front to report directly to Lincoln and his assembled cabinet. After the war Wing moved to Iowa where he served as a Methodist minister.

Captain James W. Cooke: On April 7, as Union troops neared his ship works on the Roanoke River, Captain James Wallace Cooke put the torch to the new ram under construction at Edward's Ferry, North Carolina. Little is known of Cooke's post-war years. He died on June 21, 1869 and is buried in Cedar Grove Cemetery,

Portsmouth, Virginia. His tombstone reads simply: James W. Cooke, Captain CSS *Albemarle.*

The Crew of Picket Boat *No. 1*: Ensign Gay, William Howorth, and many of the men who accompanied Cushing on his mission to destroy the CSS *Albemarle* survived the raid, only to be captured by the local Confederate garrison. They were held in various Confederate prisons in North Carolina and Virginia until paroled in late February, 1865 from Libby Prison, Richmond.

Gilbert Elliott: The young Southern shipbuilder, Gilbert Elliott, survived the war and later worked as an attorney in different cities across the country. His recollections of the construction and initial fighting of the *Albemarle* were published in *Century Magazine* in July 1888, and form the cornerstone of historical knowledge on the Confederate ironclad. Elliott married, reared a family, and died in New York in May 1895. He was laid to rest in Green-Wood Cemetery, Brooklyn, New York.

CSS *Albemarle:* Lt. Alexander Warley scuttled what remained of the vaunted Confederate ironclad shortly after Cushing's raid put her on the bottom of Roanoke River. The *Albemarle* was then thoroughly inspected by Federal engineers, and later raised by the Union Navy. After the war the ram was towed to Norfolk, Virginia, where it was condemned by a prize court in Washington, D. C. After condemnation, the vessel remained moored in ordinary storage until 1867 when the *Albemarle* was sold at public auction to J. N. Leonard & Co., in all likelihood for little more than scrap.

William Barker Cushing: William Cushing received orders detaching him from the *Monticello* on February 24, and was from that point forward relieved of active command until the end of the Civil War. After the war Cushing remained in the navy, rose to the rank of commander, married and fathered two daughters. During the remainder of his naval career, Cushing sailed the globe and was often recognized in ports all over the world as "Albemarle" Cushing.

His subsequent naval career was essentially uneventful. However, in November 1873, while in command of the six-gun American steamer *Wyoming,* Cushing would play a critical role in the freeing of American and British civilians seized improperly from the neutral steamer *Virginius* and sentenced to death by the reining Spanish authorities in Cuba; a typically bold action on his part that saved many innocent lives.

The wounds and physical hardships suffered during the Civil War would unfortunately take their toll on William Cushing's post-war health. He would suffer from increasing illness until his death in 1875 at the age of only thirty-two, and his valiant exploits on the rivers of Virginia and North Carolina would fade, to a great extent, from public memory. Yet those who knew of his feats would not soon forget his accomplishments. It was Admiral David Farragut, for instance, who once remarked to Gideon Welles that "young Cushing was the hero of the war." William Barker Cushing was laid to rest at United States Naval Academy, Annapolis, Maryland.

About The Author

Jim Stempel

Jim Stempel lives with his family in Western Maryland overlooking the Blue Ridge. His wife, Sandie, is on staff at nearby McDaniel College where she teaches astronomy and physics, while his three children – a daughter and two sons – have moved on to professional careers. A student of the human condition, he is the author of six books including satire, psychology, spirituality, and scholarly works of historical nonfiction. He is a graduate of the Citadel, Charleston, SC.

Jim is considered an authority on the Eastern campaigns of the American Civil War, having published two scholarly works on the subject and numerous articles, and his most recent book, *The Nature of War; Origins and Evolution of Violent Conflict* has been well received by an international audience.

If You Enjoyed This Book

Please post a review in locations such as Amazon, Goodreads and wherever else you can. These reviews are much more important for the author than you might think as they really help to sell their books. Reviews also assist other would be readers to make a choice so this is your opportunity to help the author. It only takes a few minutes but it makes a difference.
Thank you.

Lonestar Rising:

The Voyage of the Wasp

by

Jason Vale

Fans of Alternative History celebrate! Jason Vail's compelling novel, *Lonestar Rising: The Voyage of the Wasp*, is must-read literature.

The American rebellion has failed. George Washington is dead. The surviving revolutionaries have retreated to Tennessee, only to be routed again. In 1819, John Paul Jones, Jr., a smuggler, plies the waters off the coast of New Spain, while a new generation of rebels have settled in Spanish territories and the wasteland called Texas.

But Andrew Jackson is not content to be a Spanish subject. He dreams big. Texas must be free and independent from the corrupt old empires of Europe. But with no army other than the Texas Rangers, and no navy, Texas has no hope of opposing the mighty forces of Spain. No hope, that is, until David Crockett recruits the sardonic Jones. Together they buy and refit a broken down warship to become the first ship of the Texas Navy. With a handful of Crockett's men and a dubious crew of French pirates, they set sail to seize Spanish treasure and remake history in a ship called the *Wasp*.

Clear Lower Deck

By

Roger Paine

Learn where the expression 'grog' comes from and what happened when the admiral's parrot was seasick.

Read about a cat called Oscar who was sunk with the German battleship *Bismarck* in World War II but survived to be sunk twice more in the ships which rescued him!

In **CLEAR LOWER DECK** Former Royal Navy officer, Roger Paine, charts the ups and downs of life, both ashore and afloat, together with recipes for rum punch and rum Christmas cake! Plus the traditional RN toasts for each and every day of the week!

This delightfully irreverent, and occasionally indiscreet, collection of 'yarns' is here to be savoured and treasured.

Shortlisted for a Mountbatten Maritime Media Award, 2010

Surfmen

by

Charles Marshall

As lightning cracks over a roiling sea, a young boy clings to life amidst the waves. His family, his friends, all that he's ever known have been taken by the storm. Drifting in the sea-tossed wreckage, the boy is unexpectedly rescued and given a new chance at life on the sands of the Outer Banks of North Carolina.

Thirty years later, thirteen years after the Civil War, on that same far-flung spit of sand at Cape Hatteras, seven men of courage face the sea and its storms as men of the United States Lifesaving Service. Recruited and trained by that same boy grown to manhood, Confederate blockade runner Captain Thomas Hooper, the men of Cape Hatteras Station are the only hope for sailors in distress at the treacherous Diamond Shoals. As Thomas Hooper readies his men to fight the sea and tries to keep them from fighting each other, he realizes that while they save the lives of others, the souls they save may very well be their own.

CPSIA information can be obtained at www.ICGtesting.com
Printed in the USA
LVOW01s0031060515

437392LV00013B/185/P